Of BLOOD AND MONSTERS

Piper Lancaster Series
Book Three

Other books by D.G Swank:
(Denise Grover Swank)

CURSE KEEPERS WORLD
(Urban Fantasy)

Curse Keepers Trilogy
The Curse Keepers
The Curse Breakers
The Curse Defiers

Of Ash and Spirit Trilogy
Of Ash and Spirit
Of Fire and Storm
Of Blood and Monsters
Of Death and Ruin (September 2019)

CHOSEN
(Urban Fantasy)
Chosen
Hunted
Sacrifice
Redemption

Book of Sindal
Coming Summer 2019
Descended from Shadows
Reign of Mist
Crown of Blood

dgwank.com

For more information about
Denise Grover Swank's mystery and romance books
go to
denisegroverswank.com

OF BLOOD AND MONSTERS

A Curse Keepers Novel
Piper Lancaster Series Book Three

Denise Grover Swank
writing as
D.G. Swank

CHAPTER ONE

Ellie

I don't like this," Collin said, peering out at the street through the blinds in my cousin Piper's living room. At over six feet tall, he exuded a confidence most men aspire to, most likely because he was extremely good-looking, and he knew it.

"I don't either," my boyfriend, David, said from the sofa, "but we only have two choices—go back or wait." I didn't care much for what he was saying, let alone how defeated he sounded, but it didn't matter what he said—everything he said come out sounding good in his sexy British accent.

"Wait for how long?" Collin asked, turning to face me. "If Okeus killed her, she's never coming back."

"He won't kill her, and you know it." David's voice hitched. "But he might keep her."

We all knew Okeus, the god of war and destruction, wanted heirs, and he thought my cousin and I were strong enough to bear them. I'd tricked him into agreeing to leave me alone, at least for the immediate future, but Piper had no such deal.

"Which means there's no point waiting around here," Collin said, shaking his head. "I'm going back to look for her."

That caught me by surprise. "Really?"

Collin Dailey was notorious for looking out for only one person—Collin Dailey. Historically, the guy was compulsively self-centered. Admittedly, he'd changed since I'd first met him two months ago, but I never could've predicted that he'd step between Okeus and Piper, trying to protect her. And now this? I could hardly reconcile this man with the Collin Dailey I first met.

"We can't sit in limbo," he said gruffly. "And if Okeus got her pregnant…do you really want a baby Okeus running around?"

"There already is a baby Okeus running around," David said. "Only he's all grown up."

"And is a complete and utter asshole," Collin said. "We never should have agreed to leave her there with the two of them. We should have stayed, if for no other reason than to destroy the Great One."

Part of me agreed with him. We had spent the last few weeks tracking down the demon who'd killed my stepmother, and hours ago it had been within spitting distance. But Okeus had suddenly appeared out of nowhere. His arrival, plus his discovery that Abel, Piper's self-appointed protector, was the son he'd never known, had kind of steamrolled my plans to destroy the demon. For now. "We didn't stand a chance against Okeus. The two of us against a literal god and a higher-level demon? We could barely fend off the lower-level ones."

"Then why do you wield the Sword of Galahad?" a small, rough voice asked.

I turned to see an eighteen-inch-tall, hairy man with a bushy beard standing in the entrance to the kitchen.

Tsagasi.

My blessing and my curse. My new counselor in all things supernatural. My greatest source of verbal ass-kicking.

"You have got to stop sneaking up on me like that," I groaned.

We all remained silent for several seconds, until David finally spoke. "Do you think Ellie's ready to take on Okeus?"

"What is ready?" the little man asked, walking closer to us. "And you waste your time going back to the warehouse, Curse Keeper." He narrowed his eyes at Collin. "She isn't there."

"So Okeus took her?" Collin asked, his voice rough with dread.

"No, *she* took Abiel."

Collin cocked his head and narrowed his eyes. "What do you mean she took Abiel?"

"Just what I said," Tsagasi said in a bored tone. "She took him after the demigod killed the Great One."

The Great One was dead?

I felt dizzy, and David seemed to sense it. He got to his feet, wrapping his arm around my back.

"Abiel killed the Great One?" he asked. "Are you sure?"

Tsagasi released a grunt. "Are you calling me a liar?"

"No...of course not," David stammered.

Collin stepped in. "So Abiel killed the Great One and Okeus let them leave?"

"No," Tsagasi said, drawing the word out as though he were talking to a simpleton. "She created a world and took him with her to escape."

"That statement leads to so many questions, but we'll focus on one," Collin said, shaking his head. "What do you mean she created a world?"

"It is one of Piper Lancaster's titles," the little man said. "Kewasa, shepherd to lost spirits, witness to creation, slayer of demons and gods...creator of worlds."

"What exactly does creator of worlds *mean*?" I asked, still processing that Abel had killed the Great One. The demon who'd killed my stepmother was gone, and I hadn't been the one to end it. The thought left me feeling hollow.

"Her power is growing daily. For now, she can create small worlds in dimensions adjacent to ours. She's created one in the attic above our heads," Tsagasi said matter-of-factly. "She was hiding in it when we first arrived last evening."

"A pocket dimension," David murmured.

"What's she hiding in the attic?" Collin asked in an accusatory tone.

"None of your damn business," Piper's friend said as she descended into the living room from the staircase by the front door. She was shorter than me and had sleek blonde hair cut into an angular bob with pink streaks. The terrified look she'd worn hours ago in the warehouse had been replaced with fierce determination.

"Rhys," I said. "It's nearly dawn and you're supposed to be resting after your...ordeal."

"It's my second kidnapping in two weeks," Rhys said as she focused a laser-sharp glare on me. "Not to mention some demon or god killed my girlfriend to mess with Piper's head, and a body-snatching asshole killed our friend Hudson and impersonated him. Right now, Piper is with those *things*, which she willingly undertook to save our collective asses, I might add, and I come downstairs to hear you accusing her of *hiding something from you?*"

"Rhys," I said gently, lifting my hands toward her. "No one's accusing her of anything."

"Bullshit," she ground out through gritted teeth.

Jack—Piper and Rhys's friend—appeared behind her on the stairs. He put a hand on her shoulder, then turned to me and said, "Piper's been looking for you for weeks. And even if she hadn't been looking for you, she doesn't hide from things. She faces them head-on. Even if they're demons."

"Then what's up in the attic?" Collin demanded.

"None of your damn business," Rhys snarled.

Collin took a step toward the staircase. "If you won't tell me, I'll just go find out for myself."

Rhys blocked his path, her body shaking with anger. "I don't think so."

He stared down at the much shorter woman, ready to muscle her to the side when Tsagasi shouted, "Enough!"

Collin took a step back and turned to face the supernatural creature.

"The world in Kewasa's attic is no concern of yours. It is for her alone to deal with."

"Kewasa," David said, clearly eager to change the topic and hopefully defuse the situation. "Deliverer. I recently read about Kewasa in a translated Middle Ages text about demons. I've done more research on the title while we've been waiting, but I'm not sure what it means exactly. Do either of you know?"

Jack shook his head. "I was surprised he saved her last night," he said, narrowing his eyes. "He told her that he wouldn't kill a demon for her."

"The demigod killed the Great One," Tsagasi said. "In front of Okeus, breaking his vow to not kill demons. He did it in retaliation for killing her friend. And to keep her secret."

"What secret?" Collin asked.

Irritation filled Tsagasi's eyes. "That she can create worlds, dense one."

Collin pointed his finger at the little man. "You better not try to make that an official title."

Tsagasi only smirked.

My gaze landed on Collin, and he turned serious as he stared back at me. He'd made a deal with Okeus to leave the demons alone, but he'd also broken that vow to save me. "He cares about her."

"Kieran Abel is only capable of caring about himself," Jack said. "He's allowed demons to walk around unchecked, refusing to help Piper stop them. If it weren't for him, she wouldn't be in this position—and her friend would likely still be alive. Abel had a reason for killing that demon, but I suspect it had nothing to do with avenging or protecting Piper and everything to do with his own selfish motives."

His words seemed to confirm my growing suspicion. He had feelings for my cousin, but she had feelings for the son of Okeus, whether she wanted to have them or not. And it was obvious from the exchanges between Piper and Abel that things were very complicated between them.

Rhys remained painfully quiet.

"You think he's lying to Piper?" I asked Jack.

He paused, then turned and met my gaze. "Kieran Abel is literally the son of the devil incarnate. He's not to be trusted. With Piper's heart or her life. And right now, she's God knows where with him." He moved toward the front door. "I'm going to go find her."

"She disappeared five hours ago, Jack," Rhys said. "How are you going to find her?"

"She disappeared yesterday morning at a client's house. She came back to the exact place she disappeared from. I'm going back to the warehouse."

"I'm going with you," Collin said, surprising me again.

Collin had clearly taken a special interest in my cousin, but was it possible for his interest to be anything but purely selfish?

CHAPTER TWO

Piper

W hat the hell had I gotten myself into?

I stole a glance at the man standing next to me on the balcony of a luxury home built into the side of an Appalachian mountain. I'd told Abel to think of a place that made him happy before I whisked us off to another world, and while I'd expected to appear in some ancient time and place, he'd thought of the house he'd brought me to the night before.

"How safe are we here?" I asked, trying to ignore that the demigod next to me was still shirtless, and seemed even more attractive than ever. He was tall, with dark hair and eyes, and rippling muscles that seemed too perfect—was it because he was a demigod or because he worked out? Maybe a little of both.

"You mean from the demons?" he asked. "This is your creation. You're the expert."

I scowled. "You're the one who thought of this place, Abel."

"The world is yours, Waboose. Whatever is here is what you've created."

"So it's *not* real."

He reached for me, wrapping an arm around my back and hauling me to his chest. "You feel real."

My hands splayed over his hard pecs, and I couldn't stop my thumb from brushing the skin next to the light pink scar slightly beneath his heart. The deep wound I'd put there a little over an hour ago had nearly healed. I was suddenly very aware that I was only wearing my bra and panties—along with my belt holding my daggers and my sword—but instead of dissuading me from touching him, it made it more difficult to restrain myself.

"Do you think Okeus is waiting for us in the warehouse?" I asked.

He lifted his hand to my cheek, brushing a hair away with his fingertips. "He won't stay there himself, but I'm sure he's left his minions there to wait for us."

"So he knows I can create pocket universes?"

"I have no idea what he thinks." His face lowered to the base of my neck. "But we need to be prepared for anything when we leave."

I sucked in a breath as a shiver ran down my spine. I knew I should stop him—the night before he'd told me that if we had sex, we ran the risk that I'd be dragged to hell with him when he died, but I couldn't bring myself to pull away.

His tongue slid over the bite mark on my collarbone…the bite mark he'd given me hours before to lay claim on me. I felt a jolt of energy shoot down to my core.

He grunted, now sucking on the mark as his hand skimmed down my back to my butt cheek. His fingers dug in deep as he hauled me closer, making it clear he was very aroused.

"Abel…"

His face lifted, and his eyes were like pools of ink. "You're mine now, Piper."

While his words stoked some primal part of me that I recognized as supernatural, the feminist part of me bristled. "Excuse me?"

His mouth covered mine and his tongue parted my lips. My hands lifted around his neck and I clung to him as a passion I'd never experienced before took complete hold of my senses. It was like this man was the other half of me, even though my logical mind rejected the thought as ridiculous.

He deftly unfastened the belt on my hips, and it dropped to the concrete floor with a dull thud that barely registered. His other hand cupped my breast as he dragged his mouth away from my lips, sliding it back to my collarbone. His thumb brushed my nipple as he sucked on the bite, and my knees buckled from a wave of sensation.

Somewhere in the back of my mind, I knew what I was feeling wasn't normal, but he was a demigod and I was his Kewasa. Was that why I was so attracted to him? Or maybe it was the bite that he'd given me to assert his claim.

I shoved him, pushing him about six inches away from me. "What does that bite really mean, Abel?"

His eyes darkened, and irritation wrinkled his forehead. "I told you. It claims you as mine."

"But what exactly does that *mean*?"

He studied me for a second, then sat down on one of his outdoor chairs, tugging me with him. I ended up straddling his legs. I knew this was a bad idea, like when you feel the urge to eat a leftover cupcake at midnight, yet I couldn't seem to stop myself.

"It means you're mine, Waboose," he said softly, the palm of his hand skimming my shoulder and down my back.

He was talking in circles, and I suspected he was doing it to get me to let the subject go. "What did Okeus mean when he asked if you'd bound me to you?"

Pushing out a sigh, he skimmed a hand down my bare arm, the contact sending a chill down my back. "From my understanding, it's an eternal, supernatural bond, only it's not as equals, Kewasa. It's more like slave and owner."

I pulled away and sat upright. "You want to control me?"

Releasing a heavy sigh, he reached up to caress my cheek. "No. I would have said anything to Okeus to protect you. It's more like I've marked you as a member of my team."

My brows shot straight up, my irritation rising again. "Your *team*? As in, you're the owner?"

"No, more like the team manager."

Then it hit me what "team" actually meant.

"You can claim others?" I demanded, surprised by how jealous it made me. And then a new thought hit me. "Have you *already* claimed others?"

A grin spread across his face, a hint of the Abel I'd first met appearing. "Would it bother you if I have?"

I wasn't sure why, but the mere thought filled me with irrational rage. It felt like I should be the only one. I needed to be a grown-up and let this go—of course Abel had claimed others; he'd been alive for hundreds of years—but the image of him holding another woman and biting into her flesh made me want to throw something.

And so I did.

I scrambled off his lap and picked up a candle on the table next to me, tossing it at his head.

He easily batted it away, chuckling in amusement.

"Asshole." Needing space, I stormed through the open door leading inside.

Abel was behind me in an instant, grabbing my wrist and spinning me around to face him, still grinning. "My Waboose has sharp teeth."

"I can bite too," I snarled, eyeing the dip at the base of his neck. I could feel myself salivating at the thought.

What the hell was happening to me?

He groaned and tugged me closer. "There's nothing wrong with you. Our blood bond is even stronger after I tasted your blood again a few hours ago. It makes us irresistibly drawn to one another. If you bite me and drink my blood…it will only strengthen our bond."

My anger bled out of me, replaced by fear. "As in *forever?*"

He hesitated. "Perhaps."

I reached my hand up to the bite on my collarbone. "Abel. I should have had a say in this."

"Bite or no bite, I've claimed you, Piper Lancaster," he said in a gravelly voice. He reached for my left palm and gently opened my still-clenched fingers. With his index finger, he traced the circle and square in the center of my palm, supernatural symbols that had appeared there as my powers unfurled.

"Because I'm Kewasa?" I asked, fighting the shiver skating down my back.

"No, because you're you."

I shook my head. "What does *that* mean?"

"It means I've waited my entire life for you, Piper, and fate's cruel hand has made you my Kewasa." He closed my fist and then covered it with his hand. "Together, we defied Okeus. We tricked him, and for that alone, he will seek us out and punish us. But if he doesn't already know what you can do, he'll find out soon enough. Tsagasi did. Okeus will enslave you, Piper. We have to find a way to keep the crescent moon from appearing on your hand so I can help protect you. If we don't, I worry he'll punish you for killing me, or if the mark appears when you're locked up, you'll go mad trying to get to me to kill me."

All of which sounded terrible. "We have to go back."

He slid his arm around the small of my back and pulled me closer. "Not yet."

"You know time moves more slowly here. Twenty minutes means hours there."

"That's one reason why I want to wait." He kissed me again, his lips possessive but gentler than before. I plastered myself against him and demanded more, grabbing his face and holding him in place. His arm wrapped around my lower back like a vise. Every bit of me was pressed against him, yet I craved more.

He jerked his head up and took a breath as though he'd been underwater, his eyes hooded with lust. "*This* is the other. I keep trying not to touch you," he ground out as his fingers dug into my flesh, "but you have a gravitational pull I'm powerless to resist."

Cradling his face in my hands, I searched his eyes, wishing I knew what was going on behind them. Wishing I knew everything he did about my role in this mess. That ring he wore dulled our blood bond, and part of me wanted to pull it off his finger. The tension in his arms loosened. For a moment, I thought he was pushing me away, but he took the ring off and slid it onto the thumb of my left hand.

Find your answers, Waboose, he thought, staring at me with an intensity that stole my breath. But something else caught my attention.

"I thought the ring blocked us from reading each other's thoughts."

He gave me a wry grin. "That wasn't entirely true." *The ring allows the wearer to read the other's thoughts as well as to transmit thoughts to them.*

While part of me was pissed that he'd lied, I needed to focus. "So I can read your thoughts, but you can't read mine?"

Can you see my entire history before you knew me?

The answer was no. The ring didn't give me full access to his mind, only his thoughts, which were very X-rated as he engulfed me in his embrace. His mouth lowered to the side of my neck, his tongue darting across my skin.

"You're not going to make this easy for me, are you?" I asked. Desire washed through me in steep waves, making me want to claim his mouth and make it mine.

"Ask your questions, Kewasa," he prodded. His warm breath feathered the curve where my neck met my shoulder blade, sending shivers down my back. "While I still have coherent thought."

I was never going to find my answers this way. Bracing myself like I was leaving a warm shower to walk into a freezing room, I stepped away from him.

That's good, he thought even as I felt his profound disappointment and longing for me. He hadn't been lying—he craved me. His eyes lifted to mine and I found myself falling into them, needing to touch him again.

"This attraction isn't normal," I said, panting to regain my breath. "I can see you feel it too. What is this?"

I'm not sure, but it's supernatural.

"Soul mates?" I asked cringing at the clichéd term.

His thoughts stumbled as though he were trying to sort it out himself. *Deeper than soul mates, I think.*

"What does that mean?" I asked.

"Soul mates is a human concept," he said, struggling to explain. "In the supernatural world, there is an alpha and his or her followers. The concept of equality is unheard of. Unnatural."

"You mean there has to be one person in charge while the others obey?" I asked.

He nodded. "But you and I don't have that hierarchy. I've tried to exert supernatural authority over you, yet it never works."

"You *did* mean to control me with that bite, didn't you?" I asked, reaching up to brush it with my fingertips.

"I won't apologize for it," he said, holding his head high. "You were walking into a trap with the demons, which meant near-certain death, and I was helpless to stop you."

"And if I'd died, you would have lost your chance to put a stop to this endless life," I said, but the feelings rolling off him seemed to be more about me than him.

"There is that," he said with a cocky grin, but the ring helped me see beyond his brash attitude. Despite having courted death for centuries, he was willing to live longer if it meant protecting me. He genuinely cared more about my life than his own, and no one was more shocked about that than Abel himself. His feelings for me were a curiosity that he longed to study and explore. He loved puzzles and unanswerable questions, and I was a whole package of oddities and unexplained phenomena he wanted to figure out.

"Do you really think you'll drag me to hell if we sleep together?" I asked.

My question was like a cup of water tossed onto a bonfire. "I'm destined for hell, Piper. That is a fact. Given our supernatural attraction, sex is sure to bind us. Which means you'll go by default."

I frowned, following his reasoning but looking for a loophole. Then an idea sparked to life. "You said the supernatural world doesn't have equals. There's always an alpha."

"Yes."

"What about the curse keepers? You said they represent the land and the sea. Equal but different."

A sardonic grin twisted his lips but didn't reach his eyes. "That's not entirely true, is it? Ellie's clearly in charge."

"Only because Collin allows it," I countered. "I can feel it. He loves her and he betrayed her. He only yields his control because he's trying to pay for the pain he's caused her."

He shook his head, squashing the hope that had begun to blossom. "You don't know that for certain. You only wish it to be true."

He had a point, but I'd seen them together. "I think he could reclaim his share of the power anytime he chooses."

"Where are you going with this, Kewasa?" He didn't like thinking about Collin. He didn't like the way the curse keeper had insinuated that he was interested in sleeping with me. The more he thought about it, the deeper his anger tunneled.

I placed my hand on his chest, staring up into his eyes. "There is only one man for me, Abel. You."

His anger dissipated at my touch. "I am no man, Piper," he said in defeat. "I am a demigod. It would be better for you if we could sever this connection."

I gave him a sad smile. "Don't waste your time. Don't waste *our* time. There's no one else I want."

"You're young. You don't know that. If we appease Okeus, you could live many more decades."

Yet I did know. Although neither of us knew the how or why of it, Kieran Abel was supernaturally stamped upon my soul.

I slipped the ring off and put it on his finger, wanting him to hear my thoughts so there could be no misunderstandings. His eyes widened. "Piper."

"Shh…" I placed a soft kiss on his lips, certain about something else as well.

"No," he said, trying to pull away. "I will not be responsible for damning you to hell."

"Don't underestimate me. The curse keepers are equals, and so are we. You can control every creature on multiple planes, and yet you can't control me. I am your Kewasa." I pressed my hand to his cheek, reveling in the feel of his stubble against my palm. "I'm your equal, Abel, and I'm a witness to creation. Surely that serves some purpose in all of this. What if instead of you dragging me to hell, I pull you up to heaven?"

His eyes turned glassy, and I didn't need the ring to know that I'd given him hope. He hadn't considered it before, but here, in this world I'd created, he believed it might be possible. "It's a theory at best, Piper, a pipe dream at worst."

"And yet I believe it's true." I smiled at him. "The ring proves it. It works both ways—if we weren't equals, I couldn't use it to read your thoughts."

A wry grin quirked his mouth. "For someone who's only known about the supernatural world for a matter of weeks, you have a lot of opinions about it."

"I suppose I do. I'll stand by them until I'm proven wrong."

"By then it will be too late."

He was right, but I was certain the bond between us had a deeper purpose. I wasn't Abel's Kewasa to send him on his merry way to hell. I was truly his deliverer, capable of saving him from his fate.

"I agree that there is more to this than your role as Kewasa," he said, "but I'm not willing to take the chance."

"But I am."

CHAPTER THREE

Piper

Y ou can't be serious," Abel said. He stared at me, stunned, and I took advantage of his stupor to kiss him. I slipped an arm around his neck and clung to him as I pressed my mouth to his, licking his bottom lip.

"Piper," he growled.

"It's okay," I murmured against his mouth.

He leaned back again, his lust-filled eyes trained on mine. "I know I should tell you no, but every part of me burns for you."

"Abel," I said with a soft smile. "Let me be your real Kewasa."

His mouth crashed into mine in a frenzy of teeth and tongue and heat, the intensity taking my breath away. He pushed me backward toward the door into the house, but when I stumbled, he scooped me up into his arms and strode across the living room and down a short hall to his room, still kissing me until I was panting.

He lowered my legs until my bare feet touched the wood floor. It struck me that the room was fully furnished—a large bed, nightstands, a sitting area in front of a fireplace. Floor-to-ceiling windows looked over the valley. Had these details been pulled from my mind? I'd never been in Abel's bedroom before, so I didn't know if the room was a perfect replica.

But I didn't have time to ask. Abel lowered his mouth to my neck as his hand cupped my butt, hauling me up against him.

I lifted my hands to his shoulders, my fingers tracing his firm muscles. It wasn't enough—nothing could be. I pressed a kiss to his chest, over the hour-old scar—then licked it and a shudder rippled through his body.

Sliding his hand down to my thigh, he hiked my leg up and around his hip and pressed me into the bulge in his pants. He released a low groan.

Lifting my mouth to his, I bit his lower lip, then licked it.

He groaned again. "I'm about to throw you onto the bed and take you."

My core tightened and desire washed through me, stealing my breath. "So do it."

Dropping my leg, he took a step back, his chest heaving. "Take off your bra and panties."

The side of my mouth lifted into a grin. "What happened to throwing me onto the bed and taking me?"

He flashed a strained grin as he reached for the button of his jeans. "I'm determined to make this last longer than a seventeen-year-old boy's first time."

I reached behind my back with both hands and unhooked my bra but hesitated before I let it drop. Abel was a demigod, more physically perfect than any mortal man. I'd spent the last two weeks working out twice a day, three hours at a time, with the men Abel had hired to train me to defend myself against demons. I'd lost my former softness and replaced it with muscle. He'd told me two nights ago that he preferred my appearance before.

"Waboose," he purred, reaching for the straps and nudging them over my shoulders. "I prefer you strong and alive." He paused as the bra dropped and his gaze fell to my breasts. "You're absolutely beautiful." Sensing I wasn't totally convinced, he said, "I only said that to aggravate you. I was fighting my feelings for you, Piper. I knew it would make things easier for both of us if you were pissed at me." His hands lowered to cup my breasts. "If I made you feel less desirable, I'm sorry."

I sucked in a breath as he tweaked my nipple and a new rush of lust washed through me. "Jeans off. Now."

He quickly unfastened his jeans and pushed them and his boxer briefs down. When he stepped out of them, the only barrier between us was my panties, yet he still didn't reach for me.

"Are you absolutely sure?" he said, his voice strained. "If I were a better man, I would tell you no and that would be the end of it, but my father is the god of hell. His power flows through my veins."

I hooked my thumbs under my panties and pushed them over my hips, letting them drop to the floor.

"Let me be your Kewasa, Abel," I said again.

His jaw tightened and his hands fisted at his sides. "You're risking your soul on a hunch, Piper. Think this through."

I closed the distance between us and placed my palms on his chest, slowly sliding them down his abs until I took him in one hand with a slow, firm stroke. "The only thing I need to think through is protection." Then I remembered something he'd told me the day before. "Then again, maybe not. Since you're sterile and you said you can't contract sexually transmitted diseases, right?"

He hardened even more in my hand as I continued to stroke. "And if I tell you I'm a cesspool of disease, would that change your mind?" he said through gritted teeth.

I grinned, thrilled that I could make Kieran Abel lose control.

My thoughts spurred him into action. He pulled me onto the bed and lowered himself beside me, slipping a hand between my legs and claiming my breast with his mouth. My back arched as he set every nerve ending in my body on fire.

"There's so much I want to do to you," he ground out as he kissed his way to my other breast. "But my need for you will soon win out."

I knew what he meant. While I was eager to savor every part of him, there was a hunger deep in my soul that demanded to be satiated.

"This won't last long, Waboose, and for that I'm sorry." And with that, he rolled on top of me, shoving his arms under my back and gripping my shoulders as he braced himself on his forearms. He looked deep into my eyes as he prodded my entrance. "You are a witness to creation, Kewasa—" He entered me with a short stroke.

Everything in me cried out for more. "Abel…"

"You think I'm perfect, but in the supernatural world, that makes your soul pure." He retreated and pushed deeper. "And me unworthy."

I cried out, wrapping my arms around his back and trying to pull him in deeper. "No," I said, my voice tight. "Opposites. Equals."

His eyes searched mine again. "That remains to be seen, but I'm powerless to stop now."

He filled me with a hard thrust, fully seating himself. His eyes closed, and he paused to suck in a breath.

"Then don't stop," I said in a low, sultry voice as I squeezed around him.

His eyes opened, filled with raw hunger and power. My left palm began to burn, and I snatched it from his back to see the marks had begun to glow. My gaze shot up to Abel's. He leaned over and placed a kiss on my palm, sending a bolt of electricity straight to my core, and I cried out in surprise and pleasure.

The human part of Abel seemed to be replaced by his supernatural half as he growled, digging his fingers into my shoulders, and began a rhythm of long, hard thrusts, yet he no matter how deeply he thrust, it wasn't deep enough.

Grunting in frustration, he grabbed my right leg and pulled my calf up over his shoulder, then plunged even deeper.

I cried out again as he shifted his weight, hitting all the right spots that wound me tighter, yet it still wasn't enough. I needed more. "*Abel.*"

I felt a wave of power flow from him. As always, my body responded, craving him, but this time my own power rose up to meet the surge. I heard him gasp in surprise, just before he lost all control.

I fell into myself, surrounded by his power and the thrusts that pushed me higher and higher until I fell apart, crying out his name.

The room began to spin, plunging into a black void. I was nothing, surrounded by nothing.

Fear raced through my head, but then an explosion of energy and light blinded me. It flooded me with more power than I was sure I could hold, but I realized my body wasn't present, only my consciousness. A combination of vapor and energy exploded and then another and another, forming red and blue and white balls of light, erupting with violence everywhere around me. Everything began to move at a speed I struggled to comprehend, yet I had a sense of déjà vu, like I'd been here before. Then the déjà vu found a foothold in my soul, in the memories imprinted in my DNA, and I was overwhelmed with awe.

I was witnessing the birth of the universe.

I continued hurtling through space until I finally slowed down, and I began to orbit an explosion of yellow and orange light. Somehow I knew it was a dying star. It began to spin, creating a vortex that threatened to suck me in, then exploded into a blinding light, and I knew I'd witnessed the birth of our sun.

The explosion shot debris into the cosmos, and me along with it, but the sun's gravity pulled us to a screeching halt. The particles began to clump together to form a molten ball, which spun while orbiting the sun.

The birth of the Earth.

Debris from space began to plummet to the surface until a rock carrying a drop of water hit the lava, then another and another. A crust began to form, and then water. Power rose from the juncture of land and water, and a being was born.

Ahone.

I'd never seen him, but I knew it was him more surely than I knew my own name.

He created plants and animals and man, along with a host of other supernatural creatures to keep him company. Then the wind gods became jealous of his power and Ahone split himself in two, creating Okeus, his brother. His twin. Ahone kept the better parts of himself—compassion and love—and gave his brother only the insidious parts—greed and evil.

Okeus was jealous of his brother's creation of humans and he strived to create his own, but managed only to form monster after monster until he found someone who could help him—a woman in a Croatan village who had been a witness to creation. Enthralled by Okeus's tremendous power, the woman gave herself willingly to the god of war to give him a child worthy of inheriting his kingdom.

But then Manteo and Ananias Dare created the curse—at Ahone's bidding—locking Okeus and all of his supernatural creatures deep in hell while Ahone alone remained free.

Until a baby was born eight months later.

Ahone watched from above as the woman gave birth, nearly dying from blood loss. He considered killing the baby—his brother's perfect son—but quickly changed his mind.

He could use the boy for his own benefit. His brother would eventually break free, and how perfect would it be for Okeus's long-desired son to reject him?

My consciousness hurtled forward in time, to my own creation. I must have had some control over the vision, thankfully, because I didn't see my parents doing the deed. My view was from outside the window in their bedroom. But I sensed an unseen force present at my conception, injecting my soul, a witness to creation, into my physical being.

Abel and I had both been controlled from the very beginning. We were pawns on a celestial chessboard.

I was hurled forward in time to Okeus, who sat on a throne constructed of bones, surrounded by hundreds of souls—humans and monsters. Some, the chosen few, were naked and emaciated and bound to his throne with heavy chains. They wailed in agony, and Okeus soaked up their misery as if it were a drug.

A malevolent smile lit up the god's face. "Let Ahone orchestrate his games. I shall plan my own. Abiel will be mine, and his succubus will bear many children while he is forced to torture her as punishment for defying me." His eyes darkened and his voice filled with power. "Just as I will make the son of the land pay for his own betrayal. He will watch me kill the daughter of the sea after I endlessly torture her, and I will soak in every scream, every wave of pain. Then I will kill him too and chain their souls to my throne to torment them for the rest of eternity." His eyes narrowed, and it felt like he could see me, like he was staring into my very soul. "I will find you, *Kewasa*." He spat my name as though it left a bitter taste on his tongue. "I will send my army to find you and drag you to hell where I will make you into *nothing*."

Just as quickly as I'd been sucked into the creation of the universe, I was back on Abel's bed, in his arms, as he urgently called out my name.

I stared up into his eyes, and I knew what we had to do.

We had to kill Okeus.

CHAPTER FOUR

Piper

Abel searched my face with worry-filled eyes.

"How long was I out of it?" I asked in a low tone.

"Nearly a minute," he said, his hands running up and down my arm. He was sitting up and he'd pulled me onto his lap, my side pressed to his chest and abdomen. "I worried I killed you."

I released a shaky chuckle as I tried to pull away from him. "Someone's full of himself."

His arms tightened around me. "This isn't a time for joking, Piper."

My humor fell away. "No. You're right. It's a time for plotting."

His head tilted as his eyes narrowed. "What are you talking about?"

"We have to kill Okeus."

His body stiffened. "You passed out and woke up delusional."

"I didn't pass out, Abel. I saw it." When I realized he didn't know what I was talking about, I grabbed his hand. "Creation. I saw the creation of the universe. The birth of the gods."

His jaw slackened and he hauled me closer. "Piper. You've received a tremendous gift."

"You couldn't sense it with the ring?"

"No."

"Ahone played you, Abel," I said softly. "He was there when you were born—*I* was there when you were born. Your mother nearly bled to death. Ahone was about to kill you, but he decided to turn you against your father instead."

Abel didn't react.

"You knew."

His hand began to lightly stroke my arm. "I've suspected."

"When he told you about me," I said, "what was his purpose? Why would he want you to die?"

"To get even with my father?" he said in a monotone. "Obviously, he wanted to use me to hurt him. Maybe he hoped you'd have to kill me in front of my father. Give me to him, then take me away."

"But Okeus rules hell," I said. "He'd still have you."

"He wants a son to rule the earth while he rules the underworld. Once I'm dead, I can't come back. And then I become a threat to his throne."

"He's currently harboring a grudge the size of Mount Everest."

"Of course he is." Then he stiffened. "You saw something." When I didn't answer, he said, "You saw Okeus."

"He sat on a throne made of bones, Abel. I heard him announce his plans for you and me and Ellie and Collin." I paused as a shiver of fear trailed down my back. "He intends to torture us for all of eternity. He knew my soul was there. He told me that he was sending an army for me."

Abel's face paled.

"So we kill him instead," I said in a flat voice.

He leaned back and stared down at me. "You say that like you're suggesting we go to the store to buy a loaf of bread." He shook his head. "You can't just kill a god, Waboose. They are immortal. The best you can hope to do is bind their power. And even *that* is next to impossible. Neither one of us is even close to strong enough."

"What about the curse keepers?" I asked. "I'm sure they want to kill Okeus too. Collin hates him."

"You think the curse keeper would kill him for you?" he asked in a rough voice.

I turned and grinned up at him. "You're cute when you're jealous."

"I'm not jealous."

My grin spread. "The ring told me differently, Abel."

His hold on me tightened as he lowered his mouth to mine, his lips and tongue possessing me.

I wrapped an arm around his neck, losing myself to passion.

He lifted his head with a frustrated look. "I'd hoped that I'd find you less distracting after we consummated our relationship, but I only want you more."

He was right. I was overwhelmed to the point of distraction too, but we needed to get back to the subject at hand. "Your jealousy is wasted. Collin doesn't want to kill Okeus for me, and you know it. He'd do it to save himself and Ellie, but mostly for Ellie." I paused. "I suspect he'd move heaven and earth to save her."

His eyes narrowed to pinpoints. "Are you insinuating I wouldn't do the same for you?"

His question caught me off guard. "I don't know…maybe. But Collin *loves* Ellie. They have a relationship, albeit a dysfunctional one. They've known each other for months. We've known each other for a couple of weeks, and you've purposely stayed away from me."

He stared at me and I wished I had the ring to know what he was thinking right now.

"Abel, you disagree?"

"You're correct," he said, sounding stiff and formal. "We haven't had the time they've had."

He sounded hurt or insulted, or perhaps both, but for the life of me, I didn't understand why. While our supernatural bond was indisputable, it was pointless to compare us to Collin and Ellie. Abel's desire to leave the mortal plane was what had initially driven him to me, and although our connection had grown into something more, something much deeper, it wasn't love.

A dark look crossed his face. "Perhaps you're correct that our supernatural bond and my need for you to kill me motivated me in the beginning," he said, "but do not for one moment dissect emotion out of this."

His statement gave me pause. "I never said—or *thought*—that there wasn't emotion involved. I know you care about me, Abel, and I care about you. But it's not love."

Not yet.

I knew that, given more time, I would love him.

Something flashed in his eyes, but he promptly changed the subject. "If my father is sending an army for you, then we have two choices—we either hide here or go back. I opt for staying here."

I stared at him in disbelief. "You want me to hide? Are you kidding me?"

His jaw tightened. "Make no mistake, Piper, you and your safety are now my highest priority."

"But if we stay here, we leave the curse keepers vulnerable. And what about Jack and Rhys? You want me to just leave them there?" And what about the perpetual five-year-old ghost boy hidden in my attic? I wouldn't abandon Tommy. "No, Abel. We have to go back. We can't run from our problems, and I don't want to spend my life in what amounts to a pretty cage."

"I have to protect you at all costs."

"And I have to protect my friends and my cousin."

His rigid back and tense body suggested he had no intention of budging. I needed to take a different approach.

"Abel," I said softly, pressing a kiss to the base of his neck.

His body stiffened. "I know what you're doing, Waboose. I'd know even if I weren't wearing the ring."

I didn't let him deter me as I pressed another kiss on his chest.

Some of the tension left his body, replaced by an entirely different type of tension as I trailed kisses across his chest and down to his nipple.

"Why am I so drawn to you?" I asked in all seriousness, already wanting him as much as I had the first time…maybe more since I now knew how amazing it was with him.

His answer was to press his mouth to mine and roam my body with his hands, leaving me panting for more, the seductee now the seductor.

"We have to go back, Abel," I said breathlessly. "We can't stay here."

He stilled, his face hovering over mine. "I know," he whispered, "but let me have you one more time."

I looked deep into his eyes filled with longing and possessiveness.

"You're mine, Piper Lancaster."

"And you're mine," I said, testing the words and feeling the weight of them on my soul.

He pressed me back on the bed and took me, hard and fast, and I clung to him, meeting him at every stroke. As we lay panting afterward, he hung his head close to mine and said, "At least you didn't pass out on me this time."

I grinned up at him. "You must be losing your touch."

He smiled back and brushed some stray hairs from my cheek. "I want more time with you, Piper. Just you and me."

My heart ached. I wanted that too, but we'd already spent too much time here. "We have to go back. The sooner the better."

His smile fell and his gaze held mine. "I can't stop thinking about what happened in the warehouse. You could have been killed."

I gave him a wry look. "But I wasn't. And it's the only way back. We need to recruit the others before Okeus sends his army, and at the very least, Ellie and Collin deserve to know Okeus's plans." I nudged him to roll him to the side. "But first I need to get dressed. I'm presuming all the clothes you bought me are in the guest room."

"It's your world, Waboose. If you wish them to be there, they will be."

I pushed him off me and slid out of bed. "If I put on clothes I created in a parallel world, will I still be wearing them when I go back to ours?"

He propped up on his forearm, his lusty gaze following my movement. "I guess we'll find out."

Rolling my eyes, I decided to wear my original undergarments—just to be safe.

"Good idea," he murmured as he got out of bed too. "I don't want anyone else seeing you. Especially the curse keeper."

I liked this version of Abel, the one he became when we were alone together—warm, affectionate…lust-filled.

A fire lit in his eyes and he glanced down at me as a small grin played at the corners of his mouth. The mouth I very much wanted to kiss again. Would I ever get my fill of him?

"I am always full of lust for you, Waboose, whether you have me to yourself or if we're in a room full of people. I plan to spend the next century proving it to you."

His declaration stole my breath, but also reminded me that he could read every thought that passed through my head. I reached for his hand. "No more wearing the ring unless we both agree."

"I don't approve of that plan," he said in a sullen tone. "I need to know where you are and what you're thinking."

"Our connection tells you where I am," I countered. "And if you want to know what I'm thinking, just ask."

He considered it for a moment, then said, "Let me keep it on when we go back to the warehouse. We may need the connection if we encounter demons."

I frowned up at him. "Fine, but there's no reason for you to have it on now."

I slipped the ring off his finger, then stretched up and placed a quick kiss on his mouth before I walked out.

I headed to the guest room, refocusing my thoughts. I wondered how big this world actually was. The world I'd created for Tommy had pretty severe limits, but this world seemed to encompass Abel's entire house. And the surrounding mountainside.

The guest room closet was still full of clothes, and it struck me as odd that I'd recreated a closet full of items I'd barely paid attention to before.

I put on a pair of jeans and a black T-shirt, plus a pair of shoes from the back of the closet, and headed back out to the living room, surprised Abel hadn't followed me to the guest room.

I found him on the balcony, wearing a charcoal colored T-shirt that clung to his chest and arms, and fresh jeans that weren't stained with blood.

Kieran Abel liked to pretend he was a soulless monster, but I knew better. I'd seen the frayed edges. I'd experienced his concern for my emotional well-being. Maybe his soul had gotten dusty after centuries of not caring about anyone other than himself, but he was capable of caring about people. He obviously cared about me.

What had I cost him by forcing his hand to save me at the warehouse? Okeus now knew he had a son and, worse, a son who defied him. Whatever the price, I refused to be sorry for going to save my friends. It may have been a trap, but if we hadn't sprung it, Rhys and Jack would likely be dead. Just like my best friend Hudson.

The thought of Hudson sent a wave of grief through me. I'd failed him. How had the Great One killed him? Had he been tortured?

I'd been in too much shock to pay close attention to the state of his body.

His body, bloodied and beaten, likely still lying on the warehouse floor.

Abel turned to face me, his eyes burning with a different emotion this time. Compassion. While I'd suspected Abel had the capacity for it, I had seen little evidence of it before. No, that wasn't true. He'd shown me compassion before, but never to this degree.

I continued toward him and he held out his arms, enveloping me in his embrace when I was within reach.

This embrace was as different from what we'd just finished as night and day. He was giving himself to me now without wanting anything in return.

It only made me more certain that I was right about him.

"It's only natural that this would be overwhelming," he said. "Do you have regrets?"

"No," I said. "That's not it. Hudson's body is still lying on that warehouse floor. Like his death meant nothing. Like no one cares."

He kissed the top of my head and I broke down into tears that quickly turned to sobs.

"I killed him, Abel. I killed Hudson."

"You didn't kill him, Waboose. The demon killed him."

"It killed him to hurt *me*."

He was silent for a moment. "The demons and gods will use everyone you love and care about to hurt you and break you. It is the destiny that comes with your ability," he murmured softly in my ear. "It's not fair, yet there it is."

I wanted to argue with him, but I knew he spoke the truth. I looked up at him and gave him a weak smile. "I need you to keep doing that."

Confusion filled his eyes. "Doing what?"

"Telling me the truth."

"I will, Waboose. Even when it hurts." He frowned, then turned to look down at the dark valley below his house. From the balcony of his real house, I'd seen the lights of Asheville in the distance. Now I saw only a black haze. The air was unnaturally still. This place wasn't real, even if it felt like it.

"We need to be prepared to fight the moment we step into that warehouse," he said.

I swallowed, glancing at my belt laid out atop the small balcony table. Abel must have set it there after I headed to my room to change. "I've only had a couple hours of training with this sword. I saw those demon lions. I don't know that I can fight them."

His eyes darkened. "You can, and you will."

My eyes shot to the sheath hanging from his belt. "You only have one sword."

His lopsided, arrogant smile reappeared. "Why would I need anything more?"

I laughed despite the drying tears on my cheeks. In this instance, I was glad Abel was so cocksure.

"So we go back to the warehouse and then head to my house. I told Ellie and her men to bring Rhys and Jack there." My voice broke as I thought again about Hudson's broken body.

"Hey," Abel said in a soft voice as he picked up my belt. "You can handle this." He wrapped it around my back and fastened the buckle.

My stomach knotted. "How can you be so certain?"

"Because you have no other choice."

He finished with my belt, then took my hand and pulled me close. "Do we have to be in an embrace to go back, or can we just be touching?"

"I don't know. I didn't even know if this would work," I said, brushing my hair back in frustration. "I made a universe in my attic by walking through the door to the staircase leading up to it. This was completely guesswork."

He stared at me in disbelief. Then his expression darkened. "We'll discuss *that* issue later, but the takeaway is that *you* set the rules, Piper."

I nodded, not quite believing it. "I make the rules."

He cupped my chin and leaned close. "Get us back, and I'll deal with the rest." He gave me a deep kiss. "Now give me back the ring. Then turn around and draw your sword."

The ring was in my fist, so I grabbed his hand and slid it onto his ring finger. I looked into his eyes, hating how much I was depending on him to protect me. For the past few weeks, I'd understood exactly why he was helping me—because he wanted me to kill him. Now we were on new ground. He wanted to survive so he could protect me. I had no choice but to trust him, although I'd almost feel better if there were something concrete he wanted or needed from me.

"You have no reason to doubt me, Waboose. My loyalties *have* changed, and *you* are my priority now." He smiled, his smug smile that usually pissed me off, but once again, it filled me with reassurance, if only because it would be a massive blow to his ego if a demon killed me.

"Abel, promise me one thing."

Fear flickered in his eyes. "What?"

"Don't let your father capture and torture me. I need the blood vow you made about the demons to extend to your father."

His mouth parted and he hesitated before he said, "You want me to kill you if my father is about to capture you?"

My mouth turned dry, and I swallowed. "Yes. I know the hell he has planned for me. You have to spare me from that, Abel."

I didn't think he was going to agree, but finally he said, "If I think there is no hope, I'll kill you before letting you suffer for eternity."

"And I'll find a way to save you from eternity in hell. I swear it."

A smile lit up his eyes. "If anyone is capable of it, it's you."

I reached up and gave him a gentle kiss. "Let's do this." Then I spun around and pulled out my sword, holding it in a defensive stance.

Abel pressed his back to mine and grabbed my left hand with his right one. I glanced over my shoulder to look at him. "You're not left-handed."

His smug grin spread wider. "I'm a demigod. I can be whatever I want to be. Now go."

CHAPTER FIVE

Piper

I knew we were back in the warehouse before I opened my eyes. The air was thick with the stench of blood, decay, urine, vomit, and shit. Surprise, surprise, none of the demons had bothered to clean up. I heard snarls and my eyes flew open as Abel dropped my hand. The mark in the palm of my left hand felt like it was on fire.

As if I needed the mark to tell me we were surrounded.

We'd dropped into carnage. There was a pile of human body parts about ten feet in front of me, remnants of the members of the Guardians who'd been ripped to literal shreds by the demon lions, a name I'd bestowed upon the bulldog-faced demons with the bodies of gigantic lions. Their black fur made a great camouflage in the dark warehouse, but their red eyes glowed in the dark. I knew this because one of them sat on its haunches in front of me, beside an axe-wielding demon that looked a lot like a minotaur.

Oh. Shit.

"Abel..."

I could feel his back shift to the side as he glanced over his shoulder. He then quickly turned to the side, dragging me with him. It only took a second to understand why he hadn't turned to completely face the mythological creature—he'd been facing two demon lions of his own.

Twenty feet behind them lay the crumpled, naked body of my best friend.

I felt my knees buckle and my stomach churn. While I'd guessed his body would probably still be here, knowing it and seeing it were two entirely different things.

Piper, stay strong, Abel said in my mind.

"Son of Okeus," the minotaur said in a deep, rumbling voice, pronouncing the god's name as Okee. "Your father insists you join him." His gaze shifted to me. "And that you bring your succubus with you."

My eyebrow shot up high on my forehead. "*Succubus?*"

Again with the succubus. Was that the supernatural word for slut?

"Not now, Waboose," Abel growled in a low tone.

"Waboose?" the minotaur said with a laugh. "She looks like a warrior, not a waboose."

What the hell was a waboose? I'd thought it was some made-up nickname he'd given me, not another supernatural title.

Abel quickly took control again. "Tell my father we decline his offer."

The minotaur lifted the ax and dropped the end of the handle into the curled palm of his hand. "Tell him yourself after we drag you to him."

Abel turned to face the minotaur, full on, with his uplifted sword.

"How did you know we'd come back?" I asked. I needed to find out what they actually knew.

"We didn't," a male voice said from the dark shadows next to the stage. "But Okeus told us to wait to see if you returned."

"You didn't go to my house?" I asked. Ellie and her crew could take care of themselves, but I wanted to know if Rhys and Jack were safe.

"He was certain you would return here," the hidden monster said. "We were less sure."

And likely pissed to be stuck here waiting for us. It made me wonder if Okeus already knew about my ability to create worlds—and its limitations.

"We have no quarrel with you," Abel said, "as long as you let us go."

The minotaur laughed. "If we let you go, Okeus will punish us for a hundred years."

I suspected he meant that literally.

"One hundred years of punishment is better than an eternity in the abyss," Abel said matter-of-factly. "And I have no intention of letting you have Kewasa, so prepare to die."

The minotaur laughed. "You can't kill me, half-breed."

"You're a half-breed yourself, Theos," Abel said, his voice calm and even, a sharp contrast to my hammering heart.

I didn't dare take my eyes off the demon lurking in the dark shadows by the stage.

Your sight is not your only defense, Kewasa. Use your power, Abel's voice spoke into my head.

He was right, but I still wasn't sure of all I could do with my power. I did know I could sense out demons with the mark on my palm, so I concentrated on that. The burning in my hand shot up my arm to my chest, and something inside me seemed to ignite, bursting to life. Suddenly, I could feel every demon in the warehouse—all twenty of them.

We're surrounded by twenty demons, Abel.

Steady, Waboose, we shall defeat them.

I was happy he had such a positive attitude, but then I remembered that he could use his power to freeze demons in place. If he did that now, we could escape.

No. There are too many for me to freeze. And they know too much. They must all die.

41

Well, shit.

Take the two demon lions, he said. *Move to the first demon lion's left side and pierce its heart. Then kill the second one while I take Theos.*

I nearly snorted. Like it would be that easy.

He chose to ignore my pessimism. *On the count of three. One.*

I took in a breath and willed myself to calm down.

Two.

"Okeus said to bring you alive," Theos announced. "He never said either one of you had to be in perfect condition."

On that note, Abel thought, *Three.*

He lunged first, charging the demon lion next to the minotaur. I was a half second behind him, leaping for the pair of lions only ten feet in front of me. They reacted quickly, hunkering down to pounce, but I jagged to the left and jumped up on the stage. They turned toward me in confusion, one of them releasing a roar. The other simply watched me.

Now what? They had to be killed and I wasn't about to wait until they came up. With another leap, I hopped off the stage, landing hard on the non-roaring demon lion and straddling its back, surprised at how cold its body felt.

It took a second to react, shaking its body in an attempt to dislodge me. I grabbed a handful of the hair at the base of its neck and briefly considered killing it straight off, but I was on its back and out of the way of its mouth—it wasn't such a bad place to be. Instead, I lunged for the demon lion next to me, shoving the sword into its side, knowing full well the blow wouldn't be deep enough to reach its heart but hoping a wound would slow it down.

I'd hoped wrong.

The demon lion roared in anger and swiped its massive claws toward me. I slid my leg out of the way in time to narrowly miss being clawed, but the demon's claws sank into the side of the demon I was riding.

My mount roared, bellowing in pain, then rose up slightly on its hind legs. I dug my knees into its sides and held on tight with my left hand to keep from getting bucked off—then changed my mind as I realized it was preparing to charge the other lion. I sank my sword into its back, finding its soul. The demon disintegrated underneath me, covering me in ash, but I was more concerned with the demon advancing on me. I shifted St. Michael in my left hand, arced back my arm, then plunged the blade into the demon lion's right eye.

It roared, taking a swipe at me, but I cut off its left paw with my sword. The demon fell onto its chest and I stabbed the sword into its left side, striking its soul. It collapsed into ash, and I pierced the rising orb that looked like a translucent ball of fireflies, taking a second to watch the souls float into the air.

As I got to my feet, I could see that Abel had already killed his two demon lions and was now surrounded by a circle of a half dozen demons of various shapes and sizes. The minotaur stood on the outside watching.

A quick count established that there were still four unaccounted-for demons, not including the one lurking in the shadows.

"Come out, come out, wherever you are," I sing-songed, moving closer to the dark recesses of the enormous room.

"Come and find me, slayer," called the demon in the shadows.

I knew I should stick close to Abel, but something in this demon's voice called to me, making me want to find him.

Was he like Caelius? A sex demon that drew power from sexually aroused creatures? No, the lure wasn't sexual, and it hit me that he wasn't drawing me with a power of his own.

My power sought his.

That was new.

"Do you have a name, demon?" I asked as I took purposeful steps toward it.

It had been close, but I could sense it backing up, moving toward a small group of three lesser demons. More lions.

I drew in a sharp breath. I'd been lucky with the other two. What made me think I could handle three more demon lions and the unknown demon?

"I have a name," the demon said in a humorous tone, "but I prefer not to give it."

Smart. Names held power in the supernatural world. My cousin Ellie claimed powerful supernatural titles could scare off demons, but none of these bad boys looked like they were going anywhere, and I was pretty sure they knew my titles. Well, hopefully not *all* of them.

"Then I'll give you a name," I said. "But first I have to see you."

The demon laughed. "Then come find me, little bunny."

That caught me off guard. Was it calling me bait? But I ignored the verbal taunt and focused on the demon's whereabouts. It was obvious it thought it was hiding from me, completely unaware that I knew exactly where it and every other demon in this warehouse was located. But I still needed to see it to attack. Too bad this power didn't come with night vision.

I followed the demon's presence down a long, dark hallway along one side of the building, which was illuminated by the moonlight shining in through broken windows. The demon lions were in front of him, all four heading in the same direction.

Leading me away from Abel.

I was stupid to follow. This was obviously part of their plan, which likely involved using me as bait for Abel, but the spot deep in my soul, the newly awakened part of me, was hungry for their souls.

And that scared the ever-loving shit out of me.

Had I been wrong about my soul saving Abel's? Had I doomed myself instead?

The demons had finally stopped moving. I couldn't see them, but I knew they were waiting for me in a loading dock.

"Demon," I called out with the authority of the slayer I was. "Show yourself." I walked through the door to the dock, knowing that three demon lions stood between me and the unknown demon.

Piper, come back here! Abel shouted in my head, and while part of me acknowledged that was a really good idea, the dark part in my soul refused to consider it.

What the hell was happening to me?

Moonlight shone through the busted metal overhang, giving me a glimpse of my adversary. I hadn't expected it to look like a man, even though Caelius had resembled a man too, a wickedly handsome one. This demon was no less handsome, but he looked younger. Less experienced. He was blond, with a baby face, and looked to be no more than eighteen, but I knew that meant nothing. He was probably eons old.

"What are you?" I asked him, my right hand holding my sword and my left hand clutching my dagger, St. Michael, which I'd named after the carving of a sword-wielding angel on horseback.

He grinned. "I'm that which you seek."

I resisted the urge to roll my eyes. "Cut the bullshit."

"How do you plan to get to me, slayer? That was a neat trick with the leonals, getting them to turn on each other, but it won't happen with these three. They may tend to be more beastly than human, but they're smart. They learned from the others' mistakes."

"Why haven't you had them attack me yet?" I asked, sounding more confident than I felt.

"You heard Theos. The boss man wants you alive."

"And what do *you* want?" I asked.

"I want to know where you went."

I just stared at him. He'd have to wait forever for that answer.

He gave me a sly look. "Okeus will find out. He has his ways. Ways you won't find so pleasant."

I had no doubts about that. A shiver ran down my back, but I kept up my cocky attitude. "Why would he care where I went?"

He grinned again. "You're not that stupid, slayer."

I found it interesting that out of all my titles, he'd chosen to call me slayer. It was probably the only one that mattered to him, yet neither he nor the leonals had attacked me yet. He was waiting for something, and that made me nervous. "Why aren't there more demons here with us? Why are the rest with Abel?"

He laughed again. "Maybe you are that stupid. They wish to subdue the god's son. They all want to be the one to bring him to his father."

"You got stuck with me, huh?" I asked with plenty of sass.

"Oh, on the contrary, *Waboose*," he leered. "I *chose* you."

Well, crap. That didn't sound good.

"I want you to take me where you took the son of Okeus," he said.

I snorted. "That's not happening, which means you chose incorrectly. Especially since I have to kill you. Instead of dying at the hands of a demigod, you're about to get killed by a lowly human. How embarrassing."

He laughed again. "You'll definitely be fun."

Somehow I didn't think he meant he'd enjoy bringing me to Okeus.

"Okeus will kill you if you don't hand me over to him."

"He'll never know I took you." Turning aside, he said something in a language I didn't understand, and the leonals began to move. Within seconds, I had one on each side and one directly in front of me.

I reached out to Abel, trying to sense how many demons were left in his part of the warehouse. There were only two and Abel was moving quickly toward me.

Great. I'd never hear the end of it if he saved me like I was some damsel in distress. I needed to gain control of the situation, and quickly.

The greatest threat from the demon lions was their front claws. The demons at my sides were only a few feet away, so I lunged left with St. Michael, plunging it to the hilt into the demon's side. The tip barely reached the demon's soul, but the effect was the same—it was rendered into a pile of black ash. Having already withdrawn my weapon, lunged to the right, bringing my sword down across both of the demon's legs and chopping off its paws.

The leonal in front of me hunched back, then leapt for me. I dove forward, sliding across the thankfully smooth concrete floor, and jammed my sword up into the demon's chest.

The blade didn't quite reach its soul, but the demon's forward momentum continued, taking my sword with it.

Hopping to my feet, I drew my other dagger, Ivy, from its sheath. I spun around to face the demon with the amputated paws. Black blood covered the floor and the demon roared in pain as it tried to hobble toward me, but I knew it wouldn't die. It would eventually stop bleeding and begin to heal. The only thing that would kill a demon was to plunge a spelled blade into its soul. And while this demon could no longer claw me, its huge mouth full of teeth could do some serious damage.

The third demon lay on its side, the sword still stuck in its chest. I really needed that sword back, so I resheathed Ivy and rushed for the demon, plunging St. Michael into its side as I pulled out the sword. The dagger hadn't gone deep enough, so I stabbed it with the sword again, this time penetrating its soul. As the demon disintegrated into ash, the souls of all the animals and people it had killed floated away, looking like fireflies in the darkness.

Withdrawing the sword, I plunged it into the last leonal, striking true this time. Hundreds of souls floated up as the demon turned to ash.

"Impressive," the remaining demon said with a slow clap.

"Are you going to tell me your name?" I asked. "Or am I going to have to give you one?"

He laughed. "And give you power over me, slayer? I'm not stupid either."

"Have it your way, Boy Band," I sneered as I shifted to face him.

"Boy Band?" Another laugh escaped from him.

I shrugged. "If the hair fits…"

He moved toward me and I remained still, holding both weapons to my sides.

"Why aren't you afraid of me?" I asked, holding his gaze.

He didn't drop eye contact as he closed the last few feet between us. He stood in front of me, big and bold, and I could see by the triumph in his eyes he thought he had me under some kind of spell.

"You will come with me now, Piper," he said in a low tone, reaching for my sword hand.

"Where will we go?" I asked, trying to keep my voice even and maintain the illusion that I was in his thrall.

My grip tightened on St. Michael. I knew this demon likely had supernatural speed, which meant I had to move quickly, no hesitation.

But then his gaze lifted over my shoulder, and I heard Abel behind me.

"Kewasa. I see you've met Adonis."

Adonis? As in the Greek god? How did Abel know? My brows lifted as Adonis took several steps backward.

"Son of Okeus, it's an honor," he said, only the sneer on his face suggested otherwise.

Several growls sounded behind us, and Abel cursed under his breath. "Piper, run out the back and let me deal with this."

Was he joking? I wasn't running from anything. Even if I'd wanted to go, my new hunger for the demons' souls wouldn't have allowed it.

But I didn't have time to argue as the two demons he'd left behind advanced toward him, one of them the minotaur with the axe. I hopped down to the loading dock driveway and Adonis followed, looking pleased with himself.

"Piper!" Abel shouted, clearly irritated with me.

I held up my sword as I took several steps backward. "I'm not going anywhere with you, so you're wasting your time."

"I realize you won't voluntarily take me there now, but I'm certain you'll be more agreeable later."

Ah, so he wanted me to take him somewhere. I had a pretty good idea of why.

Grunts and clanging metal sounded behind me, but I kept my focus on Adonis. "Your spells don't work on me. Why would I help you?"

"Because I know how to stop the inevitable from happening."

My heart skipped a beat, but I played ignorant. "I don't know what you're talking about."

He rolled his eyes. "Don't play dumb, Kewasa. You're Abiel's deliverer, but it's obvious you care about him."

I couldn't let him see my hope roaring to life. "What makes you think so?"

A knowing grin spread across his face. "You know my name, human. You know what I am."

"And I suppose you want me to take you to where I went in exchange for this information?"

His grin spread. "Maybe you aren't so dumb after all."

"What about Okeus? He won't like you making this side deal."

"He'll never know."

I shot a glance to Abel, who was now in a fierce battle with the minotaur. Blood streamed down the side of his face. This was why he wasn't reacting to my thoughts—he couldn't spare the energy.

I sucked in a breath.

"Theos won't kill him," Adonis said. "Okeus would torture him for centuries. He'll want the glory of bringing Abiel to his father."

"But Theos might capture him."

Adonis cast Abel a speculative look, then shook his head. "No. The son of Okeus is wily. He'll prevail." He turned back to me. "But we only have a short window to do this. Do you wish to save the son of Okeus or not?"

"How do I know this isn't a trick? How do I know you'll fulfill your end of the bargain once I take you there?"

"You don't, but I suspect you want to save him enough to take the risk."

I was tempted…so tempted, but the dying sounds of the minotaur made my decision for me.

Adonis lifted his shoulder into a slight shrug. "I see you need to give this some thought." He took a step backward. "I'll give you some time to consider it, but I'll come to you soon, in your hour of need, and perhaps you'll be more willing."

"And if I'm not?"

His response was to disappear into a black mist and fade out of sight.

Chapter Six

Piper

I told you to stay behind me!" Abel roared from the dock above my head. The entire left side of his face was covered in blood as was his right arm. His shirt was drenched with it.

"You're hurt," I said, sounding as panicked as I felt.

"They aren't mortal wounds," he said in irritation. "Where is Adonis?"

I repressed thoughts of the demon's offer, not wanting to tell him quite yet. I knew he'd think Adonis's offer was a trick, and he'd likely be right, but I wasn't ready to rule it out quite yet. "He turned into smoke and left."

Rage filled his eyes. "He'll run to Okeus."

"No," I said. "He won't want to admit he failed in capturing us. I suspect he'll hide and figure out what to do next." When I saw that didn't appease him, I added, "He didn't know where I took you. He asked me several times to tell him."

The tension in his face eased slightly. "I suspect you're right and there's nothing to be done about it, so now we'll address your disobedience."

"Excuse me?" I said in disbelief. "My *disobedience?*"

"Good to see you're not blindly following him," Collin Dailey said to my right.

I spun to face him as he walked into the loading dock area with a drawn sword. Ellie and Jack followed him, and I could barely make out Rhys and David in the darkness beyond them.

I ignored Collin and ran to Jack, throwing my arms around his neck. "Are you okay?"

He hugged me back. "Other than my pride, I'm fine. I'm the one who should be asking you."

He stepped back, and Rhys nearly tackled me as she surged forward and wrapped her arms around me.

"Piper" was all she said, but the way she said it conveyed so much feeling.

I closed my eyes and buried my face into the nape of her neck, breathing in the scent of my own shampoo. "I'm so sorry, Rhys. Can you forgive me?"

"None of this is your fault. There's nothing to forgive. I'm so, so sorry I hurt you."

I squeezed her tight, holding on for several seconds, before I said in a broken voice, "I failed Hudson."

She pulled back and grabbed my upper arms, giving me a hard look. "No. You had no idea the demon would kill him."

"But I knew a demon was kidnapping people. I should have gotten him protection sooner. I should have insisted he stay home."

Her grip tightened until it hurt. "This is not your fault, Piper. I'm sorry I blamed you for Abby's death, but I had to blame someone, and unfortunately, I wrongly chose you. I'm *so* sorry."

"This place you fled to—where did you go, exactly?" Collin asked from several feet away.

I turned to face him, surprised to see he was addressing Abel, not me.

Abel gave him a dark look and refused to answer.

Collin turned to me. "Where did you go? Were you there all this time?"

"Leave it," Ellie warned.

"I'm just curious about the specifics, that's all," he said.

I shot Abel a glance, then turned to the curse keeper. "I took Abel away from this place, but the demons were waiting when we returned."

I shot Abel a glance, then turned to the curse keeper. "I took Abel away from this place, but the demons were waiting when we returned."

"That doesn't really answer my question, does it?"

"Collin," Ellie groaned. "Enough. Perhaps there's a reason she chose not to answer."

"If we're going to help her, then we have a right to know."

Ellie put her hands on her hips, but not from irritation—it looked like she needed help with her balance and could have been blown over with a feather. "You want to help her?"

He turned to face her, his brow wrinkling in irritation. "You *don't?*"

"Of course I do. She's my cousin and Okeus is after her. Either would compel me, but the two together make me doubly committed. The real question is why *you* want to help her."

"You think I'm that much of an asshole?" he asked, sounding displeased.

"Your babble is pointless," Abel said in a harsh tone. "We need to leave. Now."

Ellie turned her glare on him. "Forgive me if I don't fall over myself to follow the orders of Okeus's son."

"Enough," I sighed, already weary of their argument. "Let's go home."

"Piper's right," David said in a dignified voice, made all the more so by his accent. "We should leave. Okeus could send more demons to intercept us at any moment."

Abel frowned. "I'll take Piper to my mountain home. It's secure from demons."

"We're sticking with Piper," Ellie said in a no-nonsense tone. "I need to talk to her before you haul her to God knows where. We've secured her house. We'll be safe from the demons there."

I stared at her in disbelief. "You secured my house from demons? How?"

"I'll teach you how to protect yourself." She narrowed her eyes at Abel. "And much more."

While I knew Abel's house was a fortress, I needed the comfort of my own home, at least for a few hours. I felt close to Hudson there. I also needed to check on Tommy, and I really, really needed to talk to Ellie.

"We'll go to my house," I said to Abel.

"The demons will look for you there first," he said. "You need to hide."

"Hide?" I spat in disgust. "I'm not hiding."

"Piper," Abel growled.

"They'll never know she's there," Ellie said. "Collin and I left our marks on the door. Our power will hide hers."

"You underestimate her power," Abel said. "It's growing by the hour."

I held Abel's gaze. "Everyone's tired. Okeus doesn't know we've come back and killed his demons. We'll be safe for a few hours."

He gave me a dark glare but didn't argue, just resheathed his sword and gave me a nod that acknowledged we were equals.

Everyone started to head out, and I took a moment to catch my breath as a sharp pain gripped my heart.

Hudson.

I couldn't just walk away and leave his body. This place was abandoned. Who knew when he'd be found? What would his parents do? They'd turn to me for answers, and I wouldn't be able to tell them a blessed thing.

"I'll arrange for someone to find him," Abel said softly. "Besides, he's not really there."

A new horror struck me. He'd been killed by a demon. Had his soul been trapped?

Abel blocked my path as I spun around to go back inside. "I knew your cousin wished to kill the Great One for herself, but I slayed him instead to free your friend," Abel said. "If he hasn't moved on, I suspect his spirit is at your house."

Why hadn't I considered that? "All the more reason to go home." I dropped my gaze to his hand. "But you're handing over that ring first. I'll hold on to it for safekeeping."

I held out my left hand. He placed it on my palm, then stepped closer as he curled my fingers around it, looking deep into my eyes. "There might come a time when I need this ring, Waboose."

"If I think you need it, I'll give it back," I said, giving him a smug smile. "You can feel me, and I can feel you. That's enough for now."

I started walking away from the building toward where we'd left Abel's car, surprised to see it in the parking lot next to Ellie's car, not several blocks away where we'd originally left it.

"Rhys and I took Abel's car," Jack said as he opened the back door. "I thought the four of us would fit better. Plus Abel had weapons in the back…" He held the keys out to the demigod.

Abel took them, wearing a scowl as he opened the driver's door and got in.

The four of us were silent for the first couple of moments of the short drive. Finally, Abel broke the silence and quizzed Jack and Rhys about the curse keepers' behavior at my house.

Both said David and the curse keepers had stayed in the living room, waiting for us to return. It was Jack who'd led the charge back to the warehouse, but Collin had readily followed.

"What about the Cherokee immortals?" Abel asked. "Did they join you?"

"I never saw them after we left the warehouse," Jack said. "But one of the Nunnehi Little People came to the house—Tsagasi—and he told us you'd disappeared into a world."

"You can really create worlds?" Rhys asked me in awe.

"Looks like it," I said, still uncertain about my newest gift.

The sun was rising when Abel pulled into my driveway, parking next to Ellie's car. Everything had changed over the last few hours, yet my house looked remarkably the same. As I got out, I noticed the dark charcoal marks covering the door into my kitchen. "What the…"

"Ellie claims they're marks of protection," Jack said softly as he fell into step beside me, his gaze on Abel. "She says no demon can cross the threshold."

I shot a glance over to Abel, who was studying them as well. "Can you go in?"

"I'm not a demon," he said in a low tone, his gaze still on the marks, then mumbled under his breath, "They're Croatan."

The marks were Croatan?

"That's because they're Collin's," Ellie said, standing next to the door. David stood beside her. "Ahone taught him how to draw the marks before he broke the curse. Collin and I can infuse our power into them. We can do it separately, but sometimes together if we're especially nervous. They've held up until now. They even stop the gods."

"Abel has to come inside," I said in a tone that brooked no argument. "Can he enter or not?"

Ellie shuffled her feet before meeting my gaze. "We're not sure."

"Not sure isn't good enough," I said sternly. "If Abel can't go in, we'll go to his house in the mountains."

"Ellie," Jack pleaded. "We need to stick together." His tone lacked any heat, but I could hear the recrimination hidden in it. How could I choose Abel over the rest of them?

"You can invite him in," David said, "or at least we think it works that way. Ellie received nightly visits from gods and demons who could never enter. But Okeus asked for entrance once. Which leads us to believe you can issue an invitation."

I took a breath to calm down, surprised by my deep need to protect Abel. Was this normal or was it supernatural? "Will it hurt him if he tries to go in?"

"No," David said. "At least I don't think so. It's more likely he'll be incapable of going through. But none of the demons ever tried to force their way in, and I'm certain they would have if it were possible."

I glanced back at Abel. "Do you want them to remove the marks?"

"The marks stay," Abel stated solemnly, then turned to me. "We must keep you safe at all costs."

I shook my head. "But you—"

His mouth tipped up into a lopsided grin. "Await your invitation."

I followed Ellie through the door, then turned back to face Abel.

He stepped up to the entrance and stopped, his expression ruminative. "The markings put up some type of impenetrable supernatural wall."

I held out my hand to him. The curse keepers and demons seemed keen on titles, so I figured it couldn't hurt to include his. "Abel, son of Okeus, enter."

He took my hand and walked over the threshold.

"Did you feel anything?" I asked once he was safely inside.

"An electrical charge across my skin," he said, glancing down at his arms. Sure enough, his hair stood on end.

"Can you teach me to use the marks?" I asked, whirling on Ellie.

"That's a good question," she said as David ushered Jack and Rhys inside, then followed them in. "I'm not sure if they would work for you. Only Collin and I have successfully used them." She gave me an ornery grin. "But then, you're not like most people."

"What do the symbols mean?" Jack asked as he leaned back against the counter. Rhys stood next to him and he wrapped an arm around her shoulders, pulling her close.

David spoke up. "The symbols on the outside ask the wind and moon and earth to protect the occupants. Ellie and Collin use their own symbols for daughter of the sea and son of the land on the inside to seal the protection. While you're a demon hunter, we're not sure you have the same power they do."

"She's also a witness to creation like I am," Ellie said. "And she bears the curse keeper mark on her left hand—the circle in a square, the crossing of the earthly and spiritual worlds. I'm sure she has plenty of power of her own." She turned to me. "Have you seen the creation yet?"

I resisted the urge to shoot a glance to Abel. I wasn't ready to tell anyone that we'd slept together, and I wasn't sure how it was typically seen. However, I needed to tell them about Okeus's plans. Just as I started to speak, Collin walked inside.

"That sounds like a big fat no," he said, closing the door behind him. "The Nunnehi are outside keeping guard."

Ellie's face looked drawn. "Does it count toward one of the seven times we're permitted to call upon them?"

"No," Collin said softly, trying to ease her concern. "They're here of their own accord. They still don't trust Piper, and they're curious."

David gave me a tight smile. "Ellie made a pact with Tsagasi and his friends. They've pledged to help her seven times in exchange for her agreement to defeat Okeus. She's used them twice now. Once when we faced the Guardians and the Great One at the botanical gardens on Roanoke Island and again last night. But sometimes they show up of their own accord and it doesn't count toward her limit."

"They don't trust Piper because of her association with me," Abel stated rather than asked.

"That and they claim she created a world upstairs," Collin said. "They're leery of what she can do."

I wasn't surprised, but it worried me that they knew what was upstairs. Hopefully they couldn't tell what—or rather who—was inside.

"If they know I created a world," I said to Abel, "then wouldn't Okeus know too?"

"I don't know," he said. "I can sense a disruption, but I wouldn't have known it was a pocket universe. I would have suspected you'd found a way to tear through the veil between this realm and the afterlife." Then he added, "You do send ghosts on their way, so it would be within your skill set."

"Then how does Tsagasi know?" I asked.

"It's like his superpower," Ellie said. "He just seems to know things, but the others can't perceive as much as he does."

"How do I know I can trust *them*?" I asked. "You may have made a pact with his people, but I haven't. How do I know they won't try to take Abel to Okeus themselves as some kind of trade?"

"We don't," Collin said. "The jury's still out as to what they plan to do about him."

I gripped my sword hilt. "They'll have to go through me to get to him."

Abel put his hand on my shoulder and said gently, "Easy, Waboose. You need allies. Especially when the mark appears."

I spun around and looked up into his face. "I *will* stop that mark from appearing, Abel."

A teasing grin played on his lips. "If anyone could do something based on pure willpower, it would be you, Waboose, but I need assurances that you will be protected."

"Why do you keep calling her a baby bunny?" Collin asked.

My brow shot up to my hairline. "A *bunny*?"

Waboose meant baby bunny? No wonder the demons found the nickname amusing.

Abel shot Collin a death glare before turning back to me. "The Croatan used it as a term of endearment. Like the French call loved ones a little cabbage."

I didn't respond, unsure what to say. Abel had called me a waboose from the very beginning, before he really knew me...no, that wasn't true. He'd started calling me that after we faced a demon together at Helen's Bridge.

Ellie shook her head, looking startled. "Wait. *You* were a Croatan. You were there hundreds of years ago. You saw the aftermath of the curse."

"I was born eight months later," Abel said. "By the time I was old enough to remember anything, it was old news. Manteo and his son were closemouthed. My tribe spoke of the curse in hushed tones. My mother was a conjuror of spirits, and she told the tribe that the demons and gods were gone, leaving only ghosts behind. Which my tribe soon became. The English moved in and destroyed everything in their path."

"You knew his son who carried on the curse keeping duties?" David asked, looking thoroughly fascinated. "Were you related to them?"

"Manteo was my mother's brother," Abel said. "My uncle."

Ellie shot a glance from Abel to Collin. "You and Abel are cousins, Collin. Many times removed."

Collin didn't look too happy with that turn of events. Abel seemed equally unimpressed.

"You probably know more about the curse than Collin does," Ellie said.

Abel shook his head. "As I said, the curse keepers weren't forthcoming with the information. I suspect my mother knew more than she told me but didn't want to taint me against my father. She taught me to respect Okeus but to fear his brother."

"Ahone?" I asked.

"She said he would try to deceive me...to convince me that my father was evil. And she was right. After I hit my late teens, I started aging very slowly. My people feared me, so my mother sent me away. I lost track of the Croatan keeper when I left. Shortly afterward, my tribe scattered."

"Where did you go?" I asked, trying to imagine what he'd been through.

He turned to me, his eyes softening at the compassion in my voice. "England. Manteo had taught me English at my mother's urging. Ahone came to me there."

"What did he want?" Collin asked, sounding far less sympathetic.

"To let me know he was willing to guide me when needed. I only had to call out to him, and he would come."

"So of the gods, you're loyal to him?" Collin asked in a hard tone.

"I'm loyal to only one," Abel said. "And she is not a god."

"Piper?" Collin asked, sounding incredulous.

Abel didn't respond, but it was answer enough.

Ellie must have decided to change the subject. "You were talking about stopping a mark. What's that about?"

I started to tell them, but Abel grabbed my left wrist and lifted my hand. "While Piper bears the mark of the spiritual plane, more marks keep appearing, giving her new titles. We're trying to stop them."

I shot a questioning glance up to Abel, but he avoided my gaze as Ellie stepped forward to examine my left palm.

David moved closer. "Collin and Ellie are like two parts to a whole. The son of the land and the daughter of the sea. Yin and yang. Do you have a counterpart?"

I started to answer with Abel's name, but he spoke first. "Piper is Kewasa."

"Deliverer," David said. "What is she to deliver?"

More like who, I thought.

"Enough about the marks and her title," Collin said, turning to me with his sharp gaze. "I want to know what you're hiding upstairs." He moved to the doorway to the dining room.

"What's upstairs is none of your freaking business," Rhys said, darting in front of me. "And this conversation feels a lot like déjà vu."

Collin turned his piercing gaze on my friend. "If we're staying here, then we have a right to know."

"Feel free to stay somewhere else," Rhys said, practically nose to nose with him.

"We can't stay here long anyway," Abel said, sounding exhausted. "Even if the marks keep Okeus from entering, he can simply wait outside. Human time is nothing to him. I suspect we'll only be safe until nightfall. If even that long." He cast a glance to me, prompting me to tell them what I had seen in my vison…or not.

"We need to come up with a plan," I said.

Collin narrowed his eyes. "A plan to do what?"

"To kill Okeus."

He burst out laughing. "Are you insane?"

"No. Okeus is sending an army for us, and soon. We need to take the offensive."

"How do you know this?" Collin asked, some of his skepticism fading. "Did he tell you in the warehouse?"

I wasn't ready to tell them I'd seen Okeus in a post-orgasmic vision. Collin would likely dismiss it completely. "It doesn't matter how I learned about it. Okeus said he would torture and kill you and Ellie, then chain your souls to his throne of bones to torment you for eternity."

Collin's face paled.

"What about you?" Ellie asked. "What does he plan to do to you?"

I forced a sarcastic grin. "Lucky me, I get to have his children while Abel is forced to torture me."

"She can't know this for certain," Collin said. "Okeus is waiting for the six month agreement to lapse so you can have his babies too."

"Collin," Ellie said, wearily "We've defied him multiple times. I'm not surprised if he's decided I'm not worth the effort."

Collin stared at her, speechless.

"Ellie's right," David said. "Okeus isn't the forgiving type. Even if he does play the long game, he likely intends to kill you both."

"We're nowhere near strong enough to consider killing him," Collin insisted. "Last night was proof of that."

"He didn't give a timeline," I said, "but I suspect he's not going to wait long. We need a plan."

Abel put a hand on my shoulder. "Everyone is exhausted. As much as I dislike the idea of lingering here, you all need rest."

"I agree," Ellie said. "We can get a few hours' sleep then figure out a plan."

Collin folded his arms over his chest, but if he disagreed, he didn't say so.

"I have plenty of rooms upstairs for you all to sleep in. I think we need to stick together for now." I shot a glance to Rhys and Jack. "You two included. I won't risk either one of you getting kidnapped again."

Jack grimaced. "Thanks for reminding me."

"I'm not going *anywhere*," Rhys said. "I plan on sticking so close to Piper that she'll think I'm her actual shadow."

I pulled her into a tight hug. "That's good, because you're staying with me from here on out. I'll barely be able to let you out of my sight." I considered suggesting a slumber party in the living room. Rhys, Hudson, and I had done that very thing soon after we'd discovered that I was a demon hunter. We'd been too scared to sleep alone.

And now Hudson was dead.

A bakery box on the counter caught my eye. Had it only been two days ago that Hudson had bought me a donut for my birthday? Tears flooded my eyes, and I felt dangerously close to losing it.

"We'll meet down here at one," Abel said. "That will give us time to come up with a plan before nightfall." Turning to Rhys, he added, "I'm sure you're familiar with Piper's house. Can you help assign rooms?"

"Of course."

Part of me wanted to protest that Abel was taking charge when this was obviously *my* home, but I was too overcome with fresh grief over Hudson to deal with practical issues. Besides, something told me that he had another reason for sending the others off.

CHAPTER SEVEN

As everyone headed upstairs, I let Abel wrap his arms around me and hold me close.

"Is he here, Waboose?" he whispered into my ear.

I didn't need to ask who he was asking about. "I don't know."

"Call him."

I leaned back to look up at him. "What if he hates me? What if he blames me for what happened to him?"

"If he loved you as much as you've led me to believe, he won't hate you."

"Rhys hated me after she found out her girlfriend had been killed to give me a lame message from the great beyond."

"It doesn't look like Rhys hates you now." Abel ran a hand down my arm. "What's really holding you back?"

I gave him a look of surprise.

"You don't hide from a challenge, Piper. You face them head-on, so I have to wonder why you're hesitating now."

My stomach churned. If I called Hudson, I might have to help him cross over. One of the last ghosts I'd helped cross over had gone to hell. Even though Hudson had done nothing to earn eternal damnation, I wasn't sure I could bring myself to send him there if it came down to it.

But Abel was right. It was time to call my best friend.

"Hudson," I said in a soft voice, hoping the others didn't hear me. Selfishly, I didn't want more of an audience when I saw him.

If I saw him.

"Hudson, are you here?"

Seconds later, he walked into the kitchen, wearing pants and a dress shirt, the top two buttons undone like he'd just come home from work. "Took you long enough to get here." He stopped in front of me and held my gaze. "Tell me you killed the bastard demon."

Tears flooded my eyes. "Not me, but Abel did."

Hudson shot a glance to Abel, who was standing behind me. "Maybe you're not so bad after all."

Abel gave him a grim smile.

"Huddy," I said, starting to cry. "I'm *so* sorry."

He pulled me into a hug, as substantial as he'd been in life, only I'd seen his body on the floor of that warehouse. Twice. This felt like a lie. A cheat. "Don't cry, Pippy. It's okay."

"It's not okay," I sobbed into his chest. "Nothing about this is okay."

"You're right. It's not okay, but we'll make it work."

I shook my head and stared up at him like he'd lost his mind along with his life.

"Pippy," he said patiently. "I can see a lot of things more clearly now, and none of this is your fault." He shot Abel a dark look. "And, contrary to my previous opinion, it's not his fault either. This has been in motion for centuries. You're both pawns—and so are the people who are helping you now."

I blinked hard and pulled out of his embrace. "How do you know any of this?"

While I'd only started seeing ghosts a few weeks ago, I'd seen plenty ever since. Few of them even realized they were dead, let alone had information about the spirit world.

Confusion flickered in his eyes. "I don't know."

"What else do you know?" Abel asked. "Do you know Ahone's plans? Or Okeus's?"

Hudson turned his attention to the demigod. "No."

"What can you see?" Abel asked in a patient tone that surprised me.

"I can see what Pippy's true purpose is."

I held out my left palm. "You know?"

His mouth lifted into a smile. "It's so much more than killing Abel."

I shot a look at Abel—could this be confirmation that I was to be his deliverer in truth?—then shifted my attention back to Hudson. "Then what's my true purpose?"

His expression turned sad. "I can't tell you, but I can guide you along the way."

I narrowed my eyes. "Guide me how?"

"I made a deal to help you."

Panic raced through my veins as I grabbed his arm, my nails digging into his impossibly corporeal flesh. "What kind of deal?"

He stared down at me, his eyes full of love and devotion. "I couldn't leave you, Pippy. You need all the help you can get."

"That didn't answer her question," Abel ground out. "Was your deal with Okeus?"

"Why would Hudson make a deal with the devil?" I countered.

"Okeus has a way of making his deals sound enticing," Ellie said from the kitchen door, startling me. "Trust me, I've been offered enough of them to know."

How many times had she encountered Okeus?

"I'm sorry," she said, taking a step into the kitchen. "He's here now, isn't he? Your friend that the Great One killed?"

I hesitated, wiping my face with my fingertips, but decided it wouldn't hurt to tell her. "Yes."

She hugged herself, running her hands up and down her arms. "That explains why I felt a chill." Sympathy filled her eyes. "You need answers about the deal he made. Okeus is a tricky bastard. He tried to get me to make a deal with him multiple times and in multiple ways. He even had something pretend to be my deceased father. Are you sure you're talking to your real friend now?"

I cast a glance at the man who claimed to be my friend. Ellie had a point. How could I be sure it was Hudson?

"What did I say to you the first day we met?" I asked.

A soft smile lit up his face. "You asked me if I was going to eat the canned peaches on my lunch tray or if you could have them."

Tears filled my eyes again. "It's him."

"Then ask your friend who he spoke to," she said.

I reached out a hand and wrapped it around her wrist, tugging her arm free. "Ask him yourself."

Her eyes flew wide as Hudson came into view for her. She instinctively pulled back, but I gently drew her closer.

"Hudson, this is Ellie Lancaster, the cousin you helped me find. Ellie, this is my best friend in the whole world, Hudson Maine." My voice broke on the last part. I still couldn't believe he was dead, although he clearly wasn't *gone*.

Hudson reached his right hand out to hers, then hesitated when he realized I was holding Ellie's right wrist.

I moved my hand to her shoulder, and she stiffened.

"Whoa. He disappeared for a second."

"You have to touch me to see him."

"He's a ghost," she said, keeping her arm at her side. "How can I shake his hand?"

"Try it," I coaxed.

She lifted her hand to his and he grasped it firmly. "It's an honor to meet you, Ellie Lancaster, defier of the gods."

She jerked her hand away as though she'd been electrically shocked. "How do you know that title?"

"He told me."

She held perfectly still. "Who?"

"I haven't seen him. Only heard him. He told me I had a choice to stay here on this plane of existence to help Piper or to move on to the afterlife. I told him if I could help her at all, I would stay."

"You said you made a deal," Ellie pressed. "What kind of deal?"

"That sometimes I would do his bidding. He assured me it would never be anything I'd find morally offensive."

I shook my head in horror. "Hudson."

He'd made a deal with the voice. The one that had been ordering Jack and I around for months. Years. The one that had killed people to deliver cryptic, pointless warnings to me.

Only one other being could command such power.

"You don't know who the voice is?" I asked.

"No, although if I had to guess, I'd say it's Ahone."

"Yeah. Me too." I released him and pressed my lips together. Although Ahone was a lesser evil than his brother, he was far from trustworthy, and he'd shown an utter disregard for human life. What had Hudson gotten himself into? For me. The guilt was suffocating.

Hudson's dark gaze held mine and a smile wobbled on his lips. "He assured me he'd never kill anyone else to send you messages. That I could deliver them instead. No more guilt over needless deaths, Pippy."

Hudson probably knew me better than anyone, so he knew how much I'd agonized over their deaths. He would never have turned down the chance to protect me in whatever way he could from hardship. But what would it ultimately cost him?

A sob escaped from my chest. "*Hudson.*"

"Pippy, please don't cry. This was my choice. You know I've wanted to help you, and now I can. He's assured me I'm not trapped by the bargain. I can leave any time I choose."

"But you can't be sure of that. What if he lied to you?"

"I can trust him in this. I know it." His face turned somber. "Just like I know that you and Abiel are meant to be."

My breath caught in my throat. "What does that mean?"

"Don't be so dense, Pippy. You know what it means. Soul mates." His gaze turned to Ellie. "Just like you're soul mates with the other keeper."

I couldn't hide my gasp of shock. Although I'd sensed Collin's feelings for her, it was obvious Ellie was in love with David.

"Some of us defy more than the gods," Ellie said in a hard tone. She lightly brushed my hand off her shoulder. "I'm interrupting your private time with your friend. I only came down for a glass of water, but I can get it upstairs." She bolted from the room before I could stop her.

"I upset her," Hudson said, sounding worried.

"You didn't tell her anything she didn't already know," Abel said.

It felt intrusive to discuss Ellie's love life, so I changed the subject to a far more pressing matter. "We need to keep the crescent moon from appearing on my hand, Hudson. Do you know how to keep it from appearing?"

He hesitated, then said, "No."

My heart sank. "Are you sure?"

"No one has forever, Pippy," he said quietly. "Not on the earthly plane. Just take what you're offered, even if it's only for a short time."

"Our souls are bound," I said. "Abel's worried he'll drag me to hell with him."

Hudson shook his head. "Your soul is yours and yours alone. While you and Abel have a bond, he can't determine your soul's fate. Only you can."

"Did Ahone tell you that?" Abel sneered. "Demons can drag their victims' souls to hell. How can you be certain that I won't do the same? Forgive my cynicism, but why should we trust your mysterious voice?"

Hudson held out his hands in surrender. "I know certain truths without knowing why or how I know them. You don't have to take my word for it. There is another way to be sure." He turned his attention to me. "You warded the staircase to the attic against demons."

My mouth dropped open. "I didn't tell you that."

"You didn't have to. I could feel it as I walked by. Only someone powerful could make such a strong ward. She can make sure your soul is yours and yours alone." He paused. "And possibly help you with other things."

I glanced down at my hand. The mark. "We need to talk to Deidre."

"You have to think bigger than saving Abel, Piper," Hudson said. "The demons are coming for you and for Okeus's son. They've found a new gate. A larger one that allows more of them to come through."

The army Okeus had mentioned. "Where?"

He shook his head. "I'm not sure, but I *do* know they will be emerging soon."

I turned to look at Abel. His jaw tightened, but he said nothing.

"What's in the attic, Piper?" Hudson asked.

My lips parted to tell him, but for some reason, I felt the need to keep Tommy a secret for a little while longer. I had to be certain that Hudson hadn't been compromised by his connection to the voice, especially if it did belong to Ahone. "I can't tell you now, but I will later."

I'd expected him to protest, but he nodded then disappeared.

"Did I upset him?" I asked, more to myself than Abel.

"No," Abel said. "I suspect he had nothing more to say." He wrapped an arm around my back and steered me to the door. "Now you need to go get some sleep."

"Sleep?" I said, digging in my heels. "You've got to be kidding me. You heard what he said. We need to see Deidre."

His eyes darkened. "I've yet to see a ward that can protect someone from their fate. Besides, I'll take his recommendation with a grain of salt. For all we know, he's an unsuspecting pawn. I meant what I said earlier. We have to prepare for the army my father is sending, which means you need to be at your best."

I stared up at Abel, searching his eyes. "I'm not going to be at my best if I'm worried some stupid mark will appear on my hand and force me to kill you." Flustered, I shook my head and huffed out a breath. "Why are you fighting me on this?"

Emotion flickered in his eyes, making me wish I could slip on the ring without him noticing. "I don't trust the seer."

No shit.

"Then who do you trust?"

"I only trust one person. You."

I sighed in frustration. "We have to trust someone, Abel. I don't know how to stop it and neither do you."

He stared at me for several long seconds before nodding. "We'll go to the seer." A sardonic grin lifted his lips. "But may I suggest a phone call first?" He held out his phone, a number preloaded.

"Why do you have her number pulled up?"

"Surely you've figured out that I don't like surprises. I suspected you'd insist on visiting her, and I like to have contingency plans for everything."

I made a face as I took his phone and pressed send. "Then you must hate me. I'm nothing but one big fat surprise after another."

He tilted his head, studying me. "To my consternation, I find you to be a breath of fresh air."

"You just needed someone to shake things up," I said as the phone began to ring.

The call picked up, but silence hung over the line. For a couple of seconds, I thought we'd been disconnected, but then Deidre said, "What do you want, son of Satan?"

My brows shot up to my hairline. How did Deidre recognize Abel's number? Had they been in contact before? Abel had told me she couldn't be trusted. Did he know that from personal experience?

On the flip side, had Deidre known Abel was the mystery man she'd seen in my fortune reading and purposefully hidden it from me?

"Deidre, it's Piper. I need your help." I glanced up at Abel. "*We* need your help."

There was a pause before she said, "You're with the demigod." Another pause. "So you trust him."

She'd told me the mystery man was using me for his own purposes. Another part of the reading had indicated that someone close to me would betray me. Abel may have considered betraying me in the past, but I did trust him now. "The answer to both of your questions is yes, and I need your help."

"No."

It took a second before it registered that she'd refused. "*Deidre.*"

"I'll help *you*, demon slayer, but I won't help the demigod."

"Can we at least come in to discuss it?"

"Do you know what time it is?" she snapped.

I honestly didn't, but the layers of pink and orange sky in the distance suggested the sun was starting to rise. "I'm sorry. I promise we wouldn't be calling right now if it wasn't important."

Abel grabbed the phone from my hand and hit the speaker button. "Seer, agree to meet with us, and I'll give you an ounce of hart's-tongue fern."

She was quiet for a few moments, then said, "I can see you at noon. Don't be late." Silence punctuated her words—she'd hung up.

I handed Abel his phone. "How did you know she'd want hart's-tongue fern?"

"It wasn't hard to figure out. She's a seer who makes wards. It's an endangered plant."

"Then how do *you* have it?"

He gave me a pointed look. "As I mentioned, I like to have contingency plans."

"How'd you know we'd need help from a seer? You planned for me to kill you, so there's no way you could have anticipated you'd want to stop the mark from appearing. Besides, you were against me asking Deidre for help."

"I've visited seers before, Kewasa. I know how to bargain with them." A grin played on his lips. "How do you think I found you?"

That caught me by surprise, but I didn't see the point in pursuing the matter. I yawned, suddenly overcome with exhaustion.

He wrapped his arm around my back and led me to the living room. "You need sleep. We need to be at the top of our game if we want to deal with the seer."

I needed to be at the top of my game for a whole lot more than that.

CHAPTER EIGHT

Ellie

In the beginning, Collin had tried to convince me that we'd restored the natural order by opening the gate. Demons and supernatural creatures were supposed to roam the earth with us. Ahone had upset the balance when he'd tricked Collin's ancestor, Manteo, into locking them up.

I wasn't sure what to think of any of it back then. I'd blown off my father's teachings, and by the time Collin grabbed my right palm on that hot July afternoon, unlocking the four-hundred-year-old curse and freeing the gods and monsters, my dad was suffering from advanced Alzheimer's. Most days he hadn't even known who I was, let alone the details of the curse. Which meant Collin took on the role of teacher.

Or so I'd thought. Collin had become a curse of my own.

When I'd refused to pledge myself to Okeus, Collin had abandoned me, leaving me defenseless against the demons intent on consuming my witness-to-creation soul. Until he'd finally changed his mind and turned his back on the god.

Collin had saved me then, and a few weeks ago, when the Guardians had nearly killed me, he'd saved me once again—pressing our marks together and infusing me with his power as the son of the land. Before that, my body had yearned for his anytime he was near, making my relationship with David even more difficult, but that night had changed everything. As I lay bleeding out onto the grass, staring at the starry sky above the botanical gardens, he and I had witnessed the birth of creation together. I didn't understand why, but my desire for him had burned away that night, leaving only hollowness in my soul.

I loved David with every fiber of my being. He was the one who'd picked up the pieces of my heart after Collin's betrayal. David was the one who'd convinced my heart to love again. He'd supported and encouraged me every step of the way—he'd even taught me the things Collin should have about Native American belief systems. But worry burrowed into my marrow, making my bones ache with a foreboding that made it difficult to breath.

Something was on the horizon, and I feared for David. I was worried something was coming for him, and I felt powerless to stop it.

I headed up to the bedroom Rhys had assigned us, the master bedroom. I didn't stop to ask her why Piper wasn't in the master. I figured it was none of my business. She'd said there were four bedrooms on the second floor. Piper's was near the staircase, her friend Hudson's had been across from hers (which was where Rhys and Jack were staying), and a guest room and master were separated by the staircase to the attic. David and I were staying in the master, and Collin was staying in the guest room—only right now he was standing by the window of our room while David sat on the bed.

After hearing the ghost's words downstairs, the sight of Collin sent a spike of pain through my heart. Hudson hadn't told me anything I didn't already know. What made it even worse was that David knew and loved me anyway. He stayed with me despite the fact that he would never have all of me.

Collin's mouth was set into a thin line. "Something's off with those two. I feel it."

It took me a moment to realize what he was saying.

"Piper and Abel?" I asked, overcome with exhaustion.

David reached for me and I went to him, letting him pull me down to sit next to him on the bed. He wrapped an arm around my back and tugged me close.

I saw the flash of agony in Collin's eyes before irritation flushed it out. "They're not telling us everything."

"And *we're* not telling them everything, Collin, so what's really got you worked up?"

His scowl deepened. "I'm not comfortable forming an alliance with the son of Okeus."

"And I'm sure he's not happy about working with the curse keepers *who let Okeus out*, so that evens things out."

"Don't be stupid, Ellie," he spat out. "You know that Okeus will do everything and anything to enslave you—and according to Piper— now kill you. What's to stop him from sending his son to do his dirty work?"

"He would have betrayed us last night if that was his plan."

"He might be playing the long game. Do *not* underestimate Okeus."

I pushed out a long sigh. "You're right, Collin. He might be, but his concern for Piper feels genuine."

"And where was that concern last night when we were going into the warehouse? He let her walk right into that mess. He could have helped us from the start. *You* might have been able to kill the Great One."

I had to admit the Great One's defeat felt hollow since I hadn't shoved the blade into its heart. But dead was dead. At least that's what I told myself.

"And you tricked me into keeping the gate to hell open instead of locking it shut, yet here you are, standing in front of me," I said, regretting my impulsiveness as soon as the words were out of my mouth. It was not only a reminder to Collin of his betrayal and my father's sacrifice to Ahone, but a reminder to David that he was only with me because of Collin's near-mortal sins. Groaning, I got to my feet. "I'm sorry, Collin. That wasn't necessary."

His face hardened. "But it's true, isn't it?"

"Collin's right about Abel," David said, sidestepping the rehashing of past issues. "We can't trust him."

"And I never said we should. But we need to stick close to Piper and she's attached to Abel, for better or for worse." I lifted an eyebrow as I studied Collin. "I'm surprised you want to stick around."

He started to say something, but stopped and then said, "She's your cousin."

"We all know there's more to it than that."

He hesitated again. "Tsagasi says she's important. He said we should stay."

I shook my head. "When did he say that? I was with you whenever you were with him."

"Just trust me, Ellie," he said, running a hand over his head. "We need to stay with her."

Collin usually had some smart-ass comment when he wanted his way, so his sincerity caught me off guard.

"I'd planned on staying with her anyway, so no need to convince me," I said.

He nodded, then turned to look out the window at the rising sun. "Okeus's son is going to try to take control. We need to decide if we're going to let him."

I blinked. "Piper seems to be running the show there, and he's going along with it. She's pretty strong-willed."

He flashed me a smile, but it seemed sad. "Just like her younger cousin." His smile faded and he turned serious. "Nevertheless, there's going to be a power struggle between our groups. The question we need to consider is whether it's worth a fight to be in control."

"We're all on the same team, Collin."

He took several steps toward me, his face stony. "And that's why you need me, Ellie. You think we all want the same thing, but everyone always has their own agenda. Your naïveté leads you to overlook that."

My eyebrows shot to my hairline as anger exploded through me. "*Naïveté?*"

"Ellie," David said softly, gently reminding me that the others were up here and the last thing I wanted to do was let them know there was disharmony between us.

Collin held up a hand with a sheepish look. "Naïveté was obviously the wrong word choice. I should have said optimism."

I shook my head, suddenly feeling the full effects of going a day and a half without sleep. "I am far from optimistic, Collin."

"It's not a bad thing, Ellie. You just tend to see the good when I see the bad."

"It's the yin and the yang of the curse," David said with a yawn. "I've mentioned before that the curse is based on duality. You both need each other." He gave me an apologetic look.

"If I were *optimistic*, I wouldn't be scared shitless that Okeus has lost all patience and plans to kill us. I don't know about you, but I'll take a hard pass on spending eternity chained to a throne made of bones."

Collin's face tightened. "We've always known Okeus was our enemy."

"But he wanted to be my baby daddy, so we thought we had time. Now…I'm not so sure."

"Our options are limited," he said. "I still say we're nowhere near ready to take on Okeus. Even with Piper and Abel. We all saw what happened last night. Abel didn't even try to take on his father, which means he's either incapable of standing against him or he's playing his daddy's long game." His eyes narrowed. "Which means we need to convince Piper to hide with us."

"Until we figure out what to do," I said.

"No. Permanently."

"That's not an option," I insisted in disgust. "If we hide, there will be no one to stop the demons from doing what they damn well please. Is that really acceptable to you?"

"I don't know, Ellie." He sounded exasperated. "Do *you* think we're ready to defeat Okeus?"

"No." I shook my head in frustration. "I don't know." I tugged on the chain at my neck and pulled out the ring hanging from it. "We need to look at all our options. We have the ring that sings." My mother had taken the ring from the Ricardo Collection, an assortment of supernaturally powerful weapons and artifacts owned by the Guardians. That ring had gotten her killed—Collin's father and his cohorts had shown up looking for it. I doubted they knew it had been blessed by a Croatan conjuror hundreds of years ago for the Manteo curse keeper to use at the main gate to hell.

"*We're* not even sure what it does," Collin said with a scowl. "You thought it would close the gate to hell, but all it did was make an annoying noise."

I rolled my eyes. "Ahone told me the ring's purpose is to give me an advantage over the demons."

"Sure, it momentarily stuns them, but it doesn't kill them. It won't help us with the likes of Okeus."

I got up and walked over to a duffle bag by the window and started to remove a wooden box. "We have the watches."

"We don't even know what they do, Ellie," he said in frustration.

My father had left me three pocket watches of varying ages. I had no idea what they were supposed to do, but I believed they had *some* purpose in all of this. I popped open the lid, partially to make sure they were still there. "The Guardians had an identical watch in the Ricardo Collection. That has to mean something."

"I agree, but until we know their purpose, it's kind of beside the point."

I closed the box and returned it to the bag. "I haven't forgotten about my vision of the end."

I'd seen how we ended this, in a vision when I'd almost died. I'd seen Collin and me standing at the gate to Popogusso, me wearing the ring that sings and holding the Sword of Galahad while Collin held the spear. My power had made the gate blast open in blinding light. I hadn't forgotten that I was the alpha and the omega.

Collin was silent.

I glanced over my shoulder at him. "We still haven't found the spear."

In the spiritual world, we'd learned, most everything had a counterpart. The spear was the counterpart to the ring that sings. The Guardians had agreed to bring it to the meeting at the botanical gardens, but they'd reneged. Now that the Great One was gone, maybe it was time to look for the spear. It had definitely figured into my vision of the end.

"We don't even know where to start," Collin protested. "For all we know, the assholes never had it to begin with."

"The only way we can rule it out is if we search their treasure trove." I stood and gave him a wry grin. "Sounds right up your alley."

He shot me an unamused look.

"There has to be a way to kill Okeus."

"There's no killing Okeus," Collin said. "You can't kill a god. Tsagasi said so himself. You can only take their power."

I moved closer to David. "Then why does Piper have the title 'slayer of demons and gods'?"

"Maybe she only has the power to slay demigods and minor gods," David said. "She killed Caelius, the sex god, last night." He lifted his gaze to Collin. "I suspect Collin's right about Okeus. I don't think he can be killed." He gave me an apologetic look. "But I'd suggest we hold off on making a decision about whether to work with them until we hear more about their plan." He took a breath. "The Great One has been our focus for weeks. Now that it's gone, we need to decide what comes next."

Collin studied him for a second, then nodded. "He's right."

David continued. "I think the best thing we can do is get some sleep and get up early enough to discuss this with clearer heads before we meet with them. We need to present a united front."

I ran a hand over my head. "You're right, David."

I leaned over and pressed a grateful kiss to his lips.

"I'm going to take a shower," Collin said as he headed for the door. "Let's meet here a half hour before we meet with Piper and Abel."

"Yeah," I said as a wave of exhaustion swept over me. "See you in a few hours."

Collin opened the door and walked out, then closed it behind him, leaving me standing in front of David.

"Ellie," he said in his soft, compassionate voice. The one that made me feel loved and cherished. With everyone else I had to put up a badass front, but with David I could just be me—twenty-three-year-old Elinor Dare, waitress and heir to a bed and breakfast that no longer existed, someone completely too unqualified to be fighting demons and trying to save the world.

He slid an arm around the small of my back and pulled me close, resting his cheek on my stomach as I wrapped my arm around his head. I needed him more than I'd ever needed anyone and that scared the shit out of me. I'd learned long ago not to rely on people, not because they were unreliable (Collin being the exception), but because I'd learned at the tender age of eight that fate stole the people I loved. My mother. My father. My stepmother, Myra. Only I'd recently learned it wasn't fate at all. It was a creator god with a massive ego and a plan to use me to get even with his brother.

My fingers dug into David's hair, holding him closer as though it would keep him safe, because I knew it was only a matter of time before the gods stole him from me too.

"Hey," he said, tilting his head to look up at me. "It's going to be okay."

Collin was so wrong. I wasn't an optimist at all.

David's face became blurry through my tears, and he stood and began to gently remove my clothes. "Ellie, love, you need sleep."

My tears began to flow down my cheeks as David swiftly and tenderly undressed me, placing kisses everywhere he touched, not out of desire, although I knew he had that too, but because he knew I was empty inside.

"I wish Abel hadn't killed the Great One," I finally whispered in shame. "I needed to do it myself."

"I know, love," he said in his soothing tone as he pulled off my pants, leaving me in my underwear. "I know."

I started to quietly sob. "Why can't I just be happy it's gone? What is *wrong* with me?"

He stood and gathered me in his arms, and I realized he'd undressed too. "Because the demon stole the last family member you had. I know you loved Myra as though she'd given birth to you herself, and trust me, Ellie, she loved you too, more than anything. But she'd hate for you to become consumed by hate and vengeance." He tilted my face up to look at him. "Collin's right. You see the good in things. In people. You're a glass-half-full person."

"And maybe that's what got her killed," I choked out. "Maybe if I'd been more cynical, I would have…"

"Would have what?" he asked as he placed a kiss on my temple. "You would have noticed sooner that the Great One had killed her and used her form? The damage was already done, love."

"So I'm supposed to just let the demons do whatever they want?" I asked, my voice full of bitterness.

"No, Ellie, you keep fighting. You keep fighting to save the people you love and to save the people that other people love, because you, Ellie Lancaster, are destined to save the world. But not right now," he said, tugging me down to the bed. "Right now you need sleep."

I lay down on the cool sheets and let him fold me up in his arms and his legs. Out in the real world, I was the person standing between evil and the man I loved, but behind closed doors, he was the one who saved me.

CHAPTER NINE

Piper

I woke to a kiss pressed to the nape of my neck and evidence of Abel's arousal pressed against my backside.

"What time is it?" I murmured, still in shock at the turn of events that had led to Abel sharing my bed.

"Early enough for me to have you again before we leave to see the seer."

"And what does that translate into in *real* time?" I asked with a grin as I rolled over to look up at him.

"Eleven." A shadow crossed over his eyes. "I confess to my inner struggle between letting you sleep and devouring your body again." He pressed a kiss at the top of my head. "But I've warned you before, Waboose. Self-sacrifice is not my forte."

"In this instance, I'm glad you were selfish."

A predatory look filled his eyes, one that stoked a fire deep in my soul. His mouth covered mine, hot and demanding. Our connection felt like a vast ocean, and we'd barely swum below the surface.

He lifted his head, searching my face in wonder. "What is this thing between us?"

I didn't need to ask what he meant.

"You would be in a better position than me to know," I said, already breathless.

He straddled my waist, pinning my arms next to my head. "I very much like my current position."

He kissed his way down to my breasts, still holding me down and making me squirm with frustration.

"Abel."

"I'm just getting started, Waboose."

His mouth trailed over my stomach and down between my legs. I gasped as white-hot heat spread through me. "*Abel.*"

"Piper," he murmured in a low tone. "You are perfection."

He brought me to climax, then rose over me.

"My turn," I said, trying to lift up and push him off me. "I get to taste *you* now."

He gave a slow shake of his head as he spread my right leg out. "I need to be inside you. Now." Then he pushed in with one long, deep stroke.

I arched up to meet him, already on the cusp of another orgasm. What is this hold he had on me? Every part of my body sang for him.

"You are mine, Piper Lancaster, Kewasa, shepherd to lost spirits, witness to creation, slayer of demons and gods, creator of worlds. You are mine and I am completely and utterly yours."

We didn't talk after that. The pleasure was too great for me to do more than gasp and call out his name, and I didn't need the ring to know the same was true of him.

Afterward, we lay on my bed, wrapped in each other's arms.

"Do you think Deidre will have the answer?" I asked softly, my hand resting on his chest.

Surprise filled his eyes. "You're suddenly uncertain she does?"

"Unlike you," I said, "I'm uncertain about a lot of things. And Deidre is a wish and a prayer. If she doesn't have the answer, I'm hoping she'll give us a shove in the right direction.

"You don't have any other ideas?"

"I've never given it any thought," he said with a frown. "I've been waiting centuries for the mark to appear. Never once did I wonder how to keep it from happening."

"You've really wanted to die for centuries?" I asked, overcome with sadness.

He flashed me a soft smile. "Cheer up, Waboose. I haven't been moping for hundreds of years, only about the last forty or fifty. I knew my window of opportunity to move to the next phase would be appearing, and I was watching for it."

"Still, Abel…forty or fifty years…"

He turned silent, then said, "We have to come up with a contingency plan in case we can't stop the mark from appearing."

I sat up. "What? *No.*"

Abel rose too, turning to face me. "Piper. We have to be realistic, and you have to be prepared."

"No!"

He reached up to cup my cheek. "Waboose, hear me out."

I moved to get out of bed, but his hand encircled my wrist and tugged me back.

"You can't run from this," he said, his voice full of a sentiment I wasn't used to from him—compassion.

"I don't run from danger, Abel," I said bitterly, "but I refuse to discuss killing you." I pulled from his grasp and slid out of bed before he could stop me.

"We need a plan, Piper," he said, sounding anguished. "*I* need to know you have a plan in case we can't stop this."

His sincerity caught me by surprise, and I stopped to face him.

Relief washed over his face when he saw I was listening.

"Fine," I said, feeling like the word was a betrayal. "We can discuss it if Deidre can't help us."

"That might be too late," he said, getting out of bed. "The mark will likely appear without warning."

My anger surged again as I turned my attention to my rumpled sheets. "You can't expect me to have this discussion after…" I gestured helplessly to the bed "…*that*."

"Sex?" he asked with a smirk. "I never took you for a prude, Piper."

"I'm not. I'm perfectly capable of calling it sex, but that wasn't sex," I said. "I'm not sure what that was." It wasn't love. I hadn't known him long enough for it to be love, yet it was supernaturally powerful.

He took a step toward me, grabbing my wrist and tugging me to his chest. His face was expressionless as he reached up to tuck a lock of hair behind my ear. "Each time we're together, our bond becomes stronger. More permanent." A sad smile filled his eyes. "If I were a better man, I would stay away from you until the mark appears. Then I would find a way to anger you, a betrayal so deep you would feel no guilt or remorse for killing me, yet…" A soft sigh escaped his lips as he lowered his mouth to my ear and whispered, "I find myself unable to resist your siren song."

He bit my earlobe, then licked it, sending a shiver down my spine.

I slipped an arm around the back of his neck. "I don't want you to stay away. I want you here, so stop talking like that." I took a deep breath. "I need a shower and then I need to check on Tommy before we leave." I put a hand on his chest, pushing him back when he made a move to follow me. "I'm showering alone. It will take twice as long if you join me."

"I want to visit your pocket world."

I opened my mouth to protest, then stopped. "Why?"

"I want to see your first creation. I want to meet the ghost that has captured your heart."

I raked my teeth over my lower lip as I considered it. "I'm not sure it's a good idea. Tommy might be afraid of you."

"What if I agree to leave the moment he shows any sign of distress?"

"You would do that?"

"Of course."

I narrowed my eyes. "Why do you really want to see him?"

"I told you already."

Something felt off, but I couldn't figure out what ulterior motive he could have other than curiosity.

"Let me think about it," I said, turning to my dresser to get clean underwear. When he didn't say anything, I glanced over my shoulder at him. "No rebuttal?"

His gaze had drifted to my bare ass. "I was too distracted by the view."

ALTHOUGH I WOULD HAVE LIKED nothing more than to savor the hot water until it turned to cold, I decided moments after I stepped into the shower that I didn't want to take Abel up to see Tommy, so I rushed to get out, hoping to make my way up to the attic without Abel even knowing. While I was worried about the five-year-old ghost's reaction, my main concern was Abel's eagerness.

I didn't feel great about my decision—I'd literally bound my soul to Abel's mere hours ago, and here I was sneaking around behind his back—but I also knew that he would go to questionable lengths to do what he thought necessary to protect me.

With that in mind, I stuffed my bathrobe in the linen closet and opened the door to the hall, making sure the coast was clear. My bedroom door was still closed, so I tiptoed down the hall to the door to the attic staircase, reminding myself that ten minutes in the attic was equivalent to an hour here. I could only stay a few minutes at most, and even then Abel and I would likely still be late to see Deidre. I knew I should probably wait, but I hadn't seen Tommy since the night before.

I opened the door to the attic, worried when I didn't see the ward Deidre had made to help keep demons away. I'd left it on the steps. Who had moved it? Abel?

I was starting to panic when I heard Collin say, "Looking for this?"

He sat at the top of the stairs, holding the cotton bag on his upturned palm.

Closing the door behind me, I put a hand on my hip. "You're just dying to know what's so special about my attic, huh? I take it you've already done a thorough search and found nothing else of interest?"

Still seated, he tossed the bag into the air then caught it. "I suspect your secret has something to do with this?" He took a deep breath, and his cocky grin faded. "Tsagasi says it's none of our business what's up here, but our fate seems to be tied to yours right now and you have a giant bullseye painted on your back. Throw in the fact you're sleeping with Okeus's son...let's just say I need to know what you've got hidden up here before I decide if I'm willing to risk Ellie's life on this."

"Not your own?"

A scowl spread across his face. "I deserve whatever I get, but Ellie..." He sat up straighter. "Ellie is too trusting and the Great One killed the last family member she had, and then you pop up..."

"You don't trust me," I finished.

"I want to, Piper," he said, and I heard the sincerity in his voice. "I really do, but while Ellie's the trusting type, I'm more of a doubting Thomas."

Collin wasn't leaving, and the only way I could make him leave was to create a scene, which I wasn't willing to do.

I let out a sigh. "You have to come down here."

His eyes hardened. "I'm not taking no for an answer."

"I'm not asking you to leave. I'm taking you into the world I created, but you have to come down here and touch me so you can walk in."

Surprise filled his eyes. He'd probably expected me to put up more of a fight. The fact that I was taking Collin and not Abel wasn't lost on me, but I doubted Collin would do any damage. I suspected he'd be too shocked at what he found.

He slid past me on the stairs and put his hand on my shoulder. "Now what?"

"Well," I said, taking the ward from him and dropping it onto the step beneath us. "Usually I open the world from outside the door, but I confess, this is all new to me and I'm learning as I go."

"What do you mean open the world?"

I glanced over my shoulder. "You checked out the attic already, right? You saw my father's office."

"Yeah."

"I created something else. Hold on to me and I'll see if I can make this work from here. When I start to go upstairs, you keep holding on and follow until I say you can let go."

"Okay…" He sounded skeptical, not that I blamed him, but he wouldn't be for long.

I closed my eyes and focused on the attic playroom I'd created, on the little boy waiting for me there.

"Okay," I said, opening my eyes and putting my hand over Collin's hand on my right shoulder.

I took a step, waiting for him to follow. Then we slowly ascended the staircase. I pushed out a sigh of relief when I saw the playroom I'd created for Tommy a few days ago, after he was threatened by a demon in his own home.

"What the fuck…" Collin gasped as he caught his first glimpse.

"Piper!" Tommy threw his arms around my legs, nearly tackling me in his enthusiasm. "I missed you."

I dropped to a squat so we were at eye level. "I'm sorry I was gone so long. Do you know how long I've been gone?"

His nose crinkled as he seemed to think about it. "I don't know."

I flashed him a smile and touched his nose with my finger. "Don't you worry your cute little head about it."

In fact, I was relieved he still had little sense of time. Most ghosts had no concept of it, thinking years were days, which I supposed was merciful. Many of them were clueless that the homes they haunted were no longer their own. Tommy seemed more self-aware than most. I suspected he'd been awakened by the demons who had tried to use him to get to me.

"Who's that?" Tommy asked, wrapping his arm around my thigh as he hid behind it.

I turned to Collin, who was staring at Tommy in shock. My breath stuck in my throat as it occurred to me what this meant. Collin was seeing a ghost without touching me.

"This is Collin Dailey," I said to Tommy, my mind racing at the implications. "He's a friend of mine. Collin, this is my friend Tommy Whitfield."

Collin swallowed, keeping his gaze on the boy. "Piper, why are you hiding a little boy in your attic?" Then horror swam over his face. "Are you doing this for Abel?"

Tommy looked up at me with innocent eyes. "Who's Abel?"

"Why would I do this for Abel?" I asked.

Collin squirmed in place, then gestured toward Tommy. "A little boy… Abel's father is a god… you know…" He shot another look at the boy and started to spell. "S-A-C-R-I-F—"

"Oh my God!" I gasped. "You think I'd be a party to sacrificing a five-year-old? Are you out of your mind?"

"No, Piper," he said in a cold tone. "But I hardly know either of you."

Tommy tugged on my jeans. "Piper," he said with his cute lisp. He'd lost his front teeth before death and would never have them. "What's a sacwifice?"

I shot Collin a glare, then relaxed my face before I turned to the little boy. "Don't you worry about it. What have you been doing while I was gone?"

"I pwayed with the Wincon Wogs. I made a fort. Wanna see?"

I walked over to the table, still pissed that Collin thought I'd do something so heinous, but then, he had no idea Tommy was a ghost. It would be pretty suspect of me to hide a kindergartner.

Collin started to wander around the room, picking up objects and setting them down, a look of awe in his eyes. "You made this place? How? Why?"

"Tommy needed protection and the safest place was my own house. The ward on the steps keeps demons out. The attic used to be my mother and grandmother's playroom. I thought about what I'd seen in photos, and when I came up the stairs, it was here. As to how…" Tommy was absorbed in fixing something on his fort, so I walked closer to Collin and lowered my voice. "The other day while I was on a home visit, I walked into a ghost's dimension."

His eyes widened. "A ghost?"

"I talk to ghosts, Collin. You knew that. I help them cross over to the other side. Some are too stuck in their past reality to move on." I leaned into his ear and whispered, "Like Tommy."

Collin's face paled and he pointed to Tommy. "He's a gh—"

I put my hand over his mouth. "Shh… he doesn't know. He was stuck in his house, but between a demon who used him to draw me out and a bitchy homeowner who hated him, I had to move him somewhere, so I brought him here."

"Why don't you help him move on?" he asked, genuinely curious.

"Whenever I bring up his accident, he gets anxious," I whispered. "I'm worried he'll be traumatized if I just tell him. But he's looking for his mother, who's already crossed over, so he has unfinished business until I can figure out how to fix this."

He looked surprised by that but took it in stride as he walked over to Tommy's Lincoln Logs and picked up a log. "Cool fort, dude."

Tommy glanced up at him with a huge smile. "Thanks." He paused. "Will you be my fwiend?"

"You bet."

"Want to see my crayon drawings? I'm not supposed to show Piper."

My heart skipped a beat, and Collin's worried gaze lifted to mine as he nonchalantly asked, "Why not?"

"He said I shouldn't."

Collin looked alarmed, but I had to give him credit for keeping his voice neutral. "He who?"

The boy ignored the question and looked up at me. "You can't look, Piper!"

"Okay," I said, trying to keep my voice from shaking, but I pinned my gaze on Collin. He nodded as though assuring me he'd take care of it, then followed the boy to the bookcase.

Tommy saw me staring. "Piper!" he said, his tone verging on a whine.

I realized he didn't want me to see his hiding place. I gave him an apologetic smile, then walked over to one of the dormer windows. The curtains were drawn. On my last visit, Tommy had shown me an apocalyptic world outside this pocket universe. Asheville before it had been inhabited hundreds of years ago—a valley surrounded by mountains and storm clouds with fire raining down from the sky. Holding my breath, I pulled the curtains open, prepared to see the valley again, but my yard was out there instead. It looked like a bright, sunny day.

Thank God.

"That's some picture, Tommy," Collin said behind me, his voice strained. "Who's the girl with red hair?"

"I don't know," Tommy mumbled, "but that guy's you."

"That's me, huh?" Collin asked.

I was dying to look over my shoulder to gauge Collin's reaction and perhaps catch a glimpse of the drawing, but I didn't want to upset Tommy.

"And the guy with the dark curly hair?" Collin asked.

"Dunno," Tommy said. "I think the girl likes him."

"The one with brown hair?" Collin asked.

"No, the girl with red hair."

Collin took a couple of seconds before he asked, "Who's the girl with brown hair?"

"Miss Piper."

"What's in her hands?"

"Swwards," he said. "Have you seen Piper's swwards? She has pictures on the handles, but they were too hard for me to dwaw."

"Yeah," Collin murmured, sounding distracted. "I've seen them. They're really something."

"She kills monsters." Tommy's voice broke. "She killed a monster that wanted to eat me."

"Piper obviously likes you very much," Collin said.

"Yeah," he said, shyly. "She's wealy bwave. A bad, bad monster wants her. He's badder than all the other ones."

Tommy had told me pretty much the same thing before, but I'd presumed the bad monster was the Great One. Was he talking about Okeus?

I was even more certain that I had to kill Okeus. Abel thought it foolhardy, and while I had to agree with him, we weren't the only pawns for the brothers. We all were—every single god and demon and human on this plane.

When Tsagasi had called me a slayer of demons and gods, I'd presumed it was yet another indication I was fated to kill Abel. Now I wondered if he'd had a bigger target in mind.

"Will you help Piper fight the monster?" Tommy asked.

Collin hesitated, and for a moment, I thought he was going to tell the boy no, but then he said, "Yes. I've already promised that I will."

Who had he promised? Ellie? When I glanced over my shoulder, Collin's dark gaze was pinned on me. It didn't take a genius to see he wasn't happy.

"No peeking, Miss Piper!" Tommy shouted.

I held up my hands in surrender and moved to the next dormer window to let more light into the space. I threw the curtains open with more force than I'd intended and prepared myself for a face full of dust, but nothing flew out. One more reminder that this place had sprung from my imagination.

Only, I hadn't created what was outside the window.

I gasped and took a step backward, face-to-face with a demon.

CHAPTER TEN

Piper

It stood on the roof outside the window, its sharp claws digging into the shingles. It looked to be about five feet tall, with dark gray skin, long claws, and lots of teeth.

Why did they have to have so many teeth?

When it saw me, its eyes lit up and its mouth dropped open, drool dripping onto the roof. The roof sizzled and steamed. Acid.

I reached for my daggers, ready to go on the attack, then realized I hadn't put them on. The curse keepers had assured me I was safe in my own house, but then, I wasn't in my house anymore. I was in a pocket dimension of my own creation, and I'd been arrogant to think it would be safe.

Collin was at my side in an instant, but I knew he hadn't brought his sword. We were weaponless.

"What the fuck?" he murmured under his breath.

Tommy ran over and wrapped his arms around me, burying his face into my legs.

"Tommy," I said, trying to pry him off me. "Go hide under the bed."

"He can't huwt us," the little boy said, shaking violently.

Collin urged me and Tommy back several feet, then jerked the curtains shut.

"Have you seen him before?" I asked.

"He likes to watch me thwough the windows. He's looking for you. You should stay away from him."

My heart sputtered and I tried to think through my options. Should I take Tommy downstairs to safety?

Collin must have worked out his own plan, because he pulled a piece of charcoal out of his pocket and started drawing on the walls surrounding the dormer window. "Piper, take Tommy downstairs and grab my sword. I'll mark the windows and hope it doesn't get in before I finish."

"It can't get in," Tommy said. "It gets mad when it twies to break the window and climb in, but something keeps the monster out."

Finishing the first mark, Collin glanced back at Tommy. "How many times have you seen him?"

"I can't count that high."

Collin's gaze jerked up to mine. "How long has he been up here?"

"Two days, but time moves much more slowly here." I sucked in a breath of horror. "Oh shit." Then I cringed as I realized I'd cursed in front of Tommy. "Ten minutes here is an hour in our time. How long have we been here?"

Collin went back to marking the wall around the window. "Ten...fifteen minutes."

"Abel's probably frantic with worry." Then again, he could put two and two together. He'd know I was here, and with Collin, neither of which would make him happy. A new thought struck me. "We're late."

"We weren't supposed to meet the others until one," Collin said. "And we came up here about 11:45. If we're late, it won't be by much."

"That's not the meeting I'm talking about." I considered asking Collin to stay and finish the markings so I could go to find Deidre with Abel, but I wasn't sure if he could leave without me, and I didn't want him to leave them half-finished. Even though Tommy had claimed the monsters couldn't get in through the windows, I felt reassured that Collin's markings were added insurance. Especially with the many hours Tommy spent here without me.

"I want to know what other meeting you had planned," Collin said as he moved to the second window.

"It's none of your business."

"After the drawings I just saw over there"—he nodded his head toward the table—"I think it's very much my business."

My stomach dropped to the floor. "What did you see?"

He shot me a leer. "You're not supposed to know."

"Cut the crap, Collin. Do you treat Ellie like this too?"

He spun around to face me, anger blazing in his eyes. "How I treat Ellie is none of your goddamned concern."

"Little ears!" I shouted, getting pissed.

"He's not even real!"

Tommy's body stiffened, and he looked up at me with tears in his eyes. "Am I weally not weal, Miss Piper?"

I could kill Collin Dailey. Why had I thought I could trust him when I knew full well he'd betrayed my cousin?

I dropped to my knees and put my hands on Tommy's arms, holding his gaze. "Do you feel my hands?"

He nodded, tears falling down his cheeks.

I wrapped my arms around his back and pulled him close, his face nestling on my right shoulder. "Do you feel me hugging you?"

He nodded, his chin tapping my shoulder.

"If you weren't real, you wouldn't be able to feel me, and I wouldn't be able to feel you. Or smell you." I sniffed his hair. "You smell like summer. You'd smell like nothing if you weren't real."

"Summer has a smell?" he asked, leaning back to stare at me with wide eyes.

Collin leaned over and sniffed Tommy's head, then squatted next to us, giving the boy an apologetic smile. "It smells like grass and sweat and pool chlorine."

Tommy wrinkled his nose. "Sweat?"

"The good kind," I said. "Sweet little boy sweat." A wave of protectiveness and affection washed through me, catching me off guard.

Collin put a hand on Tommy's shoulder and held his gaze. "That was a stupid thing I said. You're real. I guess I was jealous." He winked at the boy, but he looked strained.

"You were jeawous of *me*?" Tommy asked in shock.

"Well, yeah…" Collin said. "You keep hugging Piper, and she's never once hugged *me*."

"That's because she's not yours," Tommy said matter-of-factly. "She bewongs to the monster."

My breath caught in my throat. "I thought you wanted me to stay away from the monster," I forced out.

He stared at me like I was a simpleton. "There are wots of monsters, Miss Piper."

Collin's mouth pinched before he said, "I'm really sorry, little dude. Do you forgive me?"

Tommy nodded with a solemn look.

"I know you said the monsters can't get in, but I'm going to make extra sure, okay?"

Tommy nodded again.

Standing, I took Tommy's hand and gently squeezed. "Want me to read you a book before I leave?"

He looked up at me with innocent eyes. "Can you wead me the story about the puppy again?"

"Of course," I said. "Why don't you go sit on the bed and I'll get the book."

"Okay."

I had an ulterior motive. I felt horrible for using him, but I really needed to see what was in that drawing he'd shown Collin...only it wasn't on the table.

Where was it?

As I picked up the book, I cast a glance at Collin, who was halfway through the second window. Had he taken it?

I sat down next to Tommy, and he asked, "What are those things Collin is scwibbling on the wall? Mommy told me I couldn't color on the walls."

"I'm not entirely sure myself, but Collin and his friend Ellie say they'll help keep the monsters away."

"Okay, Piper. Can we wead the book now?"

"Yeah." I started reading about the puppy, glancing up every few seconds to keep an eye on Collin. Tommy yawned and lay down on the pillows, and I pulled a blanket up to cover him. By the time I finished the story, Tommy was asleep and Collin was working on the final symbol on the third and last window.

I got up and put the book away, glancing around for the drawing, but there was no sign of it.

Collin sent a quick glance at Tommy and asked, "Is he really asleep?"

"Yeah."

"You really like him, don't you?"

I studied the sleeping boy, my heart swelling at the sight of him. "Yeah. I do."

"What do you make of the demon outside the window? Do you think it's real?"

"I created this world in the attic, but I didn't create what's outside it. The last time I was here, I saw some kind of vision, but this time... that demon..." I took a breath. "I think it's real."

Which meant the demons knew I could create worlds and they were trying to get in.

Which meant my secret was officially out.

"I need to tell Abel." I headed toward the stairs, but Collin slid over and blocked the staircase.

"What's the mark you're trying to stop from appearing?"

"That's none of—"

"Cut the bullshit, Piper. I might let Ellie get away with it, but I've got no reason to cut you the same slack."

If we were laying all our cards on the table, so be it. "Because you love her?"

He worked his jaw, his Adam's apple bobbing. I was sure he was going to deny it, but he looked me in the eyes. "I know I blew it. I've accepted it, but now everything I do is for her."

"Because you feel guilty?"

"Because I ruined her life. I broke the curse, tricked her into fusing the gate open instead of closing it, then abandoned her."

I wasn't sure what to say, but Collin didn't wait for a response.

"Her father and stepmother both died because Okeus tricked me into breaking the curse. My own bastard of a father killed Ellie's mother while he was trying to kill her." Anguish filled his eyes. "Did you get that? My *father* went to Ellie's house to kill an eight-year-old girl." He ran a hand over his head, then dropped it to his side. "How fucking messed up is that?"

"You're not responsible for your father's actions."

He released a bitter laugh. "I'm not telling you all of this for you to absolve me of my sins. I want you to understand what I'll do to protect her." He paused and his eyes turned cold. "I won't let anything or anyone hurt her."

I could have reacted with anger—Abel would likely have ripped him apart limb from limb for threatening me, but I understood his reasoning and took no offense. "I barely know Ellie, but I hope to get to know her. I understand what it's like to feel alone in the world. I have my grandparents, but we aren't close. Hudson was my best friend, the one who'd kept me grounded since we were twelve, and now he's gone. Because of me." I held his gaze and said emphatically, "I have no intention to harm Ellie—or you or David. My job is to help people—ghosts—continue on their journey. The one time I sent someone to hell…" I took a deep breath. "It hurt my soul. It's not in my nature to hurt people, Collin, especially people I care about."

"Can you say the same for Abel?"

I wanted to be truthful, but I needed to tread lightly. "I confess, Abel's sole focus is me, but we're working on that. He's finding his humanity."

"Forgive me if I don't feel comfortable betting Ellie's life on that testimonial."

"Look, Collin," I said. "I understand your concern. When we have our group meeting, if you and the others choose to leave, I understand. I'm not going to try to talk you out of it."

He hesitated. Maybe he'd expected me to try to convince him. "What about Okeus? Don't you need us for that delusional plan?"

"Yeah, but I refuse to coerce you to stay and help. I'm not delusional enough to think it will be easy."

"Do you have any plan at all?"

I wasn't about to confess I didn't have a shred of one. Instead, I gave him a sardonic grin. "I guess you'll find out in a few minutes when we meet with everyone else." This chat had likely cost us another hour. "I'm going downstairs now, Collin. Whether you leave limping is entirely up to you."

He let out a sharp laugh. "If I had any doubts that you were really Ellie's cousin, you've just convinced me. That look in your eye reminds me of her." His smile dropped. "But I still need to know about this mark, so if you want to go downstairs, it's time to start explaining."

I moved closer—inches away—and looked up at him with a defiant grin. "David seems to know what Kewasa means. Maybe he can explain it all to you." Then I used one of the moves Rupert, one of Abel's trainers, had taught me. I shoved the heel of my hand into his nose—although I didn't use enough force to do permanent damage—then grabbed two middle fingers on his right hand and pulled backward.

Collin cried out in pain and surprise, blood flowing out of his nose as he arched back and attempted to free his fingers. "What the fuck!"

I gave him a deadly gaze. "I warned you."

"You said I'd be limping," he said, lifting his free hand to his nose. He wasn't fighting me, but I wasn't about to let go of his fingers until I was ready to make my exit.

"Where's the drawing Tommy made?"

"On the table." He pulled his hand from his nose and studied the blood on his fingers. "I think you broke my nose."

"I didn't use enough force to break your nose." I hoped. "And the drawing's not there."

"It was there when I walked over to the windows."

"It's not there now," I said in frustration. "What did he draw?"

He studied me for a second. "Do you think he was drawing a premonition?"

"I don't know," I said. "I'd be better equipped to tell you if I knew what you'd seen."

He shot me a smirk. "Tommy doesn't want you to know. I'd hate to break a promise."

"That smart-ass comment might be more effective if you weren't gushing blood out of your nose," I said, rolling my eyes.

Abel's distant voice carried up the stairs. "Piper!"

The smile slid off Collin's face. "Can Abel walk into your world?"

"As far as I know, I'm the only one who can cross the threshold, but this is all still pretty new. When I crossed into the ghost's realm, I could hear Abel's voice. He helped me find my way back."

"Well, the demigod sounds pissed," Collin said, a combative look settling over his face. "Let's go."

I started to nudge past him. "Be sure to touch some part of me as we walk down the stairs."

"Like your ass?"

I glanced over my shoulder, my brows shooting high. "I dare you to try it. Your bloody nose will feel like a hangnail."

He chuckled. "Do me a favor—don't teach Ellie those moves."

"No promises."

He grabbed my elbow and we descended the stairs. One second the door at the bottom looked closed, then the image blurred and shifted, revealing an open door with Abel standing on the bottom step. When I saw the fury in his eyes, I considered going back to Tommy's universe to play hide-and-go-seek with the demon outside.

CHAPTER ELEVEN

Piper

I would ask where the hell you've been," he said in a deadly calm voice, "but it's more than obvious, and I can see you took the curse keeper with you." He saw Collin's bloody face then, and his eyes began to glow. Literally. "He dared to touch you?"

I held up my hands. "Slow down. It's fine. *I'm* fine."

"*I'm* not fine." Holding his hand to his nose, Collin stepped off the bottom step, pushing past Abel.

Ellie walked out of my parents' bedroom, her eyes wide with shock, and David stepped out behind her. "What happened?"

Collin shot her a look, then said, "It was a misunderstanding. I'm going to clean up."

He started for the bathroom, but Abel blocked his path. "Did you touch her?"

"For God's sake, Abel," I groaned. "I'm a grown fucking woman perfectly capable of handling myself. Your trainers have done their job. Let it go."

Abel refused to budge, instead glowering at Collin, who gave as good as he got.

"You are not to touch her," Abel growled, his hands fisted at his sides.

I stepped between them, putting my hands on Abel's chest and shoving hard, but he barely budged. "Let it go, Abel. It's not what you think, and we have much bigger issues than this."

"Such as the fact you disappeared for nearly two hours and neglected to tell me you were leaving? Or that you took the curse keeper with you when you knew I wanted to accompany you? Or that we missed our appointment with the seer and she called and said she refuses to meet with us now?"

My mouth dropped open. "I can't believe she really meant that. I'll talk to her. But yes, this might be bigger than all of that." I paused. "The demons know I can create worlds."

His nostrils flared, fear flickering in his eyes. "How do you know this?"

"Because there's one outside the window of the attic I created. Tommy said it's been looking for me."

He grabbed my wrist and dragged me to the door. "Show me."

I jerked my arm from his grasp. "Let go of me, Abel, or I'll give you a bloody nose like the one I gave Collin."

He growled. "So he *did* manhandle you."

"Oh, for fuck's sake…" I sucked in a deep breath and counted to three before I said, "I'm not taking you up there. We need to see Deidre."

"Hold up," Ellie said with an upraised hand. "Slow down and start from the beginning. Where were you two?"

"In Piper's attic," Collin said from inside the bathroom, his voice muffled. "Except it wasn't like it is now. It was a playroom, and there's a ghost boy up there."

"Why are you hiding a ghost up there?" Ellie asked.

"She said demons were after the kid," Collin said from the bathroom doorway, holding a wet washcloth to his face. "They used ghosts to draw her out."

Her nose wrinkled with confusion. "But you send ghosts to the afterlife, Piper. Why not just send him too?"

"He's not ready to move on. I'm still trying to figure out how to help him."

"Is that why you won't let me up there?" Abel asked. "You're afraid I'll upset him?"

I shot him a glare. "You're not exactly known for your sensitivity."

He scowled. "Get to the demon part."

"Tommy's world is my attic, but reimagined. When I opened the curtains to one of the windows, there was a demon outside. Tommy says it wants me, but there's some kind of barrier keeping it out." I motioned to Collin. "Collin marked the walls around the dormers to add extra protection."

"To keep a ghost safe?" David asked in a neutral tone.

"Yeah," I said with a hint of attitude. "To keep a scared little boy, who happens to be a ghost, safe."

"You're thinking the boy is an apparition," Collin said, lowering his washrag, "but he's like a real kid. I touched him."

"When you were touching Piper?" Abel asked, narrowing his eyes at me. "He did *touch* you."

I rolled my eyes. "Focus, Kieran. He saw Tommy without touching me."

His eyes widened. "Your powers have grown again." He pondered that for a moment, then added, "But more importantly, the demons can find the worlds you create."

"Maybe the kid told them," Collin said. "He knows things a mysterious 'he' told him."

"He?" Abel asked in alarm. "Do you have any idea who it is?"

"No," I said, "but something tells me it's the same 'he' who's been talking to Hudson. I suspect Ahone. Tommy says the bad monster wants me."

"But he also claims she belongs to another monster," Collin said.

"That monster could be you, Abel." I turned to him, not surprised to see the outrage on his face. "No offense, but your father *is* a monster."

"No," Collin said, tossing the washrag into the bathroom sink and walking into the hall. "I'm pretty damn sure Abel was in Tommy's drawing, and he referred to him as a man, not a monster."

"What drawing?" Ellie asked.

Collin lifted his chin. "Do I smell coffee? I need coffee."

He headed down to the kitchen before anyone could stop him.

"Collin!" Ellie called out.

A dark look crossed Abel's face. "What drawing?"

"I never saw it," I said with a sigh. "Tommy was eager to show it off to Collin because the voice told him he couldn't show it to me. Collin asked Tommy about it, but he refused to tell me what he saw."

"Which prompted you to give him a bloody nose?" Ellie asked, looking pleased.

"Not exactly, but it was related." I studied her in a new light after Collin's confession. Did she have any idea of the level of devotion he had for her? It wasn't my place to tell her. "I'm fairly certain you were in drawing. And David. Collin quizzed him about a red-haired woman and the guy with curly black hair who she liked."

David self-consciously ran a hand through his wavy dark hair.

"Why is it such a secret?" Ellie asked.

"I don't know," I said, "but Tommy drew my daggers too. He said he couldn't get the details of the carvings right."

"I'm not coming back up there," Collin called up from downstairs. "So if you want me to be part of this conversation, you'll need to come down."

Abel's face reddened—he didn't like taking orders from anyone—and I had to admit Collin's cockiness was grating. Still, he wasn't the only one who needed a caffeine fix.

Without saying a word I headed downstairs, leaving the others to follow or not. Part of me was grateful for the reprieve. After my encounter with Collin, I was pretty sure I was going to have to come up with a compelling argument to get them to help me kill Okeus, and I didn't have a clue how to do that.

Collin was sitting on the sofa, nursing his coffee with a satisfied grin, but I gave him a smug look as my gaze landed on the blood spots on his shirt.

I headed into the kitchen and poured a cup of coffee. As I took my first sip, the stupid donut box caught my attention.

Hudson.

Tears sprang to my eyes again. "I'm sorry I failed you, Huddy."

"You have to stop talking like that," he said, suddenly appearing a few feet away.

I turned to face him, not surprised he'd shown up, yet feeling incredibly sad at the sight of him. "I miss you."

He flashed me a smile. "I'm right here, Pippy. Not the same as before, but I'm here."

I set my coffee cup on the counter and hugged him.

"Hudson." I released him and leaned my hip against the counter. Shooting a glance up to the ceiling, I said, "Have you met Tommy yet?"

He frowned. "Who?"

"The ghost boy hiding in the world I created in the attic. He knows things he shouldn't, just like you do, and a mysterious voice talks to him too. I doubt there are two of them."

He didn't look as surprised as I would have thought he'd be. Maybe death, the greatest mystery of all, takes the edge off other surprises. He just nodded. "I should try to talk to him. Maybe he wants a friend."

"I think he'd like that," I said. "Time moves much slower up there, but I have a feeling I'll be gone for long stretches. I hate to think of him being all alone."

"I'll see what I can do," he said.

"Thanks, Huddy."

He reached over and picked up the bakery box and held it out to me. "I've seen you looking at this. You have to take it outside and throw it away." When I frowned, he said, "Pippy, we can't change the past. We can only move forward. This stupid box upsets you, and you have much bigger things to worry about."

"Like what?" I asked, still refusing to take the box. For some reason it felt so final to throw it away. Like I was accepting his death.

"Piper," he said, his tone serious. "Throw it away."

I shot him a look of frustration, but I wouldn't refuse him. He had every right to make demands of me. I lifted an eyebrow. "Can I eat the donut first?"

He rolled his eyes. "If you want to eat a stale donut, then by all means."

I opened the lid and hesitated when I saw a maple bar covered in bacon bits. Hudson's favorite. "It's yours."

"What was mine is now yours. Everything. But life is too short for stale donuts, so throw it away. You have work to do."

I narrowed my eyes. "What do you know about the work I'm supposed to do?"

"Just take it outside, Piper."

He was being weirdly persistent, and although he'd always been a clean freak in life, I doubted this was about trash.

Shooting him a suspicious gaze, I took the box out the back door toward the detached garage where I stored the trash bin. I'd dumped it into the bin when my left hand began to tingle, alerting me to a presence in the trees behind the garage. I cursed myself for leaving the house without my weapons, but the presence felt neutral. Familiar.

Tsagasi walked out from behind a tree.

"Did you have Hudson send me out here?"

"The ghost?" he asked, sounding bored. "No. I have been waiting for you, but I have had no contact with the ghost in your house. Either of them."

That worried me, even if I didn't care to admit it to Tsagasi. "Are you pissed that I saved Abel?"

"No. The son of Okeus has proven himself loyal to you. He was necessary, but he's fulfilled his role. You need to stop your quest."

"You're saying I shouldn't try to prevent the mark from appearing on my hand?" I asked, my tone hard and unyielding. "You want me to kill him?"

"Nothing lives forever," he stated matter-of-factly. "Your friend is proof enough of that. Now that Abel has fulfilled his role, it's time for him to move on to the next plane."

Fear gripped my heart, but then I asked myself how this supernatural being knew so much. "Who made *you* the authority on the future?"

"I do not know the future, only the present and the past. His role here is complete." He paused. "Ask the seer if you like. Ask her what she sees in her bones. Abel has fulfilled his role. Yours is only just beginning."

I started to freak out. Tsagasi knew so much he had no way of knowing—did that mean he was right? But the little man was clearly biased against Abel, and he himself had admitted he had no knowledge of the future.

I shook my head. "*No.* I won't accept that."

"He's known this was coming for centuries, Kewasa. He accepted his fate until he met you."

"Am I supposed to apologize for that?" I asked with a sneer.

"No," he said, his eyes full of sympathy. "There is no need for apology. Only acceptance."

I shook my head and took a step backward. "Fuck that, Tsagasi. Maybe you've convinced Ellie and Collin to follow along with whatever you say, but I don't have to accept it. I'll fight it until my dying breath."

"I knew she was too stubborn and foolhardy," said a voice say from the woods beyond the garage.

This new presence was neutral too, which was why it hadn't pinged on my radar, but I chastised myself again for not being more alert.

"Who the fuck are you?" I called out. A rude approach, sure, but he'd shown up without knocking and acted rude to boot. "And why should I care what you think?"

Another little man appeared out of thin air at Tsagasi's side. He looked up at me with a glare. "You don't have to give a fuck about us or what we think, but my brother thinks you're crucial for our salvation."

"The only person I'm interested in saving is Abel," I said. "And if you can't help with—"

"The demons are coming," Tsagasi said, his voice lowering. "They are advancing tonight. You need to stop wasting time on the son of Okeus and prepare for a battle."

"Tonight?" I'd hoped we'd have more time. "I'm not sure Ellie and Collin will join us. Will you?"

Tsagasi turned to stare at the little man next to him. "My brother and the others have yet to decide if they wish to take this risk."

"Take your time," I scoffed. "No hurry, but I don't think we can face an army on our own. Even with Collin and Ellie." I studied him for a moment. "I know there are four in your group who have sworn fealty to Ellie, but are there more of you?"

Tsagasi's brother snarled, "Our numbers are no concern of yours."

I slowly shook my head. "Not true. I suspect you have an army and we need your help. You said you think I'm part of your salvation. I'm not much good to you if I'm dead."

"You only fight to save your skin from Okeus," Tsagasi's brother said in disgust. "You don't give a damn about our cause. You don't give a damn about the abuse we've suffered for eons."

His words sank into my marrow. I'd never once stopped to consider how Okeus had treated other supernatural creatures. "You're right," I said, softening my tone. "I haven't, but in my defense, this is entirely new, so there are a lot of things that have never occurred to me. All I know is Okeus is evil incarnate, and he has to be stopped. Permanently."

Tsagasi's brother's skepticism was palpable. "You plan to permanently stop Okeus?" He released a snort. "How?"

I straightened my back and hoped I exuded more confidence than I felt. "I plan to kill him."

Tsagasi's brother parted his mouth in shock. "You wish to kill the god of war?"

"I know it sounds crazy—"

"Have the curse keepers agreed to help you?" the brother barked.

I hesitated. "No. Not yet."

"Do you have a plan?"

Oh crap. "No, I—"

He turned to Tsagasi. "She has no plan. She has no pledged allies. Why did you ask me to come meet her? This is madness!"

Tsagasi placed his hand on his brother's arm and searched his eyes. "Tsawasi. She is the one. I can feel it deep in my soul. Can you not feel it too?"

Tsawasi's jaw clenched. Then he turned his hardened gaze on me. "She is inexperienced. She is foolhardy."

"She is strong and grows stronger by the day. She is the one, I'm certain of it."

Tsawasi sucked in a deep breath, then pushed it out. "You risk much on a hunch, my brother."

"Have I steered you wrong yet?" Tsagasi asked quietly.

Tsawasi released a long string of curses, but when he finally turned to me, pointing his hairy finger at my face, he said, "If the curse keepers agree, and if you come up with a plan, we will fight with you."

I couldn't hide my shock. "You will?"

Still pointing at me, Tsawasi turned to his brother with a look of disgust. "She is no leader. She will be the death of us all."

"She is the slayer of demons and gods." Tsagasi turned and gave me a long look. "She is our Kewasa."

Dread washed over me like a bucket of cold water. "Abel said I'm *his* Kewasa."

"The son of Okeus is not the only supernatural creature whose life hangs in the balance," Tsagasi said. "I believe you are Kewasa to all."

I shook my head. "No. You're wrong. That's Ellie and Collin. They're the warriors who guard the gate."

"The gate they opened," Tsawasi spat. "The gate they have failed to close."

"But you were trapped," I said. "They let you out."

"True," Tsagasi said, "but many supernatural creatures do not trust them to guard it anymore. We've been waiting for a savior."

"History has not been kind to saviors," I said. "Saviors are often sacrificed for the greater good."

"And yet, it may be the only way you can find that which you seek," Tsagasi said quietly. "You wish to free the son of Okeus, do you not?"

"I wish to free him from my curse," I said, my voice shaking as I held out my left hand. "I wish to save his soul."

Tsawasi tilted his head. "If you defeat Okeus, you will have to rule the underworld."

"*What?*"

Tsagasi shot his brother a dark glare but remained silent.

"You or an appointee of your choosing," Tsawasi amended.

"What are you talking about?" I asked in confusion.

"It is how monarchies have been ruled for eons," Tsawasi said with a partial smile. "The winner takes the kingdom *and* the crown. If you defeat Okeus, you can change the rules." He pointed to my hand. "You can save the son of Okeus."

"Can it really be that easy?" I whispered.

Tsagasi burst into mirthless laughter. *"That easy?"* He shot Tsawasi a glare. "What have you put into her head?"

"The truth."

Tsawasi took two steps forward, craning his neck to look up at me. "If you convince the curse keepers to help you, we will bring our own army to the gate at Helen's Bridge. We will fight Okeus's army, but you must fight him to his death."

Or mine, it went without saying.

"I will do my best," I said solemnly.

Tsawasi shook his head in disgust, then headed back to the trees, muttering, "Let's hope your best is enough."

CHAPTER TWELVE

Piper

Abel was waiting for me when I walked in the kitchen door, and he looked furious. "Why were you outside?"

"It's not important. We need to talk to the curse keepers."

He grabbed my arm as I tried to pass. "Not yet. Why did you go outside?"

I suspected he wouldn't appreciate the fact that Huddy had been the one to send me out there. Had Hudson known the Nunnehi Little People would be waiting out there for me? Had he known what they would offer?

When I tried to break free from Abel's hold, his face hardened. "You can't trust the curse keepers, Waboose. They have their own agenda."

"Agreed, but if we all ultimately want the same thing, does it matter?"

"I suspect they want similar results, but their tolerance for collateral damage is likely different from ours."

"This is bigger than all of us, Abel. Trust me."

He searched my face, then nodded toward the doorway. "You'll find them in the living room, but they're growing restless."

I started to pull free but stopped and looked up into his worried face. "I know how to fix this now." I held out my left hand. "I know how to fix everything." Then I placed a hard kiss on his mouth and headed into the living room, leaving him to follow.

Collin sat on one end of the sofa and Ellie on the other. David had taken the chair next to Ellie, and Jack and Rhys sat on two dining room chairs that had been pulled up to the sofa.

"Did you go to Costa Rica to pick the coffee beans for the coffee you're not drinking?" Collin asked in a smug tone.

He was right. I'd left my coffee in the kitchen. Two could play the smart-ass game. "Yeah," I said back, "it's a shame the beans weren't to my satisfaction."

David chuckled. "So it's not just Ellie who doesn't take Collin's shit. Must be a Lancaster trait."

His comment pleased me more than I would have expected. Maybe I was grateful to know I had a connection to Ellie that went beyond our last names and our supernatural gifts.

"Time to talk plans," I said, realizing there was no easing into this. "I just spoke with Tsagasi and his brother Tsawasi outside. They believe Okeus's army is coming tonight."

Everyone was silent for a moment before Collin said, "Tonight?"

I nodded.

"And they're coming for you and Abel?" he asked.

"They're coming for us too," Ellie said in a tone that suggested Collin was an idiot. "We *know* that."

Collin got to his feet and swept his arm in my direction. "The only reason we know that is because *Piper* told us that's part of Okeus's plans, and she said he plans to kill us." He leaned forward, his gaze piercing my cousin. "But think about it, Ellie. Okeus's goal has always been to impregnate you. You only bought a reprieve. One year is nothing to him. He'll wait. You're worth *far more* alive to him than dead."

Ellie cast me a worried glance before looking up at Collin. "I know, but—"

"But why would Piper lie to you?" he asked, his voice full of understanding. "I understand your confusion, but consider this: If you were in her position, would you trust that a near stranger would agree to fight an army of demons if her life weren't on the line? Maybe she told you that as insurance."

"Collin!" Ellie protested.

Abel took a step forward, about to protest, but I put a hand on his chest and shook my head. "Let them talk it out."

"You're presuming everyone's just like you, Collin," Ellie said, getting to her feet. "Cynical, jaded, and in it for themselves."

If he was hurt by her statement, he didn't show it. "And you always trust too easily, which is how the Great One deceived you for so long."

Now David got to his feet, anger hardening his features. "You're out of line, Collin."

"Am I?" Collin asked in a harsh tone. "You're just like her."

"Enough," Abel said in a low voice, but his word exuded a supernatural power that swept through the room and silenced everyone.

Collin turned to Abel, livid. "What the fuck did you just do?"

"I stopped a pack of squabbling children." His gaze surveyed each of us in turn. "Piper has no cause to lie about any of this. She saw what she saw."

Collin held up a hand, his skepticism returning. "Wait a minute. What do you mean *she* saw it. You *didn't*? Where were you when she learned all of this from Okeus."

"No," I said, realizing they thought Okeus had told us his plans in the warehouse. "I saw it in a vision."

Collin threw his hands up in the air. "Oh! A vision! That's *so much* more trustworthy."

"Collin, stop," Ellie snapped. Her face softened as she turned to me. "What vision, Piper?"

"I saw creation," I said, awe at the experience bleeding into my words. "I saw the creation of the universe and the Earth and Ahone." I glanced back at Abel. "I saw Abel's birth and Ahone's plan to use him against his father." I turned back to Ellie. "I saw my own conception, and at the end, I found myself in hell. Okeus sat on a throne of bones, surrounded by hundreds, likely thousands of souls, some chained to his throne. That's when he announced his plans." I paused. "But he knew I was there watching, and he told me he was coming. It was real."

Everyone was silent for a moment. Then I said, "Tsawasi has pledged to send an army of his own to help us fight the demons."

My cousin and her two men stared at me in shock. Then Collin swore under his breath about Tsagasi being the most deceitful creature on the planet, sprinkled with much more colorful words.

"He pledged an army just like that?" Ellie asked in disbelief. "Did you make a blood oath?"

"No," I said, "but I promised to kill Okeus."

Abel looked stricken. "Waboose, how could you?"

"It has to be done anyway."

"What happens when you don't kill him?" Collin asked in a snide tone. "Did you doom us all with your promise?"

I swallowed my fear. While standing with the two Nunnehi Little People, I'd been full of bluster and bravado, but standing here in my living room, surrounded by the people whose help I needed, I realized I was in way over my head.

"We discussed no punishment," I said. "I said I would kill him, and I meant it. It was already my plan, so what difference does it make?"

"You can't just kill a god, Piper!" Collin shouted, then turned his attention to Abel. "Do you really not give one ounce of shit about her? How can you let her run with this delusion?"

"I do not control her," Abel said, his voice booming off the walls. He was clearly pissed Collin was questioning my sanity.

"So you approve of this suicide mission?"

"No." Abel hesitated. "But she's right about Okeus. He will never let any of us go."

"I have a sword that subdues gods, Collin," Ellie said in a cajoling tone. "Tsagasi insists I need to use it."

"I thought Tsagasi was on our side," Collin countered, pissed off anew. "Now he's sending us off to a battle we're certain to lose?"

I almost told him that it was Tsawasi's plan and that Tsagasi seemed to want no part of it, but the last thing I wanted to do was give him another reason to ridicule the idea.

"If they're providing an army to fight against Okeus, then they have skin in the game too," David said.

Collin spun to face him. "Surely you don't think we stand a chance of winning. Do you know how many demons are in an army?"

A grin tipped up the corners of David's mouth. "I'm guessing a lot."

"This is crazy!" Collin shouted, gripping both sides of his head.

"An army of demons spilling out onto the earth," Jack said from his chair, his gaze on me. "Sounds like the apocalypse."

My stomach dropped. He was right. "What do you think about all of this, Jack?"

He took in a deep breath, and the philosophical look on his face reminded me that my young, fit friend really was a priest. "Let's say you take Collin's advice and you flee, you then have to ask yourself several questions. One, when *will* you be ready to fight them?" He gave me a sad smile. "Make no mistake, I have no desire to see this battle happen now or in the future, but it seems inevitable."

I nodded. "I know."

"And two, what happens if no one is there to stop this army of newly emerged demons? They'll be hungry. There are nearly one hundred thousand men, women, and children in Asheville. This city will look like a slaughterhouse."

I felt the blood drain from my head. He was right.

"Three, do you have any idea how to kill him? Because once you're close enough to try, there will be no turning back, Piper."

"I know, and no. Not yet. But my power is still growing."

"All the more reason to wait," Collin said, but with much less conviction.

"The people, Collin," Ellie whispered with tears in her eyes. "All those people."

Collin turned to face her, looking close to tears himself, but I knew they weren't for himself or even the citizens of Asheville. They were for her. "I know."

We were all silent for a moment. Then Collin pushed out a sigh of acceptance. "I'd suggest we take a vote, but I don't see the point." He turned to me. "Good job. You've convinced us all to march off to certain death, so what's your plan?"

I sucked in a breath, my newly bolstered confidence fading. "That's just it. I still don't have one."

Collin burst out laughing. "You want us to help you kill the god of war and you don't have a plan?" He shook his head, then turned to Ellie. "Your cousin is nuts."

"So we *make* a plan," Jack said. "We'll need weapons. We're going to need holy water. Gallons of it."

I gave him a look of gratitude and mouthed *thank you.*

He nodded. "I'll figure out a delivery system."

"You expect Jack to fight?" Rhys demanded, speaking for the first time. "Are you insane, Piper?"

"I'm not going to stand back and do *nothing* while the others fight," Jack said in a stern tone. "This is what I was destined to do."

Rhys's eyes grew wide. "How are you going to defend yourself? Holy water didn't save you the last time you were attacked by a demon."

"I know where you can find weapons," Hudson said in the dining room, appearing behind Jack and Rhys.

Jack spun around and jumped to his feet. "Hudson?"

"You can hear him?" I asked in shock.

"I can *see* him."

I shook my head. "How?"

"I don't know," Jack said.

"You," Abel said in a grave tone. "Your power's stronger than before."

"What does that have to do with Jack being able to see Hudson?" I asked.

"Jack has always had a predisposition to see the supernatural plane. He saw flashes of the demon that attacked him. Your own power is like an amplifier, boosting his."

"Will it boost our power too?" Collin asked.

Abel stared hard at him for several long seconds. "Yes."

"Pippy, he's right," Hudson said. "Your power is still growing, but you'll need something more to kill Okeus."

"You said you know where we can get weapons?" I asked.

"The Guardians had spelled weapons." He gave me a knowing look. "Your grandfather's friend had some in his house."

"How do you know that?" I asked. "Did the voice tell you?"

"The Guardians took me to Robert Corden's house. The ceremony for the Great One took place there. They talked about the weapons."

One of the Guardians who'd been killed by the lion demons was a friend of my grandfather's—someone who'd apparently been spying on me my entire life. And it sounded like he'd also played a significant role in Hudson's death. I would have killed Robert myself if he weren't already dead.

"They took you to his *house*?" I asked in horror.

"I take it she's talking to her ghost friend," Collin said.

"Shut up, Collin," Ellie grunted.

Hudson gave me a sad smile. "If you seek revenge for my death, save it for the demons and Okeus. Robert Corden had at least twenty weapons you can use against them." He turned to look at Collin. "Including a spear that sings."

I realized Collin couldn't hear him, so I said, "Collin, does a spear that sings mean anything to you?"

Collin and Ellie exchanged a knowing look before she asked, "I take it your ghost knows something about it?"

"He knows where it is."

Her face paled.

Hudson turned his attention back to me. "You'll need to go soon, Pippy. His widow has just returned from out of town, and the police haven't made the house a crime scene yet."

"Why would they make his house a crime scene? Robert was killed in the warehouse." Nausea washed over me as the truth hit me hard. "You were murdered there."

"In his basement," Hudson said calmly, as though we weren't discussing his death. "But there's no reason for you to go down there. The weapons are in the display cases in his study."

"How are we going to get into Robert Corden's house?" I asked.

"We have the perfect cover," Jack said. "He was one of my parishioners—a new member of the church."

"Which means they were watching you too," I said.

He gave me a grim nod. "But his duplicity is to our benefit. And the fact that he and his wife were friends of your grandparents purchases your admission. We have the perfect excuse to drop by for a visit."

"That's presuming she knows he's dead," I said.

Jack pushed out a sigh. "Olivia called me about an hour ago." He held my gaze. "The police know."

My stomach fell to my feet.

"They're investigating the scene. They've notified Robert's widow."

Which meant they'd found Hudson's broken, naked body. I felt my chest tighten.

Hudson walked over to me and squatted, placing a hand on my knee. "I'm not there, Pippy. I'm here with you."

I shook my head, his face growing blurry with my unshed tears. "I should have protected you."

His hand tightened on my knee. "Enough. I can be more help to you dead than I ever was alive."

"Don't say that, Hudson."

"But it's true." He stood. "You need to deal with more important things, like getting the weapons."

"He's right," Jack said. "The sooner we go the better."

"I'll be going as well," Abel said.

"No," Hudson said. "They know Abel is part of the spiritual world. Corden's wife will never believe it's a sympathy call if he's anywhere near the house. It needs to be you and Jack."

"But if his wife knows about Abel, won't she slam the door in the face of the man they kidnapped and the woman they planned to use?"

"She doesn't know about Jack. She was out of town and he was a last-minute addition to the plan. And as for you..." He grimaced. "Her reaction could go either way."

"I'll play dumb," I said. "I didn't know anything about Robert's involvement until I saw him at the warehouse, and she has no way of knowing I was there."

I snuck a glance to Collin, who cast a suspicious glare in my direction. Collin clearly didn't trust me, but based on what he'd told Tommy in the attic, he'd stick around anyway because of Ellie. I didn't totally trust him, so perhaps it would be best to keep him close, even if Collin wasn't truly our enemy. I hoped.

"I want to bring Collin with us," I said.

Both Collin and Abel exclaimed "What?" at the same time.

"If there are a lot of weapons, we'll need help carrying them," I said. "Not to mention, Collin apparently has experience with this kind of thing."

"I don't like it," Abel growled.

Hudson glanced between me and Collin, then said, "I think it's a good idea, but be wary of the son of the land, Pippy. He doesn't have your best interests at heart."

"I'm going too," Abel said, making it clear he wasn't taking no for an answer.

Hudson's gaze narrowed. "You need to go to the seer and make amends. She holds an answer you seek."

Instinctively, I glanced down at my left hand and noticed Abel did the same. Our gazes met and I whispered, "You have to try."

If my plan worked, we wouldn't need her help, but for all I knew, the mark might appear before the battle.

"She'll refuse to speak to me," he said. "It will be a wasted trip."

"Hudson says you should go, and besides," I said with a grin, "it will give you something to do while we're gone."

He leaned his face close to mine and whispered, "I don't want to let you out of my sight, Waboose."

"I know how you feel," I whispered back, "but this is the best plan and you know it."

Holding my gaze, he nodded then gave me a gentle kiss. "Get your weapons and hurry back to me."

I planned to, because after my chat with the Little People, I was pinning all my hope on defeating Okeus.

CHAPTER THIRTEEN

Piper

I'd half-expected Collin to resist going with us, but he was on board from the start, which I found slightly troubling, but not enough to make me change my mind.

We grabbed a quick lunch from the kitchen before we piled into the car. I was worried Abel would flip out at the last minute and try to stop me from going, but he watched in grim silence when we left.

Jack climbed into the passenger seat, and Collin sat in the back wearing a ball cap. He had a duffle bag filled with what he'd called "necessities." I started the car and headed to South Asheville.

"Do you know the neighborhood well?" Collin asked, lowering the bill of his hat to cast a shadow on his face.

"I've had a few clients there," I said.

"Ghost clients," he said in a disparaging tone.

"It's better than petty theft," I said, then cast a glance over my shoulder. "Yep, we know about your prior arrest. Hudson researched you."

Jack chuckled. "What do you want to know about the neighborhood, Collin?"

"Is there much traffic? How easy is it to blend in?"

"Not much traffic," I said, "and from what I can tell, most of their neighbors are gone on the weekends. We should be good."

"Is there an alley behind the house?"

I grimaced. "I'm not sure. I've been inside their house before for Christmas parties and the like, but I didn't exactly scout it out. There aren't many alleys in that neighborhood though, so I would guess not."

"It's okay," Collin said. "We'll make do." He glanced out the window. "Here's what we're going to do. You'll let me off around the block, and I'll head to the back of the house. One of you will excuse yourself to the bathroom and open a back door or window to let me in. I'll take the loot, toss it out back. If it's too big or too conspicuous to haul to the car, I'll hide it and we'll pick it up later."

"I'll let you in," I said. "I know the house. I can let you in through the kitchen and point you toward the study with the glass cases."

"Sounds good," Collin said. "I'll try to finish within five to ten minutes, but I'll need you to keep the homeowner busy so she doesn't walk in on me."

"We can do that," Jack said. "Text us when you're done so we know when to leave and pick you up."

"We'll determine the pickup location after we drive around the neighborhood," Collin said. "Ideally, we wouldn't do this all on the same day, it's too damn suspicious, but time is not on our side." He grimaced as he glanced out the window again, then turned back to look at me. "So how much do you make on a ghost gig?"

I frowned. "I didn't charge in the beginning. My clients just gave me tips, which was sometimes cash, sometimes homemade jam, sometimes a gift card to Bed Bath & Beyond."

"Back when you were a fraud?" Collin asked with a smug grin. "You and I aren't so different."

Unfortunately, I couldn't argue with that.

"But you charge now," he said.

"Piper provides a great service," Jack said defensively. "She not only lets people say goodbye to their loved ones, but they can see and touch the ghosts. Of course she charges."

Collin looked amused that Jack had come to my defense.

I just shrugged. "It's my job now and I have bills to pay."

"Lucky you that you *have* a job," Collin said in a snide tone. "Ellie lost her bed and breakfast in a fire created by the Great One and David had to take a sabbatical."

"And you?" I asked sarcastically. "What gainful employment did you give up?"

He leaned back in his seat with a lazy grin. "I'm a fisherman. Got a boat and everything."

I laughed. "I struggle to see you with a rod and reel."

"Nets, woman," he teased. "Real fishermen use nets."

"Have you seen Ahone?" Jack asked abruptly, turning to look at Collin.

Collin's grin fell. "Yes, but I heard him before I saw him. He called out to me on my boat." He shook his head with disgust. "The fucking bastard ruined my life."

"He told you to break the curse," Jack said.

Collin looked startled but nodded. "Yep."

"A voice told me to quit law school," I said quietly.

"And a voice has been guiding me as well," Jack said, "one I fear I've followed too blindly."

"A word of unsolicited advice," Collin said. "Do not listen to that asshole. Take what he tells you to do and run in the opposite direction."

Jack shot me a dark look. We'd both let that voice rule our decisions—me for a year, but Jack for most of his life. How did we rectify that now?

The two men talked about Ahone, who'd appeared to Collin and Ellie as an older man with a long white beard and robes like he'd stepped out of a biblical adaptation. I'd seen that version of him in my vision, but he hadn't started off that way. He'd walked out of the ocean as a young and virile man, and I couldn't help thinking the old man image was a ruse, a way to appear less threatening.

When we approached the neighborhood, their conversation fell away as they studied the houses lining the street.

"That's it up there," I said, pointing down the street. "There's no alley, but there's a road that runs behind it."

"So the houses opposite it face the backyard," Collin said. "Is there a fence?"

I drove past the front of the older, Tudor-style house, relieved to see a tall wooden fence surrounding the property.

"Let's hope there's a gate at the back," Collin said. "I'm not sure scaling a six-foot privacy fence in broad daylight is the best idea."

"Do you want me to drive down the road behind the house?" I asked, shooting a glance at him.

"Sure, but first let's stop and put up a sign announcing that we're thieves," he sneered.

"Look," I barked. "I've never broken into a house before, so forgive me if I don't know all the rules."

Collin looked like he wanted to say something, but he pressed his lips together and frowned. "Just try not to look too conspicuous, okay? Drive down the damn street and don't slow down or look at the house. Let *me* check it out."

I pulled up to the stop sign at the end of the road, then cast a sideways glance at Jack. He gave me a slight nod, so I made the turns onto the road behind the Cordens' house. I drove to the stop sign at the end of the block, looking straight ahead. When I pulled to a stop, I glanced at Collin in the rearview mirror. "Well?"

"We're good. There's a gate. Let me out here."

"Are you serious?" I asked.

"As a fucking heart attack. Give me fifteen minutes, then let me in the back of the house." Before I could respond, he hopped out of the car, carting his bag of goodies with him.

"Should we trust him?" I asked Jack as I turned right, catching a glimpse of Collin heading down the street we'd just driven down.

"I was about to ask you the same thing. You were the one who suggested we bring him." Then he shot me a wicked grin that told me he thought I'd made the right decision.

As I continued on toward the next stop sign, it struck me that I hadn't been alone with Jack since our world had been blown to hell. This was my chance to talk to him, and the way things were going, it was unclear whether there'd be another. "How are you doing with all of this? You've been through a lot over the past twenty-four hours. Hell, you suffered a head wound a couple of days ago." Sitting up straighter, I tried to look in his hair. "Do your staples hurt?"

"I'm fine," he said dismissively as he glanced out the passenger window. "It's nothing."

Instead of turning right toward the Corden house, I went straight.

"What are you doing?" Jack asked in alarm.

"We've got fourteen minutes and thirty seconds before I need to let the petty thief in the back of the house. We can spare a few minutes."

Jack looked surprised by my statement. "Don't you think we should go talk to Mrs. Corden?"

"Hudson suggested she was with the Guardians, which makes her culpable in Hudson's death, so forgive me if I don't feel like offering my condolences for her bastard husband's much deserved death or chatting it up with her in her fancy living room."

Understanding washed over his face. "I didn't even consider that. Maybe I should go in alone."

"It was my idea to come, and I need to open the back window for Collin. Your job is to keep her entertained."

Jack nodded but didn't look happy about it. Then he sat upright, looking startled. "Do you think Robert Corden's ghost will be there?"

Well, crap. I hadn't considered that. "He was killed by a demon, but I slayed the demons that killed him, so I set his soul free."

"So that's a yes?"

I made a face. "It's a maybe." I gasped. "That's an even better in."

His face scrunched with confusion. "What are you talking about?"

"I'll tell Loretta I'm there to offer my condolences"—I made a retching sound—"and then I'll offer to talk to his ghost."

"No," he said. "Keep the ghost whisperer stuff out of it. I doubt she'll want him giving you a heads-up that the house was a murder scene. Our best bet is to go in and play dumb."

"And if his ghost shows up?"

He pushed out a sigh. "We'll deal with it then."

I drove another block before turning right.

Jack shifted in his seat, looking uncomfortable as he said, "So you and Abel… I take it you literally kissed and made up."

There was no sense in denying it. "We reached an understanding." I eyed him for as long as I dared before shifting my attention back to the nearly empty road. "Do you believe we determine the fate of our own souls?"

I hadn't planned on asking him, at least not yet, but it had been tugging on the back of my mind ever since Abel and I had returned to the warehouse.

A frown creased his forehead. "What prompted you to ask that? Collin telling us not to trust the voice?"

I wanted to be truthful with Jack, but I also didn't want to hurt him. I had to be careful about how I handled this. "Something was different when Abel and I came back to the warehouse."

"What do you mean?"

I swallowed, not sure I wanted to admit it, but I needed the peace of mind I hoped Jack would offer. "My soul craved the demons we were fighting."

He was silent for a couple of seconds before he asked, "What exactly does that mean?"

"That I wanted to kill them and possess their souls."

He turned to look at me. "As abhorrent as killing something— even a demon—must seem, they *are* demons. They're pure evil."

"It was more than that, Jack. It was like every fiber of my being needed them."

He was silent again. "This morning was the first time it happened?" He didn't give me a chance to respond before following up with another question. "What about the demon outside the attic window? Did you crave its soul?"

I sat up in surprise. I hadn't considered that. "No."

He gave me a reassuring smile. "I suspect it was a heat-of-the-battle type thing. The demons had captured your friends and killed Hudson. You had a need for vengeance, thus your thirst for their souls."

"But it felt like more than that, Jack. It felt almost…evil."

He was quiet again. "Do you think your close association with Abel has changed anything?" He made a face, clearly uncomfortable. "I couldn't help noticing that you slept in the same room as him."

My face heated. Keeping my eyes on the road, I said, "If you're asking if we slept together, the answer is yes."

There was a long pause before he said, "I see."

When he didn't say anything else, I said, "You don't approve?"

"It's not up to me to approve or disapprove, Piper."

"But you think it was a poor choice."

"It's making you question the state of your soul, so you tell me."

I gave a slow nod, biting my lower lip as I focused on heading back to the Corden house. "Hudson assures me that my soul is my own to save or lose."

"Obviously you don't quite believe it if you're asking me."

I hesitated to put all my cards on the table, but he knew the hardest part. Might as well tell him the rest. Casting a long look at him, I said, "The supernatural world calls me Kewasa. What if I'm not supposed to deliver Abel to death? What if I'm meant to deliver him from his fate?"

"How so?" he prodded, seemingly interested in my theory.

I told him what I'd learned about the power structure in the supernatural world—how there was always an alpha, except when there wasn't: Collin and Ellie balanced each other, and the same was seemingly true of Abel and me. "What if I can save him, Jack?"

"If we're truly masters of our souls," Jack said, "then it stands to reason that Abel would be able to choose his fate."

"He's certain he's destined for hell because of his father. He said his father prefers him alive because if he's dead and dwelling in hell, he's a threat to Okeus's throne."

"Does he want Okeus's throne?"

I paused on that question. The Little People told me if Okeus was defeated, someone would have to rule in his stead. Did Abel want the job? Somehow I doubted it. "I don't know."

"That's usually one of those prewedding questions I ask couples," Jack said with the first hint of snark I'd heard since our conversation had started.

I grinned. "You ask your couples if they want to rule hell?"

He laughed. "Okay, not exactly that question, but we discuss long-term goals and dreams."

"It's not like we were getting married," I countered in my defense.

Jack turned serious. "But surely you weren't naïve enough to think sex with him would be without consequence."

He was right. "I hoped I was saving him from hell." I grimaced. "It didn't feel wrong, Jack. It felt very, very right."

It was his turn to make a face and look away. "I can do without the details."

My face flushed. "Not like that. In my soul, Jack. It felt like we were destined to be together." Then I addressed the elephant in the room, my previous attempt to prove fate wrong by kissing Jack. "I think we both know you and I aren't meant to be. We proved that the other day when we kissed and felt nothing."

He swallowed, his gaze fixed on the windshield and his face expressionless. "Speak for yourself, Piper."

I started to protest, but he held up a hand to stop me. "I think we should head back to the Corden house now."

He was right and it was obvious he was done with this conversation, but it felt wrong to leave things this way. "Jack, I'm sorry."

"I'm doing my best to counsel you, Piper," he said with a hint of disgust, "because I feel like that is part of my destiny, but please don't patronize me by apologizing."

I started to protest, but I didn't want to hurt him any more than I already had.

We were silent for the rest of the short drive back. I pulled into the driveway and started to get out, but Jack placed a hand on my forearm.

"Piper."

I turned to look at him, tears in my eyes.

"I'm still your friend," he said with a sad smile. "I'm still here for you. I'll try my best to rein in my own issues."

"Jack—"

He shook his head and opened his car door. "We're good, but don't dry your tears. Save them for our visit with Robert Corden's widow."

It was showtime.

CHAPTER FOURTEEN

Piper

Before we went inside, I opened the trunk of my car and grabbed a sage stick and a lighter, dropping them in the pocket of the jacket I'd worn to conceal the daggers strapped to my thighs. Jack watched in silence.

I shrugged. "Just in case."

Loretta Corden opened the door after the first knock. She held a wad of tissues in the hand that wasn't clutched around the handle. Alarm filled her eyes. "Piper. Father Jack."

Jack offered her a warm smile. "Loretta, I just heard about Robert and rushed over to make sure you were all right."

Her wide eyes darted back and forth between us. "How did you hear? They haven't made it public yet."

"I have a friend in the police department," Jack said. "She clued me in."

Loretta's gaze landed on me.

I knew I should say something, but her and her husband's betrayal stilled my tongue. I'd known them for years. My grandparents trusted them implicitly. Hell, they'd babysat me several weekends while my grandparents were away.

And then they'd made me a sacrificial lamb.

"Piper was with me when I found out," Jack said. "And she insisted on coming."

"I was worried about you," I forced out, stuffing my anger down deep. "I know Nana and Granddad will be devastated when they find out."

"Can we come in?" Jack asked.

Flustered, Robert's widow took a step back. "Uh…"

"Loretta, you must be in a terrible state of shock," Jack said, walking over the threshold before she could refuse us. "Let us sit with you for a bit."

I followed him in and shut the door behind us as Jack grabbed her arm and gently guided her to the front sitting room.

"Did the police give you any details about what happened?" Jack asked. He sat on a formal, white brocade sofa and pulled her down with him.

"Uh…no."

Jack shook his head. "Do *you* have any idea what happened? What was Robert doing at the warehouse?"

I tried to hide my shock. After telling me to play dumb, Jack was certainly skirting the edge with his questions.

She looked startled and cast a glance at me. "I don't know."

"It's okay, Mrs. Corden," I said softly, fighting the urge to verbally attack her with everything I knew while simultaneously wringing her neck. "I'm sure this is all shocking and disorienting. I'm surprised you haven't called anyone to come sit with you." My smile tightened. "Then again, Nana and Granddad are your closest friends and they're still on their cruise."

A new thought hit me. Had Robert purposely timed the attack for when they were gone? I was pretty sure Nana had told me they'd booked the trip at Loretta's suggestion. Then my stomach turned as I recalled Nana informing me they'd be gone over my birthday, on a cruise their friend Robert helped them arrange.

Loretta licked her bottom lip and sucked in a deep breath. "I…"

"It's okay," Jack said, placing a comforting hand over hers, which rested on her jiggling knee. "We can just sit here for a moment. Did you and Robert make prior funeral arrangements? Do you need help with that?"

She looked up at Jack, her lip trembling. Her eyes were wide with panic and a hint of fear. What was she afraid of? The police? Us? Fallout from the Guardians?

I felt no pity for her, this woman who had made me cookies and given me birthday and Christmas gifts. All I felt was hatred, pure hatred filling my soul. My hands twitched, aching to wrap around the hilts of Ivy and St. Michael and help Loretta join her husband in hell.

"Piper," Jack said in a voice slightly too loud and sharp, and I realized he'd been trying to get my attention.

I stared at him in horrified silence. I'd been seriously contemplating murdering this woman. What the hell was wrong with me?

He forced a smile, then said, "I was just saying that Loretta could use a cup of tea, and since you're so familiar with the house, perhaps you could go make us all some."

"Of course," I said, my voice tight as I got to my feet. "I'll be right back."

Hurrying out of the room, I could hear Jack's soft baritone soothing Loretta as he offered his assistance in anything she needed. I stumbled down the hall, sweat beading on my forehead as I realized how close I'd been to murdering her.

Had I tainted my soul? Had I doomed myself rather than saved Abel?

I could dwell later, when I wasn't midway through a theft attempt. Instead, I hurried through the family room at the back of the house and to the right. I found the tea kettle in a cabinet next to the stove and glanced out the window at the back of the house as I filled it with water. I didn't see Collin standing around, but it hadn't been a full fifteen minutes yet, and besides, I hoped he'd be more discreet. There was no telling with him. Collin was a complete wild card.

After I set the kettle on the stove and turned on the burner, I headed to the back door and stepped outside, scanning the perfectly landscaped yard. Collin was crouched between the house and a large lilac bush in front of the study windows.

He glanced up at me and I motioned him inside, then shut the door behind us.

"Took you long enough," he muttered. He lifted an eyebrow when he noticed the tea kettle. "Good to see you've got your priorities straight. It *is* close to teatime."

"Shut up, Collin," I hissed under my breath. "My ruse is I'm making tea, so I'll be expected to show up with a pot. Loretta will be listening for the hiss of the kettle."

He frowned but didn't say anything.

"Come this way," I whispered, heading through the family room.

He followed and waited behind me when I stopped at the entrance to the hall, listening to Jack's comforting voice. I couldn't hear what he was saying, but he had Loretta preoccupied, so I led Collin into the main foyer then down a side hall toward the study at the opposite end of the house.

Stopping in front of the study door, I started to reach for the knob, but Collin batted my hands away. It was then I realized he was wearing a pair of gloves.

"Don't touch it," he said, moving in front of me and grabbing the handle. "Fingerprints."

He was right and I felt like a fool. Sure, I was here because Loretta had let us in, but I had no excuse to be in the study.

"It's locked," he said, then reached into his bag and pulled out a small packet, which he quickly unwrapped to reveal small tools. It took him several seconds to pick the lock then push the door open. "We're in."

We walked inside the study, and unwelcome memories washed over me. I'd visited this house more times than I could count, starting before my parents were killed. I remembered my own father sitting on the leather settee in front of the windows that overlooked the backyard, bouncing a preschool-aged me on his knee while he talked to a group of men. I'd asked him why Mr. Corden's house smelled like the mountains, and he'd told me it was the oil on the wood paneling. The smell was hitting me now, full force, and I swallowed the pain it brought with it.

Robert Corden had pretended to be a family friend, but he'd been our ruin. He'd had my parents murdered.

Had my father figured it out before he and my mother had been shot?

"Piper," Collin whisper-shouted. "Come on."

He was standing in front of multiple glass cases that contained close to a hundred weapons of various kinds—swords, antique guns, daggers, and several antique pocket watches.

"Holy shit," Collin muttered, intent on the watches. "It's identical to Ellie's."

"A sword?" I asked, scanning the case, but he ignored me, now working on picking the lock of the first case.

"We have a decision to make," Collin said as the lock clicked. "Do we take them all or only a few?"

"We don't know which ones are spelled," I said. "But if we take them all, the robbery will be reported sooner."

He nodded in agreement, a grim look on his face.

"I can help," Hudson said from behind me, and I squelched a shriek as I spun to face him.

"You're here," I said in shock. "You can leave the house?"

He gave me a sad smile. "I'm self aware, Pippy. Which means I'm free to roam. And I can help."

"How?"

Collin shifted, clearly uncomfortable. "I hope to God you're talking to a ghost and not your imaginary friend."

I took a couple steps backward, blindly reaching back to grab his arm.

He jolted. "Holy shit."

While Hudson had been at our meeting, the only people who had seen him were me, Abel, and Jack. "Collin, meet Hudson, my best friend, who has offered to help us determine which weapons are spelled."

"No offense," Collin said in a sarcastic tone I was becoming well acquainted with, "but how can you tell which ones work?"

Hudson's mouth twisted into a small grimace. "I can't, but Pippy can."

"What?" I squeaked out. "No, I can't."

Collin snorted. "Pippy?"

Resisting the urge to shove my elbow back into his solar plexus, I instead shook my head. "I can't do that, Hudson."

"You can," Hudson said, shooting Collin a dark glare. "You only have to try."

I released Collin's arm and turned to study the weapons in the case. "They all look the same to me."

Hudson put his hand on my shoulder. "Focus on your power, then study the sword at the top left. The second from the top."

"How do you know that one's spelled?" I asked, glancing back at him. "You said you can't tell."

His eyes darkened, and I remembered how he'd known about the spelled weapons in the first place. Had they threatened him with that sword?

I bit my lip and nodded at him before turning back to face the weapons. My gaze roved over them again, and I said in frustration, "Nothing."

"Don't look directly at it," Hudson said. "Look at the surface. Do you see it now?"

I narrowed my eyes and saw a faint sheen that glowed, but it quickly faded. "I think I saw a flash of it."

"Saw what?" Collin asked.

I returned my focus to the sword, surprised when the sheen came back into view. It was brighter now and stayed in focus. Maintaining my concentration, I turned to examine the entire case and gasped when multiple weapons lit up like a Christmas tree.

"What?" Collin asked.

"I'll point out which ones are spelled, and you remove them from the case."

"How many are there?"

"About seven in this case," I said after I did a quick count, then turned to glance in the one next to it. "About fifteen in the next one. Close to twenty, just like Hudson had told us." I pointed to an ornate watch on a middle shelf. "Plus that watch."

Collin reached for the watch first and shoved it into his jeans pocket. I started to protest, but he'd already pulled a thick blanket out of his bag and was laying it on the floor.

"Aren't you worried about cutting yourself when you're done?" I asked, nodding at the blanket.

He shot me a glare that suggested I was a fool as he removed a large, crumpled-up duffle bag from his smaller one. The new bag looked long enough to hold the swords.

Collin was a pain in the ass, but I knew we needed him on our side. I also knew what he'd seen in the attic had scared him, yet he was here anyway. "I know Tommy showed you something you didn't want to see in that picture," I said. "I don't know exactly what it was, but I know it's supposed to happen if you fight the bad monster with me."

He didn't respond as he stood upright, so I took that as a yes.

I needed him to trust me enough to tell me, which meant I needed to offer something in return. "I'm going to tell you about the mark I need to stop from appearing."

He raised his eyebrows and waved a hand. "Please continue."

I held out my left hand, showing him the marks on my palm. "While we share the circle and the square, I have marks you don't." I pointed to the diagonal lines on the upper right corner of the mark. "Abel says this one means demon slayer. It indicates I can cross spiritual planes." I looked up into his eyes. "I'm waiting for another, the reason Abel sought me out. The mark that makes me Kewasa."

"Deliverer," Collin said.

"Abel's deliverer." Did I tell him that Tsawasi thought I was their deliverer as well? I wasn't sure his ego could handle it right now. I needed to ease him into it.

He scowled. "What does *that* mean? Are you going to make him king of the world? His daddy's successor?"

"The opposite. My destiny is to deliver him *from* this world." The blank look on his face told me I'd need to be more direct. "When the mark appears, I'll kill him."

Shock filled his eyes. "Damn, Piper. That's cold."

I rolled my eyes. "I don't *want* to kill him, you fool. I'll be compelled to. I won't have a choice. That's why Abel's so worried about his father locking me up. If the mark appears while I'm imprisoned, he says I'll go mad trying to obey the pull of the mark."

"And if you kill him…"

"Okeus will be furious and make me pay many times over."

"Fuck."

"He sought me out because he was ready to die, but now we're trying to figure out a way to stop it. Or at least slow it down. I'm hoping the seer will know, but Tsagasi pretty much told me not to waste my time. He said Abel's job is done, presumably now that he helped me open my witness to creation magic."

Collin remained expressionless as he digested my information.

I gave him a determined look. "I don't give a fuck what Tsagasi said. I'm going to find a way to stop it."

"You can't fight fate, Piper," he said with a weary sigh. "Trust me, I've tried."

"Bullshit, I'll fight it kicking and screaming all the way."

A smirk lit up his eyes. "You're a lot like your cousin."

"I'm gonna take that as a compliment." I paused. "There's something else you should know if you're going to fight with us." When I was sure I had his attention, I said, "Tsawasi thinks I'm their deliverer too."

He stared at me for so long I was sure he'd gone into some kind of trance, but finally he answered. "I know," he said, sounding older than time.

"You *know?*" I asked in shock.

"Tsawasi and I have had our own conversation, and since I'm not a touchy-feely, share-my-feelings-with-you-and-braid-each-other's-hair kind of person, all I'm going to say is that Tsawasi convinced me we need to stay with you." The tone of his voice made it clear he resented this turn of events and likely me along with it.

"Collin—"

"Which swords?" he asked, his face hardening as he gestured toward the case.

We worked for the next several minutes, restricting our conversation to the task at hand.

"Where's the spear?" Collin asked after we'd pilfered most of the weapons. He was rearranging the weapons to make the collection look less picked over. "You said the ghost told you the spear was here."

I turned to Hudson with a questioning glance.

"It's here," he said, sounding subdued.

"But it's not in the case," I said. "Is it in a cabinet or closet?"

"No," Hudson said, then paused. "It's in the basement."

A cold sweat broke out on the back of my neck. Then something ignited in my chest, a white-hot energy that began to build. "They used it…" I swallowed. "On you?"

He didn't answer, but the expression on his face said it all. My rage didn't stop to dwell on the fact that I hadn't seen any blood on his body.

"The spear's in the basement," I said, barely recognizing my voice.

Collin's head jerked up. "Piper?"

"I'm going to get it."

"You can't go yet," he said, sounding pissed. "We have to pull the rest of the swords. Since you can see them and I can't, why don't *you* get the swords, and *I'll* find the spear?"

"No," I said, the heat growing more intense. "It has to be me." I started for the door.

"You can't just leave," Collin barked. "We're not done, and I have more claim to that spear than you do."

I turned back, surprised at the dark anger in his eyes.

"It's *my* fucking spear," he spat. "It's meant to be wielded by the Manteo keeper. Now help me grab the rest of the damned swords for this fucking battle you insisted on."

The pressure in my chest disagreed with this plan, but I stopped to think how I'd feel if my daggers were in the basement. I wouldn't want Collin leaving me behind while he retrieved them.

I strode over to the cabinet and pointed out three more swords while I grabbed one off a shelf.

"Fingerprints, Piper," he snarled. He grabbed a pair of gloves out of his bag and tossed them to me. "I hope to God we don't get caught, but if we have to ditch the weapons, we don't want to leave a damned calling card."

He was right, and I knew it, but part of me didn't care. I was too enraged to care about anything other than going to the basement to see where Hudson had been murdered.

"Piper, you don't need to go down there," Hudson said in a surprisingly calm tone.

"Yes, I do," I said as I shoved a hand into a glove.

"Jesus," Collin said as he grabbed one of the swords I'd pointed out to him. "You freak me the fuck out talking to that ghost."

"You fight demons, but you're afraid of ghosts?" I asked, the tightness in my chest easing slightly.

"I can *see* the demons," he barked, then gestured to the case. "And I'm not afraid of ghosts. What else?"

There were only a few more spelled weapons left, so we grabbed them together. Collin wrapped all the spelled weapons in the thick blanket he'd laid on the floor, then stuffed them in the larger bag.

"What will you do with them now?" I asked, pulling off the gloves and stuffing them into Collin's bag.

"Toss them out back then head to the basement. You and Father Jack can swing back and pick me up as soon as you're finished with your chat and tea." His eyebrow shot up. "Speaking of tea, don't you think you need to get back?" He wanted to find the spear on his own.

I hadn't planned on staying this long, and I knew I needed to get back, but there was no way I was skipping out on the basement. Although I didn't want to see the place where Hudson had taken his last breath, something down there was calling to me.

"Yeah," I said as I headed to the door.

"Dammit," Collin groaned. "You're not going back to make your pot of tea, are you?"

"Not a chance." I shut the door behind me, realizing that I'd never told Collin where to find the door to the basement. He'd figure it out on his own.

I headed to the kitchen with Hudson following behind me. "Piper, do *not* go down there."

"He's down there, isn't he?" I asked, not bothering to keep my voice down.

"Piper, please," Hudson pleaded.

The closer I got to the kitchen, the more the heat in my chest bloomed. I couldn't stop myself if I'd wanted to. The teapot was starting to whistle, so I turned off the burner and slid the kettle to a different burner. As I headed for the basement door, I noticed a salt and pepper shaker set on the counter. Grabbing the salt, I dropped it into my coat pocket, then closed the distance to the basement door.

"Nothing good will come of this," Hudson said as I started down the stairs.

I stopped halfway down and turned back to look at him. "You're not coming?"

He shivered, his face drawn. "No."

"Good. I don't want you anywhere near this. Wait for me upstairs," I said as I grabbed Ivy and pulled it from my thigh strap. "This won't take long."

I'd only been down to the Cordens' basement once. When I was a teenager, Nana had sent me down to get a bottle of wine from their makeshift wine cellar, which was really half the unfinished basement.

The basement was an odd assortment of concrete walls, half of which were still lined with racks filled with wine bottles, but the pentagram drawn on the floor was a new addition, as well as the unlit candles lining one section of the space. A spear was propped against the corner, but I wasn't interested in the spear. Not anymore.

"Come out and play, Robert," I growled, the pressure in my chest making it difficult to breathe.

He didn't answer at first, not that I was surprised.

"Why am I not surprised that you're a fucking coward?" I sneered. "You had my father killed, but you made sure not to dirty your own hands. Hell, you couldn't even kill Hudson, could you? You let the demon attack him instead."

"It wasn't my place to kill Jack," a man's voice said behind me.

I spun around to face him, Ivy at the ready.

"You can't kill me," Robert said, looking slightly amused. "I'm already dead."

I slowly slid St. Michael from its sheath and held it out toward him, the hilt lying across my palm. "Did you ever see the daggers? The ones you had my parents killed over?"

His gaze lowered to my hand, and I could see he was dying to get closer.

I held Ivy out the same way. "So much trouble. So much heartache over two stupid knives," I said, my words heavy with bitterness. "And you never even got a chance to see what I could do with them."

He took a step forward and the mark on my hand began to burn. I stood up straighter, and my soul leapt at the prospect of facing a demon.

"Come out to play, little demon," I said, wrapping my hands around the hilts of my daggers as I took a step back and surveyed the room.

"You're not supposed to be here," the demon answered from the dark recesses of the basement. I took a few steps closer and saw a dog-like demon trapped in a small pentagram in the corner.

I turned to Robert, flashing an evil grin. "Keeping a demon as a pet, Robert?"

He started to speak, then stopped. "It belonged to the Great One."

"Lies," the demon spat.

"You're the liar," Robert shouted. "You said our plan would work, and now you're trapped there forever, because I'll *never* let you go."

"I don't believe either of you," I said. "And neither of you will be trapped for long." I lifted a dagger for Robert to see. "Watch what you sacrificed my parents for." Then I turned and killed the demon with a single thrust.

It fell into a pile of ash, leaving behind a glowing orb. I pricked it and watched as dozens of souls floated free like fireflies. My own soul ate the energy in a greedy gulp, hungry for more. Much more.

When I turned back, Robert looked stunned.

"Why so surprised? You wanted me to be a demon slayer, am I right?"

His gaze lifted to mine. "Not entirely."

"Then what was your purpose?" I asked, taking a step toward him. "What noble cause did my parents die for?"

"Our plan was to control the demons. To harness them for our own purposes. *You* can control them."

"Well, aren't you the fool?" I laughed bitterly. "The only control I have over them is life and death."

He stared at the pile of ash, suddenly looking uncertain. "Sometimes that is enough."

"You and your buddies really thought you could harness demons?" I asked in disbelief. "You truly were deluded."

He grimaced and gestured toward the remains of the dead demon. "Things got out of hand."

"You think?" I said. "Now, let's move on to the real reason I came down here…to send you on to your great reward."

He gave me a defiant look. "You can't send me if I'm not ready."

"Oh, Robert," I said in a lilting tone. "You know absolutely *nothing*." I shoved both daggers into their sheaths and pulled the sage stick and lighter out of my jacket pocket.

Collin hit the bottom of the stairs just as I lit the stick, white smoke wafting into the air.

"You're a little early with the congratulatory cigar," Collin said.

"You're standing about six feet from a ghost destined for his eternal reward," I said, dropping the lighter into my pocket. "I suggest you get your spear and get out before shit gets real."

Collin grabbed the spear, jolting as soon as he touched it. His eyes were fixed on Robert. "Who's your friend?"

"You can see him?" I asked in shock.

"Yeah." Then disgust washed over his face. "Fuck. It's the damn ghost, isn't it?"

"Take a closer look at him," I said.

Collin studied his face. "The joker from the warehouse. What are we going to do with him?"

"Don't worry about that. I have it covered." I handed Collin the salt shaker. "Pour this across the bottom step, then leave or stay at your own risk."

"I'll stay," he said as he poured the salt.

Robert licked his bottom lip, his eyes darting from me to Collin. "Piper, I'm sure we can work something out."

"Yes," I said as I walked to the corner by the stairs. "We definitely can."

"Do you want money?" Robert asked, his voice rising in pitch.

"How the hell can you give her money if you're dead?" Collin asked with a short laugh.

"Loretta—"

"Won't give me a dime," I said. "Not even if I let her see you. She's currently crying her crocodile tears over your death." I started to chant, hoping the saging would work without my shell and feather, but somehow I knew it would. "Fire, earth, air, water. Cleanse this place of negative energy."

"Can I do anything to help?" Collin asked, sounding less cocky and more respectful than before.

"Yeah," I said. "Stand behind me and guard my back."

He gave me a questioning glance but said nothing as he walked behind me, keeping his gaze on Robert. "He looks more real than I expected."

"You expected a translucent, shimmering image? They used to be like that in the beginning, but now they look and feel real. Like Tommy," I said, wafting the smoke along the wall with my free hand.

"But different than your friend in the library," Collin said.

His comment reminded me of my own observation of Hudson, how his spirit was different from the others. I was about to ask Collin to explain, but Robert cut me off. "You look like an intelligent young man. You were a great leader in the warehouse." When he saw he had Collin's attention, he said, "I meant what I said about money. I have a lot of it. It's no good to me dead, but you are very much alive…"

"How much money are we talkin'?" Collin asked in an exaggerated drawl.

I glanced back at him to see if he was serious, and he gave me a wink.

"Millions," Robert said. "All you have to do is get control of Piper and stop her from doing this."

Collin laughed. "Control Piper…"

I could feel the pressure in the room build as I continued chanting and saging the walls. I'd saged houses for months, but this was the first time I'd felt the physical effects of it.

Abel was right. I was changing and growing stronger. I wasn't so sure if it was a good thing, but I was powerless to stop it…if I even wanted to. Besides, we needed all the strength we could get for the battle tonight.

Robert was becoming more desperate in his negotiations with Collin, raising his bribe with my every chant.

When I was halfway around the room, I could feel the atmosphere change again, both physically and psychologically. The pressure was now making my ears hurt and my soul ached for something I couldn't define. Robert must have felt it too because he began to curse.

"You fucking bitch!" He grabbed a bottle of wine from the rack and threw it at me. "You're not sending me to hell!"

Collin pushed on my shoulder, dropping me to a squat right before the bottle hit the concrete wall. Glass shards sprayed outward, landing in my hair and splattering me with red wine, which ran down the wall.

"Holy shit," Collin said, momentarily relaxing his grip on me as I stood upright and continued my chant. "Things took a turn for the ugly. Forget your meds, Robby?"

"You need to go," I shouted at Collin as the sound of wind began to fill the room. "All this noise is going to get Loretta's attention, and you can't be caught here."

"No," Collin said. "You need me to watch your back. I'll go out the storm cellar door when you're done."

I hadn't known there *was* a storm cellar door, but I only cared insomuch that it was a potential exit for Robert, not that he seemed to be rushing for it.

I reached the third corner, wafting the smoke of the sage stick toward the wall. "Fire, earth, air, water. Cleanse this place of negative energy."

Robert began to shriek as a mass of dark gray swirling clouds appeared on the last wall.

"What the *hell* is that?" Collin shouted.

I shot him a grimace. "Correct word choice."

Robert was furious. He grabbed another bottle of wine and threw it at me, but Collin shoved me to the side at the last moment, holding me up with his firm grip on my arm.

"Fire, earth, air, water. Cleanse this place of negative energy."

Robert began to wail, his face elongating and contorting, and I felt a shift in the air around us. A tear in the veil that separated our plane of existence from the spiritual.

"Holy fuck," Collin said, taking a step back. "Is that what I think it is?"

I cast a quick glance to the vortex and stifled a gasp. The last time the portal had appeared, the interior had been hazy and undefined, all-black clouds threaded through with flashes of fire and lightning. Not so this time—I saw a barren landscape studded with countless stone pillars. Thousands of emaciated people were chained to them, while giant birds swooped down and pecked at their heads and bodies. Lightning flashed across the angry red and blue streaked sky, and a terrible coldness seeped from the opening, chilling me to my marrow. But it was the wailing that set my nerves on edge, thousands and thousands of sobbing, moaning, begging souls.

"Yep," I said. "It's absolutely what you think it is."

Robert began throwing things in earnest, but to Collin's credit, he protected me, using the spear and his forearm to block the wine bottles. As I reached the last corner, the vortex wide open now, I began the final line of my chant. "Fire, earth, wind, water. Clear this place of Robert Corden."

He released a scream and I barely recognized his face as I advanced on him with my sage stick. Collin walked beside me as though he were my second in battle.

"It's time for you to meet your destiny, Robert," I said, my voice calm and clear. The first time I'd sent a spirit to hell, the guilt had nearly choked me, but now I felt only pure satisfaction. The bastard was moving on to his great reward.

"No!" Robert shouted, reaching for my neck with both hands.

Collin started to thrust at him with the spear, but there was no need. The vortex began to spin, creating a wind that spun loose debris on the floor and pulled Robert toward it.

"No!" Robert shouted again, reaching for a steel pole and holding on.

I considered repeating the chant, but deep in my soul, I knew it wasn't necessary. It was nothing but a medium for the power that lived inside me. The power that had been hidden for so long, but which was now burning like an ember of coal, setting my entire body aflame.

"Piper," Collin said. "You're…"

Glowing. My entire body was glowing as I struggled to contain the power inside me.

"Go," I said. "You need to get out of here."

He gave me a questioning look, and for all his previous bluster, I knew he'd stay with me until the end if I asked. I could have attributed it to his promise to Tsawasi, but I knew his conviction went deeper than that.

"Go," I said with a reassuring nod. "We'll meet you in the back."

He nodded, then shot to the dark recesses of the basement, taking his spear with him.

My control over the vortex was stronger than I would have thought, because the wind only picked up once I was sure Collin was gone. Bottles of wine shimmied loose from the shelves and began flying around the room, smashing into the walls. My hair whipped around my face.

Robert let go of the pole and leaned forward against the wind, trying to walk toward the stairs.

"Robert Corden," I said in a grave tone. "In life, you committed yourself to the advancement of evil. First you paid with your life, now you must pay with your soul." I withdrew Ivy from its sheath and pointed it toward him.

"I won't go!" he shouted. He now resembled the demons he'd worshipped. He'd commune with them again soon enough.

I gave him a hard shove toward the vortex and the wind caught him.

"No!" he screamed, grabbing hold of the edge of the wall and hanging on as his feet were swept into the air. "Piper! Have mercy!"

I moved closer and gave him a cold stare. "I'll show you the same mercy you showed my father and mother."

I swung my hand in a wide arc and shoved Ivy into his gut.

His eyes flew wide and he sucked in a pained breath.

"I'll show you the same mercy you showed Hudson as you watched the Great One kill him and possess his body." I withdrew the blade and tucked it into my belt beneath my long coat, then started to pry his fingers from the edge of the concrete wall.

A horde of demons approached the portal from the other side, scuttling across the desert by the hundreds and reaching for his legs.

"You're supposed to save us!" Robert shouted, his face pale and his eyes round with fear. "You're Kewasa!"

"Deliverer," I said in a tone so cold I didn't recognize my own voice. "I'm delivering you to where you belong." The demons were pulling on him now, trying to tug him in, and I pried off the last finger. "Enjoy hell, Robert."

He fell into the horde, and the last thing I heard as the vortex closed were his screams of agony.

My soul rejoiced.

I didn't have time to deal with my horror over my reaction.

"Oh my God," I heard Loretta say from the staircase. I wasn't surprised she'd come to investigate, but I wasn't prepared to come face-to-face with Detective Lawton, the Asheville officer who'd questioned me about Gill Gillespie's murder. While the staircase was hidden from most of the basement, it had a front-row seat to the spectacle I'd just performed, which must have made me look like a crazy person.

Jack stood on the steps between them, pure horror in his eyes, and I couldn't help wondering what had put it there. The fact that I was likely about to get arrested for destruction of property, or had he seen the portal? Was he horrified by what I'd become?

"Piper Lancaster," the detective said with a smirk. "Long time no see. A few weeks, if I remember correctly."

I had no idea how much they had seen and heard. Had they seen Collin? I sent Jack a questioning look, but his face remained grave. *Dammit.* I'd better presume the worst.

"Hello, Detective Lollis," I said, purposely getting his name wrong. "What a surprise to see you here."

He descended several steps. "Likewise. We've been working an interesting case. Incident that happened in a warehouse along the French Broad River, and I dropped by to talk to Mrs. Corden about her husband. Imagine my surprise when I found out Father Owen already knew."

"I told you," Jack said in a sharp tone. "I have a friend in the department."

"Nevertheless…" the detective said, eyeing me like I was a twenty-pound turkey on Thanksgiving Day. "I was just thinking to myself, 'I wonder who might know something about this mess,' and your name rose to the top of the list."

Lucky me. "You don't say."

"What are you doing in Mrs. Corden's basement?" he asked.

"Don't answer that," Jack said, walking past the detective and stopping next to me. "At least not without an attorney present."

Detective Lawton gestured toward Jack with an amused grin. "New Tinder date? Looks like you've been a busy girl."

"That's *woman*," I said, "and who I sleep with is no concern of yours."

"True," Detective Lawton said, "but I suspect you have something to do with what happened at that warehouse, and that most certainly *is* my concern. And I'm sure the mess you've created in this basement is a concern to poor Mrs. Corden."

I felt the color leach from my face.

The detective removed a pair of handcuffs from his jacket pocket. "Ms. Lancaster, you're under arrest for vandalism. Anything you say can and will be used against you in a court of law."

"Don't say a word," Jack said as the detective gleefully finished giving me my Miranda rights. "We'll get you an attorney."

It came as no surprise when Abel's car sped to stop at the curb as the detective hauled me out the front door, my hands cuffed behind my back. I wasn't sure if Jack or Collin had called him or if he'd just sensed I was in trouble.

Before the detective had hauled me away, Abel had pulled me into an embrace and whispered, "Don't say a word to him until my attorney arrives. Not even a yes or no. And only answer then if she thinks you should."

"I very nearly became a lawyer, Abel," I replied, trying to hide my fear. "I know the rules."

He gave me a dark look. "Just because you know the rules doesn't mean you follow them, Waboose. *Promise me.*"

I nodded, and the next thing I knew I was in the back of Detective Lawton's unmarked sedan, heading to the police department. It was only then that I noticed the familiar weight of my dagger belt was absent. My daggers were gone. I twisted to look out the back window, and there stood Abel, solemnly watching our car drive away, my dagger belt dangling from his hand.

Never underestimate a demigod.

CHAPTER FIFTEEN

Piper

Detective Lawton was chattier than I'd expected on the drive to the station, asking me question after question about the most mundane things—what was my favorite breakfast spot in Asheville? Who was my favorite band?—in an attempt to pull me into conversation. He even spent two minutes describing the flavor of the French toast at his favorite breakfast hole, and two more talking about how much he liked the Electric Monkeys. The entire time, he chided me for holding my silence. I had to admit it was hard not to respond, if only to tell him to shut up.

My mind was racing with what they'd seen, what *he* had seen. He hadn't mentioned seeing anyone with me in that basement, so I presumed, or at least hoped, Collin had gotten away.

In the brief lulls in the detective's monologue, I found myself thinking about what had happened in the Cordens' basement. I'd stabbed him and sent him to hell. Had he not been dead, I would have happily killed him. If I were truly truthful with myself, I'd acted out of revenge. I tried to find comfort in the knowledge I hadn't chosen where he'd gone—fate had decided; I'd only been the guide—but it still left a bad taste in my mouth.

When we got to the station, Detective Lawton stayed with me, still talking nonstop while I was processed, then shoved me into a room and closed the door behind me.

A woman stood from the table and held out her hand. She was my height and thin and not much older than me. Her highlighted blonde hair was pulled back into a smooth chignon. She wore a pale beige skirt suit and a white silk blouse. Her three-inch beige leather slingbacks looked fairly expensive. "I'm Mary Chambers. Mr. Abel has hired me to be your attorney."

From her clothes alone, I could tell Abel had paid her good money. The haste with which she'd arrived led me to believe he'd put her on a huge retainer, although I was sure his charm had helped sway her.

"The homeowner has decided not to press charges," she continued. "She said her husband was like a grandfather to you and you were overcome with grief."

My jaw dropped in surprise. "So I can go?"

"Not quite. Now that you're here, Detective Lawton wants to hold you for questioning. I've told him there's no need for that, that you'll answer his questions out of your own desire to assist the police so they can find out what happened to Mr. Corden."

If he knew about Robert, then he also knew about Hudson. But she was right. There was no time to spare. I needed to cooperate so I could get out of here. "Okay. Let's get this over with."

She went to the door and told the guard that we were ready to talk to the detective. He led us down a hall to another room, this one empty and with a one-way window.

I sat at the table with my attorney.

The door burst open and Detective Lawton strode in looking a little too happy with himself given that Loretta had decided not to press charges.

"Recognize the room?" he asked in a cheerful tone.

I did. This was the very room where he'd questioned me about Gill's death just a few weeks ago.

"How do you know Robert Corden?" he asked.

"He and his wife are friends with my grandparents."

"How close?"

I hesitated. "Very close. Best friends."

"And you saw them often?" he asked.

"When I was a kid, yes. They held an annual Christmas party and my parents were always invited. My mother had been going since she was a young girl."

"You saw them more after your parents were killed," the detective said, not a question but a statement of fact.

"Yes. I moved in with my grandparents, and as I previously mentioned, they were best friends."

"How often would you say you saw them?"

I shot Mary a glance, and she gave me a slight nod. I had to wonder where Detective Lawton was going with this, but I saw no reason not to answer. "Probably once a week or so until I was about sixteen."

"And then how often?"

I shook my head. "I don't know. I stopped going to their weekly dinners. Maybe once every few months until I went to college."

"So it's fair to say you weren't around the Cordens much after you went to college."

"Yes," I said. "That's right."

"And when did you start your affair with Robert Corden?"

I stared at him as though he'd sprouted a third eye in his forehead.

My attorney stiffened. "Piper, do not answer that." Her eyes narrowed at the detective. "What evidence do you have to reach such a speculation?"

"I'm just trying to determine why Ms. Lancaster would be filled with so much grief that she would shatter over a hundred bottles of wine with an estimated value in the thousands."

Mary put a delicate hand on the table, but her voice was as firm as iron. "We've already established that Piper was close with the Cordens as a child. That alone entitles her to her grief."

Detective Lawton started to say something, then stopped and forced a grin. "Let's shift to another topic. What do you know about the slaughter at the warehouse down by the river?"

I nearly cringed at the word slaughter, but I knew I had to show surprise. I only hoped I could pull it off. "*Slaughter?*" I asked in alarm. "I heard about what happened at the warehouse in Fairview. Is this different?"

He leaned back in his chair, feigning a relaxed position. "Come on, Ms. Lancaster. You're telling me you haven't heard a peep about it? It's been all over the news this afternoon."

I shook my head. "I haven't listened to any news in days. It's nothing but doom and gloom lately."

"You would know about doom and gloom, wouldn't you?" He flipped open the folder in front of him. On top of a stack of papers was a photo of Gill's dead body—naked and covered in so many deep gashes he was barely recognizable.

I sucked in a breath and shrank back in my chair, tears stinging my eyes.

"Crocodile tears, Ms. Lancaster?"

I blinked and jerked my gaze up to him. "What does that mean?"

"It's no secret you had a contentious relationship with Gill Gillespie. You had an ugly breakup with him."

My attorney cleared her throat. "The autopsy report says Mr. Gillespie was killed by a wild animal, likely a bear, and seeing as Ms. Lancaster neither owns nor controls any bears, her past relationship with Mr. Gillespie is irrelevant."

Apparently, Abel had filled her in on my history. Hell, he'd probably hired her weeks ago as a contingency plan.

"Tears for a man to whom she was heard saying, 'I'm going to make you pay for what you've done' mere hours before his murder?" the detective countered. "It seems like a stretch."

"It's called empathy, Detective Lawton," Mary said in a cold, direct tone. "A trait you seem to lack. And it was an *accidental* death…unless we're charging wildlife with murder now." She wasn't taking shit from the detective. I liked her already.

Detective Lawton eyed me for several more seconds before he slid Gill's photo to the side and revealed the naked body of Abby, Rhys's girlfriend who had killed herself at the urging of the mysterious voice.

"That's Abby," I said, my tears returning. "Rhys's girlfriend."

"So you knew her?"

"No, but I was with Rhys and Jack when we went to her apartment to check on her."

"Abby's death has been ruled a suicide," my attorney said. "My client had nothing to do with it."

"True," the detective said. "An animal attack. A suicide." He slid out another photo from deeper in the stack, and my stomach twisted when I recognized Jack's back from his own demon attack. He'd shown me the fresh scars the day I'd met him. "Do you recognize this man?"

"From his back?" Mary asked dryly.

He winked. "She does get around."

"My client's sexual history has nothing to do with any of these murders."

"Humor me anyway," Detective Lawton cajoled, sliding the photo closer to me. "Take a guess."

I saw no reason to hide my knowledge. "There's no reason to guess. That's Jack." I gave him a tight grin. "The *priest* you mistook as my Tinder date at the Cordens' home. Jack was attacked before we met."

The detective put one fingertip on Gill's photo and another on top of Jack's. "Two men associated with you were attacked by the same animal."

My attorney was getting pissed. "We've already established that Piper doesn't own a bear. She didn't even know Father Owen until a few weeks ago, *after* his unfortunate attack. The link is coincidental."

Detective Lawton's eyes narrowed. "Is it, though?"

"What's that supposed to mean?" my attorney asked, irritation biting through her words.

"Why did you seek out Father Owen?" he asked me. "*You* went to *him*. The receptionist at the church said you made an appointment."

I studied the smug man in front of me. He'd obviously spent some time investigating me even after I'd been cleared of any wrongdoing.

"I'm considering converting," I said evenly. "I wanted to ask him questions about the Episcopalian faith." I tilted my head forward and lowered my voice. "But don't tell my grandmother. She'll be furious if I leave the Methodist church."

Hate filled his eyes. "You think you're so clever." He slid out another two photos, this time of the partially burnt garage and destroyed kitchen from one of my ghost jobs. "What can you tell me about this?"

"The truth?" I asked with a raised brow.

Detective Lawton shifted in his seat. "Honestly, Ms. Lancaster, the truth would be a refreshing change from you."

"That kitchen"—I tapped the photo—"is the result of a ghost who was reluctant to go to the next plane, not that I could blame her. I opened a portal to hell, and she didn't go quietly."

He gave me a look that said *give me a break*. "You opened a portal to hell...?"

"It was my first. To be honest, I wasn't happy about it either. Usually they're glowing lights."

"Glowing lights," he repeated in a dry tone.

I lifted my brow. "This will go a lot quicker if you stop repeating everything I say."

My attorney leaned into my ear and whispered, "I suggest you leave the attitude to me and refrain from mentioning ghosts and portals to hell."

I frowned but bit my lip. She was right. Most people weren't receptive to talk about the spiritual plane, even if more people were believers after the Lost Colony of Roanoke had reappeared a few months ago. "Did the homeowner have a complaint?"

"No, the fool claims you rid her home of a mischievous ghost. She was grateful, despite the destruction to her property."

I was relieved she hadn't changed her mind.

"What about the garage?" the detective asked.

"Looks like it caught on fire," I said.

"Did you set it ablaze to chase out demons?" he asked with a wink.

The demon had set the fire to get to me, but I kept that to myself. "I didn't set that fire, Detective."

"Uh-huh," he said, pulling out another photo.

This one was full of blood—on the floor and all over multiple severed body parts.

I'd been in that warehouse. Twice. But for some reason seeing the carnage in photos made my stomach roil.

"What do you know about this?"

I looked away, feeling like I was about to throw up. "I need a trash can."

"Do you?" he asked, holding up the photo. "Or is that an act?"

"She's seen the photo, Detective Lawton," my attorney snapped. "You got the reaction you hoped for, now put it away."

"You have no idea what reaction I was hoping for," he countered. "And I'm not done." He pointed to something in the gore. "Do you recognize this?"

I squeezed my eyes shut.

"Look at it again."

I shook my head, refusing to speak.

"That's a leg belonging to Robert Corden, the man who was supposedly like a second grandfather to you. What a coincidence."

A metallic taste coated my tongue.

"That's enough, Detective!" my attorney shouted.

"Look at the photo, Piper!" the detective ordered.

You are Piper Lancaster and you don't hide from anyone or anything, I heard Abel say in my head. *Look at the photo, Piper.*

My eyes flew open in shock. He must have found the ring in my jeans pocket. But he was right. I was a fucking demon slayer. Why was I letting this man cow me? I steeled myself as I stared at the photo.

"Do you recognize him now?" the detective asked.

My gaze lifted to his cold expression. It struck me that this man hated me, truly hated me, and I had no idea why.

"How could I recognize a leg?" I asked in a reasonable tone.

His mouth pinched to the side. "True…" he said in a thoughtful tone. "Maybe this photo will help." He pulled out a photo of Robert's head, the stump of his neck still attached. His look of horrified shock was still on his face in death. "Recognize him now?"

"Yes," I whispered.

"Detective Lawton!" my attorney cried out.

"I'm sorry," he said. "I didn't quite hear your answer, Ms. Lancaster."

"Yes," I said more clearly.

"He was obviously ripped to shreds by *something*," Detective Lawton said, trying to sound nonchalant. "Another bear?"

"That's outside my area of expertise," I said, trying to sound rational, but I knew he was saving his prize photo for last—going in for the kill—and I needed to prepare myself.

"So to recap," he said, spacing out the photos. "We have three people dead who you personally knew—"

"I didn't know Abby."

"And one man who survived." His cold eyes lifted to mine. "I'm sure you can see why my interest has been piqued."

"If you're looking for a high body count," I said, my voice hardening, "I'm surprised you didn't bring my parents into it."

"Oh, that's right," he said, shuffling through the stack. He slowly removed several photos and placed them directly in front of me. One wide shot of my parents together, lying on the asphalt, their clothes bloody from their gunshot wounds. The next two showed my parents' faces in death. My mother's anguish. My father's disappointment that he'd failed to protect me. That he'd underestimated the Guardians.

Tears flooded my eyes as I stared at them. They'd died for me. They'd died for *nothing*.

"This is cruel and unnecessary," my attorney said in disgust. "My client was ten years old when her parents were brutally murdered in front of her. Are you suggesting she plotted to kill them?"

"Did she?" he asked. "Stranger things have happened."

My attorney got to her feet. "My client has been nothing but cooperative and compliant. Suggesting she had something to do with her parents' murders is cruel. Mrs. Corden has chosen not to press charges, which means my client is no longer under arrest." She turned to me, then said in a gentler tone, "You don't have to answer anything else, Piper. We're leaving."

Everything felt like it was in slow motion. I couldn't pry my gaze from my parents' faces. I couldn't help feeling like I'd failed them.

That's nonsense, Piper, Abel said in a short tone. *The Guardians were responsible for their deaths. Not you.*

Abel was right—*of course* he was right—but their faces...

"I have one more photo to show you," the detective said, his smug tone back. "Then we'll be done."

I steeled myself, knowing what I was about to face.

Detective Lawton pulled out another photo and placed it in front of me without commentary.

Hudson's naked body lay on the concrete floor. Thankfully, he was lying partially on his stomach, and the position provided him with some semblance of dignity in his death.

"You don't look all that surprised," the detective said, sounding pleased with himself.

I still didn't say anything.

"Do you know who this is?" he prodded.

"Hudson," I said, my voice breaking.

"So you *do* know him," the asshole said. "There was some question since he was naked and had no identification on him, but I recognized him from when I dropped by your house a couple of weeks ago." He pointed to the corner of his eye with his fingertip. "I never forget a face, and apparently *you* have a thing for your lovers' naked backs." He grinned and winked.

I stared up at him in disbelief. My best friend was dead—murdered—and he was making light of it.

"Were you born a monster or did you become one?" I asked in disbelief.

He laughed. "I'm no monster, Piper, but *you* definitely believe in them, don't you? You truly believe demons walk the earth." He paused. "In fact, you believe demons were responsible for all of these attacks, am I right?"

My mouth gaped open in shock at his callousness.

Do not answer him. He's trying to entrap you.

"Come on, Piper." He paused. "May I call you Piper?"

I shook my head. What was his game now? "You already have been."

"True enough." He settled back in his seat. "Did you know your best friend was dead?"

I took slow, steady breaths.

"He was living with you, correct? Why didn't you report that he was missing?"

"Because I saw him just yesterday afternoon."

"Was he going somewhere last night? Meeting friends?"

Tears were streaming down my cheeks. "I don't know. We both went to our rooms to take naps in the early afternoon, and when I got up, he was gone."

"And when was that?"

"Late. Maybe eight or nine."

"That's quite a nap," he said in a derogatory tone. "What did you do after that?"

"I was with Kieran Abel."

"At your house?"

"No," I said, then lied. "We were at his house in the mountains." I took a breath, trying to gather my wits about me, then went on the offensive. "Why didn't you tell me about Hudson first? My attorney's right; you're cruel. What's your game, Detective Lawson? Is this *fun* for you?"

He leaned forward, staring into my face. "No, Piper. Murder isn't fun." He cocked his head. "Or is it?"

"How would I know?"

I heard my attorney's shoes scuff slightly, like she was preparing to get up.

"Did you even realize Mr. Maine was missing?" the detective asked. "Or were you busy screwing your multiple Tinder dates?"

My attorney shot to her feet. "And with that, we're done."

I got to my feet too and followed her around the table.

Detective Lawson turned in his chair. "Do you really think your ex-boyfriend and the priest were attacked by bears? Or were they attacked by demons?"

"Do not answer that," my attorney said as she pounded on the door.

The detective got to his feet and turned to face me. "You said you were sending a ghost to hell in that trashed kitchen. How did you know it wasn't a demon?"

I pressed my lips together.

"Did you go to that warehouse to fight demons?" he asked. "Was your friend collateral damage?"

I kept quiet as my attorney pounded on the door again. "We're ready to leave, Detective."

"Sure, but give me just a few more moments." He paused. "Isn't it funny that these bear attacks started after the Lost Colony appeared? Didn't your ghost business pick up around that same time?"

My attorney turned to face him. "My client will not be answering any more questions," she said. "So if you're not holding her or arresting her for something outside the vandalism charges Mrs. Corden dropped, I strongly suggest you let us go."

"But Ms. Lancaster's barely told me anything." Detective Lawton watched us for a few more seconds, then sighed. "Let them out."

I heard the lock click and my attorney opened the door, waiting for me to walk out first. We were heading down the hall toward the door to the reception area when I sensed a ghost close by.

Great.

My attorney opened the door, and I saw Abel pop up from a chair, looking very much like he had the first night I'd met him in this exact same spot, only this time he looked concerned rather than cocky. Had he been worried the detective might arrest me? Or was it because of the ghost standing next to him? The young man who watched me with panic in his eyes.

"I have more questions for you, Ms. Lancaster," Detective Lawton called from the open doorway. "We need to schedule a time for you to come back in."

I ignored him as the ghostly young man approached me. "You're her."

I started to walk past him, but he grabbed my arm and pulled me to a halt. "Please. Help me."

"I'm sorry," I said under my breath. "I can't."

"*Please*," he begged. "I don't want to be here anymore."

This situation was odd for me, and it wasn't just because I was standing in the police department waiting area being observed by the detective who was sure I was a murderer. Ghosts didn't usually seek out my help. Most of the time, I had to convince them they were ready to move on. It unnerved me that this one not only knew who I was but wanted my help.

"I'm sorry," I said, pulling free. "I can't."

"Who are you talking to, Ms. Lancaster?" the detective asked in a smug tone while still standing in the doorway. He was several feet away, but still watching me closely.

The ghost grabbed my arm again and held on tight. "Please," he said. "I need you to tell my girlfriend I'm sorry and I didn't mean it."

"Go tell her yourself," I whispered.

"I can't leave the police station." The ghost held up his hands, letting his long sleeves fall a few inches down his arms to reveal a pair of handcuffs. Had the handcuffs bound him to this place?

"Piper," Abel warned in a low tone. "We must leave. Now."

He was right, of course. The sooner I escaped Detective Lawton's watchful eye the better, but I also couldn't leave this man who was begging for my help.

"What's your name?" I whispered, casting the ghost a quick glance then pretending to talk to Abel.

"Tyler Miller."

"And your girlfriend's name?"

"*Piper.*" Abel started to wrap an arm around my back, but I pushed him away.

Relief filled Tyler's eyes. "Vicki Daniels."

I was going to regret this, but it was too late to turn back now. "I need to know more. What did you say to her? And can you give me something specific to help her believe me?"

Tears filled his eyes. "I told her I was sleeping with my boss, but it wasn't true." He rubbed his forehead with the heel of his palm. "She was jealous, and I was pissed and drunk and I told her that to piss her off. I left then, only I was stupid and crashed my car. They brought me in on a DUI, but I choked to death on vomit and died in my cell."

He looked over my shoulder, to where Detective Lawton was standing. "I was in bad shape, but not just 'cause I'd been drinking. When they brought me in, I fell to the floor with handcuffs on and"—he gestured at the detective—"he kicked me in the ribs. Don't trust that one."

I'd had no intention of trusting him before, but now...

"I never got to tell her I was sorry," Tyler said. "She still believes I cheated on her. Will you tell her?"

"Yeah," I said softly. "I'll tell her. Are you ready to move on?" Part of me was scared to send him to the afterlife, lest the wrong door open for him. He'd died in a jail...his chances of a fiery afterlife were higher, but he was ready to move along.

He nodded and a bright white light appeared in front of the receptionist's window. He gave me a worried smile. "You promise you'll tell her?"

"Yes," I said, my knees nearly buckling with my relief. "I promise." Then I watched as he walked into the light and the bright vortex swallowed him whole.

Abel grabbed my arm and started dragging me toward the exit.

"Hold up there," Detective Lawton said as he took several steps closer. "What was all of that?"

Abel shot me a warning look, but I turned back to face the detective. "What was what?"

"All that." He waved his arm in a wide sweep. "Who were you talking to?"

"She was talking to me," Abel said in a tone so low it sounded like a warning.

"Nooo…" the detective said, dragging out the word as a gleam filled his eyes. "She was talking to someone else."

"Piper's officially done answering questions," Abel said, tugging me to the door.

The detective darted for the door and blocked our exit. "Were you talking to a ghost just then, Ms. Lancaster?"

Abel shot me another warning look.

"Ms. Lancaster, if you can't be more cooperative, then I'll be forced to hold you until you're more willing to chat."

"You can't be serious." Abel's mouth dropped open, and it would have been humorous if my freedom weren't on the line.

"I'm afraid I am," the detective said in his arrogant tone.

"On what grounds?"

"All I need are my suspicions, Mr. Abel, and right now those are pretty high."

Abel turned to my attorney. "Mary." Her name was said as an order.

She finally jumped in, lifting her chin and somehow managing to look down on the man even though he was taller than her. "Detective, the charges against my client were dropped, but she agreed to cooperate. She was more than happy to answer questions, but you didn't really ask questions, did you? You were intent on shocking and upsetting her. She would have been far more cooperative had you been less adversarial."

"Would your client like some milk and cookies and a bedtime story before she confesses?" he asked, his voice mimicking a small child.

"My client would like to be treated respectfully and not be subjected to gruesome photos of incidents that have absolutely nothing to do with her."

The detective turned to me. "You're a ghost hunter, right?"

I almost didn't answer, but it was on my website for anyone to see. "Not a hunter, per se."

"Oh, that's right," he said, snapping his fingers. "You call yourself a gentle ghost whisperer."

"That's right," I confirmed, earning another glare from Abel. I saw no reason to deny it. I saw no reason to deny it when I advertised the fact online.

"And you purport to communicate with ghosts and spirits? People hire you to talk to them?"

Why was he asking me all of this? I'd already admitted to it during both of my visits here. I had a very bad feeling, but I still found myself saying, "Yes."

I wouldn't lie about something so easily proven.

"Are the ghosts real, Ms. Lancaster, or are you making them up and committing fraud by charging people money to talk to them?" He grinned. "That's right. I've done more looking into you. I know you charge now."

The first time I was here, I'd gotten out of the fraud allegation by telling him I didn't charge for my services, but that strategy wasn't really an option this time around. "And your point is?"

"Either you're tricking those poor grieving people into giving you money to 'talk'"—he used air quotes—"to their loved ones, or you truly believe you are talking to dead people. Which is it?"

"Detective…" my attorney said in a warning tone.

The police officer turned to her with outstretched hands. "What? She has a website advertising that she talks to ghosts. Does she believe it or not? Why won't she answer the question?"

"I'm not a fraud," I said. "I talk to ghosts. I help them with their unfinished business."

"Were you talking to a ghost just now?" he asked, his eyes glittering with malice.

"Yes. His name was Tyler Miller and he died here. He'd been arrested on a DUI and choked on his own vomit."

For a second the detective's expression froze, but then he said, "Anyone could have come up with his name. It's a matter of public record."

"He said he was wearing handcuffs when you kicked him in the ribs."

The color leached out of his face, but then his eyes filled with rage. "Piper Lancaster," he said as he drew out his handcuffs, "you're under arrest."

Abel stepped in front of me and released a snarl. "What are the charges?"

"No charges yet," the detective said with a slimy grin. "But she's an obvious flight risk. I can hold her for forty-eight hours until I get the charges nailed down."

"Detective Lawton," my attorney said, her voice strained. "My client's entire life is here in Asheville. She has a home, family, friends, a business...she's no flight risk. There's no need to hold her while you're on your witch hunt."

"I disagree," he said. "Ms. Lancaster is obviously deluded and a danger to herself and others. For all we know, her delusion got her friend Mr. Maine killed."

Abel's body vibrated with rage. "She's not deluded."

Detective Lawton's eyebrows shot up in amusement. "And you've known her how long? Just a few weeks ago, you told me you were her Tinder date."

"Mr. Abel," my attorney said, placing a hand on his arm. "Let me handle this."

"Then handle it!" he shouted.

"I can arrest you too, Kieran Abel," the detective said. "I'd love to. Just keep giving me a reason."

My attorney started arguing with him, so I took advantage of his distraction.

"Abel," I said in a calm voice even though I was panicking. I put a hand on his arm. "Abel, listen to me."

He jerked his gaze down to meet mine. He was furious and I wouldn't put it past him to physically attack the detective to keep me out of jail.

"Abel, you can't get arrested too. Have you talked to Deidre yet?"

"No. She's avoiding me." His eyes hardened. "She'll never work with me, Waboose, but she'll work with you. Let me take you from this place."

"No. I can't just leave." A new thought hit me and I lowered my voice. "Oh my God. The demons are coming tonight."

"Yes. Which is why we need to go. You're in danger if I leave you here." I could see he was considering something drastic.

"No, Abel. *Don't do anything stupid.*"

"Like leaving you here to face the demons alone and weaponless? *That* would be stupid." He cast a dark glance at the detective. "I can kill him without even touching him."

They weren't empty words. He could make the detective's heart explode in his chest. "No. Don't. I'm already under suspicion. You can't be too."

Although the gate between the worlds had been opened, there was still a tenuous separation between them. My gut feeling was that we needed to maintain that as long as possible. No public use of power.

"I'm not leaving you here, Waboose. You'll be completely unprotected—weaponless, wardless... *No.*"

"I'm sure you hired that hotshot attorney for more than just her pretty face." The dark look he shot me suggested he wasn't amused. "Use the legal system, Abel. You could break me out, but I'd be running from the law for God knows how long."

"Following human laws does me no good if you're dead."

I didn't respond because while his statement sounded callous, I knew he was worried because he cared about me, not because he needed me for his original purpose.

"I'll let this play out for now," he said in a tight voice. "But if they keep you here past dark, I will walk right into this place and get you out, human laws be damned." His eyes narrowed. "Do not think about arguing with me."

I forced a smile. "You like me."

I'd told him the same thing weeks ago, much to his aggravation.

"I love you," he said without hesitation. "I've waited hundreds of years for you, Waboose. I won't lose you this way."

I stared at him in shock. Never in a million years would I have expected Kieran Abel to admit he loved me, but before I could respond, the detective ended his argument with my attorney and slapped a pair of handcuffs on my wrists. He pushed me out of the waiting room while he read me my rights again.

He hauled me to an empty holding cell at the end of a long hall full of empty cells and shoved me inside, shutting the door behind me.

He stood on the outside, his gaze piercing me with so much venom I could practically feel it.

"Why do you hate me so much?" I asked softly. "What did I do to you?"

"You did *nothing*. That's the problem."

He started to walk away, and I stared after him in confusion. What was he talking about?

Before he could turn the corner, he stopped and abruptly spun around. "Did he beg for mercy?"

I blinked then cautiously asked, "Who?"

"My brother."

Then he turned and walked away.

CHAPTER SIXTEEN

Ellie

Something's wrong," I said, pacing Piper's living room floor. "I can feel it."

"If anyone can take care of himself, it's Collin," David said, glancing up from his book.

I stopped pacing. "I could be worried about Piper and Jack."

He gave me an understanding smile, but didn't call me a liar.

"They're back," Rhys called out from the kitchen, and I raced in there in time to see Jack and Collin walk through the door, each carrying a handle of a large bag. They dropped it on the kitchen table with a loud thud.

"What took so long?" I asked, looking both of them over for signs of injury, relieved when I saw none.

"We ran into a little trouble," Collin said, refusing to look me in the eye.

Rhys leaned out the still-open kitchen door. "Where's Piper?"

Neither man answered.

"Where's Piper?" I asked with a sharp edge in my voice.

"She hasn't been hurt," Collin said, finally glancing up at me.

I put my hands on my hips. "But that doesn't tell me where she is, does it?"

"Where's Abel?" Rhys asked as she closed the door. "His car's not out there."

"I suspect he's at the police station," Jack said with a heavy sigh. "A detective showed up at the Cordens' house. He found Piper in the basement just as she was helping Robert Corden cross over. He arrested her for vandalism and took her to the station."

"Vandalism?" Rhys asked. Then her shoulders sank. "If Corden was anything like her ghost last Friday, he didn't go willingly."

"There were wine bottles involved," Collin said. "Many."

I was still reeling from the news. "You two were gone for nearly two hours. What took so long?"

"I was stuck waiting on the priest," Collin said, trying to sound nonchalant and failing miserably.

"And you couldn't call or text me with an update?"

He shrugged. "Piper sent me out of the basement when the wine started flying around. She knew she was going to be discovered, but she wanted to finish what she'd started. I got out through a storm cellar door and hauled the bag of swords to the back of the property. I saw no need to get in touch until I knew what was going on. It would have only worried you. We're here now, and we have the swords and the spear."

I couldn't help noticing he hadn't brought the spear inside—the bag they'd carried in wasn't nearly long enough to hold a weapon with that kind of length—but I didn't call him on it. Not yet. I was still trying to wrap my head around the fact that Piper had been arrested. "So she's at the police station now?"

Collin nodded, his face grim.

"Hopefully not for long," Jack said. "Loretta said she didn't want to press charges."

"Why didn't you call, Jack?" Rhys asked, sounding pissed.

"I had to wait for a police officer to question me about Piper," Jack said. "Why we were there. Why she might have gone down to the basement. Why she'd smash nearly a hundred bottles of wine. I didn't dare call any of you. But like I said, Loretta Corden agreed not to press charges, which means they should be releasing her soon. Abel should be here with her any minute. He was going to the police station to pick her up."

We all stood around for nearly a minute, each of us quietly trying to process this unexpected turn of events when Abel walked in the kitchen door.

"Where's Piper?" Rhys demanded. "Why isn't she with you?"

"If I'd had my say, I would have her with me now," Abel said, standing outside the open kitchen door. "Detective Lawton is holding her."

"On what grounds?" Jack asked in outrage.

"Does he need any?" Abel asked in a quiet voice that sent a shiver down my back. He rubbed the heel of his palm over his eye, growing agitated. "He made up some bullshit allegation about her running a fraudulent ghost hunting business to detain her. Asshole has every intention to hold her the entire forty-eight hours. My attorney is working to get her released, but it looks unlikely that will happen."

"The demons…" I said.

Abel looked like he was about to spontaneously combust. "I'm going to break her out of there," he said in a calm voice, but his body radiated violence.

"You can't just break her out," David said, his first comment on the sorry situation. "Let's think this through."

Abel turned his cold gaze upon my boyfriend. "I already *have* thought this through. The Little People said demons are advancing on Asheville tonight, and Piper is currently locked in a cell, completely unprotected. Okeus could try to take her and she will be powerless to stop him."

My stomach tightened with fear. "He's right. Unless we can surround her with salt or symbols, she's a sitting duck."

"But if Abel breaks her out, he'll be wanted by the police too," David said. "Think about the long-term implications, Ellie."

"I'm pretty sure Abel doesn't care about the long-term implications if Piper's dead," Collin said dryly as he sat down on a dining room chair. "He's a fucking demigod."

"There's one more concern," Abel said. "I made a blood vow to kill her if her life is threatened by demons. If I can't save her, I'll be powerless to stop myself."

"Why the hell did you make that stupid vow?" Rhys asked.

His jaw clenched, but he remained silent.

"It is what it is," I said with a sigh. "We've all done things we regret. That doesn't matter now—what matters now is figuring out how to get her out of there with as little damage as possible. Or at the very least, figure out how to keep her safe."

"We've befriended an Asheville detective," Jack said. "The one who gave me the heads-up about the police discovering the warehouse. Olivia knows what Piper can do—well, not about the creator of worlds thing, but she knows the ghosts and demons are real and dangerous. She's a believer and I'm sure she'll help us however she can."

"Then call her," Abel snapped. "But if Piper's not out by nightfall, I'm taking matters into my own hands."

"Worst-case scenario, she can create a world to escape into, right?" Collin asked, perking up. "That's what she did at the warehouse."

"True," I said, "but she'll disappear. I'm sure they have cameras in the cells, so how do we explain that away?"

"Why do we need to?" Rhys said. "If she disappears on camera, it'll prove she's legit."

"With Detective Lawton, I wouldn't count on it," Jack said, but he looked relieved by Collin's suggestion.

Abel only looked slightly appeased.

"We still have to deal with the demons, whether Piper is released or not," I said. "Which means we need a plan. We should call Tsagasi."

"I'm already here," the little man said, appearing in the doorway into the dining room.

I stared down at him, trying to temper my irritation. He and his brother had promised Piper an army in exchange for absolutely nothing—okay, in exchange for killing Okeus, which she'd already planned on doing—while I'd had to swear a blood oath to get seven favors from four of them. I wasn't totally surprised. Tsagasi was always quick to remind me that I had yet to use my sword for its intended purpose—to subdue gods—but I was of a mind that it was pointless to use it if I knew I would fail. I'd told myself this wasn't a contest, but part of me was still pissed.

"I know you promised Piper an army," I said. "Where will you make your stand?"

"*My brother* promised the slayer an army, and that's why I'm here. He's rescinded his offer."

"What do you mean he's rescinded his offer?" Collin demanded.

Tsagasi looked up at him. "The slayer is locked up. No slayer. No army."

"The demons are coming with or without Piper and your army," I protested. "There will be no one to stop them. You can't do this. Tsagasi."

"It was not my army to promise," he said. "It is up to Tsawasi."

"Then let us talk to *him*," Collin said.

"He's adamant. No slayer. No army."

Collin turned to me, trying to hide his relief. "We don't have any choice. We need to hide."

"That sounds pretty convenient," Jack sneered.

"Abel plans to get Piper out," David said. "Can't you tell Tsawasi that?"

"It might not be as easy as that," the little man said. "Did you stop to think about why she was locked up in the first place?"

"Because Detective Lawton hates her," Jack said.

"Humans are merely pawns in this game. They are not what is important," Tsagasi snapped.

"Than what is?" Collin asked.

"Must I spoon-feed you everything?" he snapped. "The answer is in the attic." Then he disappeared.

"What's he talking about?" Collin asked, turning to face David.

"I think he's suggesting the source is supernatural."

"And I suspect he's not talking about Piper's father's office," Rhys said.

"How do we get into the world in her attic?" I asked.

We were all silent for a moment, before Abel said, "I might be able to enter."

Everyone looked at him.

"Why are you still standing outside?" Rhys asked.

His brow furrowed. "I can't come in without an invitation."

I started to speak, but Collin held up his hand. "Do we really want to let him in?"

"Collin," I groaned, then said, "Abel, son of Okeus, enter."

He swept past us, shooting Collin a dirty look, and headed straight for the living room. The rest of us followed him like he was the Pied Piper. When we reached the door to the attic, he opened it and stood at the opening for a moment.

"There's the ward," he said, staring down at a cotton bag on the second step up. He turned to look at something we couldn't see beside him. "Can you go up there?"

"What is he talking to?" I said to no one in particular.

"Hudson," Jack said. "He's telling Abel he can't go up either."

"But Abel didn't even try."

"I suspect it's more like he can feel it," Jack said.

"The priest is right," Abel said, turning around with a grim look. "I can't walk in."

"I'll try," Collin said. "I went in with her this morning."

Abel stepped back and made a sweeping gesture toward the stairs, but he looked pissed.

"First of all," Collin said in a cocky tone. "You have to remove the ward." After tossing the cotton bag over his shoulder, he stomped up the stairs.

I followed him up the stairs, stopping next to him at the top.

"Damn," he grunted. "It didn't work."

I glanced around at the office setup. "This was Piper's dad's?"

"This isn't supposed to be here. It's supposed to be a kids' playroom with a little boy."

We headed back downstairs and tried it again. And again. And again. Finally, Collin admitted defeat.

"You were up there earlier," David said to Collin. "Did you see anything significant?"

"Like I said, it was a playroom with a kid," Collin said in frustration. "We saw the demon outside the window."

"Do you think that's what Tsagasi was talking about?" I asked David.

"It's hard to say, but I doubt it unless it was a special demon," he said.

"Was it special?" I asked Collin.

His eyes narrowed. "It was a fucking demon that had acid for saliva. What does that tell you?"

"Nothing much," Jack said. "There has to be something else."

Collin's gaze hardened. "There was nothing else. Now will you agree to hide? We can't face an army without Piper, and from the sound of it, she's not going anywhere anytime soon."

"I won't be hiding," Abel said in disgust. "I will break her out of that prison, but in the meantime, there might be another way to get into the world in the attic. The seer will likely know. I need to see her anyway, and this will give me the excuse I need to show up at her doorstep."

"I'm going too," I said.

"No," Collin barked. "We need to get as far away from this place as possible. If we leave now, we'll put hundreds of miles between us and the horde of demons.

"I'm going with Abel," I repeated in a tight voice, resisting the urge to shout at him.

Abel shot me a dark look. "I'll go alone."

"I'm coming, Abel," I said in a no-nonsense tone. "Think of it this way—you might need me. Rumor has it the seer can't stand you and likely won't help you, and frankly, I still don't trust you."

His glare would have made a lesser woman cower in fear.

"Then I'm coming too," Collin said, sounding pissed. "I don't like the idea of you being alone with Okeus's son." He didn't have to spell it out for me. Abel was bound and determined to save Piper. What if he tried to trade me to Okeus in her place? Collin gave off a devil-may-care attitude, but he was careful when it came to my safety.

"I'll go too," David said.

"No," I said in a firm tone. Someone needed to take charge here, and it might as well be me. "We can't all go, and I think the son of Okeus and I could use a little bonding time."

"No," Collin protested. "I won't allow it."

"Won't allow it?" I demanded, getting in his face. "You don't have a say in this, Collin. I'm going."

He started to protest, then stopped, even though he was obviously biting his tongue.

I turned to David. "We need someplace else to stay tonight. Maybe you can look into it. The sooner we move the better."

David nodded. "On it."

Abel spoke up, although I could see the reluctance in his eyes. "You can stay at either of my places. I have a loft apartment downtown and a secured home in the mountains about fifteen minutes away. Both places are warded against demons."

"How about Ahone and Okeus?" Collin asked.

His gaze darkened. "The wards keep them out as well. Both places are secured and at your disposal." He hesitated as though thinking something through, then added, "But first you must promise me something in return."

I narrowed my eyes. "What?"

His face softened and I saw the hint of fear in his eyes. "If something should happen to me, you must promise to stand by Piper's side. Don't leave her to face the demons alone."

His request caught me off guard. "Are you that worried about your father?"

"More worried than you know."

"Your bargain is a safe house in exchange for protecting Piper?" I shook my head. "I'd stick by Piper's side, deal or no deal. Even if she weren't my cousin. She can't do this alone, and while I know her friends are helping her, they don't have any supernatural power, even if Jack can see ghosts now." I remembered Rhys was listening and shot her an apologetic smile. "Sorry."

"It's the truth," Rhys said, "but I don't want to be that annoying friend who needs saving. Let me help. Let me come with you to the seer."

I started to tell her no, but she'd clearly been through hell and didn't want to be treated like a victim. Sitting in this house wouldn't help her, and it wouldn't help us either. "Okay, but you have to do as Abel and I instruct."

I expected Abel to protest, but he gave Rhys a long look then nodded. "Yes. You should come."

Rhys looked grateful for his response, but Jack was less than pleased. The thoughtful, compassionate air he usually gave off turned deadly. He pointed his finger at Abel. "If anything happens to her...."

I expected Abel to give him crap for challenging him, but he gave Jack a solemn nod. "She's important to Piper. I'll protect her."

I couldn't help thinking that he should have protected her out of human decency. But then, he wasn't fully human.

I'd do best to remember that.

CHAPTER SEVENTEEN

Ellie

Collin grabbed me before I walked out the door, making sure that we were both alone.

"Ellie, wait."

"You can't talk me out of this."

"I know, but you need to see this." He reached into his pocket and pulled out a dull-gold pocket watch. It was etched with a four-pointed star surrounded by smaller stars.

I stared up at him in confusion. "You took Daddy's watch with you?"

"No," he said. "I found it at the Cordens' house. We'd heard the Guardians had one identical to your father's, and I found it in the case with the swords."

He handed it to me, and I was amazed by how similar it looked to one of the watches in the box upstairs.

"There's something else, Ellie. Piper could see which swords were spelled to kill demons. She said the watch glowed too."

"The watch can kill demons?" I asked in surprise.

"I have no idea, but Piper said it glowed, so that means it can do something." He held my gaze and lowered his voice. "Maybe the seer can tell you what to do with it."

IT WASN'T A LONG DRIVE to downtown from Piper's house. It was a Sunday afternoon in late summer, which meant downtown Asheville was buzzing with tourists. We had to park in a garage several blocks away and walk to the crystal shop the seer owned, not that I was complaining. The thought of facing a bunch of demons tonight had me on edge and walking at the brisk pace Abel set helped take the edge off my anxiety. I snuck a glance at Rhys, who was having a harder time keeping up with her shorter legs, but she wasn't complaining either. If anything, she looked determined.

I was busy taking in the sights. While I'd heard about the quirkiness of the liberal "hippie" town in the mountains, I'd never been. Until a few months ago, I'd hardly been anywhere, sticking to Roanoke Island and the Outer Banks. I'd always assumed my reluctance to leave the island could be chalked up to agoraphobia, but after I met Collin, I realized it was because of the curse. It made sure I never strayed too far from the main gate to hell—a centuries-old tree in the St. Elizabeth Botanical Gardens, not that I'd believed the stories my father had told me since before I could talk. Especially after my mother was murdered because of them.

But now that Collin and I had broken the curse, I was free to go anywhere without feeling like I was about to suffocate. The curse was broken. There was nothing left to protect.

In theory…

Now it felt like the world was on a precarious balance.

Abel stopped at the door to the crystal/New Age store and frowned as he grabbed the door handle and jerked hard. The door remained firmly shut.

"It's closed," Rhys said, pointing to the sign hanging in the middle of the door.

"Seer!" he shouted as he pounded on the door, his voice booming loud enough to draw the attention of people on both sides of the street. A lot of people.

"Abel," Rhys said, glancing around nervously. "Stop!"

He turned on her with a vicious look. "I have to see her."

"And if she truly hates you, you're not exactly endearing yourself to her," I said with a sigh, pushing him out of the way.

He took several backward steps toward the curb while I pressed my face to the glass and peered inside the window. While I saw rows of shelving with candles, books, crystals, and all things New Age, there was no one inside.

I turned to him. "Maybe we should come up with a plan B."

"There is no plan B," he said.

I dug out my phone to look up the store's number, but Abel stopped me. "I have her private number, but she'll be more likely to answer if you call instead of me."

He rattled off a number and I punched it into my phone and pressed send, just as anxious as Abel to get things rolling.

"How did you get this number?" a woman answered after several rings.

"That's not important," I said cautiously, not wanting to sound too eager. "What's important is I need to use your services."

"We're closed."

Abel's gaze shot up to the second-story window over the door.

"I can see that. I'm standing in front of your shop." I glanced up too. "You saw my cousin Piper two nights ago. I'd really like to meet with you."

She was quiet for several seconds, and I had to pull my phone from my ear to make sure she was still on the line.

"You're a curse keeper," she finally said, her tone grave and not a little surprised.

A chill ran down my back. "Yes," I said breathlessly. "Will you see me?"

She hesitated. "I'll see you, but the demigod must wait outside."

I shot a glance at Abel. "I'm good with that."

He clearly had superhuman hearing because a dark look crossed his face.

"I'm coming down," the seer said before she hung up, and I was left with a scowling demigod.

"She says she won't see you," I said.

"I heard." But he didn't seem resigned to it. If anything, he looked more determined.

Rhys eyed Abel warily, as though she wasn't sure what to expect but wanted to stay out of the line of fire.

About thirty seconds later, a woman came into view from the back. Dressed in a long, flowing pink shirt and jeans, she had mocha-colored skin and long thin braids tied in a loose ponytail at the nape of her neck. She was younger than I'd expected—in her early forties—but the expression on her face suggested she wasn't going to take Abel's crap.

She unlocked the door and pushed it open about a foot, staring straight at Abel. "I told that fool girl noon sharp, and then she didn't have the courtesy to call and apologize, and now Luna's gone for the day." She pointed her finger at him. "And no, I won't be seein' you, spawn of Satan."

That caught me by surprise. Did she know about Abel's parentage? Piper had only learned of it last night.

"She would have apologized," Abel said in a tight voice. "But she's currently being held in the Asheville police station."

The seer did a double take. "What on earth for?"

"Fighting demons comes with a high body count," Abel said. "It doesn't help that Piper has caught the attention of a sadist."

His announcement made my stomach clench. Poor Piper. I'd understood his urgency before, but even more so now.

She studied him for a moment before her face hardened. "You're still not comin' in." Then she turned her attention to me, looking me up and down. "You may enter."

I took a step closer to Rhys and linked my arm with hers. "Rhys is coming in with me."

The seer waved her hand in a beckoning motion. "You may both come in." Her gaze darted to Abel. "He may not." Then she pushed the door open wider.

"I have something you want," Abel said as I ushered Rhys inside before me.

"I'm in need of hart's-tongue fern," the seer said, "but I'll wait until the slayer comes with you."

"She may not have that long," Abel called out as I walked inside.

The seer paused and seemed to consider his words.

"I'll consult the bones," she said at last. Then she shut and locked the door behind us and led the way to the door at the back of the shop.

"Did she say she'll consult the bones?" Rhys whispered.

"Uh…yeah."

I had no experience with seers, although Tsagasi had told me about their existence. Many were frauds, but others had real power to see things. When I'd asked him if my concern for David's safety was legitimate, he'd tried to blow me off by saying everyone must die. But when I'd pressed him, he'd told me a seer would eventually cross my path and to inquire with them. They were the ones who could divine the future.

Could he have meant Deidre?

We followed the woman down a hall toward a staircase, where we climbed to the second floor. I hesitated when we entered a living room, but she continued on down another short hall into a dark room that was empty but for a small round table with two chairs on one side and one on the other. Two candles on the table provided the only light.

"Sit," she said with a graceful sweep of her hand toward the visitors' chairs. She picked up a lighter and began to light some of the candles on the floor, arranged around the perimeter of the room.

"Wouldn't it be easier to turn on a light?" Rhys asked in a dry tone as she watched.

She wasn't lighting all the candles, just enough to provide light… and mystique. I was sure part of this woman's "magic" was illusion and suggestion.

"Who's Luna?" I asked.

"My daughter."

"Do you need her?" I asked.

"We shall see."

She started lighting candles along the back wall. "So you found her?"

"Excuse me?" I asked, wondering if she was talking to me.

Bending over, she glanced up at me. "You found your cousin."

"How'd you know I was looking for her?"

She snorted. "I know you weren't the one searchin'." She paused, and her next words were filled with worry. "The real concern is why I didn't see you comin' to me."

I shot a glance to Rhys, who remained expressionless. What did that mean? I wasn't sure how her talent worked, but if she hadn't seen me coming, then it seemed unlikely she'd be able to read my future. Maybe she couldn't help me after all.

I gave her a tight smile. "I didn't have an appointment."

The woman moved to the wall to my left. "That isn't how I'd know, child."

My gaze drifted to the table in front of me. In the center was a small animal skin, along with a small wooden cup. I resisted the urge to dismiss her. Sure, this seemed backward and archaic, but over the last few months, I'd learned that the most powerful things were sometimes the simplest.

She lit a few more candles, then sat down opposite me and Rhys. Taking a deep breath, she studied both of us.

"You're her friend," the seer said as her gaze landed on Rhys.

"You must not be that good," Rhys scoffed. "I barely know Ellie."

The seer gave her a look of annoyance. "Not her. The slayer. You're the one whose friend died."

Rhys's face paled.

The seer either didn't notice Rhys's reaction, intent on shifting the candles on the table so they were on opposite sides of the animal skin, or she ignored it. I was going with the latter. What with all the candles and the cryptic pronouncements, she seemed fond of the drama.

"Is that cowhide?" I asked, hoping it was fake.

A tiny grin played on the corners of her lips. "It's deer—a doe who had recently given birth to twins."

"And you killed it?" Rhys asked in horror.

"Not me personally. I paid a hunter to do so. The recent birth of twins amplifies the power."

Rhys sat back in her seat as though the hide carried a deadly disease.

The seer stopped fussing with the things on her table and looked up into my face. "My name is Deidre, and I am, in fact, a seer."

"But you just said you didn't see my visit," I said. "Is that unusual?"

She made a face and picked up the cup. "Do you believe in seers or are you a skeptic?"

"Shouldn't you be able to tell?" Rhys asked dryly.

Deidre gave her a deadly glare.

I pushed out a sigh. Why was nearly everything in the supernatural world so adversarial? "After everything I've experienced the last few months, I believe there are people with supernatural gifts, but there are also people who exploit others."

One side of Deidre's mouth tipped up. "Let's see what I can see."

She shook her cup, then dumped out the contents in a diagonal line across the animal skin, starting toward Rhys and drawing the cup toward herself. Small animal bones and seashells spread out across the skin.

"Oh my God!" Rhys cried out. "Are those real animal bones?"

The seer ignored her, focusing her attention on the scattered objects with a frown. "This is curious."

My chest tightened. "My entire life is filled with curious. What do you see?"

"Your future is murky; your past is as well."

"What do you mean my past is murky?"

She looked up at me with a curious stare that seemed to see deep into my soul. "It means things have purposely been kept from you."

"I know that," I said with more of an attitude than I'd intended. "A god has been manipulating my life for his own purposes since before I was even born. He caused my mother to miscarry multiple times until I was conceived."

Her lips pressed into a thin line. "Yes, this has the feel of the hand of a god."

"What *do* you see?"

"I see great tragedy and loss, but your past is blurred with your future, makin' it hard to see which is which."

Great. "I need to know if my boyfriend will be safe."

She gave me a sympathetic look. "No one is safe."

"I need to know if the gods will kill him." My voice broke. "I need to know what to do to protect him."

"I can't see that, my child."

Tears stung my eyes. "I need to know."

"Give me your hand." She reached out her hand, palm up, and I slowly gave her mine. She turned it over, and her index finger traced the lines. "This is the path you were destined to lead, one that cannot be changed or altered. In your case, it's clearer than the bones."

"What does it show?"

She gave me a sad smile. "It shows much of what I've already seen, only it gives a clearer timeline." She pointed to the line that ran along the side of my palm by my thumb. "This is your life line and it shows the tragedies of your life." She pointed closer to the start of the line. "This marks a tragedy when you were quite young—around seven or so."

I swallowed the lump in my throat. "My mother's murder."

She nodded then studied my hand again. "Here are two deaths, very close together and recent."

"My father and my stepmother. But do you see another soon?"

She traced the scar on my palm, the diagonal slash Collin had made during the ceremony he'd tricked me into helping him with—the one that had permanently opened the main gate to hell. The slash went through my life line directly below the marks of my parents' deaths.

"If there was something here, it's now gone," she said.

My anger at Collin sprang back to life, but I'd spent weeks pissed at Collin and he'd since realized he'd majorly screwed up. Being angry with him wouldn't do me any good, as David had pointed out more than once—it only made me bitter and stole what little happiness I'd found in this dangerous and exhausting world.

"I'm sorry," the seer said, sounding like she meant it. "I can't find the answer you seek. Some things aren't meant to be known."

"What if Piper hides him in a world?" Rhys asked. "She placed the ward at the opening to the world she created for Tommy's ghost. Why can't we do the same for David? That way you'll know he's safe while you're fighting the demons."

I hadn't considered the implications of Piper's ability. Only been incredulous that she possessed it. Rhys's confidence in the plan was contagious.

But my excitement was deflated by another realization. "He'll never go along with it."

"He stayed out of the warehouse last night," Rhys protested.

"That was a special circumstance," I said. "The demon possessed a power to make him lose his mind to lust. I convinced him it was safer to stay outside."

"Then find a way to convince him to stay away this time. Surely you can come up with something."

How could I possibly convince David to sit out on a battle this potentially big? Then it struck me that the answer might just be sitting next to me. "You. You're the answer."

She shook her head. "Me? How?"

"Even though Collin and Jack came back with the Guardians' spelled weapons, you don't know how to use them. You'll be in danger." I was beginning to believe this might work. "But David has a sword and he very much wants a purpose—a way to be useful, a real one. He can protect you."

She opened her mouth as though she was about to protest, then stopped, sinking back into her chair. The look on her face suggested that she was considering my suggestion. "If I agree to this plan, does it make me a coward?"

"God, no," I said, reaching over and grabbing her forearm. "Collin and I use the duality of our marks to share power. I can be killed and injured, but he can heal me. I nearly died twice and he saved me both times. As far as I know there's no doing that for you or David." Then a new worry hit me. "What about Piper?"

She frowned. "Abel saved her after the first time she fought the demons. I'm not exactly sure what he did, but her shirt and leather jacket had been ripped to shreds and she was covered in blood, yet there wasn't a wound on her." Rhys paused. "Given the state of her clothes, I'm positive the blood was hers, yet she seemed completely fine."

I nodded, not surprised. "You and David have no fail-safes like Piper, Collin, and I do. If we're fighting demons, I'd rather make certain you and David are safe."

"And Jack," Rhys said with worry in her eyes.

"And Jack." Although I was certain he wouldn't agree to any such plan. I got the impression he planned to be front and center—and that maybe we should let him.

"The priest will insist on fighting," Deidre said, making me realize we'd just spilled a lot of information about our world.

"Do your bones tell you that?" Rhys asked, her upper lip curled.

"No, but I've met him and know he'll never leave the slayer's side."

"Because he's in love with her?" I asked. Motivation was everything and I needed to know his, but Rhys sucked in a breath at my question.

"That's one reason," Deidre said. "But the other is that he sees it as *his* purpose. He may lack your power, but he was born to slay demons and he won't shy away from that."

Rhys tilted her head, her eyes narrowing with suspicion. "When did you meet Jack? Does Piper know?"

Deidre gave her a long look. "He came to see me a couple of weeks ago."

"I thought he was in Charlotte a couple of weeks ago," Rhys said. Deidre shrugged.

I studied Rhys for a second, wondering if it was a simple mistake or if Jack had intentionally deceived her. I turned back to Deidre. "Can we trust the priest?"

"Of course we can trust him!" Rhys protested.

The seer gave me a wicked smile, her eyes glittering with mischief. "You have the same goals and purpose."

"That doesn't exactly answer my question, now does it?" I prodded.

She continued to give me her Cheshire Cat grin.

She wasn't volunteering anything more and I'd have to accept her answer for now, as much as I hated to leave it at that. "Can you tell us anything else?"

Deidre slowly turned to Rhys. "Unlike the curse keeper, *your* future is clear as a summer day. Would you like to know it?"

Rhys gave the mat on the table a squeamish look. "I take it you'll use the animal skin and bones?"

Deidre grinned. "I can read your palm if you'd prefer, but I usually get much more information from the bones."

Rhys started to offer her hand, then pulled it back. "No. I don't want to know. If I'm getting killed by demons tonight, I don't want to spend the rest of the day worrying about it."

Deidre gave her a look of approval. "I might see that you live to the ripe old age of ninety-two. Then your worries will be relieved."

"Not really," Rhys said. "I'll still worry about Piper and Jack." She turned and gave me a sad smile. "I'll still worry about Ellie, Collin, and David."

"But not the demigod?" Deidre asked with undisguised curiosity.

Rhys hesitated. "Piper seems attached to him, for whatever reason, so I'll worry for her sake."

Her comment reminded me of Piper's mission to visit the seer. "Deidre, I know Piper arranged to see you earlier."

"I know why she wanted to see me," Deidre said in a firm tone. "But I refuse to help the son of Satan."

"I understand that," I said. "And while I'm not too fond of him myself, he's important to Piper. Besides," I added. "She needs him supernaturally. He's her Collin."

Deidre shook her head. "No. She no longer needs him. He's served his purpose."

"Do your bones tell you that?" I asked in frustration.

She sat up straighter. "As a matter of fact, they do."

"Deidre," I pleaded. "I know you don't like him, but she needs her supernatural counterpart." I gestured to Rhys. "You heard what

Rhys said. He saved her life before, and she's bound to be hurt again in the battle tonight. *Please.*"

Deidre pushed out a massive sigh and placed her hands on the table. "Curse Keeper, you place more faith in me than you should. True, I don't like the creature, but that's not what's stoppin' me from helping him or the slayer. It's the fact that I have no idea how to stop the mark from appearin'."

"So she's destined to kill him?" I said in defeat.

Deidre slowly nodded, compassion easing the hard lines on her face. "Yes. The best thing you can do for her is to prepare her for that."

"It will destroy her," Rhys said, her voice cracking. "She'll never get over it."

"She *will*," Deidre said with plenty of confidence. "She must. The son of Okeus's purpose on this earth is endin', but for the creator of worlds, it's only just beginnin'." She paused and lowered her voice. "But she has a dangerous road ahead. She will need her friends to protect and guide her."

"We'll be there for her," I said solemnly. I couldn't imagine being compelled to kill Collin or David. I wasn't sure I could survive losing either of them, let alone at my own hands. "I won't leave her."

Deidre nodded with a pleased look in her eyes. "Good. Now let's address the real reason you're here."

"Do you know what that is?" Rhys asked.

"Not entirely," Deidre admitted. "It's hard to read anything about the curse keeper. It's as though she's been covered with a veil."

I didn't like the sound of that, but I wasn't surprised. "We want to enter a world Piper has created," I said. "Without her. I know you created a ward to keep demons out, but can you create one to let us in?"

"You hold the power to enter on your own," she said. "You have it on you now."

I glanced down at myself in confusion. What did I have on me? Then I remembered the watch Collin had given me. I pulled it out of my jeans pocket and showed it to her.

She reached for it and turned it over in her hand. "There is great power in this piece."

"I don't think that's it," I said. "Collin had this in his pocket earlier, but he couldn't enter the world."

She gave me a look that made it clear she thought I was harebrained. "The other keeper isn't a witness to creation, now is he?"

Could it really be that easy? "No, I guess not."

"Can you give us some wards to help repel demons?" Rhys asked.

Deidre gave her a warm smile. "Come with me."

When we headed downstairs and followed her into her workshop, I could still see Abel standing on the street corner.

"He could break in and demand that you help him," I said. "He *is* a demigod."

"He could try, but I've created wards to keep him out," she said as she started to gather her materials. "But I'll be the first to admit he's changed."

"So you have met him before," Rhys said. "Why do you hate him so much? On principle or because he pissed you off?"

"Both."

"Part of the reason he's here is because Piper wanted to ask you how to stop the mark," I said.

"And the other part?" Deidre asked, focused on her work.

"To get into the attic."

She jerked her head up. "Why does the son of Satan wish to invade Piper's world?"

"Tsagasi told us that an answer we need is in there."

Her face remained expressionless. "The Little Person?"

"Yes," I said. "I met him weeks ago, when we first formed an alliance. His brother has offered to help us, but only if Piper is free, and he says the answer we seek is in the attic." Then I added, "And Abel is desperate to save her."

A scowl darkened her face. "You want me to let the son of Satan in, don't you?"

"Or at least speak to him."

Deidre cursed under her breath and shot me an irritated look. Without another word, she dropped the pestle in the mortar and marched to the front door.

Rhys and I stood back in the hall, watching as she opened the door and called out, "Kieran Abel."

He moved closer but gave her several feet of personal space. I could hear quiet murmurs pass back and forth between them before she pushed the door open and let him in.

After what she'd said about the shop's protections, I'd expected him to hit some kind of barrier, but he walked right through and headed toward us with a determined look.

Deidre walked past us and headed upstairs, leaving the three of us in the hallway.

"Did you piss her off so much she refuses to help any of us now?" Rhys asked.

"No," Abel said with a frown. "She's gone to consult her bones and shells."

Rhys's mouth formed an O of surprise. "What about?"

"Piper." His tone was short, irritated, yet I could see it was concern that made him that way. I understood that well enough.

Five minutes later, Deidre returned, looking exhausted and haggard. She walked past us into the workroom and started mashing leaves again, but with a lot more force than she'd used before.

To my surprise, Abel stayed in the hall, silently watching her work. Why hadn't he asked her what she'd seen?

The silence continued for nearly ten minutes as she made five wards—five small white cotton bags filled with herbs and a few bones—much to Rhys's disgust based on the way she cringed at the sight of them.

She handed a bag to Rhys. "Keep this with you at all times. Put it in your pocket if you have one. Or put a cord around it and wear it under your shirt. It will last about three weeks before it begins to wear off. It will hide you from demons, but if they see you, they can still kill you."

Rhys lifted the small bag up to her nose and sniffed it. "It stinks."

"It's not perfume," Deidre scolded, then handed the other bags to me. "The rest of you need to wear these too."

I glanced down and did a quick count. "We need one more. Not counting Abel, there are six of us, and there are only five bags."

She shook her head. "The slayer is trapped behind bars. Those are for the rest of you."

I snuck a quick glance to Abel, who remained expressionless, then back to her. Hell, he might not want to ask, but I had no problem doing so. "Could you see her future? Will she be released tonight?"

"I will see to her protection," she said, then turned around to remove more dried plants from her shelves.

"That doesn't answer my question," I said. "What did you see?"

She gave me a deadly cold look. "What I saw is no concern of yours. Not yet, but the time will come very shortly when you will need to know. Now let me work in peace. I have to get this right."

I was dying to ask more, but her anger seemed to be boiling beneath the surface, so I kept quiet, instead sneaking glances to Abel, who watched her intently. The concern in his eyes worried me.

What had Deidre seen in Piper's future and why wouldn't she tell me? Worse, why wasn't Abel demanding she share it with him?

Deidre made another bag. Wiping a fine sheen of sweat from her brow, she handed it to Abel and looked deep into his eyes. "I think you know what to do with this."

He stared down at it as though it were a rattlesnake about to jump out and bite him. "You're positive she will need this?"

"The bones don't lie."

"But will it protect her?" he asked, worry in his eyes.

She lowered her gaze to the bag in her hand. "What you asked of me is tricky."

"That's why I'm here. You're the best."

She lifted her gaze with a smirk. "I've already made the ward, son of Satan. Flattery isn't necessary now."

With a short nod, he carefully took the bag from her. "I will see to it that you get the items I promised."

He turned and headed for the front door.

"Kieran Abel," she called out after him as she moved past Rhys and me into the hall, wiping her hands on her apron.

He stopped and slowly turned to face her.

"I am truly sorry."

To my surprise, she sounded like she meant it.

CHAPTER EIGHTEEN

Piper

My holding cell included a single cot—with no bedding or pillow—and a toilet in the corner. I was unlikely to have a roommate, and I was grateful I wouldn't have to share a cell with some hardened criminal. There was no window or clock to clue me in to what time it was, yet I was sure it was already after sundown. I could feel it in my bones. When the demons emerged, I knew they would come for me, and if any of them were as humanlike as Adonis and Caelius, they'd be able to maneuver through the human world well enough to find me. Once they did, I was toast. They had one mission—to take me to Okeus—and a few police officers and locked cells wouldn't get in their way.

A guard brought me a tray with inedible food that looked like it was supposed to be mashed potatoes and a hamburger covered in gravy, but I left it on the floor by my cot as I paced.

I was torn between hoping Abel wouldn't do anything stupid, like trying to break me loose, and wanting to get the hell out of there.

There was nothing I could do but wait.

About ten minutes after the guard had brought my dinner, Detective Olivia Powell appeared in front of my cell, wrinkling her nose as she looked down at the tray. She wore a pair of dress pants and a sports jacket over a white button-down shirt. "I swear the food they serve is a form of torture."

I didn't respond. She was likely right.

She took a step toward the cell, wrapping her hand around one of the bars. "How are you holding up?"

I forced a smile. "I've had better days."

"Yeah, I bet." She glanced around to see if anyone was listening, but the only guard in sight was outside the holding area down the hall.

"How'd you find out I was here?" I asked, walking up to her. "Was Lawton bragging about his catch?"

She grimaced. "I admit he's pretty pleased with himself, but Jack called me first."

I leaned my hip against the bars. "Jack."

"He's worried about you, Piper. He asked me to check on you."

I nodded. I was worried about me too.

Opening her jacket, she reached in and pulled out half a sandwich covered in plastic wrap. "I thought you might be hungry."

I didn't feel hungry, but it might be a while before I had another opportunity for edible food. I needed to choke down the sandwich. Taking it from her, I quickly unwrapped it and took a bite.

"Turkey and cheese," I murmured around the food in my mouth.

"I figured that was safe," she said under her breath. "Everybody likes turkey."

Not Rhys, who was a die-hard vegan, but I was too busy eating to correct her. Now that I'd taken a bite, my stomach was demanding more.

I finished the half sandwich in less than a minute. Olivia held out her hand and took the ball of plastic wrap, which she stuffed in her jacket pocket.

"Jack's petitioned to see you as your religious counselor, but Lawton's refused the request. The only one who will be able to see you is your attorney, and he's even pushing her off."

"Can he do that?"

"Not really, but he's finding excuses to stall." She gave me a grim look. "I doubt you'll be getting out of here tonight."

I swallowed my rising anxiety. She hadn't told me anything I didn't already suspect, but it still sucked to have my fears confirmed.

"I brought some salt," she said, glancing down the hall again before pulling a plastic salt shaker from her pocket and passing it through the bars. "It's not much, but Jack says a line of salt might make a difference if demons show up." She worried her lip, clearly distressed. "Jack was hesitant to tell me all the details, but he seems to think you're a primary target for them."

"Well." I couldn't tell what she wanted—reassurance that Jack was wrong or confirmation that Jack was right? I went with option C. "Jack is a worrier." Forcing a smile was too difficult, even a fake one, so I avoided her gaze, asking, "Do you know if Jack and the others have encountered any demons yet?"

Worry filled her eyes. "Not that I'm aware of."

I nodded. "That's good."

Surely the police would know if an army of demons was slaughtering people to consume their souls as they emerged from their new gate to hell, wherever that turned out to be.

"Jack thinks Abel will show up to protect you," Olivia said with worry in her eyes.

"If the demons show up, he'll fight them," I said, my fear rising again. No one other than me could kill him, but what would the police do if they found him brandishing his sword in the police station? Especially if the demons made themselves invisible.

"Piper, you need to know that Lawton is pushing the DA hard to pin all of this on you."

"On what grounds?" I asked, then shook my head. "I think I might know why he hates me, although it's pretty vague." I grimaced. "He thinks I did something to his brother."

"His brother?"

"Do you have any idea what he's talking about?" I asked.

She paused. "No."

"Has his brother been hurt or injured?" I asked. "Or maybe he disappeared?"

"He never talks about his personal life. But I'll do some digging."

"Do you think he's putting on an act?" I asked. "Do you think he believes in ghosts and demons? Maybe he—"

She shook her head. "He's been so adamant you're a fraud. Those are the grounds he's currently holding you on until he can drum up more charges."

"What more could he possibly accuse me of?"

Her grim silence sparked an even grimmer thought. He hadn't shown me those gruesome photos for nothing.

I huffed out an angry curse. "You've got to be kidding me. Does he honestly intend to try and pin those deaths in the warehouse on me?"

She pushed out a breath. "The public is upset. He needs a scapegoat, and you fit the bill. A woman masquerading as a ghost and demon hunter who loses her mind and slaughters people." She lowered her voice. "If he finds out you have weapons…"

"He'll say I used them?" I asked, incredulous. "Those people were ripped apart by an animal and shredded with claws. Any forensic expert could tell you that a knife blade didn't make those wounds."

"Piper," she said, lowering her voice to a soft whisper, "I think we both recognize animals aren't the only possible explanation here." She made a face, and I got the hint. The thought that this was the work of demons had crossed her mind. "You're right, though, that no knife wound could make those wounds, which is to your advantage, but you're not going to make it to trial. You'll be a sitting duck in jail because they'll refuse to allow a heinous monster to post bail, which leaves you at the mercy of the demons."

Her eyes narrowed. "How'd you know the people in the warehouse were ripped apart anyway? You were there, weren't you?"

Crap. Luckily, I had a decent excuse. "I saw the photos. Detective Lawton made sure to give me more than enough time to examine them."

She cringed. "That guy is a cruel son of a bitch. But...why do I get the sense you were there?"

I gave her a defiant look. "Those demons took Hudson."

Her eyes filled with understanding. "You went to get your friend."

While I thought I could trust Olivia, I wasn't one hundred percent sure. And if there was a sliver of doubt, I'd do better to lie. The cops wanted confirmation I'd been at that warehouse, and I couldn't give it to them—not even to Olivia. "I want the person responsible for Hudson's death brought to justice, and that's not happening if Lawton thinks I'm involved."

Disappointment washed over her face, but she nodded. "I understand."

I only hoped she did.

"Do you have a message for me to give to Jack?" she asked.

I considered her question before I said, "No."

"You don't trust me."

"Not entirely, but if you keep proving yourself, I'll get there. But in this instance, I really don't have anything to tell him. Not yet." I glanced down at the salt shaker in my hand.

"Pour your salt. Then hand me the shaker. The less evidence left behind to implicate me, the better."

She was right, of course, so I started at one end of the bars and poured a thin line of salt all the way to the other wall.

Olivia studied it for a few moments, then nodded briskly. "It's not noticeable, and I doubt anyone will be coming in or out of your cell tonight, so it should remain undisturbed."

That was simultaneously reassuring and depressing.

"But if the salt gets disturbed and you're at risk..." She stopped, a war waging in her eyes. Then she pushed out a sigh and lifted her gaze to mine. "Jack said to remind you that you can escape like Tommy."

I'd already considered that option and decided to only use it as a last resort. I'd never be able to explain disappearing, and it would put me in heaps of legal trouble. Not to mention I'd be trapped. If the demons knew I had disappeared in this cell, they'd be waiting for me to reappear. If I was going to go with that option, I might as well let Abel bust me out of this place, which I was seriously starting to consider.

"Do I *want* to know what that means?" she asked. "Isn't that the little boy ghost you went to go rescue when Jack was in the ER?"

She definitely had a good memory. "Yeah."

"How did Tommy escape?" she asked.

I gave her a grim smile. "Let's hope you never have to figure it out."

She twisted her mouth, then stared off into the distance for several long seconds, lost in thought. "I'm going to see if I can pull some strings and get you sprung tonight. Sit tight."

She gave me a grim smile before she started down the hall.

"Olivia," I called after her, and when she turned around to face me, I said, "I don't know if Jack told you what's coming, but you should really take cover. Maybe leave town."

She stopped and studied me for several seconds. "I'm not running from this, Piper, and I'm not leaving you here as demon fodder. I'll be back."

CHAPTER NINETEEN

Ellie

The sun was close to setting by the time we got back to Piper's house. Abel was disturbingly quiet during the short drive from downtown. Rhys was annoyingly talkative, but I knew she was nervous. So was I. Deidre was certain the pocket watch would gain me admittance to the attic, but I wasn't convinced. It hadn't helped Collin.

David was in the kitchen when I walked in, and I was sure he'd been watching for us from the living room window. "Any luck?"

"Let's hope so," I said as I set the wards on the kitchen table. Fingering the watch in my pocket, I headed into the living room. David followed me. "Where's Collin?"

"He said he was going to look for Tsawasi and talk some sense into him."

I stopped at the base of the stairs and looked back at him. "What does that mean?"

"It's Collin," David said with a shrug. "I was lucky he told me anything at all."

He had a point, but I didn't like it. "The car's still outside. He couldn't have gone far."

David's face softened. "The sun's setting. Given what we know is coming, he won't have gone far."

"Which means it's now or never if I want to try the attic again. The demons will likely come here first, looking for Piper," I said.

"Agreed," David said. "I'm all packed up and ready to leave for the safe house as soon as we're done."

Abel and Rhys stood in the dining room, locked in a private conversation. Jack was at the table, pouring over a book. No doubt Abel was quizzing Rhys about what the seer had told us while he waited outside. Call me a traitor, but I decided to take advantage of their distraction.

"Come on," I whispered, then slipped up the staircase, making my footfalls soft to hide the sound.

When we reached the top, David pulled me to a halt. "You don't want Abel and Rhys to go into the attic with you?"

"I'm not so concerned about Rhys, but Abel... no." I gave him a grim smile. "I have no doubt that he will put Piper above all others, at the expense of everyone else's safety."

His grim look must have matched my own. "Like Collin."

"Exactly." I knew his stance and was powerless to rein him in...or did I just tell myself that? I pushed out a long sigh. "I want to go up alone."

Hurt filled his eyes. "You don't want me to go?"

"It's not that I don't trust you, David," I insisted. "It's that I don't know how this is going to go down. I don't know the rules. What if I take you up there and can't get you back out?"

"Ellie," he said softly, reaching for my cheek as he lowered his face to mine, pressing our foreheads together. "You can't spend your life worrying about my safety. You have to protect yourself and the world."

"How can you say that, David?" I asked, tears filling my eyes. A heavy wave of foreboding washed over me. "I love you. You're my life."

"No, my love," he said with a tender smile, pulling back slightly. "I am one part of it"—his grin turned ornery—"a significant part, but only a part."

"I can't lose you," I whispered, a tear streaking down my cheek.

"I'm not going anywhere," he said. Then his smile faded and he turned serious. "But if something out of my control should happen…" He paused and made sure he had my full attention. "I won't go anywhere. I'll stay here with you like Hudson did for Piper. I won't leave you, Ellie."

"Don't talk like that," I said, starting to panic.

He gave me a gentle kiss, but I grabbed the back of his head and held him close, kissing him with a determination that overwhelmed me.

Pulling back, he stared at me with eyes full of pride and love. "I'm not going anywhere. I have too much work to do, and so do you. Now go up to the attic before Abel realizes what you're up to."

I wiped my tears and nodded. He was right. "I have no idea how to do this."

"Perhaps just concentrate on her created world as you walk up the stairs."

I grinned. "It can't be as simple as that."

"Sometimes the simplest strategies are the most effective."

A sense of déjà vu filled me. Then I realized I'd had the same thought at the seer's. David had taught me this.

I could hear Abel calling my name downstairs, so I quickly opened the attic door, pulling out the pocket watch with my free hand. I half-expected David to comment—he'd spent weeks of research trying to determine the watches' purpose—but he simply waited behind me.

Rubbing the back of the engraved watch, I concentrated on my witness to creation power and my mental image of Tommy's playroom, then started to climb. The watch issued a mechanical click about halfway up, and when I looked at it, I saw the face had opened up, revealing a new dark blue layer beneath the original gold. Embedded in the blue was a smaller timepiece, showing the identical time. Something had happened, but I didn't dare look up until I reached the top of the steps.

When I finally did look, I gasped. The office was gone, and the room was filled with toys and a daybed on the wall opposite the front-facing dormer windows. Only I couldn't see the front yard now. The view from the windows showed countless demons pounding on the glass, trying to break in, a glowing background behind them. The walls surrounding the dormers were covered with black charcoal. Collin's marks, seeking protection for anyone within the space.

I gasped and took a step back, instinctively flexing my hand. I didn't have a weapon on me—carrying a sword around was hardly inconspicuous—but one sword against so many demons would have been like a drop in the ocean. However, if the demons managed to break in, I could use the mark on my hand to temporarily send them back to hell—a last resort given the way it drained my energy.

"They can't huwt us," said a tiny voice on the other side of the room.

I let my gaze jerk from the windows to the bookcase and a cowering little boy crouched beside it. I dropped my hand and took a cautious step toward him. "You must be Tommy."

He nodded but still clung to the side of the bookcase.

I moved closer. "I'm Ellie. Piper's cousin. She's told me about you."

Tears fell down his face, and he swiped at his cheek and runny nose with the back of his hand. "You're in my pictures."

Collin and Piper had argued over a drawing. Could this be the answer we were looking for? If so, wouldn't Collin have told us what was in it?

"So I heard," I said, moving closer still and squatting next to a table strewn with Lincoln Logs. "Can I see it?"

The little boy gave me a hesitant look. "I'm not supposed to let Piper see it."

"Why not?" I asked, trying to hide my fear, even more certain that the drawing held a clue.

"The voice told me not to."

"But I'm not Piper," I said with a warm smile. "Surely you can show me." When he still looked uncertain, I added, "You let Collin see it."

"He stole it."

I blinked in surprise. "What?"

"He put the picture in his pocket."

Why hadn't he shown it to me? He'd pretended to have no idea what answers could be hidden in the attic, when all along they'd been stuffed in his pocket.

"That's okay," I said, forcing a smile even though I was seething inside.

"But I drew more. Lots more," he said, still gripping the edge of the bookcase. "I can show you those."

My eyes flew wide. "Would you?"

He nodded, his eyes huge with fear.

"Do the demons scare you?" I asked gently. "Do you want me to shut the curtains?"

He shook his head and took a step away from the bookcase. "I told you. They can't get us."

"Then why are you scared?" I asked.

Rather than answer, he pulled a drawing pad from a shelf and carefully set it on the table.

I leaned over to watch as he flipped through it. Page after page was filled with countless primitively drawn bodies in a sea of red.

"Tommy," I said, trying to keep my voice light. "What are those drawings of?"

He glanced back at me with innocent eyes. "The world."

"The world," I echoed as fear turned my blood to ice. "Why does the world look like that?"

"The monsters," he said as he turned back to his task and continued to flip pages. Then he flipped past a page that looked different from the previous ones.

I reached out and stopped him. This one showed a primitively drawn girl with light brown hair holding what looked like two knives, facing a blue creature that looked like an ogre. A small figure cowered behind her. "What's this?"

"That's Piper and the monster that tried to eat me."

"A monster tried to eat you?" I asked in horror. Piper had told us she'd saved him from a demon, but this picture put it into perspective.

He slowly nodded. "Piper saved me from the mean lady too."

"What mean lady?"

"The lady who stole my house."

The homeowner? We'd all been in such a hurry I'd never gotten the full story as to how Tommy had been transferred from his house to Piper's.

He turned the page to a drawing that was clearly me with Collin and David, my auburn hair and David's black hair giving us away. Next to us were two little men covered in hair—the Nunnehi Little People—and two Native Americans stood behind us. The Nunnehi warriors.

"What's this?" I asked, trying to sound nonchalant.

"That's you and your friends."

He turned the page and the next picture showed the carnage in the warehouse. A pile of body parts and lots of blood, along with creatures that resembled the lion demons that had killed the Guardians. A man with dark hair and eyes stood on a stage, surrounded by rays of light. A girl with dark hair and knives stood beside him with a man with dark hair and hints of a scruffy beard. Abel? "What's this?"

"That's Piper's fight," he said.

"Who's the man in the middle?" I asked, pointing to the man surrounded by light.

He pointed to the man next to Piper. "That man's daddy."

"Do you know who he is?" I asked.

A dark look covered his face. "He wants to take Piper away from me."

My breath caught in my chest. "How do you know that?"

"*He* told me," Tommy said as though I were a simpleton. He turned the page. I could see the remnants of the page that had been ripped out, but it was the page behind it that held my attention. It was like the first pages—bodies strewn on the ground in a sea of blood, but in the middle of this one was a figure with long brown hair holding two knives, its face a horrific mask.

"What's that?" I asked, pointing to the figure.

He turned to look up at me with tears in his eyes. "That's the bad monster that eats Piper."

It took me a full two seconds to comprehend what he'd said.

"It has her knives," I murmured.

He studied me as though trying to figure out if he could trust me. Then his lip trembled. "I wasn't supposed to let you see it."

He closed the notepad with a loud slam, then held it to his chest, his chin quivering.

"I want to help Piper," I said, my heart pounding so hard I wondered if he could hear it. "But I need your help."

"I'm scared for Piper," he said, through his tears.

"I want to save her, Tommy. She's my cousin. Help me save her. What is this monster?"

"I don't know," he said, starting to cry softly.

"Can I have your picture?" I asked, pointing to his notebook.

"I'm not supposed to give it to you." But I could see the hesitation in his eyes. He wanted to give it to me, but he also wanted to follow the rules.

I gave him a warm smile. "How about you put the notebook on the table, and I'll take the picture when you aren't looking?"

"Like Collin did?" he asked, his eyes full of innocence.

I hid my renewed anger. "Just like Collin did, if you like. Then it won't be your fault."

He thought about it for a few moments, then nodded. After he gently placed the notebook on the table, he walked over to the middle window. I watched in horror as he put his palm on the glass. The demons went wild, frenzied in their attempt to get to him.

"You really aren't scared of them," I said, slightly in awe and slightly in horror.

"They won't hurt me now."

"Because you're in this room?" I asked.

He turned back to look at me with innocent eyes. "Because he won't let them."

My blood turned to ice again. "The voice?"

He nodded and turned back to the window.

"Why is he protecting you now?"

He didn't answer, instead tapping on the window as if it were a fish tank, sending the demons into a renewed frenzy.

Thoroughly creeped out, I opened the notebook and started to rip out the page, which was when it occurred to me that there were dozens of other drawings in there I wanted to study. Instead of taking the one page, I picked up the notebook and stuffed it under my T-shirt.

I only made it down one step before Tommy called back to me.

"I know you took all my pictures," he said, his back still to me.

"I…"

"It's okay," he said, tapping a rhythm on the glass. "He says you can have them."

That caught my attention. "He's talking to you right *now*?"

"He says you can have them because it's too late to stop it."

Fear bubbled in my chest. "Stop what?"

He turned to look at me with a face of pure innocence. "The monster. It's coming for her now."

"I thought you were afraid for her," I said in dismay.

A small smile lifted the corners of his lips. "*He* will protect her."

Who was the he? Abel or the voice?

I ran down the stairs, shouting Collin's name as I burst into the hallway and ran directly into Abel. I placed a hand on his chest to steady myself.

"What did you find?" Abel's entire body vibrated with the words.

I took a step back and pulled out the notebook with a shaking hand, noticing Collin pacing behind Abel and David standing behind him. "A monster is coming for her. Now."

Abel's eyes widened and he spun around, passing Rhys, who stood in an open bedroom doorway, on his way to the stairs.

"Abel!" I called after him. "Wait. There's something you need to see!"

But he ignored me, stomping down the stairs and out the front door.

"What?" David asked. "What did he need to see?"

I shifted my focus to Collin. "What's in the picture you stole from Tommy?"

"What the hell are you talking about?" he countered, but he couldn't look me in the eye.

"What's in the picture, Collin?" I said in a deadly tone.

His gaze met mine. "Tsawasi took it when I saw him just a bit ago."

"That's not what I asked, is it? What was in the picture?"

"I'm not allowed to tell you."

My temper took over and I grabbed a handful of his T-shirt and slammed him against the wall, pressing my chest to his as I glared up at him. "What's in the goddamned picture, Collin?"

A wicked smile lifted his lips, but his eyes looked dead. "This wasn't how I pictured you coming on to me in my fantasies, but I can work with it."

I kneed him in the balls then stepped back, taking only small satisfaction in the sight of him hunched over and grunting in pain. "I'm sick of not being able to trust you, Collin Dailey. Either tell me or get the hell away from me."

He twisted his head to look up at me, disbelief in his eyes. "You don't mean that."

"Try me."

He took several seconds to recover, sucking in deep breaths as he leaned over his bent legs. When he stood semi-upright, his serious gaze found and held mine. "Tsawasi made me swear not to tell you."

"Why?" David asked. "Did the picture show a monster getting Piper?"

Collin turned to him with pleading eyes. "Yes."

"Why didn't you tell us?" I demanded, pissed and hurt, and so, so disappointed.

"You have to trust me, Ellie," he said with tears in his eyes. "I'm doing this for you. I'm trying to make things right."

"Trust you?" I demanded. "How can I trust you when you're keeping secrets? *Again.*" I thought we'd finally gotten beyond the past, and here he was proving once again that he was sneaky Collin, the bastard who'd tricked me into opening the gate to hell and keeping it open.

"Ellie," David said. "What did you see?"

I handed him the notebook, suddenly overcome with exhaustion. Then it struck me that our group was one short. "Where's Jack?"

"He left," Rhys said, worry in her eyes. "He waited for nearly an hour, and when you didn't come back, he said he couldn't wait. There was something he wanted to take care of at Helen's Bridge."

"I was gone an *hour*?" I asked in dismay.

"Time moves more slowly there," Collin said. "Remember? Piper and I were gone longer this morning."

How the hell had I forgotten? I popped open the watch and saw ten minutes had passed according to the tinier watch face, but the larger one showed an hour had passed. "Is Jack coming back?"

Rhys grimaced. "I don't know, but if I were to guess, I'd say no. He told me to have you put me in the attic with Tommy, instead of taking me to Abel's house. I guess with him gone, he's afraid I'll be left alone there without protection when all of you leave for the..."

She swallowed, looking sick.

After what I'd just experienced, I wasn't so sure that was a good idea.

"What the hell is Jack doing that's more important than facing the demons?" I demanded, my temper getting the best of me again. "Deidre swore he'd stand up against them."

"I don't know for certain," Rhys said in a shaky voice, "but I think it has something to do with Helen and a promise he made her."

"Who the fuck is Helen?" Collin asked, standing more upright now.

"Helen from Helen's Bridge," David said solemnly. "He was talking about it earlier, how he could maybe see her now without Piper there to help."

"What did he promise her?" Collin asked.

Rhys shook her head. "I don't know, but the gate to hell is up there and the demons will be hungry when they emerge. They've fed off her before. Maybe he's trying to protect her."

I stared at her in disbelief. An army of demons was about to emerge from the gates of hell, and Piper was locked up at the Asheville Police Department. Abel was about to break a multitude of laws to get her out. Jack was AWOL to presumably help a ghost, and Collin had proven himself untrustworthy...once again. They said the definition of insanity was doing the same thing over and over expecting different results despite the evidence of every previous experience.

I was cured.

I turned to face Collin. "When this is over—one way or the other—you and I are done."

His face lost color. Then anger filled his eyes. "What the fuck are you talking about? You can't be done with me."

"Try me."

"We're the fucking curse keepers, Ellie. You're stuck with me, whether you like it or not," he said bitterly.

"No," I said with an icy coldness that made my hair stand on end. "You abandoned me after you turned the ceremony to close the gate on its head and left it open. I can do the same to you."

The seriousness of the situation began to sink in. "Ellie…you have to trust me."

I slowly shook my head. "No. Not anymore I don't."

"You bicker like children as the earth rumbles with the approach of the advancing demon army," Tsagasi said in disgust, appearing at the base of the stairs. "When will you get your priorities straight?"

"He's right," Collin said, his voice stiff. "We have to prepare to fight."

"Fight?" I snorted. "So you're fighting now? What happened to running off to hide?"

"My brother has changed his mind," Tsagasi said. "The son of the land made a bargain to secure your army."

"What? I felt like I'd been drenched by a bucket of icy water.

Collin gave me a bitter smile. "Maybe you'll trust me now." Then he stomped off downstairs.

Tsagasi stared up at me, shaking his head, his disappointment evident.

We   were   doomed.

CHAPTER TWENTY

Piper

I wasn't prone to claustrophobia, but an overwhelming sense of impending doom had settled in my cell and it was suffocating. I knew the sun had gone down by now and that Detective Lawton had no plans to let me out anytime soon. Sunset meant the demons were due to come out and play. I knew I needed to be alert, but my lack of sleep was catching up with me. I was about to lie down to get some rest when Detective Lawton walked in front of my cell.

"Good evening, Piper. Feeling lonely yet? Ready to talk?"

I kept my mouth shut, suspecting it would piss him off. It might not be the smartest move, but I wasn't about to cooperate with this asshole.

Detective Lawton approached the bars of my cell with a vindictive gleam in his eyes. "I hear you didn't eat your dinner. I hope you didn't think you were getting out anytime soon. Forty-eight hours is a long time." He paused, then asked, "Have you decided to confess yet?"

"Depends on what you're wanting me to confess to," I said in a glib tone. "I'll confess that I ran up my credit card at a shoe sale last month—I never could resist a strappy pair of sandals, you know what I mean?"

He shot daggers of hate at me.

"I'll even confess that you're not my favorite person, but I suspect that's not what you're looking for either."

"Aren't you perceptive?"

"Not perceptive enough." I should have been on the lookout for human threats, not just supernatural ones. I should have been investigating the detective who had an irrational hate for me, but it was too late for regrets. I had to deal with the here and now. I was dying to ask him about his brother, but I had to time it to my advantage. He'd dropped that little fun fact to let me stew on it, and if I jumped right to it, I'd be playing into his hands. Better to let him bring it up first.

Wearing an evil smile, he grabbed one of the bars. "Rumor has it demons are loose in the city." He paused. "If you believe in such a thing. But then, you do believe in demons, don't you?"

My breath stuck in my chest. I had so many questions but couldn't ask a single one. Detective Lawton wouldn't bother to answer. He'd only torment me more.

"It doesn't matter what I believe," I said. "I suppose it's a matter of whether you're afraid of the boogeyman. Are you willing to risk *not* believing?"

He waggled his eyebrows. "Who says I don't believe?"

The blood rushed from my head as I realized I'd just been majorly played.

"Perhaps I *do* believe," he said, giving me a smug look. "Perhaps the demons are coming for you now."

I stared at him in horror as he took a step backward, shoving his left hand into his pocket. "Then again, maybe I don't and I just made it all up. But what are you going to do?" he asked with a shrug and a chuckle. "The only thing *you* can do is sit there like a good little girl and wait."

"What did you think I was doing in the Cordens' basement?" I asked, needing more information from him, even though I doubted he'd spill anything.

He looked amused by my question. "Aren't I the one who should be asking *you* what you were doing down there?"

"Humor me," I said, holding my arms out to my sides. "I'm bored. Why do you think I was in the basement?"

He moved back to the bars, leaning his shoulder against them. "A number of things come to mind. The public story is that you were vandalizing a family friend's wine cellar."

"And why would I have done that?" I asked. "What motive?"

"Perhaps you were upset at his bitter betrayal."

The blood rushed to my feet as I stared at him in disbelief. "What betrayal?"

"I think it's safe to say that arranging to have your best friend killed so a demon could assume his form would be considered a betrayal."

My mouth dropped open.

"Then there's the whole pretending to be your grandparents' best friends to stay close to you, plus his possible involvement with your parents' murders. Those would both be considered betrayals as well." He chuckled. "Even so, call me crazy, but I don't think you were down there to throw a tantrum with their wine."

What the hell was happening?

"What? No quippy comebacks? That's a shock." Shoving his hands into his pants pockets, he cocked his head. "So, if you weren't down there to destroy some perfectly innocent wine, why *were* you down there?" He pursed his lips and shrugged. "You could have been looking for the spear."

"Excuse me?" I asked, sure I was hallucinating.

He pulled his hands from his pockets and held my gaze. "But that's where we run into a problem. The spear was already gone, but you were still there."

He knew about the spear. He knew about Robert Corden's deceptions and what he'd done. "You're a Guardian."

"I'm a guardian of the *law*," he joked, then turned serious. "You obviously didn't take the spear, but you know who did. You need to tell me what you know."

How had I never suspected his involvement before? But he'd been careful. He'd acted so contemptuous and doubtful, so eager to poke fun at my ghost whispering.

"I don't know what you're talking about," I said breathlessly.

His face twisted into an exaggerated expression of confusion. "That spear was there on Friday night, Piper, and when I found you this afternoon, it was gone."

He'd been there Friday night? Was he complicit in Hudson's murder?

"I didn't do anything with a spear," I said. "So if I wasn't there for revenge or for the spear, why was I there?"

He grinned, leaning closer. "To send Robert Corden's ghost to hell, of course." He gave a slight shrug. "Which is a type of revenge, wouldn't you say? Were you mixing business with pleasure?"

So he knew everything. I needed to get over my shock and deal with him. Detective Lawton was much more dangerous than I'd originally anticipated.

"If you think I'm innocent, then why am I in here?" I asked.

"Innocent?" he laughed. "I never said you were innocent. You were there when my brother was murdered. Hell, you were likely part of it."

"I've never murdered anyone," I protested.

"I bet those demons would disagree," he said.

He was probably right about that. "Why do you think I had a part in your brother's death?"

"I know you were at the bridge that night."

A cold wave of dread washed through me. The first night I'd fought—and killed—demons. The Guardians had set the battle up as

225

a test for me at Helen's Bridge, but it had gone very badly for them. I stared at Detective Lawton in stunned silence.

"Helen's Bridge?"

"Have you murdered people at other bridges?" he sneered.

"I'd bet money on that being a no," I heard Olivia say at the end of the hall.

Detective Lawton and I turned to her in surprise as she started walking toward us.

"Olivia," he said with contempt. "How much did you hear?"

"Enough." She'd changed out of her dress clothes into jeans and a long-sleeve T-shirt. If she had a gun, it was hidden—the only thing in her hands was a brown paper bag. "Enough to know you're going to let her go."

An evil grin spread across his face. "Not a chance. I've made a deal, and I plan to collect."

"A deal with who?" she asked, stopping next to him.

His grin spread and my heart sunk.

"Ten bucks it wasn't with the DA," I said. "He made a literal deal with a demon," I sighed with overwhelming exhaustion. "When will you people learn that it doesn't work that way?"

"You think you can keep them all to yourself?" he asked.

I released a short laugh. "Detective Lawton, you're deluded if you think you can control a demon."

"It's all about knowing what's within your limits. *You* control them."

"Then you're even more deluded than I thought. Who do you think killed Robert and his cohorts last night? Who do you think killed your brother?"

Hate filled his eyes. "Demons. On your orders."

I laughed again. "The demons killed the Guardians at the bridge because demons like to kill people. I couldn't have stopped them if I'd tried." No need to tell him that Abel had encouraged the attack. "And as for the Guardians at the warehouse last night... Robert pressed his luck. Higher-level demons don't like humans who think they're even close to being their equal. The Great One had the leonals attack and kill them."

Detective Lawton's confidence seemed to slip a notch.

"Who did you make a deal with?" I asked. Then the answer came to me. "Adonis? Oh, you *are* a fool."

The detective gave me a defiant look.

"What did he promise you?" I asked. "Money? Power?"

"Adonis? As in the Greek god?" Olivia asked, her eyes wide with shock.

"When's he coming?" I asked. Adonis had to know that Okeus was sending an army for me. There was no way he'd cut it too close.

"Soon," Lawton said.

I turned to Olivia. "You need to go. *Now.* You can't be anywhere around when he shows up."

"Why?" she asked with fear in her eyes.

"Because he wants something from me that I have no intention of giving him, and he's bound to throw a fit."

"I'm not leaving you here," she said, grabbing the bars.

"She's not going *anywhere*," Detective Lawton said to Olivia. "The DA agreed that we need to hold her while we collect enough evidence to formally charge her with six counts of murder."

"She'll never last that long."

He grinned. "Exactly. So no need for you to stick around."

"Olivia," I said, placing my hand over hers. "You have to go."

Her eyes went wide and she glanced down at the brown bag in her hand, which looked heavier than before, almost like it was straining to carry something beyond its capacity.

Lawton seemed to notice the bag for the first time. "Did you bring your lunch?"

"It's for Piper," she said, then shoved it between the bars before he could stop her.

I took it from her, surprised when I opened it and saw the hand I'd cut off the fire demon last week in the garage he'd immolated. I glanced up at her in astonishment.

"I don't know if you can do anything with it," she said. "I was desperate."

So much had happened since she'd taken the hand from the crime scene, an unnecessary cover-up given that most demons were invisible to the human eye. It wasn't like an investigating cop would have stumbled upon the amputated appendage.

I really didn't want to touch a demon hand—although holding a detached one was far better than holding a live one—and I wasn't sure what purpose it could possibly serve, but I pulled it out anyway.

Detective Lawton jumped back several feet, his face drawn in horror. "What the fuck is *that*?"

He could see it? Why? Because of my own increasing power or some other reason?

"This?" I said coyly as I held it out on my upturned palm. "This is the hand of a demon who thought he could control me." I tilted my head slightly, narrowing my eyes. "I don't know what kind of game you think you're playing with Adonis, but I promise you that you are in over your head. Now let me out of here and I'll do my best to protect you."

He stared at the demon hand in terror before lifting his gaze to mine. For one brief moment, I thought he was going to agree, but then a sick grin spread across his face. "I think I'd rather wait for my reward," he said as he checked his watch. "In fact, he'll be here soon, so I need to prepare." He turned to walk away, then stopped next to Olivia. "I suggest you don't try anything stupid. Demons don't like to be crossed, and I assure you that you don't have time to get her out."

Having pronounced my doom, he walked down the hall, whistling a happy tune.

Darkness burst to life in my soul, making my body glow. The demon hand began to wiggle, and a tiny blue flame hovered above the palm.

"Oh my God," Olivia gasped, stepping back from the bars.

But I paid her little attention, instead focusing on the asshole down the hall. The blue flame enlarged and jumped from my hand, shooting through the bars and flying toward the detective, hitting him in the back and making his entire body instantly burst into flames.

His screams bounced off the concrete walls.

I dropped the demon hand in horror, and Olivia watched Detective Lawton for a couple of horrified seconds before she came to her senses and started to run for him.

"Olivia! Don't touch him!"

She stopped and turned to me with wide eyes.

"It's demon fire. If you touch it, it will kill you."

She took several steps toward me, approaching me as though I were a dangerous wild animal.

It would be a fair assessment.

"How do you know that?" she asked. "Did Jack tell you?"

I gave myself a slight shake, feeling like I was in a dream, not quite here. "No. The demon told me."

"What demon?" she asked, looking a little more reassured that I wouldn't hurt her.

"The hand," I said, wrapping my arms across my chest as I stumbled backward and sat on the cot.

"Piper, are you okay?"

"I killed him," I said, looking up at her in shock. "I didn't mean to do it. The demon hand…"

"Don't touch it, okay?" she said, sounding like she was negotiating a hostage crisis, only I was both the hostage *and* the captor. "I'm going to get Jack. He'll know what to do."

Tears welled in my eyes. "I killed him."

"Piper!" she shouted. "Listen to me. Don't do anything else…Oh, shit. The cameras…"

She glanced up at it, and I just reacted, on instinct and pure adrenaline, jumping up from the cot and snatching the hand up from the floor. I sought out the camera and shot a flame toward it, sending electrical sparks flying throughout the cell, and the darkness inside the hand immediately took hold of me.

Olivia released a shriek, but I turned to face her, feeling the demon's anger and purpose coursing through my veins. *Destroy the humans and make them our slaves. Take the slayer to the Great One.* But I was the slayer and the Great One was destroyed and the demon in me was confused.

Once again, I threw the hand to the floor, at once repulsed and vibrating with an unnatural fury.

"I'm going to get Jack," she said, then turned to look at Detective Lawton's now-smoldering body. "Why hasn't anyone come in yet?" she asked, sounding equally relieved and worried.

I could feel the demon's anger and purpose fading to nothing.

"Olivia," I said through clenched teeth as I began to violently shake.

She glanced over her shoulder at me.

"Tell Jack that I was momentarily possessed by the demon's power and purpose. But it faded soon after I dropped the hand. Maybe we can use it to our advantage tonight."

"You can't be serious! You want to use a demon's power?"

I got to my feet and walked to the bars. "At any time now, an army of demons is bursting out of hell with the sole purpose of tracking down me, Abel, the curse keepers, and likely Jack, to either kill us or drag us to hell to torture for eternity. We might have a supernatural army to help us, but I have no idea how many demons are coming nor how many supernatural creatures will help. The demons will be hungry. The entire city of Asheville is in danger, and we are the only ones to stop them." My shoulders tensed. "I've never been more serious. I will do anything and everything I can to stop them."

The fear in her eyes made me question whether I should have been so blunt, but she had to understand the stakes.

"I'll find Jack," she said in an expressionless tone. "But I have no idea how we're going to explain *him*." She gestured to the still-burning body beside her.

"I'll take care of that," I said with a shocking amount of confidence. "Call Jack, then get out of Asheville. I'm serious, Olivia."

She shook her head. "You must not know me very well if you think I could just leave. I've sworn to protect the citizens of Asheville, and that's what I intend to do." Then she turned around and left.

As soon as the door clicked behind her, the horror of what I'd just done hit me full force. There was no denying or sugarcoating it now—I'd killed a man. I could claim that it wasn't my fault, that I'd been temporarily possessed by the demon, but I hadn't tried to stop it. The ugly truth was that I'd wanted to kill him. I doubted it would have happened otherwise.

Evil was brewing in my soul. Was it because I'd slept with Abel, or had the danger and violence drawn something that had been there all along out of hibernation? But I didn't have time to examine my conscience or my soul. I had to get out of here before Adonis showed up. I had to find the others. I had to protect my friends.

I had to get to Abel. He'd know what to do. He'd help me fix this.

But then I realized I hadn't heard Abel's voice since I'd been locked up in the holding cell. I knew he still had the ring, and if ever there were a situation to use it without permission, this was one. He must have tried to communicate with me since I'd been tossed in here.

So what did *that* mean?

It meant I was on my own.

But then a shimmer appeared outside of my cell, and Hudson came into sight, frowning at the still-smoldering body.

"Hudson," I cried out, rushing to the bars and wrapping my hands around them. "I don't know what to do."

"You have to get out of here, of course," he said, turning back to me with a reassuring smile, only something about him looked different. "Use the demon hand to open the lock."

My mouth dropped open. "I can do that?"

"You can do anything. You're Piper Fucking Lancaster." While it was supposed to be a confidence-boosting speech, something about his tone made me uncomfortable.

He pointed to the demon hand that lay in the middle of the cell. "Pick it up."

I shook my head. Something was off about him, and despite my perky speech about the possibility of using demon power to our advantage, I was having serious second thoughts now that the power rush was fading. "Huddy, that hand is evil. I think *I'm* turning evil."

"No, Piper. You're fighting to survive. The world is counting on you. You are Kewasa to all."

"But I killed him, Hudson. I killed the detective using power from the demon's hand."

"You harnessed a demon's power? Do you have any idea what you can do with that? This is great news!"

"How can you say that? It's *horrible*."

"You did what you had to do, Piper," he said again as though I'd confessed to swatting a fly.

I took a step back as I remembered Ellie's warning about Okeus, how he'd created something that had resembled her father but wasn't really him. "What did you give me for my thirteenth birthday?"

He blinked in confusion. "What are you talking about? Why would you bring that up now?"

Fear washed through me like thick sludge. "Hudson. Answer the question."

"That was a long time ago," he said.

"No. We were just talking about it a few weeks ago when we were discussing my birthday."

He stared at me for several seconds, and then his body morphed into that of another young man, the one I'd seen during the creation of the world, a young Ahone.

"Well, it was worth a try," he said, brushing his hands together as if trying to rid himself of Hudson's cooties.

"Why?" I asked, fighting back tears. Had I seen the real Hudson this morning or Ahone masquerading as my best friend? But this one felt different. His face looked almost plastic-like, and when I looked closely, his hair looked like a wig.

"Why did I do any of this?" he asked, moving closer. "To best my brother."

"I still don't understand."

"That's okay," he said with a patient smile. "You don't need to, but here's what you *do* need to know. You have a choice—be enslaved by Okeus or pledge your fealty to me."

When I started to tell him to go to hell, he held up a hand to cut me off. "No, I don't want your answer now. It's not time, but if you pledge fealty to me, rest assured I will save all who you hold dear."

I held out my left hand. "Can you stop the mark from appearing on my hand?"

He grimaced and hesitated. "I suspect that alone would get you to drop to your knees and worship me, but I won't lie to you, not in this. I cannot stop it. Nothing can."

"I don't believe it," I said.

A slow grin tipped up one side of his mouth. "Which part?"

"Any of it. You created the mark. You can stop it."

"The origin mark belongs to fate, creator of worlds. Some things are out of even my control."

Then he smiled again, then faded to nothing.

CHAPTER
TWENTY-ONE

Jack

The sun had sunk, setting his nerves on edge, but Jack parked his car on the side road south of the bridge. When he'd come here before with Piper to free Rhys from the Guardians, they'd parked further away, but there was no need for stealth tonight. The demons would be here soon enough.

"Helen," he called out as he approached the bridge, hoping the ward the seer had created to help him see all things supernatural wouldn't fail him.

Helen's long, sorrowful wail would have ordinarily filled him with fear and empathy, but tonight it filled him with hope.

"Helen," he said softly. "It's Jack. Remember me?"

She appeared to him then, swinging from the bridge by a rope around her neck, her white nightgown billowing around her. Tonight her face was grotesque in its death mask—her face a bluish-gray with bulging eyes, her swollen tongue sticking out of the side of her mouth. He didn't see her as solidly as when he touched Piper, but she was real enough.

"Helen," he said again. "I think I can help you."

Her swaying stopped and the gentle breeze abruptly dropped off. "Why do you think I need help?"

"Aren't you looking for Margaret?"

The haunting of Helen's Bridge at the top of Beaucatcher Mountain was famous in Asheville, and people often climbed to the top of the hill at night to try to get a reaction out of Helen. To all those people, she was a sideshow freak, but to Jack, she was a suffering soul who longed to be reunited with her long-dead three-year-old daughter. The poor girl had been burned to death in a fire, likely set by the wife of her employer and lover. While the fire might have occurred over a century ago, to Helen it was still just as fresh as though it had happened yesterday.

Helen's ghost disappeared from the bridge, and he felt his hair stand on end with a current of electricity stronger than what he'd previously felt in her presence. He was either more sensitive to her energy or she'd gotten a power boost, and as far as Jack knew, the only possible power source for a ghost was a demon.

"Why do you think you can help me, priest?" she sneered in the air around him, still invisible.

"I've been researching, Helen. I think I can help you find Margaret."

"She's not waiting for me in the light," she said with venom-laced words. "Her soul was cursed."

"I know," Jack said softly. "A seer told me."

She reappeared then, only this time she wasn't hanging from the bridge. Rather, she stood in front of him in a simple turn-of-the-twentieth-century dress. "A seer?"

"The seer's grandmother was the one who cursed your daughter."

Rage filled Helen's eyes and she released a scream that shot through the night sky, shaking the leaves. He expected to see birds take flight, but he realized that all the birds were gone. The demons had scared the remaining wildlife away.

Helen's eyes glowed as she directed her anger toward him.

Jack held up his hand, his heart hammering in his chest. "Helen, I can help you. I think I can break the curse."

"Margaret is in hell," Helen wailed. "And my soul wasn't stained enough to go to her. You cannot help me."

"I think I can," Jack said, taking a short step closer, "but we have to do it soon. The demons are coming."

A soft smile lifted the corner of her lips. "I know."

His breath stuck in his throat, but he pushed out, "How do you know?"

Then it hit him. Her increased power. Her desire to go to hell.

"Helen," he said, blood pulsing in his ears. "You do *not* want to go to hell. Trust me. I've seen it. No one wants to willingly go there."

Tears filled her eyes. "My Kieran wants to go."

"And you don't want him to go either, do you?" Jack said. "So why would you want to go yourself?"

"Margaret."

"I know," Jack said, instinctively reaching for her. To his surprise, he felt the rough weave of her dress sleeve under his hand, something he wouldn't have thought possible without Piper. "But I found a way to break the curse and pull Margaret from hell. Then Piper can send you both to the light."

Her eyes darkened. *"Piper.* She wants to kill my Kieran."

"No." Jack shook his head. "She's doing everything in her power to save him. She's trying to stop the mark."

"She wants him for herself," Helen said, "but he loved me first."

A heartsick ghost. Jack hadn't seen that one coming. "Kieran cares about you."

"But not enough." Her haunting eyes pierced his. "Piper must die."

Fear raced through his blood. "Okeus won't like that," Jack said. "He wants Piper for himself and very much alive. He won't let you into hell if you kill her."

An evil grin lit up her face. "I never said I made a deal with the god of war."

Oh shit. Icy dread washed through him. "Ahone?"

"Kieran will be mine. Kieran and I can both go to hell, but first I must purchase my admission. I must kill the slayer."

"Helen," Jack said, trying to figure out how to reason with her, but her plight had clearly driven her mad. "I've seen hell twice. It was a horrible, horrible place. You do *not* want to go there. Let me bring Margaret."

She studied him for a moment, which he took as an encouraging sign.

"Think about Margaret. I'm sure she doesn't want to stay in hell. She wants to go to the light."

Tears filled her eyes. "My baby needs me."

"Then let's get her, okay?" Jack asked, feeling his confidence return. He'd been studying this for weeks. He hadn't planned to try it yet, but if the demons were coming, he wasn't sure Helen's tenuous grasp on sanity would survive. He had to do this now. "I have the things I need to draw Margaret out of hell, but we need to hurry."

An amused look filled her eyes. "You truly believe you can do this?"

Her change in demeanor caused him a moment of pause. "Yes. At least let me try."

She nodded her acquiescence, and he started to climb the north hill, into the woods. He knew it would be easier to walk around to the other side and cross over the stone carriage bridge, but he didn't trust Helen. She seemed less excited to save her daughter than he'd expected.

"Where are you going?" she asked.

"I have to call her to the gate."

Helen looked less sure now, but she walked with him, or more like floated.

"Can you show me where the gate is?" he asked once he knew they were close. "I know the general location, but Deidre says I have to be at the mouth, and I can't see it."

Helen eyed him curiously as though wary of a trick, but she led him to a small dip in the ground. He dropped to his knees and slipped off his backpack, pulling out the supplies Deidre had sold him. Jack had hoped to have Piper help him when he did this—he would pull Margaret out and Piper would send them both to the light—but this couldn't wait. He'd altered his hasty plan to ensure he could still protect Helen and her daughter. Now that he knew Ellie could cross into Piper's pocket universes, he hoped she'd be willing to bring Helen and her daughter up to the protection of the attic before they left to face the demon army.

He could only hope there was time.

Jack set out his supplies and laid sage sticks in a foot-by-foot square on the damp ground. Once that was complete, he used a piece of red yarn to make a circle inside the square. He set small votive candles in the corners of the square, then sprinkled holy water on everything, saying a prayer to St. Michael, the archangel etched on Piper's dagger, asking for his protection and assistance guiding the lost spirit from the depths of hell.

Helen watched in silence, and he was relieved that he'd convinced her to at least try this his way.

Lighting the candles and then the sage, Jack prayed to other angels to lend their guidance. Then, when he was sure he and Helen were as protected as possible, he began the chant Deidre had taught him last week, opening the mouth of hell just enough for him to call inside.

A small black hole appeared in the air, a swirling mass of death and chaos that coated his skin with hopelessness and despair. He prayed to his guardian angel to boost his faith as he then called out, "Margaret, your mother waits for you."

A small girl's cry grew louder and closer. Helen dropped to her knees across from Jack, shouting, "Margaret, Momma's here, baby. Come to Momma!"

Jack pulled some herbs from a pouch and sprinkled them around the square. "Using the power and the blessing of Deidre, from the Savannah line, I break the curse that binds you to hell and call you forth, Margaret. Come to your mother."

A small girl's face appeared, golden corkscrew ringlets surrounding her face, but worms crawled from her empty eye sockets and her mouth was lopsided, as though it had been removed and put back on crooked.

"Momma," she said in an innocent voice, but a surge of power came with it, full of malice and hate.

Helen screamed, "That is not my daughter!"

Jack stared at the girl, wondering if he'd done something wrong, but then he reminded himself that the child had spent a century in hell. They could figure out how to fix her after they got her out.

"I need your help, Helen," he pleaded. "You have to be the one to pull her out."

"That is not my daughter!" she screamed, flinging her finger toward the horrifying face.

"She's been in hell, Helen," he said, trying to make her understand. "We'll save her and then ask Kieran how to fix her," he said, thinking on the fly.

Her face softened at the sound of Abel's name. "Kieran."

"That's right," he said as the girl made agonizing sounds. "Kieran cares about you. He'll want to help Margaret. To help *you*."

"Kieran never comes to see me anymore," she said, clutching her hands to her chest as tears welled in her eyes. "He loves her now."

"He still cares about you," Jack insisted. "I know it. Now, let's pull Margaret out and ask him what to do."

She cast a dark gaze at the girl, her brow lowering. "He said you would do anything to save her. You would go so far as to trick me."

"Margaret?" Jack asked. "It's not a trick, Helen. I swear to you that I want to save her. I'm a priest. Helping people is what I do." And in that hellish moment, all his agony about whether he'd made the wrong decision to join the priesthood washed away and new conviction flooded him. This was where he needed to be.

Her dark gaze turned to Jack as she calmly said, "Her. The slayer."

"Piper?"

"He said you were wily, that you would say and do anything to change my mind."

A knife appeared in her hand. A small kitchen knife she'd likely used in her duties when she'd worked in Zealandia Castle, but Jack hadn't expected it, and he hadn't prepared himself for her swift blow to his gut. He felt the air rush out of his lungs as she withdrew the blade. Blood seeped through his shirt.

"He said I could earn my entrance with murder." She stabbed him again, and he was too shocked to block her, but after several more swift blows, he came to his senses.

Getting to his feet was out of the question, so he turned to crawl, but she resorted to stabbing him in the back, screaming at him to die. He made it around a tree, then fell to his stomach, pain screaming through his body. His consciousness began to fade, and he realized once again that his arrogance had been his downfall.

Only this time it would be fatal.

CHAPTER TWENTY-TWO

Ellie

The sun had set. Abel was gone. Collin was gone. Jack was gone. Nevertheless, allies or no allies, I intended to stop the demons. "David, I'm going to put you and Rhys in the attic with Tommy."

One of Abel's safe houses would have been more ideal, but we were out of time to get them there, and without Abel, we'd have no idea how to find either of his homes anyway. And while the ghost had creeped me out, compared to a horde of demons, he seemed the lesser evil. The attic would have to do.

"I'm not hiding, Ellie," David said in his calm, reassuring voice.

"You can't come with me," I said.

He reached an arm around my back and pulled me close. "Then you need to hide in the attic with me."

"I can't do that!" I tried to jerk free, but his arm tightened.

"Why not?" he asked, still sounding reasonable, as though we were discussing which movie to watch on Netflix.

Because," I said, stalling, and then stammered out, "you have to protect Rhys. Just in case. She's defenseless in all this."

"Ellie. If Piper's created world isn't enough to protect Rhys from the horde of demons, what difference could I possibly make for her if the horde finds its way in?"

"No," I cried. "No." There had to be a way to keep him safe.

"Ellie—"

"It's my job, not yours," I said through tears, still trying to push him away from me, but his arm was like a vise, holding me in place.

"And what's *my* job, Ellie?" he whispered as he stared into my eyes. When I didn't answer, he said, "My job is to help you. In all things. He who guides the keeper."

"There won't be any guiding on that hill, David," I said bitterly. "There will only be death."

"Do you really think you can defeat them alone?" he asked, still sounding irritatingly reasonable.

My chest heaved with several breaths before I said, "No."

"Yet you still plan to go."

"I have to," I said, freely crying now. "It's my job."

"But if it weren't your job, would you go?" he asked with a soft smile.

"That's not fair!"

"The answer is yes. You would go, because people will die if you don't, and not even the prospect of near-certain death will hold you back. You will always choose to save people, Ellie, and I love you all the more because of it."

"David," I said, collapsing into his chest.

He held me close, his voice in my ear. "I love you so much, Elinor Dare Lancaster. You have been my greatest gift."

I started to sob, clinging to his shirt.

"I could no more walk away from you than I could will myself to stop breathing. I will stand with you until I can no longer stand." He grabbed my cheeks between his hands and lifted my face until he held my gaze. "I've always known our time was short. I'm willing to accept that."

"But I'm not!" I protested hotly. Then my anger faded and I whispered, "I'm not."

"It's not our choice."

I jerked away from him then. "Fuck fate."

A grin tipped up his mouth. "Easy to say, love, but harder to execute."

"So you do the opposite," Rhys said, sounding embarrassed. "I'm sorry to intrude on such an intimate moment, but I'm part of this too."

"I'll put you in the attic," I said, turning my back on her as I wiped my tears away. How had I forgotten she was watching? No doubt my freak-out wasn't exactly confidence-building. "You'll be safe there."

"No offense," Rhys said, "but if you and Piper get yourselves killed, I'll be trapped there for eternity with the creepy ghost kid. I'd rather take my chances out here."

I turned back to stare at her, realizing she had a point.

"So how do we fuck fate?" David asked, sounding intrigued.

"I don't know," Rhys said. "But I don't intend to get caught up in some demon's or god's plans again. Look, I don't know much about demons and gods, but I *do* know Roman history and it's chock-full of impossible battles that the Romans won because they were fearless, even when they were massively outnumbered."

"Like us," I said.

"Don't forget that Collin is getting his own army," Rhys said. "From what David told me, they're supernatural beings caught between the two gods and they've been treated like crap for eons. They're probably fighting because they don't want to take their shit anymore. Like the Russian peasants and the Bolsheviks."

"That's presuming Abel breaks Piper out of the police station," I reminded her.

"Please…" She rolled her eyes. "The guy's got it bad for her. He'll knock the building down to get her out."

"Okay," I said, giving her my full attention. "So presuming Abel gets her out and Tsawasi shows up with his army, what do you think we should do?"

"You obviously need some kind of battle plan. If you find out where the demons are coming from, you could create a funnel to keep them contained, like Gaius Suetonius Paulinus did when the rebel Britons he'd just conquered tried to overtake his small army. The super strategic Romans waited for the advancing horde of Britons in a narrow passage, where the Britons would no doubt charge in like wild animals and get choked into a narrow line, unable to attack any way but forward, basically eliminating their numbers advantage. The Britons were totally trapped in this funnel 'cause they got blocked in by their own wagon trains. So...it's not just about having the numbers..."

"The three of us won't be able to create much of a funnel," I protested. "Collin left, which means we can't count on the army showing up either."

"He didn't leave you permanently," David said. "He couldn't leave you if he tried. Just like you can't leave him."

"David," I said in protest.

He ignored me. "He'll be there when the demons emerge, taking a stand with you. Just like I will."

"And me," Rhys said. "I'm scared shitless, but I have to do something. So call him."

My phone started to ring, and I wasn't surprised to see Collin's name on the screen.

"Tsawasi says the demons won't be emerging from Helen's Bridge," Collin said, sounding breathless. "They're coming out of a crypt in Riverside Cemetery."

"*What?*"

"Nothing's happened yet, but you might want to get over here." He paused. "Have you heard anything from Abel or Jack?"

"No," I said, "I'll call them as we head over."

"We?"

"David and Rhys insist on coming too."

He hesitated, then said, "Okay. See you soon."

I filled David and Rhys in on the short conversation, and we headed downstairs to get the bag of weapons. Rhys pulled out two swords she thought she could handle, and David rigged up a belt with scabbards for her. As she looked down at her weapons, she said, "For the record, I'm ordinarily a pacifist."

I grinned at her. "Me too."

"Huh," she said, studying me for a moment. "I never would have guessed."

I liked this girl. "When this is all over, you, me, and Piper should really go for a spa day."

She beamed. "I'd like that."

"If you girls are done bonding," David said good-naturedly, "then maybe we should head out."

David had a point, but my life had been nothing but demons and heartache for the past few months. It felt good to have a normal moment for once, however fleeting.

I picked my bag up off the table, ready to leave Piper's house with everything in case we couldn't come back, when we heard a knock at the front door. All three of us froze.

"It can't be anything bad," Rhys said. "The boogeyman wouldn't just knock on the front door, right?"

I snorted. "You'd be surprised."

She crept to the living room and peeked through the curtains covering the living room windows. "It's Detective Powell."

"The police?" I asked in dread.

"Yeah, but she's Jack's friend." Rhys moved to the door. "She's his contact at the police station." She flung the door open before I could stop her. "Olivia, is everything okay with Piper?"

"She's still in a holding cell, if that's what you're asking." She made a face, then rubbed a hand across her forehead. "Is Jack here by any chance? I *really* need to talk to him."

Rhys shook her head. "No. I haven't seen him since this afternoon."

"I need to speak to him about something important." Her gaze lowered to the two swords strapped to Rhys's belt. "So it's true. There really is going to be a demon invasion."

"While I hope they're wrong," Rhys said, "it looks like it's going to happen."

Olivia hesitated. "Piper told me I need to get out of town, to save myself."

"You should follow her advice," I said in a curt tone. "Things are likely to get ugly."

She shook her head. "If the citizens of Asheville are in trouble, I'm not running from it. I want to help, but first I really need to talk to Jack. He won't answer his phone. Is that like him? Should we be worried?"

Rhys glanced back at me with concern. Turning back to Olivia, she said, "We think Jack went to Helen's Bridge, but he's been gone for a while. *I'm* officially worried."

Olivia's jaw set. "I'm going to go look for him."

Rhys gave me an apologetic frown. "Ellie, I need to go with her. I'm worried about him too."

"That's a good idea," David said. "Even if the demons emerge from the cemetery, some are likely to come out of the gate at the bridge. Find Jack, then we'll figure out whether you three should stay there or meet us somewhere."

Rhys's shoulders sagged with relief. "Thank you."

Olivia turned to leave, but I called after her, "You need a sword."

Olivia stopped and spun around with a skeptical expression. "I have a gun."

"Bullets won't kill them," I said. "You have to stab them in the heart with a sword that's been blessed to kill demons."

"Sometimes cutting off their heads works too," David added.

Olivia's brow shot up. "Blessed?"

"If you're a demon," David said, "I guess you could say cursed. But if you're going to be anywhere near them, you'll need a blessed sword to protect yourself."

Olivia seemed reluctant, but after she relented, Rhys showed her the weapons. Olivia selected a sword with a thinner blade, telling us she'd taken up fencing in college. Knowing both women were armed, I felt slightly better when they walked out the door.

"You don't think demons are going to emerge at the bridge, do you?" I asked once they left.

"One never knows," he said with a sad smile.

I walked over and gave him a kiss. "Thank you for trying to protect them."

"Other than Olivia's semester of fencing, they have absolutely no experience using a sword, let alone facing demons," David said. "I think it's safe to say I feel relieved knowing they are somewhere safer."

I couldn't help wishing I'd sent him with them.

CHAPTER TWENTY-THREE

Ellie

Collin had texted directions to the crypt they were staking out at the cemetery, but no army awaited us there. We only found Collin and Tsagasi standing in front of the mausoleum at the back of the graveyard. The opening was in a section of hill that looked like it had been carved away, with two stone walls that tapered to three-foot walls on either side. A narrow one-lane road curved in front of it, and the dilapidated wooden doors were accessible from it. David parked the car about twenty feet away.

"Trying to keep my car insurance premiums down by keeping it out of the fight," David teased, and I couldn't help cracking a smile.

When we got out, I glanced around, realizing I didn't see a car, not that Collin had one. He'd come to Asheville with us in David's car. "How'd you get here?"

Collin gave me a smart-ass grin. "Uber."

He could have easily been lying, but it wasn't worth pursuing.

"Where's Tsawasi?" David asked.

"And more importantly, where's his army?" I added

"He says he'll show up when Piper's fighting," Collin grumbled. He was sitting on a low stone wall, kicking his feet nonchalantly and looking anything but deadly, even holding his spear.

"Then let's hope Abel is successful," David said.

"Are you sure this is the back door to hell?" I asked Tsagasi. It was close to ten o'clock and my nerves were frayed.

"The night is young," he said in a snippy tone. "You must learn patience."

"We're standing in the middle of a cemetery," I countered. "I'm not impatient. I'm creeped out." Moreover, I was terrified, not that I was going to let on. I needed my false sense of confidence.

"Do you think the bastard is really going to get her out of there?" Collin asked after several moments of silence.

We all knew he was talking about Abel.

"If he thinks she's in danger, yeah. He will." I gave him a long look. "Wouldn't you do the same if it were me?"

"There *will* be danger," Tsagasi said. "I'm surprised he's waiting. Better to get her out now and prepare for battle."

"He's waiting because of her," Collin said in irritation. "He knows she'll be pissed if he just breaks her out, but she's too stubborn to admit that it needs to be done and not willing to deal with the carnage to make it happen. So instead he'll try to appease her by waiting until it's almost too late—or maybe even after it's too late—all because he wanted to make her happy."

I turned to him, propping my hand on my hip. "Why do I think you're really talking about me here?"

He lifted an eyebrow with a smirk. "If the shoe fits…"

"I'm open to a grown-up discussion, Collin," I retorted. "Why don't you try it sometime?"

"Quiet," Tsagasi barked, turning his attention to the rotting wooden double doors built into the hillside. The sides were held together by two newly added slabs of metal. Rusty wrought iron scrollwork topped the structure, and it now had a faint glow behind it.

"Collin," I said, reaching for the hilt of my sword.

"Yeah," he groaned as he slid off the wall, holding the spear in his left hand and drawing his sword with his right. "I see it."

I cast a worried glance at David. He had a sword of his own, but he had little training. Truth be told, out of all of us Piper was likely the most skilled after all the training Abel had put her through, but she was currently locked up in the Asheville jail, completely unprotected by anything other than the salt that Olivia had smuggled in to her, and whatever was about to emerge from that crypt was going to be looking for her. It would be looking for Abel too, but he could take care of himself.

The light behind the grate over the doors pulsed and brightened, and a loud moan echoed from behind the doors.

My heart kicked into overdrive as I pulled my sword from its sheath and took a defensive stance. Sure, I'd faced demons before, often, but never more than four at one time. I had no idea how many would come erupting from that tomb.

Collin fell in on my left, Tsagasi stood to his left, and David took our rear. The four of us against who knew how many demons.

"Keep them in the funnel," I said. "Try to keep the trapped between the sides of the hill and us. Just like Gaius Stutony Palley in England."

Collin shot me a look that suggested he questioned my sanity. "*What?*"

"Just try to keep them contained between the hill and us," David said. "Don't let them pass."

Collin glanced from David to me, then turned back to watch the doors.

Blinding light burst from the grate and through the cracks of the door, along with several deafening, piercing screams.

"Okeus isn't taking any chances," Tsagasi said. "He's sent the Botageria."

"What are those?" I asked, even though I wasn't sure I wanted to know.

"They are equivalent to bounty hunters and they do not fail at their task."

"Like hellhounds," David said.

"Yes," Tsagasi said, "except they don't drag their targets to hell. They drag them straight to Okeus." He paused. "Although they usually do end up there. They have one purpose—find the target and return it. They let nothing get in their way."

I was about to ask him for tips on how to fight them when the doors slammed open and three hideous creatures raced out. They were six feet tall on their haunches and several hundred pounds each. Their back legs were short and squat compared to their longer front legs, suggesting they could leap like giant frogs. Their heads were doglike, with massive jaws that could easily crush small animals or a person's arms or legs...or head. Short, shiny black fur covered their bodies.

The doglike things stopped several feet from the door, their massive heads swiveling from one side to the other—sniffing the air.

"They are smelling for her," Tsagasi murmured.

I was prepared to fight them, but also prepared to send them back to hell using the power in the mark on my hand. If Collin would agree to combine his power with mine, we could recite a chant that would destroy them completely—which was how we'd earned our 'destroyer of life' titles—but he'd only agreed to it once. Apparently, even Collin had an ethical line in the sand.

Maybe he'd change his mind for this one.

I held out my right palm. "Collin...?"

His jaw was set, and a determined look filled his eyes. "We don't have enough time."

At the sound of our voices, the demons lowered their heads and focused their attention on us, their eyes glowing with a golden light.

"But," he said in a low tone as he leaned forward, his arm bending slightly in preparation to attack. "If it looks like we can't handle them, I'll keep them busy while you send them away. We can't let them leave the cemetery."

I started to protest, but he was right. Sending them away with one mark would only be a temporary fix, but better that than the alternative. "Okay."

Collin took a breath as though preparing to run toward the dog things, but before he could launch off, several more demons emerged from the still-glowing crypt. These were even squattier—about three feet tall and maybe two feet wide—but they stood upright. They had short arms and legs and looked ridiculous, until one of them opened its mouth, revealing multiple rows of shiny teeth. I counted seven in total.

"And what are those?" I asked Tsagasi.

"Those are the Botageria's foot soldiers."

Great. "Anything important we should know about them?"

"They love to destroy for the sake of it."

Even better.

"We need Tsawasi," Collin groaned. "He may not be ready to bring his army, but we'll make him come anyway." Turning to me, he said, "You need to call in a favor. Make Tsawasi come to us and bring the Nunnehi warriors. We *cannot* let them have her."

"Piper?" That caught me by surprise. While Collin wasn't a monster, he seemed surprisingly protective of Piper. "What do you know that I don't? What was in that drawing, Collin?"

He shot me a dark glare. "For fuck's sake, Ellie. *Call them.*"

Releasing a growl of frustration, I said, "Nunnehi and Tsawasi, I need your help."

The two Nunnehi warriors and Tsawasi, armed and ready to fight, appeared in the blink of an eye.

"Would they have come to our defense without using one of my favors?" I asked Tsagasi.

He shrugged and gave me a smug glance.

Yes. "Dammit, Tsagasi," I said. "I thought we wanted the same thing."

"We do, Curse Keeper, but the Nunnehi and my brother hate the yoke you've chained them with. They are eager to shed it."

At the rate I was going through my favors, it would be a matter of days before they were free. Then what? But that was presuming we survived this attack, which wasn't looking as dire as I'd expected. They'd been spouting doom and gloom about an army. Ten demons wasn't ideal, but it was manageable.

I didn't have time to dwell on it—the Botageria's foot soldiers bolted toward us like dogs let loose on a hunt. They ran surprisingly fast given their short legs and wide bodies, and they reached us in a matter of seconds. When they were close enough to tackle us, they leapt into the air, claws extracted on both sets of limbs, and aimed for our abdomens. I begrudgingly admitted it was an effective means of attack—eviscerate your opponent before the fight even begins.

Unfortunately for the demon attacking me, I was prepared. I thrust my sword through its belly, and the weight of its body pulled my sword to the ground. The damn thing was impaled.

With the heel of my boot, I stepped on the demon's lower abdomen and pulled out my sword. The demon flung itself upward, aiming for my leather-boot-covered lower leg with a wide-open mouth and gleaming teeth, and even though I was at an awkward angle, I managed to swing my sword in an arc and remove the demon's head. It fell to the ground, its body flopping but its eyes already glazed over. One down.

I glanced up and saw the rest of my group had already dealt with the remaining foot soldiers. This had been too easy. Then I realized the Botageria were bolting across the cemetery, knocking over century-old tombstones in their haste to get to downtown Asheville.

Where Piper was being held at the police station.

"Collin!"

He glanced up from the demon he'd just killed with his spear. "*Fuck.*"

The Nunnehi warriors were already in pursuit, sprinting after them at superhuman speed.

"Go after them!" Tsagasi shouted.

There was no way we could run that quickly. Collin must have been thinking the same thing because we both headed for the car at the same time.

"I know a way to get to the back of the cemetery faster," David shouted, keeping pace with us. "I studied the map in case of a situation like this."

Collin started the car and swung it around in a wide arc, narrowly missing a tombstone. Once he was headed in the right direction, he punched the gas pedal, throwing me back in the seat. He took the sharp curves at speeds that threw me around the front, making me wish I'd belted up, but I could see the Nunnehi warriors up ahead, plus the three demons trying to evade them.

Collin skidded to a halt and we jumped out, withdrawing our swords as we advanced on them, Collin holding up his spear at his side.

"We should use our power," I said, the mark on my hand burning. There was no doubt that they were powerful. "I'm not sure we can fight them."

"We can't contain them long enough," Collin said. "If we try, we might send the Nunnehi back by mistake. We need the Nunnehi too much to risk it. Besides, the Botageria aren't interested in us—or them. They'll take off running toward Piper the first chance they get."

"We need to go to the police station," David said. "Now."

"He's right," Collin said, turning and running for the car.

"I thought we weren't letting them leave the cemetery!" I shouted after him and tossed a quick look at the fight in front of me.

The Nunnehi and the Nunnehi Little People were fighting all three demons, but it was obvious the demons weren't interested in killing the supernatural beings for the sake of it. They were only engaging because the Nunnehi warriors were in their way. Once they slipped past, there would be no stopping them.

David was right. Our best chance of helping Piper was to make a stand outside the police station.

When I jumped into the car, it was already moving toward the cemetery exit, Collin at the wheel. I grabbed my phone and called Abel.

"They're loose and about to head your way," I said, trying to look at the fighting through the back window.

"Did he send the Botageria?" he asked in a solemn tone.

"Yes."

"And the foot soldiers?"

"We killed them."

"There will be more." He sounded so sure, a rock formed in the pit of my stomach.

He was right. We'd been promised an army, and this was far from it. "Collin, David, and I are headed toward you. Jack's at Helen's Bridge."

"Why is he there?"

"I have no idea, and it's a long story, so I'll fill you in later. Are you still at the police station?"

"Yes. Send the priest here."

"I'll message him. We're coming too."

"But not soon enough," he said in a flat tone.

"Are you going to break her out?"

"I should have done it hours ago. I will not let my father have her."

I considered his options—*our* options. We would be Piper's last line of defense at the police station, which didn't look that promising since the Nunnehi warriors could barely hold the Botageria back. "Just focus on getting her out. We'll hold the demons off as best we can."

"Thank you." I was surprised they weren't empty words.

255

"Where will you take her? To a world?"

"I'll try to get her out of the cell first. If Okeus and the demons know what she can do, they'll wait there until we return, and we won't have the element of surprise we had in the warehouse. We'll be captured." He paused. "But she'll insist on fighting. Running from things is not her way."

"We're a lot alike."

"That's what worries me," he said. "If we do get captured or disappear and you need a safe place to go, I'll leave directions to my mountain house in my SUV." Then he hung up.

CHAPTER TWENTY-FOUR

Rhys

He's still here," Rhys said as Olivia parked her car behind Jack's. "So why won't he answer his phone?"

"That's what we're about to find out," Olivia said with a confidence Rhys wished she felt.

After being kidnapped twice, every little noise set Rhys on edge, and the fact that they were approaching a gate to hell? She was beyond jumpy.

"You can stay in the car," Olivia said reassuringly. "You don't have to come."

"Are you kidding me?" Rhys said. "I've seen enough horror movies to know the person who stays back gets it first." She shook her head. "I'm not getting skewered in the car. We stick together."

Olivia looked like she was fighting a grin. "Okay. We'll go together."

They got out and walked up the road toward the bridge in silence, leaving our weapons behind. Olivia said if someone saw us carrying swords they'd likely call the police.

"Is there really a ghost up here?" the detective asked.

"I've never seen her, but Piper and Jack swear she's real."

"And Jack came up here to see the ghost?"

"Yeah, I think so," Rhys said.

"Do you know why?" Olivia asked.

"No, but we went to a seer today and she mentioned Jack had come to see her. It would be just like him to go out of his way to help Helen. Plus the demons feed off Helen when they emerge and there's no wildlife left to feed on. It's totally a Jack thing to want to help her before the demons emerge."

Do you really think some of the demons will come out here?" Olivia asked. "Like your friend said?"

"Honestly, I don't know. Before I left, Ellie was trying to get me to agree to go into hiding, so I'm guessing it's unlikely. I suspect the only reason she and David readily agreed to me coming here is because they thought there wouldn't be anything to fight here."

"Is it wrong that I'm more than a little relieved by that?" she asked with a laugh.

"No," Rhys said. "This way I feel like I'm doing my part but not in the thick of the action."

They stopped in the middle of the road in front of the bridge.

"So where is he?" Olivia asked.

"Jack?" Rhys called out in a half-shout. Their voices carried in the quiet of the night.

They waited for a few seconds before Olivia asked, "Will the ghost bother us?"

"I don't think so," Rhys said with more bravado than she felt. "Helen's harmless. The worst thing she does is make it so cars can't start."

They exchanged a look.

Rhys gave Olivia a reassuring smile. "But Piper says that Helen loves Jack, so he can probably persuade her to leave your car alone."

Olivia scanned the hills surrounding the sides of the road.

"Jack!" she called out louder than Rhys had.

Nothing.

"I think we should check the woods," Olivia said.

Rhys was terrified of going into the woods—anything could be hiding in those trees—but it was obvious Jack wasn't on the road. "Yeah, good idea."

They stayed on the south side and headed up the dirt path to the bridge. The gate to the bridge stood open. The owner tried to keep it locked, but the bridge was too big of a draw to paranormal enthusiasts. Especially since the Lost Colony of Roanoke had reemerged several months ago. Trespassing was an inevitability.

Voices rose up from below, and Rhys looked down at a group of teenagers walking on the road beneath them, slightly less than a dozen by her guess. They giggled as they staggered toward the bridge, some of them loudly shushing the others.

"You'll scare her," one of the girls said.

"Yeah, right," a guy said, his words slurring.

Olivia scowled. "They're drunk."

Rhys shrugged. "It's not all that uncommon."

Olivia looked torn between going down to question them and walking over the bridge to the other side. The need to find Jack must have won out because she started over the low-walled bridge, crouching in an obvious attempt to avoid detection by the group below. Rhys followed, but halfway across, a boy shouted, "Look! There's the ghost up there!"

"That's not a ghost," another guy said with a laugh.

"No," Olivia called down as she rose to her full height. "It's a detective with the Asheville Police Department."

"We didn't do nothing!" one of the boys called up, lifting his hands in surrender.

"Looks like you've been drinking to me," Olivia said in disgust. "Lucky for me, I've got something more important to deal with. Are any of you designated drivers?"

When no one responded, she released a loud sigh. "I'll let you go, but you're not allowed to drive. Call a friend or relative who is sober to come pick you up or start walking."

The teens grumbled, but a couple girls and a guy shouted up, "Thank you!"

Olivia nodded with a grim look. "Stupid kids."

"It's not like we wouldn't have done something like that as kids," Rhys said, forcing a chuckle.

"Not me," Olivia said.

"Then when this is all said and done, we need to have a girls' night out and loosen you up, Detective Powell," Rhys teased.

"That's assuming we survive the demon apocalypse," Olivia said dryly.

"I chose to be positive," Rhys said, despite her shaky nerves.

"After the things I've seen the last few days…" She let the statement trail off as they reached the other side of the bridge.

When Olivia pulled out her phone and used the flashlight to sweep the area with light, Rhys did the same. Nothing.

"Do you think he's up here?" Rhys asked. She was scared he was and scared he wasn't.

"I don't know," Olivia said. "But I'm worried that his car is here and he's not. I could call the station and see if someone picked him up thinking he was a burglar, but I doubt they'd haul in an Episcopalian priest. They'd likely just tell him to go home."

"Unless they saw him carrying a sword," Rhys said.

Olivia cursed under her breath, then switched off her flashlight and started to place a call as Rhys wandered deeper into the woods, still sweeping the area with her flashlight.

"Jack!" she whisper-shouted, then gasped when she saw a backpack on the ground. "*Olivia.*"

Olivia headed toward the backpack, Rhys on her heels. An assortment of items were clustered together on the ground a couple of feet away.

"Rhys, what is this?" the detective asked, pointing to the yarn circle within the smoldering square and the still-lit votive candles.

A cold chill ran down Rhys's back. "I don't know, but Piper and the curse keepers have that mark on their hands. It represents the intersection of the spiritual and physical realms."

"Do you think Jack put it here?"

"I don't know. Maybe."

Olivia made a sweep of her flashlight, then squatted next to the backpack. She raked her fingers across the ground, and when she lifted them back up, they glistened red.

"Oh my God," Rhys cried out. "Is that *Jack's?*"

Olivia stood upright and put her phone back in her pocket as she pulled out her gun.

"A gun won't kill a demon, Olivia," Rhys reminded her, her heart leaping into her throat.

"We don't know that a demon did this," Olivia said, pointing her gun at the ground. "I just found out that Lawton was with the Guardians, so it could be anyone. Shine your flashlight on the ground in front of me."

"The detective that has it out for Piper is with the Guardians?" Rhys asked in shock.

"Was," Olivia said in a dull tone as she started to follow the dark spots on the ground. "He's dead."

"What? How?"

"Let's focus on finding Jack," Olivia said with a wavering voice. "We'll deal with the rest later."

They followed the trail, the drops becoming smears along the ground.

"There's so much blood," Rhys said, her voice breaking.

Olivia didn't answer.

"Oh my god." Rhys could see the sole of his shoe poking out from behind a thick stand of tree trunks. "That's his foot."

The women hurried around the tree and found him lying on his stomach, his head tilted to the side and his eyes closed. His shirt was drenched in blood.

"Is he…" Rhys couldn't finish.

Olivia squatted next to him and pressed her fingertips to his neck, scanning the trees before returning her gaze to him. "No. He's got a faint pulse. We need to call 911."

Rhys pulled out her cell phone and started to press buttons when Jack's eyes fluttered open.

"Helen," he whispered.

Rhys dropped to the ground beside him and started to cry. "Jack. What happened?"

"Helen."

Olivia's eyes widened. "The ghost?"

"I tried to help…" he forced out. "She…"

"What did she do, Jack?" Rhys asked.

"Piper… she plans to kill Piper."

Rhys lifted her horrified gaze to Olivia, who started sending a text, then stopped. "Who do we tell? Jack…"

Rhys handed her phone to Olivia. "Text Ellie and hand me your phone to call 911."

But the ground began to rumble before she made it past the nine.

"What the hell is that?" Olivia asked, her eyes wide again.

"Demons," Jack said. "They're coming."

"From *here?*" Rhys asked in a squeak.

"Oh shit." Olivia finished her text, then squatted next to Jack. "If an army of demons is coming, I don't think we want to wait for 911. We'll have to take Jack with us."

"What?" Rhys shouted. "We can't. He's…"

"Dying," Jack said. "Go. Leave me."

"No fucking way," Olivia said as she grabbed Jack's arm and started to wrap it around her shoulder. "Rhys. Help."

Jack cried out in pain and Rhys leaned back, terrified, but she knew Olivia was right. They couldn't leave him, and they couldn't wait. She had no idea if they'd get him help in time, but they had to try.

The front of his shirt was covered in blood, so Rhys slipped off her sweater and tried to hastily tie it around his abdomen to put pressure on his wounds.

"We don't have time," he said, barely audible. "Just go."

The rumbling in the ground deepened as it began to shake.

"Shit," Olivia said as they started to drag Jack toward the bridge. "We need to hurry."

The two women half-carried, half-dragged him to the bridge, and while it was the safest way out of the woods and to the cars, the old stone bridge was swaying, chunks of rock falling to the road below.

The teenagers were still there, sitting on the side of the road, laughing and screaming, "Earthquake!"

"Those stupid fools," Olivia muttered, then shouted, "Get the hell out of here!"

"Hey!" one of the girls called out in horror as she stared up at them. "He's bleeding!"

"Oh my God," another girl shouted. "What happened to him?"

"There's a serial killer loose in the woods," Rhys yelled down to them, drawing an irritated glare from Olivia. "Run!"

The teens started screaming and running for the hill.

"It seemed like the quickest way to get them to leave," Rhys said, trying to maintain her footing on the shaking bridge.

"Yeah, quick thinking," Olivia said grudgingly.

When they made it to the other side, Rhys looked Jack over. He wasn't a huge man, but he was tall enough and bulky enough that moving him was a strain. His body had begun to feel like deadweight, and his eyes were closed. They'd already lost Hudson—they couldn't lose Jack too.

"Olivia. I don't know if he's breathing."

"Let's just get him to my car," she said, sounding just as terrified as Rhys felt. Although they'd be better off if one of them had their shit together, Rhys took some comfort in the fact that she wasn't the only scared one.

They were halfway down the hill, Jack's legs now dragging behind him, when a loud roar rent the air.

"Is that what I think it is?" Olivia asked, not slowing down. Her car was twenty feet away, and she started to run, dragging Jack. Rhys struggled to keep up, chanting in her head: *Do not fall down. Do not fall down.* If she fell, they were all goners.

Rhys was too terrified to look toward the other side of the bridge. For one thing, most demons she'd had the displeasure of meeting had been invisible to her, and even if she could see them, she had no desire to meet her possible death head-on. Better to let it surprise her. Seeing a demon wouldn't make her run any faster.

When they reached the car, Olivia fumbled with her key fob, then opened the back door. She and Rhys unceremoniously dumped Jack onto the backseat. Olivia started to shut the door behind him, but Rhys slid inside, perching on the edge of the seat. "I want to sit with him."

Olivia's only answer was to shut them in and run around to the driver's door. Once she started the engine, she screeched around the corner and shot down the hill, just as a black wave emerged from the woods. Rhys had to squint to try to make out their individual forms because they moved as a pack, scuttling like cockroaches.

"Oh my God," she cried out in horror. There were hundreds of demons spilling from the woods and headed toward downtown Asheville.

Toward the police department.

Olivia's racing car seemed to be outpacing them, although Rhys didn't know how long that would last since the road down Beaucatcher Mountain wasn't designed for speeding. She turned her attention to Jack, who lay in an awkward position, unmoving. She pressed her fingers to his neck, straining to feel a heartbeat.

"Olivia," she wailed. "I think his heart stopped."

"No," Olivia cried out in agony.

But Rhys wasn't ready to let him go. She grabbed his legs and pulled his butt closer to the door to straighten out his back and neck, then started chest compressions.

"I think he's gone, Rhys," Olivia said, her voice breaking. "He's lost too much blood."

"No," Rhys said through her tears. "I can't lose anyone else." Then she leaned over and blew into his mouth before resuming compressions.

She wasn't giving up on him, even though she knew in her gut Olivia was right.

CHAPTER TWENTY-FIVE

Abel

He hung up from his call with Ellie, then pocketed his phone with the same determination and decisiveness that had ruled his life for the past two centuries, except his usual confidence had been stripped away. Control was something he had always taken for granted, but he couldn't take that risk now. While he would like to believe he could save her, he had to face the possibility that he might not reach her in time.

None of the humans in that station were a threat. Abel could kill them all in a literal heartbeat, but he knew it would destroy Piper if he killed humans to save her. She was so wrong. It wasn't his humanity she saw in his eyes, but a reflection of her own.

They meant nothing to him.

Nothing meant a damned thing without her.

He couldn't reach her with the ring, but his soul knew she was inside, just unreachable, even if he didn't have a clue what it meant.

Grabbing his sword off the passenger seat, he popped his trunk then got out of his car. He hooked the scabbard on his belt before slinging Piper's belt, her daggers still attached to it, over his shoulder. He hooked her sword onto the other side of his belt, then closed the lid. Once he reached her, she'd need a way to defend herself. He didn't have a plan other than to free her and get her the hell out of there. But it was enough.

As he strode toward the entrance, he felt the demons' power pulsing in the night, their wild and rapacious thirst that could only be quenched with human souls.

He slowly drew his sword from the scabbard. They must have been watching him from inside, because a policeman immediately walked out of the station with his gun raised.

"Lower your weapon, Mr. Abel."

Abel ignored him. If the officer shot him, it would hurt, but it would hardly even slow him down. If the officer became too much of an annoyance, he'd deal with him then.

Two large ravens landed in the parking lot in front of the police station entrance and quickly morphed into a beautiful young couple, a man and a woman.

Raven mockers.

But he could see through all other supernatural beings. Underneath their glamours, they were old with leathery, wrinkled skin, stringy hair, and rotten teeth. They appeared before the death of young healthy people, then consumed the hearts and souls of the dead to add to their illusion of youth. They were invisible to humans, so Okeus had chosen well. The police officer would think he was having hallucinations.

"Raven mockers," Abel said. "You may feast from any bodies slain in the carnage, but you will *not* get in my way."

They stood several feet from the entrance, their long claws raised toward him. "We cannot let you gain entrance, Son of Okeus. If you go to your father now, all will be forgiven."

"What about Piper?" Abel asked.

The police officer stared at Abel as though he had lost his mind. He pressed a button on his shoulder. "I need backup. He's brandishing a sword and talking to himself."

The raven mockers ignored the officer as well. "Her fate is for your father to decide."

That's what he feared.

Abel gave them a slight nod. "Then be prepared to die."

The policeman, who was standing a few feet to the side of one of the raven mockers, reacted quickly, drawing his gun and releasing several shots that pierced Abel's chest and abdomen.

Abel sucked in a breath but drew on his energy to push out the bullets and stop the blood flow, even as he advanced on the creatures that were armed only with claws and terror. They weren't a real threat to him, only a warning from his father that he was aware of Abel's intentions and planned to stop him.

Abel cut them down in two clean strokes, their bodies falling to the asphalt, but more officers had appeared at the entrance, guns drawn and pointed at him.

It would have been so much easier to kill them all, but instead he thrust his power toward them with a sweep of his hand, pushing them to the side as he walked through the door into the waiting area he'd sat in before.

He wondered again why he'd let her persuade him to trust the legal system. Piper had made him sloppy and careless when he needed to be more vigilant than ever, especially after the seer had confirmed his suspicions. His carelessness would be her downfall.

More shots rang out, hitting him in the back, but his power surged again, cutting off the blood flow as needed. He considered forming a shield of power around himself to block their bullets, but he needed to focus on the locked door in front of him. He concentrated a wave of energy on the hinges, focusing on ripping them from the metal doorframe. One by one they came loose with the whine of bending metal chased by multiple pops as the hinges were freed from the casing.

More bullets struck his back and he turned in frustration, releasing a growl as he sent a burst of energy toward the officers, propelling them out the door.

His back stung and he sent more energy toward the wounds, popping out the bullets and staunching the bleeding, but even he only had so much power. Although he couldn't die, not unless Piper killed him, he might not be able to fight at full strength if he kept hemorrhaging power.

He grabbed the hinge side of the door and ripped it open wide enough to slip through.

More officers were waiting for him on the other side. He met a new barrage of bullets, but this time he gave them his full attention, stopping them in mid-flight, then redirecting them back to the humans who had shot them.

The officers fell to the floor, confused and in pain as Abel stepped around them to get to Piper. He glanced down at them, knowing that somewhere deep in his heart he should care, but his need to save Piper obscured all else.

He broadcast a supernatural ping to search for her. She was at the back of the building, but just as he started in that direction, he sensed the demons behind him.

The raven mockers had been a token gesture to stop him, a peace-making effort, but these new demons were creatures of war. With human bodies and massive wings, they looked like biblical angels but were anything but. They were the Mohedron, part of Okeus's elite fighting guard. Or so Ahone had told him. Abel himself had never seen any of them before, and yet he instantly knew who and what they were. He even knew their names, only proving he was everything his father had hoped he would be.

"Abiel, son of Okeus," said Elius, the demon in charge, his hand on the hilt of his sword strapped to his side, "surrender to your master and all will be forgiven." He had long, pitch-black hair pulled back into a low ponytail and piercing black eyes that contrasted with his pale skin. His only clothes were a dark purple loincloth while the others wore loincloths in pale blue.

"And if I say no?" he asked.

"That is not an option. Surrender now and Okeus will let you keep the slayer as a pet."

"I wish to bring her to Okeus myself," Abel said.

"That is no longer an option," Elius said in a formal tone. "You will come with us now."

Abel sent a wave of power over the six demons. "You will let me go."

Elius's mouth lifted into a sardonic grin. "That won't work on us, Abiel. We answer only to your father."

Abel growled. Fighting them would delay him, but it appeared he had no choice.

Settling into a fighting stance, he said, "Then so be it."

He lunged for Elius first, planning to take off the head of the dragon.

Elius was a trained fighter. He would be an equal match, and the fight would become even more difficult if the others joined in.

But the others started mowing down the new police officers who'd arrived to subdue Abel. The fact that the humans could see them was to their advantage, but they still didn't stand a chance. Bullets wouldn't stop the Mohedron.

Abel forced himself to take his usual slow and methodical approach, letting his opponent wear itself out and become sloppy. After several minutes, it became apparent it would take hours to wear Elius to exhaustion, which meant Abel needed to speed up the process. He spared a moment to direct another ping toward Piper and was nearly nicked by the end of Elius's sword.

Another supernatural creature was with Piper now, and it wasn't a demon.

It was a god—a minor one—and he sensed it was the same one that had escaped from the warehouse that morning. Obviously it had come back for Piper.

His sense of urgency quadrupled.

CHAPTER TWENTY-SIX

Piper

The burning in my hand sent my heart racing. A demon was close. I bolted off the cot as a rush of hunger flooded my soul, hunger for the demon's soul. I was too terrified to let the feeling disturb me. The fact that a skimpy line of salt was my only means of defense was a bigger concern. There was the demon hand, still lying in the middle of the floor, but I'd only use it as a measure of last resort. I already felt my humanity slipping away, no sense speeding that process along.

"Slayer, your accommodations look less than comfortable," a voice said as I heard footsteps approach my cell.

Not a demon. Adonis, a minor god and major pain in the ass.

He appeared wearing a shit-eating grin as he watched me through the bars of my holding cell. "What did you do to that very helpful police officer?"

He nodded toward the burned pile that had been Detective Lawton. No one had arrived to check on him, not even after the demon-fire blasts and all that screaming, which could only be Adonis's doing. Some ally he had turned out to be for the officer.

I got to my feet and took several steps backward. "How did you get in here?"

He looked amused by my question. "The police seem to be distracted by the demons fighting the son of Okeus, so I walked right in."

"Abel is fighting demons?"

He laughed. "To save you. It's cute. He's holding his own against the head of the Mohedron right now—Okeus's elite guard. Quite the feat considering Elius has trained for centuries longer than Abiel has been alive."

I tried to swallow my fear for Abel. Sure, the demons couldn't kill him, but they could cause him pain. "What do you want, Adonis?"

"You know what I want, slayer. I want it even more after the rumors I've been hearing."

"What rumors?"

His eyes hardened. "Don't think you can try to lie to me, creator of worlds. Word has it that you have a world in your house. Okeus is there now trying to figure out how to break into it."

Fear sucked the air out of my lungs. Tommy. I had to trust that Deidre's ward and Collin's symbols would protect him. And I had to have faith that everyone living had left the house by now. I couldn't worry about any of that now. I had to get out of here and help Abel.

"So you want me to take you to a world?" I asked for clarification. "And in exchange you'll give me the information I need to save Abel? I need you to be a whole lot more specific about what you're promising."

"Oh, creator of worlds," he said with a derisive laugh. "You want to save the son of Okeus. I know how to make that happen."

"And at the risk of repeating myself…" I narrowed my eyes. "*Be more specific* or I'm not even taking you to see my fine toilet here." I gestured to the disgusting commode in the corner.

Shaking his head in amusement, he turned his attention to the metal door. A loud pop filled the space, and then he pulled the door open. He started to walk into the cell, only to step back, his grin spreading. "You *are* resourceful."

I glanced down at the salt line. Apparently, it worked on minor gods too. "What can I say? I have friends in high places."

"If you're lucky," he said, taking another couple of steps backward and getting down on one knee. "Okeus could be a friend in a high place. Perhaps he'll be in a good mood and offer you many things for your cooperation."

"And if I'm unlucky?" I asked, my stomach in knots as I watched him.

He leaned over, placing his hands on the disgusting concrete floor, then blew like he was blowing out fifty candles on a birthday cake. The salt scattered into the cell, clearing a path for him.

Pushing back up, he shot me a huge grin. "Did you really think that would work?"

I took another step back as he got to his feet, brushing off his hands.

"There's a reason the curse keepers put markings around their windows and doors. Can't blow those off." Then he walked right up to me.

The hunger in my soul roared to life and my fingers wiggled at my sides, itching to hold my daggers. Itching to kill him. I stared down at my empty hands in horror. Was I becoming one of the monsters I was destined to kill?

Adonis slowly reached for my left hand, lifting my palm up between us. He lightly traced the square and the circle in the center of my palm. "So much power for such a tiny thing." His gaze lifted to mine even as he continued to trace the lines. "Your power has grown even since this morning. Okeus will be all the more intrigued by you." He leaned into me, his mouth close enough to my ear to blow my hairs, tickling my neck. "He might make you the same offer he made the daughter of the sea." He leaned back and stared down at me, still holding my hand. "You have much to bargain with. Use it to your advantage."

I tried to jerk back, but he held tight. Something deep inside me roared to life, hungry for his soul. Hungry for his blood.

My eyes flew open in shock. *What was wrong with me?* The need to kill him was nearly overpowering.

"Ah…" he said, his eyes lighting up with excitement. "You've barely tapped into your power. I can feel so much more of it simmering below the surface. You can use it to save Abiel, slayer of demons. You're stronger than you know."

"From the demons Okeus sent to bring him back?" I asked, the power in me jumping at the chance to kill. *Consume.* "Or from his fate?"

He grinned and his beautiful features turned dark and ugly.

I tried to pull away from him again, but his fingers dug into my wrist, pulling me closer until our chests touched. "You hunger for demons. Go kill them."

The monster inside me leapt at his words, but somehow common sense prevailed. "Apparently, Abel's in the midst of fighting Okeus's storm troopers, or whatever they are. You think I can fight them? Three weeks ago, I didn't even know how to hold a sword."

A grin played at the corners of his lips and he whispered, "You don't need the sword."

My eyes flew wide as the monster in me confirmed he spoke the truth. In the beginning, Abel had told me I'd develop the ability to bind demons. Up until now, I hadn't believed him.

"Take me to a world and I'll show you how to access your power," Adonis said. "I'll show you how to save the son of Okeus. How to save yourself."

I was tempted, so tempted, but he'd never be content with simply going to a world. He'd want to control my talent, control me. "No."

"Piper," he cooed with a tenderness that should have been reserved for a woman he loved, but this was Adonis, the god of beauty and desire. He lived to seduce. (Thank you, Mr. Thatcher, for that Greek mythology unit in seventh grade English.) "Think of the things we could create together. And I'll let you keep Abel as your lover."

"*Let* me? No one lets me do anything, not even Kieran Abel."

Impatience filled his eyes. "I'll ask you nicely one last time, *Kewasa*," he said through tightly clenched teeth. "Take me to a world."

I glared up at him. "I realize times have changed, but you really need to learn that no means no."

He pushed out a sigh. "Just remember you brought this upon yourself."

Then he reached into his pocket, and before I could realize what was happening, he slapped a copper bracelet around my left wrist.

When I tried to break free from his hold, his fingers dug deeper. The monster in me pushed back, trying to shoot power at him, but it stopped at my wrist—at the bracelet.

"It worked," he said, looking relieved.

I grabbed it with my right hand, trying to pull it off, but it didn't budge. Panic washed through me as I realized what he'd done.

"You blocked my power!"

The monster inside me roared in anger and my vision turned red. I finally broke free from his grasp, taking several steps backward and jerking hard on the bracelet.

"Piper," Adonis said patiently as he watched me struggle.

"Get it off!" I roared, realizing it blocked everything. My ability to sense demons. My ability to create worlds. Would it stop me from seeing ghosts?

"Piper," Adonis repeated, but this time with a hint of impatience. "You're wasting precious time."

He was right. I forced my anger and terror down and tried to focus on him. "What do you want, Adonis?"

He gave me a pleasant smile. "You know what I want, creator of worlds. You had a bargaining chip and you chose not to use it. I had to up the ante, so to speak."

I shook my hand, trying to move the copper band, but it was glued to my skin. "You want me to take you to a world," I said in an emotionless voice. "Which one and for how long?"

"I can pick a world?" he asked in surprise.

"Yes, but I want what you promised before."

He shook his head. "Nope. You had your chance, which I thought was very generous on my part. I could have put the block on you from the beginning."

"So why didn't you?"

"I'd far rather use the motivation of giving you what you want versus using fear and intimidation. The results are usually much different." He gave me a sad smile. "Perhaps this is a good lesson for when you come face-to-face with Okeus."

"I can't create a world if I'm wearing this." I waved my arm at him.

"True, which is why I want you to make me a blood oath that you won't kill me and you'll take me to worlds whenever I wish it."

"You've got to be kidding."

"Unfortunately for you, I'm not." He pulled a small dagger from a sheath at his hip.

Fear stole my breath as he reached for my left wrist. He tugged me close and gave me an evil smile. "I hope you learn many lessons from this, Kewasa. It gives me no pleasure to inflict pain."

Then he stabbed my palm, pushing the blade deeper than necessary.

I screamed in pain, unable to stop myself.

"Piper!" Abel bellowed from somewhere in the building.

Worry filled Adonis's eyes before it morphed into determination. He left the blade embedded in my palm, his hand on the hilt. "Agree to the oath."

"No."

He twisted the blade slightly, sending another spike of pain through me that nearly made me pass out.

"Come, Piper," he cajoled. "It's so easy to say yes." He twisted the knife again, and my knees nearly buckled as my mouth went dry. "Say yes and I'll do all the work of the vow. You've already done the hard part—volunteering your blood."

Part of me wanted to give him what he wanted—anything to make the pain stop—but if I gave in to him, who else would come after me? Who else would torture me to take them to a world?

Gritting my teeth and holding back tears, I said in a direct, clear tone, "No."

"Then you leave me no choice." He pulled the blade out of my hand and, still holding my wrist in a viselike grip, pressed the sharp tip to my chest, over my heart. "Agree to the oath," he said with tightly controlled anger.

Tears stung my eyes, making his face blurry, and terror swamped my head, but I refused to give in. "No."

The knife tip dug a fraction of an inch into my skin, and I screamed again.

"Abel won't reach you in time to save you," Adonis said, lowering his gaze as he withdrew the blade. "Humans are such delicate creatures, and you, dear Piper, are still human, despite the incredibly powerful magic you possess." With a quick jerk of his hand, he plunged the knife into me, between my ribs.

I glanced down and saw that he'd indeed stabbed me. Blood began to soak my shirt.

"Eyes on me, Piper," Adonis said, but his voice sounded fainter.

I looked up.

"I can save you," he said as though he was speaking to a three-year-old. "But I need you to agree to this oath."

My head was fuzzy, and my legs were weak. Something in the back of my head confirmed what I'd already suspected. I was bleeding to death. I'd made oaths before. What was one more?

"I don't agree to the terms." My voice sounded far away.

"You're not in a position to negotiate   !" he shouted in frustration, and I realized he wanted me to live just as much as I did.

We were in a life-and-death game of chicken.

"I need a contract," I said, struggling to make my mouth move to say the words.

"Just say you agree!" he shouted, giving me a hard shake.

My knees buckled and I fell to the filthy concrete floor. Adonis knelt beside me, leaning over my face. "You, Piper Lancaster, Kewasa, shepherd to lost spirits, witness to creation, slayer of demons and gods, creator of worlds, agree to cause me no harm and to grant every request that I make." His eyes held mine. "Say I will."

I stared up at him. "No."

"Godsdammit, Piper! Just take the godsdamn oath!" he shouted.

"No." My eyelids felt heavy and suddenly I was so tired and so cold. I just wanted to close my eyes for a second.

"Drink!" Adonis shouted, and I felt him press his wrist to my mouth. His bleeding wrist.

I clamped my mouth shut. Drinking Abel's blood had linked us, and I would rather die than be linked to this god.

But the monster in me fought to drink his blood, eager to gain access to another god's power.

No! I shouted at the hunger and found the strength to turn my head.

Abel, I told the monster inside me. *Only Abel.*

Adonis cursed, and then his wrist was gone, and I was plunged into darkness.

CHAPTER TWENTY-SEVEN

Piper

"Piper."

I opened my eyes at the sound of Hudson's voice. Everything around me was gray and foggy. The air felt clammy and stale. "Where am I?"

"Pippy," Hudson said, leaning over me. "We don't have much time. Listen, okay?"

I nodded as I tried to sit up, but Hudson pushed me back down. "You have to live, Pippy, no matter what. Do you understand me?"

I started to nod, but then I remembered Hudson was no longer the Hudson I loved, but rather Ahone in a cruel disguise.

"Get away from me, Ahone!" I tried to shout. I had to evade him, but there was nowhere to go. I was trapped with him in this limbo of nothingness.

"It's me, Piper," he said. "I swear it's me."

I worked to tamp down my panic, trying to focus on the here and now, and concentrating, I could feel the difference between the image Ahone had used as a disguise and this Hudson.

"Thank God," I breathed out, sinking with relief. "Ahone tricked me before. He made me think he was you. And then I worried that maybe it had never been you."

He brushed my hair back from my forehead, frowning with concern. "Don't fret, Pippy. It was me before too, in your house. And even at the Cordens'. I did stay for you, really. And now I need you to listen to me. You have to go back, you have to live."

"There's more to this mess than just you, Piper, and you're worthless if you're dead."

"*You're* not worthless," I countered. "You may be dead, but you're here giving me a message."

"I'm pretty damn worthless if you won't listen."

I shook my head. "Huddy. I can't. I won't."

He leaned into my face. "Piper, if you could only see what I see in your future…"

"Then tell me what you see."

He shook his head and stood. "Some things are supposed to unfold with time."

"Do I at least save Abel?" I asked. "Do I stop the mark from appearing?"

Sympathy filled his eyes. "Nothing can stop the mark."

"No!" I shouted, getting to my feet. "I *know* it can be stopped. Adonis told me he knew how to stop it."

"You refused to give him what he wanted."

"The price was too high, Huddy."

"Then you made your choice."

"No!" I protested. "I don't accept that."

Hudson pulled me into a hug. "You have bigger things to worry about than saving Abel. You need to save yourself, and don't you dare pull some kind of 'Life's not worth living without him' bullshit for a man you met less than a month ago."

If I'd needed proof this was really Hudson, this would be it.

"He's not just a guy I met. It's deeper than that." But he didn't need to convince me that I didn't want to be doomed to hell with Abel.

281

Hudson searched my face, and after a few seconds, he said, "I know, Pippy. I know more than you could possibly understand."

"Then tell me," I repeated.

"The only thing I can tell you is that you need to live, and you need to tap into your power to save yourself."

"Adonis bound my power. I can't."

"Adonis bound your demon slayer power. There's more to you than that."

I stared at him as though he'd lost his mind…and then it hit me. "My witness to creation magic."

"Good. Now go live."

Hudson put his hand on my forehead and gave me a hard shove.

His push was so hard I fell backward, but I didn't hit the floor. Instead, I kept falling and falling into pitch blackness.

And then I felt Abel's presence before I felt or heard him. His arm was at my mouth, his blood dripping into my parted lips.

"Piper. Come back," he pleaded.

My eyes fluttered open, and I saw his worried face hovering over mine.

"Abel," I breathed. Then seeing my daggers hanging off his shoulder, I fluttered my fingers, trying in vain to reach for them, and he intercepted, taking my hand in his to press it to his chest.

"Kewasa," he choked out. There was no mistaking the fear in his eyes.

I wasn't rousing as quickly as I had the first time he'd saved me and I knew why. I lifted my left arm a few inches.

"Lie still, Waboose. Conserve your strength."

He was still worried, and I realized I was still dying.

"Abel," I said. "We need Adonis to remove the bracelet on my arm. It's blocking my power."

His eyes widened. "Adonis is dead."

Wrapping his hand around the band, he pushed a wave of power into it, burning the skin underneath, but I gritted my teeth against the pain. Then he grabbed the band with both hands and pulled, his face straining with the exertion.

Abel couldn't get it off either.

Panic filled his eyes as he gathered me into his arms. "I'll take you to the seer. She can help us remove it." He didn't sound convinced.

"You don't think I'll make it."

He stomped down the hall, stepping over the body of a police officer.

"I'm not losing you," he said as he walked out of the lockup area and into carnage.

Bodies were strewn everywhere—human and demonic. The stench of death was overpowering. My eyes started to close, but I forced them open when I thought I saw massive feathered wings. Sure enough, they were attached to bodies that looked human.

"Are those angels?" I asked in disbelief.

"Shh…" he murmured. "Save your strength."

So many dead. I lifted my gaze to his. "Abel…"

"Piper, don't look."

But I couldn't help it when I realized so many of the police officers hadn't yet crossed over. Their spirits were stumbling around, dazed and confused.

"Abel, stop. I need to help them."

"You need to help yourself," he barked, clearly agitated. "After we remove that damned bracelet, I'm putting you in one of your worlds to recover."

"Abel…"

"You can't help them, Waboose. Even if your power weren't blocked, you don't have the energy to send one of them to the afterlife, let alone so many."

I let him carry me through the bloody police station and out the main entry. As much as I hated the thought of leaving them, he was right—if we didn't leave now, my wounds really would kill me. Once we were outside, I tried to take in a deep breath to clear the stench from my nose, but I struggled to find the energy. My T-shirt was wet and sticky and plastered to my skin.

My hand began to burn, and Abel tightened his arms around me. Off in the distance, three abnormally large animals were racing toward us. He cursed under his breath, and I caught the word Botageria.

"I'm going to run for my car, Waboose, and then I'm taking you far away from here."

"Are those things here to collect you for your father?" I asked.

He hesitated as though he was considering whether to answer, then said, "No. They're here for you."

Horrified, I reached for the bracelet again, but I didn't have the strength to even grab the thing let alone pull it off. "We have to get it off."

But Abel ignored me as he sprinted for his car, reaching the driver's side within a few seconds. He opened the back door and dumped me onto the backseat, then dropped my daggers on the floor at my feet. He'd started to shut the door when something caught his eye over the roof of the car. His entire countenance changed, his urgency fading.

Leaning into the car, he held my gaze. "I don't have time to outrun them." He sounded anguished and gave me a long look. "Don't you dare die on me, Piper Lancaster."

I gave him a weak smile and lied. "I won't."

But he'd already slammed the door closed and taken off running, presumably to confront the creatures sent to fetch me.

Several loud roars rent the night air, and I lay sideways on the seat where Abel had dumped me, partially sitting up. My breathing was shallow, and I could feel my heart slowing down. Even if Abel could get the demons to back off so he could take me to Deidre, I'd never make it.

How could this be the end?

CHAPTER TWENTY-EIGHT

Ellie

Is that Abel?" I asked as Collin pulled the car to a screeching halt across from the police station. "He hasn't gotten Piper yet."

Abel stood in the middle of the road, facing all three Botageria with only his sword and his anger. They lunged and tried to get around him, but he held them back, getting in several good thrusts that drew blood. The creature to his left appeared more wounded than the others, but they held to their sole purpose—finding Piper.

"Ellie," Collin said, grabbing his door handle, "you and David go into the station and get Piper, and I'll help Abel hold them off. Once we get her out here, Tsawasi will send his army. We need that to happen."

I glanced back at David, wondering how we'd break her out of jail. We weren't criminal masterminds, but David gave me a reassuring smile.

"We'll figure it out," he said. "Let's go."

I nodded, then turned to Collin. I had no idea how this would turn out, and I didn't want to leave things on a bad note. "Collin, be careful."

He shot me a cocky grin. "Worried about me?"

"Yes," I answered truthfully.

His grin faded. "Don't die on me, Ellie."

"I won't if you won't," I teased.

"Good. Then get your ass in there to save the Kewasa, who's supposed to be saving all of us, while I give the arrogant demigod an assist before he takes bragging rights for holding off the Botageria single-handedly." He hopped out of the car, and David and I followed suit.

"I'll cover for you guys until you get into the station," Collin said, his sword and spear at the ready. He looked like a warrior. "If those things figure out you're going after Piper, they might follow."

"Good thinking," I said, then took off in a sprint for the station, dodging the bodies of several dead police officers in the lot.

The glass doors were busted out, so I ducked through the empty panes, nearly passing out when I saw the devastation inside.

"Oh my God," I gasped, and I felt David's hand on my shoulder.

"Did Abel do this?" he asked in disbelief.

"I don't know," I said, trying to catch my breath. I wasn't even sure how to get through the sea of dead bodies. The floor was slick with blood. "If this was him, then where is Piper?"

He took a few steps deeper into the room.

"Ellie, are those angels?" he asked as he started picking his way across the room. He reached a hand back to me, helping me find my footing as we passed through an open door into another room.

When we entered the large room full of desks, I saw the angels, their massive black wings bent and broken, their heads removed. More police officers lay in grotesque and unnatural poses, some with limbs ripped off. Some looked like they'd been shot. All of them were dead.

"I don't think Abel killed all of these humans," David finally said. "The angel's hands are covered in blood. I think they were the ones to rip some of them apart."

"Is that supposed to make me feel better?" I asked, shuddering. We were in so far over our heads I wondered how we were still breathing.

"Let's find Piper and get out of here," David said, his voice tight. He headed deeper into the building, passing through an open hallway that appeared to have several holding cells.

"Piper!" David called out as he led the way, walking past a burnt body in the middle of the hall.

"What the…" I said, walking around the charred remains, past several empty cells with closed doors.

The last one was open and the floor was covered with blood.

"Oh God," I gasped. "Do you think that's Piper's blood?"

"I don't know," David murmured, pointing his sword toward the corner of the small cell. "But I have to wonder why there is a blue hand on the floor and who it originally belonged to."

My gaze traveled to it. "I have no idea." I quickly scanned the room. "I think she was in here, so the question is where is she now?"

"I don't know," David said. "But we need to find her if we want Tsawasi's help."

Well, shit.

My phone rang in my pocket and I pulled it out, surprised to see Rhys's number.

"Rhys," I said. "Did you find Jack?"

"It's Olivia," the voice said, and I could hear Rhys in the background counting to five in a broken voice.

"What's going on, Olivia?" I asked, my heart in my throat, turning on the speakerphone.

"Jack…we found him."

Rhys's voice was counting again between sobs.

"He told us that a ghost is coming to kill Piper, but there's even worse news than that. Jack…"

"Jack's dead." I hadn't meant to be so blunt, but I wasn't sure how much more death I could take.

"Rhys is trying to save him, but he's lost too much blood." Olivia's voice broke. "He said the ghost stabbed him."

I looked up at David with wide eyes. "They can do that?"

"You'd know more about this than I would," she said. "But I have more bad news. A demon army emerged out of the hill while we were there, and they are on their way to downtown Asheville."

"We really need to find Piper," I said, fear tightening its grip on me. We needed Tsawasi's army if we had any chance of surviving this. The stakes were impossibly high.

"She's still in the holding cell?" Olivia asked in surprise. "Abel didn't get her out? Jack was sure—"

"We're standing in her cell right now and she's not here," I said, "and Abel's fighting off the demons that were sent to take her back to Okeus."

"Where could she be?" Olivia asked in shock.

"Perhaps Abel convinced her to go to a world," David said. "Especially if she was injured."

"I didn't catch that—did you say a world? Wait, why do you think she was injured?" Olivia asked, but she sounded strained.

"There's a large puddle of blood in her cell," I said.

"It could be someone else's," David said. "After seeing the rest of the station."

"Are you talking about Lawton's burnt body?" Olivia asked. "You need to be careful around Piper. She's the one who killed him."

"What?" I asked in disbelief. "How?"

"I brought her the demon hand she'd cut off a few days ago, wondering if it could help her. When she took it, a blue flame appeared on the demon's palm then shot out of the cell, down the hall, and made Lawton erupt into flames."

My mouth dropped open. "She murdered him."

"I don't think she did it on purpose, and I know she felt remorse after, but when she was in the middle of it…" She paused. "It was like she was possessed."

"The picture in Tommy's notepad," David murmured.

"What picture?" Olivia asked.

David shook his head, warning me not to mention it. "Long story, not important."

But I had to wonder if he was wrong. Maybe she could see something we were missing in all this.

She hesitated, then said, "We were going to head to the hospital, but we're coming straight there." I heard Rhys shout her protests, but Olivia's voice remained firm. "It sounds like you need the help and there's at least some chance of helping you."

She hung up before we could talk her out of it.

"Do you think Piper's becoming the monster in that picture?" I asked David. "Tommy said the monster ate her, and honestly, I was worried she'd be possessed, but maybe it's not quite that straightforward."

"What are you proposing, Ellie?" he asked cautiously.

"What if she already became the monster, and that's why she's not here?"

"Again," he said slowly. "What are you proposing?"

"I don't know," I admitted, my head beginning to ache. "But we really need to be on guard."

"And if she's truly evil?" he asked.

So much death. My psyche ached with the responsibility. "If Piper has become one of the demons we must confront we need to remember our duty—to protect humanity from evil forces. Even if the evil is my cousin in disguise."

But first we needed to deal with the advancing army.

CHAPTER TWENTY-NINE

Collin

N eed some help?" Collin asked Abel after Ellie and David had made it into the police station. He took the fact that he hadn't heard gunshots as a good sign.

"Where is the other curse keeper?" Abel asked, sounding breathless, which caught Collin by surprise.

He was an immortal demigod. While he could be wounded, he wouldn't die. But the sight of his blood-covered shirt gave Collin a moment of hesitation. He was counting on the demigod's strength to help them fight off the demon army, but that wasn't looking like a great bet just now.

"They went into the station to get Piper."

"She's not there," Abel said, then charged the middle demon.

The creature on the right tried to make a break for it, so Collin advanced, striking and partially detaching its clawed paw with his sword. The Botageria were bloody and weakened, but their drive to get around the two men was daunting. Collin suspected he would wear out long before the creatures did. But his immediate concern overrode his other worries. "Then where is she? Tsawasi won't send his army until she's up and fighting."

Abel shot him a dark glare, and the lack of concentration cost him a large gash on his arm from the middle demon's claw.

"Where the fuck is she, Abel?" Collin demanded. "Did you send her to a world?"

"She is close to going to another world, but not in the way you think." His words were heavy with grief and rage, and the demigod's attack took on a new ferociousness.

Panic jolted through Collin. "Where is she, Abel?" he shouted.

"She's in my car. Dying."

"*What?*" Collin took off for the car, resheathing his sword and tossing his spear to the ground, frantically looking in the front seat. Nothing. Then he saw her in the back, slumped over, her eyes partially open, her shirt drenched in blood. So much blood.

He jerked open the car door and slid in next to her, reaching for her wrist to feel for a heartbeat. It was there, but faint and slow. Abel was right—she was dying.

"You can't die," Collin grunted in irritation as he lifted her shirt up to search for her wound. Fuck. There it was on her breast, a slash that oozed blood. Who the hell had stabbed her? Given the location, so close to her heart, and the amount of blood she'd clearly lost, he couldn't believe she was still alive. What the hell did he do now?

A glimmer of fear for her life bobbed below his consciousness, but his need to save Ellie was his main concern. And if Piper was dead...

He pulled her bloody T-shirt over the top of her head and pressed it to her wound in an attempt to stop the bleeding, but it was a Band-Aid effort when she obviously needed a hospital.

"Tsawasi!" he shouted at the top of his lungs, and to his amazement, the little man appeared in the front seat. "She's dying!"

The little man looked her over as though she were a dead leaf blowing across the yard. "Yes."

"This is *not* what you told me would happen if I followed her into this. This is not what you promised!"

"You are like a child with your impatience."

"You call this *impatience*?" Collin demanded. "How can she save us if she's dead?"

"She's a savior for a reason."

"You promised me an army to fight Okeus, but you hinged it on Piper fighting because you knew that she *wouldn't* be fighting." Collin shook his head in disgust. "You're just like Okeus and Ahone, full of tricks and half-truths. You told me she'd save Ellie, and at the moment, she's putting Ellie in even more danger."

Tsawasi stared at him in consternation. "You never learn, son of the land. This is about far more than you and the daughter of the sea."

"That's right," Collin sneered. "You want us to save your asses while you put in as little effort as possible and we take all the risk."

"It's about your *humanity*," Tsawasi barked. "She dies in front of you, yet you have no compassion. You care only for how this will affect you and the daughter of the sea. You feel nothing for her at all."

The little person was wrong. He wanted to save her, he wanted to care, but he'd spent most of his life purposely not caring about anyone or anything until Ellie… His heart couldn't afford to be hurt anymore.

"I told you that Piper is your salvation, Collin Dailey," Tsawasi said. "But what I didn't tell you was that by saving yourself, you would also save Ellie. This was a test of your humanity, and you failed. Your lack of compassion has doomed you and, in turn, Ellie. This is on *your* head."

The car door opened, and Collin felt himself jerked backward out of the car, landing on his ass on the pavement.

CHAPTER THIRTY

Ellie

When we exited the station, I could hear the demon army. They sounded like a plague of locusts descending on the city, and the sound was growing louder, drowning out the sirens and screams in the distance.

Where was Piper and Tsawasi's army?

Then I saw Abel's car door open and Collin fly out backward onto his butt. The car door slammed shut. He scrambled to his feet and pulled a paper from his pocket, then crumpled it with his palm and threw it to the ground, his face contorted in rage.

What the hell? Why wasn't he helping Abel? I ran toward him in complete confusion. "Collin?"

I turned to look in the car and saw an unconscious Piper, her head tipped back on the seat, her chest and stomach covered in blood.

"Piper!" I shouted, jerking on the car door handle, trying to get in to help her. "*Piper!*" I jerked the handle several more times before I shouted at Collin, "Did you lock the door?"

But I didn't wait for an answer. Using my sword hilt, I pounded on the window. "Piper!"

David moved to the other side of the car and pounded on the driver's window with a fire extinguisher he must have found inside.

"It's too late," Collin said, grabbing my arm and trying to pull me away.

"She's dead?" I asked, starting to sob. "She can't be dead!" I cried. "I only just met her. There was so much more…" My anger rose, choking out my grief. "No!" I started to kick the window with my shoe, putting as much force into it as possible. My efforts had no visible impact on the car. David's strikes with the fire extinguisher hadn't even made a crack.

"What the hell?" I shouted in confusion.

Another car screeched to a halt. Olivia ran toward us then stopped, her mouth dropping open at the sight of the devastation in the parking lot and inside the station.

"We have to go," Collin insisted, grabbing my arm and giving me a hard jerk.

I turned to him, shaking my head. "What the hell are you talking about?"

His face hardened with anger, but also panic. "Tsawasi's not sending his army, and we will die here. We have to go."

I couldn't believe what he was saying. "He told you that?"

He started to say something, his eyes filled with grief and regret, but seemed to change his mind. He finally settled on, "He said we're doomed."

I took a step back, taking in the horror of the army of creatures descending toward us. There was no earthly way we could fight that many demons. Not just the five of us. Not even if Tsawasi and the Nunnehi helped.

But what would happen if we didn't even try?

"Ellie, we have to go!"

I slowly shook my head, staring up at him with profound sadness. "You always took your role so seriously, even as a child. You had the Manteo mark tattooed on your chest, and you knew every nuance of the curse. So when you met me, it disgusted you that I was so ignorant. You always considered yourself the superior curse keeper, but right now, I realize that it was all empty ritual and rules for you." I held my fist to my chest. "I was willfully ignorant, I won't dispute that, but once I accepted that role, I took it to heart, Collin. My job is to fight the demons to save humanity. You've never accepted yours."

"You're wrong," he said bitterly, his eyes filling with tears. "Once I realized what I'd done, my sole purpose was and has always been to protect you. I will never apologize for that." Anger filled his eyes. "I've accepted my guilt *and* my penance."

I sucked in a breath. I knew how he felt, but he'd never said it with so much fervor. "I'm not leaving, Collin," I said, the certainty of my impending death settling over me. The rightness of my decision filled me with peace. "I will die trying to save the world."

His jaw spasmed and his eyes hardened. "And I'll die trying to save you."

I realized David was standing off to the side, the look of hopelessness on his face tempered by firm resolve. "We all have to die sometime."

Screaming caught my attention, and I realized Rhys was beating on Abel's car window. "Piper! No!"

The agony in her scream brought fresh tears to my eyes.

Abel released a loud shout, his anger filling the air around us with a heaviness that made it difficult to drag in a breath.

So be it.

I turned to face the demon army, determined to take out as many as I could before I drew my last breath.

CHAPTER THIRTY-ONE

Piper

I was caught in the same hazy grayness I'd been in before, but this time Jack sat with me, cradling my injured hand.

"Jack," I said in surprise.

He gave me a sad smile. "Piper, you don't have much time, so listen. You have to access your power."

"I tried," I said, still confused at seeing him. "How are you here? *Are you dead?*"

"That's not important. You have to listen, okay?"

"Jack," I said, starting to cry. "No. I can't lose you too."

I lay back in the nothingness. It was all too much. So many people I cared about had died, and every single one had died because of me. The heaviness of my guilt made it difficult to pull in a breath.

"You have to find your power, Piper. You have to save them."

I shook my head. "I can't. Adonis put this bracelet on my arm, blocking my power."

"Your witness to creation magic can't be blocked," Jack said with a reassuring smile. "Find it. Use it."

Easy to suggest, but I had no idea how to access it. An orgasm had brought on that soul-deep memory, something that certainly wasn't repeatable at the moment.

Suddenly I was back in Abel's car and my pain was so intense I nearly passed out again. My breathing was ragged and shallow, and I was so, so cold. Outside I saw Ellie, Collin, and David standing in a line, their backs to me and their weapons at the ready as a demon army approached, so deep I couldn't see the end of it. There had to be a thousand of them.

Abel stood in front, fighting two large creatures, while another lay on the ground.

"If you die," Jack said, sitting in the front seat, transparent like the first ghosts I'd seen. "They die too."

"I don't know how to find it, Jack."

"The magic is in your soul."

Then Hudson appeared next to him, his image flickering as my eyesight dimmed.

I cracked a grin. "You look funny."

"And you're delirious from blood loss. Focus, Piper. Why haven't you saved yourself yet?" Hudson sounded pissed.

"Abel…" I started to say, my voice trailing off.

Hudson turned in the seat to face me. "Newsflash—Abel's not gonna save you. He can't even save himself."

"I can't find it," I said, my words slurred.

"Bullshit," he barked, obviously taking the bad cop role and leaving good cop to Jack.

Jack's gaze focused on something beyond the windshield. "The demigod must really love you to put up with the beating he's taking to save you."

Tears burned my eyes.

"Crying's not gonna help anything, Piper," Hudson snapped. "Find your power. Ellie and Rhys need you, and you're not even *trying.*"

My eyes sank closed. "I'm so tired…"

"You can't die yet, Piper," Hudson said, his voice much clearer than before. There was no mistaking his annoyance. "You said you wanted to save the demigod. Dig deep down. It's in there."

But I was too tired to dig. I just wanted to take a nap, even as part of my brain latched on to the hope of saving Abel.

I slid back into the gray place, but neither Hudson nor Jack was with me this time. I was alone.

Hudson had been with me over half my life, helping me search for answers about my parents' murders and to live through my grandparents' attempts to raise me into a compliant, dutiful granddaughter. He'd stood by my side through every life change—getting into law school, dropping out of law school, becoming a ghost whisperer, and discovering the codicil to my father's will that said I had to trace my family lineage to Ananias Dare from the Lost Colony of Roanoke—an impossible task given the fact that the entire colony had disappeared. And he'd stayed with me, even in death.

I'd only just met Jack weeks ago, but he'd made the worst month of my life bearable. He'd tried to help me figure out all the weird things happening to me with little regard for his own safety. He'd agreed to help me before he even really knew me, going so far as to disrupt his life to stay in Asheville. He'd died and I wasn't even sure what had happened, but I knew I'd be lost without him.

Maybe it was time for me to stand on my own.

But suddenly I wasn't alone. A man and a woman stood in the shadows, watching me. Fear skated along my skin. My power was bound and my physical body was impossibly weak. I was a sitting duck. "Who's there?"

They stepped forward, the shadows shifting off their faces, and I gasped. "Mom? Dad?"

They looked exactly as they had the last time I'd seen them. Mom in the blue dress Daddy loved because it brought out the blue in her eyes, and Dad in his green and white checkered shirt that Mom had tried to make him give to Goodwill. While Dad was stoic, Mom burst into tears, opening her arms in invitation. I ran into them, only I wasn't twenty-five anymore, I was ten again, so the top of my head came to the middle of her chest.

She wrapped me tightly in her arms, burying her face in my hair. "I've missed you, Pippy."

"I can't believe you're here," I said, crying into her shirt.

She kissed the top of my head. "We've come to take you home, sweetheart."

I wrapped my arms around her waist, in disbelief that she was with me. Hugging me. But my dad stood to the side, watching with an expressionless face, his arms crossed over his chest.

I pulled away from my mother and turned to him. "Daddy?"

His arms dropped to his sides. "You can't come with us, Piper."

"What are you talking about, Todd?" my mother demanded. "*Of course* she's coming with us!"

"She's not done. She's only just begun."

Mom pointed a finger at him, her face red with anger. "You never wanted her to do this in the first place. Why are you forcing her to do it now?"

"Look at her. Really look at her."

My mother looked annoyed as she studied me. I stood eye to eye with her now, once more my twenty-five-year-old self. Suddenly, her eyes widened. "Oh."

"She has to go back."

Mom started to cry. "I can't send her back to face this, Todd. It's too much. It's too dangerous."

"She's a woman now. She needs to do this."

Tears streamed down her face, but she finally nodded. "Yes. You're right."

I turned to my father in confusion.

He reached for my left hand, which was bloody again. The copper bracelet dug into my skin. "Piper. Make the bracelet fall off."

I stared up into his worried face. "I can't."

"Yes, you can. Focus on the beginning and the end. Let the power fill you."

I'd seen the beginning, but the end? He was speaking in riddles.

He cradled my hand in his, his thumb brushing the center of my palm as I closed my eyes and focused on the power embedded in my DNA.

Nothing happened.

"Piper!" I heard Hudson shout. "Find your power now!"

"I'm trying."

"Not hard enough!"

I was going to die and leave Ellie and Collin and Rhys to deal with demons. I'd never get the chance to get to know Ellie. There was now a police station full of men and women who needed my help to move on, and I'd promised Tyler to tell his girlfriend he hadn't slept with his boss. I promised Jim Delancey, Abel's security guard, that I'd tell his wife, Debbie, that he loved her and hadn't wanted to leave her. And without me to help him, or kill him, Abel would be at his father's mercy for eternity. I couldn't do that to him. I couldn't let him down. I couldn't let any of them down.

But I still had no idea how to access my power.

You can do this, Piper, the voice that had ruled my life for the past year said in my head. *Go back to the beginning. Go back to the end.*

In that moment, I understood the voice I'd been hearing hadn't been Ahone after all. It was something else entirely.

As much as I hated the voice for what it had done to Abby, its advice echoed what my father had just told me. Go back to the beginning? Creation? My birth? When I'd first met Abel?

And what was the end?

Then a memory popped into my head, one that had been buried for over a decade.

I was ten years old again, standing in front of the restaurant where my parents had been killed. The flashing blue and red lights bounced off the building and someone tried to get me to go inside, but I refused to budge, watching the EMTs work on my parents' lifeless bodies. I was waiting for them to come to me.

"You're a very brave girl," a tall, older man said. He wore a long tunic and leaned on a staff. His long white hair matched his beard, but it was the patch over his eye that caught my attention. That and the two black birds circling high over our heads. While he looked old, somehow I knew he was strong and powerful. The older, twenty-five-year-old me knew he wasn't Ahone. He stood next to me, but I had no idea how he had gotten there. I'd been standing alone. "You shouldn't be here by yourself."

I looked up at him in surprise, feeling oddly calm, like if I were patient enough, everything would be okay. "I'm waiting for my parents."

"I know," he said, his voice full of sympathy. "I'm sorry for the price you have to pay."

I blinked in confusion. "I don't understand."

"I know, and that's okay, but one day you will be even braver and more powerful. More powerful than you can understand. You, Piper Lancaster, will help save the world."

I shook my head. Superheroes saved the world and I wasn't a superhero. If I were one, I would have been able to save my mom and dad.

"It's okay if you don't understand," he said. "Someday, it will all be clear. But for now, know that I'll be watching out for you. I'll always make sure you're okay."

"Piper!" I heard my grandfather shout behind me, and I spun around and saw him running toward me. Too soon. They still hadn't come. I quickly turned around to wait, worried I'd miss them.

He squatted next to me. "Piper, look at me."

They should have appeared by now. Had they already left me?

"Piper," my grandfather said in a gruff voice that was heavy with emotion. "Look away."

Even at ten, I knew what he thought, that I was disgustingly morbid watching my parents' lifeless bodies, their blood running down the pavement and collecting against the curb like rainwater. But I'd spent my entire childhood talking to dead people. I wasn't going to walk away from my own parents.

I'd think about what it all meant after their departure.

The older man who'd spoken to me was now walking past the policeman who had refused to let me hold my mother's hand. The officer didn't attempt to stop him. The birds followed.

Suddenly, Mom and Dad's spirits were standing next to him, and the bright glowing light appeared. The older man led them toward it, but my parents stopped and said something to him. He gestured toward me and they turned to look.

I started to run for them, but my grandfather grabbed my arm and held me in place.

"Let me go!" I screamed. "I have to tell them goodbye!"

"They're already gone, my child," my grandfather said, his voice breaking. He tried to pick me up, but I flailed and kicked, trying to break free.

My parents were trying to get to me too, but the older man held them back.

"Why won't you let me see them?" I shouted at the man. "Why can't I tell them goodbye?"

"Piper." My grandfather was openly crying, fumbling to get a better grasp on my arms.

My mother's face wrenched with anguish, and I heard her voice float toward me. "Piper, I will always love you. Have a good life."

My father stood next to her with his hand on her shoulder. "I love you, peanut. I've tried my best to shield you from this, but the day will come when you have to fight the evil hiding in the darkness, when you and your daggers will play a part in the salvation of the world."

"Daddy…" I started to cry as it hit me that my parents were about to walk away from me. Forever. "I'm scared."

"I know, and I'm sorry for that. I wish I could stay and help you through this, but one day, you'll find the help you need. I've been assured of that."

"I don't understand," I said through my sobs.

Tears swam in his eyes. "I know, but you will one day. Just remember that there is greatness in you. Make me proud, Piper."

Mom put a hand on his shoulder. "You put too much on her, Todd." She turned to me, tears streaming down her face. "There are many powers in this world, baby, but don't forget the power of love."

Then they turned and walked into the light, leaving me orphaned and alone.

I fell to the sidewalk, sobbing my pain and grief.

My grandfather scooped me into his arms and started to carry me to his car, but the older man approached us.

Part of me knew I should fear him—even now in my distress I could feel his immense power—but all I felt was defiance.

"You could have saved them," I spat out.

"No, Piper," my grandfather said, his chest heaving with his own sobs. "No one could have saved them. They were already gone."

The older man walked beside us, and I realized my grandfather couldn't see him.

"What do you want?" I asked in a venomous tone. "Why are you walking with us?"

Granddad released a heavy sigh. "Piper, you're too old for imaginary friends."

But I knew they weren't imaginary, even if everyone but my father had insisted they weren't real. He had taught me to hide my "friends" from everyone, which was hard considering I often wasn't sure which of my friends were living or dead.

"I want to go to the light," I said to the man. "I want to go with my mom and dad."

Horror washed over my grandfather's face. "You don't know what you're saying. You have a place with your nana and me. We'll take care of you."

The older man shook his head with a sad smile. "You can't go, Piper. It's not your time." He gave my grandfather a long look. "Don't worry about upsetting your grandfather. This will be forgotten, by both of you, and you won't see the ghosts again until it's time."

"Time for what?" I asked.

"Time to face your destiny."

The memory faded and something deep in my chest began to burn. The heat built in intensity, and just when I was sure I couldn't handle the pain, it burst free, spreading throughout my body, stealing my breath. Then the heat focused on my left wrist, the metal burning my skin before it exploded.

I bolted upright, my eyes flying open, and I was in the back of Abel's car, completely healed and filled with so much power I could barely contain it. Fragments of the bracelet were embedded in the seats, roof, and back doors of the car.

My gaze was drawn to Abel, who stood about twenty feet in front of the car still engaged in a battle with the large demons. I could feel his simmering power, but I also felt his fatigue.

I glanced down at my left palm. The gaping wound was gone, replaced by a one-inch-long pink scar, making it look like I'd been crucified, especially when I turned my hand over to look at the scar of the exit wound. I could feel the power of the marks that were supernaturally embedded in my skin, as well as the three marks still below the surface, waiting for their moments to emerge, and I knew them for what they were.

The mark of Kewasa.

The mark of the god killer.

The mark of the mother of gods.

I stared at my palm in horror.

No! I refused to give Okeus children. I'd kill myself first.

Jack was gone, but Hudson was still in the front seat, only he was no longer translucent. He was watching the fight in front of us. "You can't save him, Pippy. You need to stop wasting your time on this and fight the demons."

"I can save him *and* fight the demons." Power was racing through my body. I could harness the power to stop the marks from appearing. I'd find a way.

But Hudson shook his head, pity filling his eyes. "You're only making the inevitable more difficult. But for now, grab your weapons and   fight."

CHAPTER THIRTY-TWO

Piper

I reached down and grabbed my dagger belt, which Abel had uneremoniously—but oh so thankfully—dumped on the backseat floor, and quickly wrapped it around my waist and fastened the buckle.

When I stepped out of the car, I saw that the demon army had come to a halt in the near distance, maybe fifty feet away, but it was Abel who commanded my attention. Who commanded all of our attention. Like the army parked restlessly at the top of the small hill, Collin, David, Ellie, and behind them Rhys and Olivia, were off to the side waiting with bated breath, weapons at the ready, and their eyes fixed with horror and awe on Abel, who was locked in fierce combat with the deadly demons—the Botageria.

He was covered in blood, but so were the doglike creatures that attacked him.

"You can't have her!" he shouted, slashing at one of the demons as it advanced while holding back another with my sword.

"Piper?" Rhys gasped when she saw me, her face covered in tears. "You're glowing. Are you dead?"

Was I? I glanced down at my body, taking in the drying blood on my bare abdomen and chest, wondering where my shirt had gone and why I was once again battling demons in only a bra. At least I had pants this time. "No," I said, still feeling out of it. "I don't think so."

"Jack." She started crying again, and it was then I noticed the blood on her own hands and arms.

"I know," I said. "He came to me."

"As a ghost?" she asked with a small wail.

I nodded, tears filling my eyes.

"Helen killed him," she said, anger filling her words. "He said she's coming for you."

I sucked in a breath. I would never have imagined her capable of killing Jack, but the rest of the news didn't surprise me. She'd made it clear I wasn't her favorite person. "She warned me that she wouldn't let me kill Abel."

"I guess she plans to kill you first."

The demons seemed like a bigger concern, but I was still only half-there, drunk with power and ready to defend the people I loved. "I'll take care of her."

A tiny part of my heart turned cold. I *would* take care of her. I'd find a portal to hell and send her there.

"Now get in Abel's car and wait for me," I said. "You have no business being out here." I turned to Olivia, who was walking toward us. "Get in the car with Rhys and wait."

"I want to help," she said with a fierce look.

"You need to keep Rhys safe. In the car."

Rhys opened the passenger door. "Piper, be careful."

I nodded, but I was already turning my attention to the scene in front of me.

"Where is Tsawasi's army?" I called out, and four startled faces turned toward me.

"Piper?" Ellie called out in shock.

But Abel looked the most startled. One of the creatures in front of him got in a blow to the head, but thankfully it didn't knock him down.

"Where is your army, Tsawasi?" I shouted, my voice booming through the night.

The little man appeared next to me, his mouth dropped open in shock. "You live."

"Observant," I said. "Tell me how to stop the mark."

His eyes darkened. "An army advances and you're concerned with saving the demigod?"

I snatched one of my daggers from its sheath and leaned over to point it to his chest. "At least I stand here ready to fight to save the world—humans and supernatural creatures alike. What the fuck have you been doing? Hiding behind your weak, half-hearted promises." I withdrew my dagger and straightened, scared of the depth of my anger and the power that accompanied it. "Call your army."

I strode toward Abel without looking back to see if he'd heeded my order.

"Piper," Collin gasped as I walked past him. "I'm sorry."

I cast him a moment's glance, unsure what he was talking about, but the only thing that mattered now was my destiny, my life, my love.

Abel.

He was fighting the two remaining creatures and I joined him, my daggers drawn and ready. In the short distance, the army of demons began to shift in masse, growing louder, then deafening, as it picked up speed, taking up rebel screams and shrieks and wild, animalistic howls as it swept toward us.

Abel sent a wave of power toward me. *Go to the seer.*

I'm not injured, Abel. I'm fully healed. "My place is with you, Abel. I stand with you." And I knew in my heart it was true.

I stood in place, staring into the eyes of one of the six-foot-tall demons. They looked like dogs with massively broad shoulders and long front arms that held them upright while they squatted on their shorter back legs. They stopped their attack on Abel and watched me.

In a cacophony of noise and barely controlled chaos, the demon army came to an abrupt halt behind the Botageria.

From the distance, they had looked to all be the same, but up close, I could see the differences. The shorter demons stood in front, reminding me of bulldogs but with more buglike faces. The next wave of demons were taller, more animallike than human, fierce with deadly claws and teeth. Behind them stood a wave of elemental demons, and a wave of winged demons lingered behind them. I couldn't see past the first few lines, but I could feel the rest of them. I knew they were there.

And my soul was hungry for every single one of them.

I was sure we looked like generals from two warring parties, meeting with our armies behind us, only Tsawasi had yet to produce the army he'd promised.

I lifted my chin and said to the Botageria on the left. "Go back to your master and tell him he's wasted your time. I refuse to go with you."

"Piper," Abel said. "The Botageria only take orders from Okeus."

One of the demons released a slow growl.

The power filling my body made me too sure of myself, but I was also a proponent of *fake it 'til you make it*, and there was no way I was going with them. "Today they take orders from me."

I could feel Ellie and Collin behind me, their life forces burning brighter than that of David, who stood behind them. Abel's was brighter than the others, no brighter than mine. I was truly his equal now, and he seemed to sense it.

He sucked in a breath. "Waboose."

Tsagasi popped up beside me. "The Botageria are fierce," the little man said matter-of-factly.

I adjusted my stance, keeping my gaze on the demons. "And so am I."

"Your power has grown significantly, creator of worlds," Tsagasi murmured. He sounded as though he wasn't certain whether that was a good thing.

"I have more titles within me."

He hesitated, then said, "I know." There was no mistaking the disappointment in his tone.

I didn't need his approval or permission.

"Where is your army, Tsawasi?" I shouted, keeping my eyes on the demons. "Or must I kill the demons alone?"

Abel shot me an incredulous stare. I knew I was drunk with power, but what better time to stare death in the face?

I pointed my blade at the fiercest looking Botageria. It seemed to be in charge. "I will kill you if need be, or you can deliver my message. It's entirely up to you."

The demon leaned back its head and roared.

"Then face your death." I didn't wait for its attack to charge.

Ride its back, Abel sent toward me. *I'll take its front.*

He charged, aiming for the demon's bloodied arm, while I ran beside it and jumped onto its back, grabbing a handful of fur as it rose to its full height and roared, trying to shake me off.

Abel charged and slit the demon's throat as I stabbed the base of its skull with my dagger.

The demon stumbled and Abel plunged his sword into the creature's chest. The demon turned to ash, its body disappearing underneath me, but I landed on my feet in a squat, piercing the glowing orb that floated into the air.

Abel stood in place, staring at me with a look of love and longing.

"I love you too," I said with a grin. "Now help me kill the rest of these demons so you can take me to bed."

A grin spread across his face. Then he turned to face the surviving Botageria, who was currently engaged with Ellie and Collin.

The army of demons stayed in place, and while I was grateful for their forbearance, I had to wonder what they were waiting for. Our own army? I heard a rumble behind me, relieved to see Tsawasi's army pouring out of a small stand of trees across from the police station.

The little man stood on top of Abel's car, shouting to them in a language I didn't understand as they emerged. They began lining up, ready to clash with the demon army, with us sandwiched between.

The sound of laughter filled the air, unnaturally loud given the chaos around us, and I dared a glance up. Okeus sat on a golden throne floating on a cloud. He wore a dark gray suit with a white shirt and gray tie. His legs were crossed, and his left forearm rested lazily on the arm of his chair. "You are a feisty one."

Abel stepped in front of me, his sword in his right hand. "Create a world, Waboose."

I held Okeus's gaze. "*No.* I'm not going anywhere." I could feel his life force and I craved it the most. I licked my upper lip as I shot the god a wicked smile. "I'm looking forward to this."

"Piper, no!" David called out behind me.

I'd known they would protest, but Ellie surprised me. She walked toward me with a solemn expression. When she reached me, she asked, "Are you sure you want to take this stand?"

"This isn't your fight, Ellie. You don't need to be here with me."

"The hell it's not." She took a breath, then murmured, "There's a reason I have a sword created to subdue gods."

"And there's a reason I have the title slayer of gods." Along with the soon-to-appear mark, god killer.

In the back of my mind, I couldn't help wondering if this was too soon…if we were really ready, but I had to protect Abel and I refused to spend the rest of my life running. I'd known it would come to this since the showdown at the warehouse, and I suspected Ellie had known for far longer.

"He is the master of deceit," Tsagasi said in a low voice behind us.

He wasn't telling me anything I didn't already know, but it was good to have the reminder.

"You plan to *kill* me?" Okeus asked, sounding amused. "How do you propose to do that?"

He had a point. He was floating on a cloud about twenty feet over our heads. How would we even get up there?

"As amusing as this is, we have other business to attend to." His eyes narrowed on Abel. "Abiel...my son. Your behavior has been disappointing...however, you *are* part human and I see her appeal." I felt naked under the god's stare. "Drop to your knees. Bow your head and swear allegiance to me and all will be forgiven."

One glance at Abel was all I needed to know he was actually considering it.

"Abel," I said, taking the half step between us to close the distance. "No. Do *not* enslave yourself to him. We can defeat him."

He turned to look at me, uncertainty in his eyes.

"No," I said firmly. "There's another way."

We can't defeat Okeus, Piper.

"Not with that attitude we can't," I teased, my stomach in knots. *Trust me.*

His gaze held mine as his hand lifted to my cheek, and he lowered his lips to mine with a soft kiss. *With my life, my love.*

He pulled away from me and turned toward the army, releasing a roar as he lifted his hand and shot a wave of energy toward the first line of demons, freezing them in their tracks.

"Charge!" Tsawasi shouted, and the army behind us advanced, swarming past us to attack the stock-still demons in the front.

"We'll take the final Botageria," Abel shouted to the curse keepers. "Get the demons that break through the line."

We both charged the remaining beast, throwing thoughts at each other as we worked to take it down. The surviving Botageria had learned from our combined attack of its partner, so it took longer to destroy, but Abel finally got a good strike to its heart. It turned to ash and I freed the souls.

Abel's eyes glittered with joy, and I realized he loved this—the war and the killing—he thrived on it. In some ways, he was very much his father's son. I knew I should be concerned, but darkness lived deep in my own soul, the perfect counterpart to the crown prince to the throne of hell.

Tsawasi's army had made it through the first line of demons and were now fighting the next tier, but I could feel the back rows of the demon army slipping around the sides.

"Abel, the demons plan to surround us. Can you freeze them again?"

"I would stun our soldiers as well." He didn't question how I knew, just ordered some of Tsawasi's army to stop them, but it soon became apparent that our army was vastly outnumbered.

Okeus watched from above with obvious glee.

The fire demons had broken through our line of soldiers and were casting demon fire toward us.

The answer struck me. I knew how I could turn the tide in our favor. "We have to capture a fire demon."

"Are you mad?" Abel shouted as he fought off a group of smaller demons.

"No. Will you help me or not?"

He shot me a dark look. "I will follow you to the end of time, Waboose."

"You can start now." I grabbed his arm and dragged him to the side of the police station. Then I pressed him against the wall and captured his lips with my own, unable to stop myself.

When I pulled back, his eyes were wide with wonder and lust. "Piper."

"I am yours, Abel. In every way. Don't hide your true self from me. Don't hide your thirst for blood, because I have a thirst of my own." I caught sight of a fire demon rushing past a police car, moving toward us. "Now freeze that demon."

He turned and stunned it in place. The demon's eyes widened in fright.

"Now what?" Abel asked.

"Can you unfreeze it at will?"

"Yes," he said hesitantly.

"When I tell you to, release it."

He started to ask me what I was doing but stopped and nodded.

I charged toward its back. I'd originally planned to cut off its hand, but I couldn't help wondering if the fire would be more powerful if the hand were still attached, and besides, I could use the demon's body as a shield. Instead, I changed course and climbed onto its back, grabbing its arm and pulling its right hand up over its shoulder.

"Piper, what are you doing?" Abel asked from beside me.

"Creating a weapon."

The demon underneath me was pissed. I could feel fury seething from its skin.

"Can you control it to do what you want?" I asked.

Yes, but I don't know for how long.

Then we'll use it as long as we can.

Abel turned the demon toward its own army, and I began to pummel the demons with fire.

CHAPTER THIRTY-THREE

Ellie

I stared at my cousin in shock.

"Do you see what she's doing?" I called out to Collin. The demons were coming at us in waves. Tsawasi's army had done a good job of holding them back, but we'd been outnumbered from the start and our numbers were thinning.

"She's riding a demon and throwing fire," Collin grunted as he prepared to fight a new group of demons advancing from the side. His spear and sword were already coated black with demon blood.

I'd believed that we could win this battle, but I was becoming less certain, especially since Okeus was watching with amusement from above, not looking remotely concerned.

David was to my right, fighting off a demon that had broken through the front line. I'd been worried about letting him fight with us, but he'd held his own, killing more demons than I'd expected.

"Jack!" I heard Rhys scream from over by Abel's car. "*Jack!*"

I turned to where she was looking, shocked to see Jack stumbling toward us, his shirt bloody. He looked around in a daze, stunned by the battle in full swing around him, but somehow he had a sword in his hand.

"What the hell?" Collin said in disbelief. "I thought he was dead."

"Olivia said he was," I said. "But you thought Piper was dead too."

"Piper's no normal human. He lost too much blood to be moving around," Collin said. "Something's not right."

I had to agree with him. Besides, I was certain Piper's own power had healed her. What, or who, had saved Jack?

"Jack," David called out. "Look out."

Jack was about twenty feet away, looking a little less dazed but still not capable of defending himself. He seemed oblivious to the group of three demons snarling after him.

David was closer, so he rushed forward to intercept the demons before they got to him. "Jack! Run to Rhys. Get in the car with her."

Jack stumbled, unsteady on his feet, and David reached for him as the demons prepared to attack. Which was when Jack's expression cleared, shifting from confused to knowing. To evil. He grabbed David's extended left hand with his own, then ran his sword through David's chest, the tip shoving out the back of his shirt.

It took a second for what I'd seen to sink in. Then I screamed at the top of my lungs, bolting for him. "*Nooo!*"

Collin's arm snaked around my waist in a firm grip, hauling my back to his chest. "Ellie, stop." His voice broke. "He's gone."

"*Nooo!*" I screamed again, beginning to wail. But I knew he was right. Jack, or the thing that was controlling him, had killed him instantly.

"David!"

Rhys's screams rang in my ears, and I heard Collin shouting at her to get back in the car and lock the doors. But all I could see was David's lifeless body on the ground.

"*David,*" I sobbed.

Collin's arm tightened around my waist and he gave me a little shake. "Ellie. I have to go protect Rhys, but I can't leave you here like this. Don't fall apart on me now. Please."

I sucked in a breath to try to calm down, but my hands shook, and my sword clattered to the ground.

Rhys continued to scream, crying out Jack's name as he shifted direction and began to advance on her. Olivia had gotten out of the car to help but was now being swarmed with demons on the other side of the car.

"Go," I said, shoving Collin's arm off my stomach. "I won't do anything stupid."

He released me and searched my face with a cold look in his eyes. "We'll kill him."

"It's not really Jack," I said in a shaky voice. "It's a demon."

"All the more reason to kill it." Then he took off toward Jack.

Rhys was just as much of a mess as I felt, but I had to get it together to help her. Bending down, I scooped up my sword and sprinted for her as a new group of demons emerged with Rhys in their sights.

"Rhys!" I shouted as I got closer. "Get in the car."

"Jack," she sobbed, clearly hysterical. "He killed David. Why would he kill David?"

"It's not Jack," I assured her, worried about how she'd react when Collin killed him. "Get inside." I opened the front passenger door and pushed her inside. "Stay in here until we tell you it's safe to come out." I shut the door behind her, hoping she'd stay put.

I heard the clash of metal and saw Jack and Collin in a sword battle. I swallowed my fear, telling myself that Collin could take care of himself. Instead, I rushed around the car to help Olivia fight off the group surrounding her.

"They're everywhere," Olivia said. "We need to pull back."

She was right, but I wasn't sure Piper would agree. I couldn't see her, but I knew she was somewhere deep in the demons, blasting them with their own demon fire.

I killed the last demon near the car, grateful for the sense of purpose, but Olivia and Rhys still weren't safe. "Olivia, there's an address in there for Abel's mountain home. You'll also find the code to get inside. Go wait for us there."

Horror filled her eyes. "I can't leave you."

"We're pulling back too," I said, partially hoping it was true. Part of me wanted to stay until every last one of them was dead, but I also knew we couldn't. We were too outnumbered.

She nodded then got in the car and wove out of the parking lot, hitting a demon in the road. It flopped over the roof of the car and landed on the road before I stomped over and slayed it.

Okeus sat on his throne in the clouds, watching me with an amused grin.

That fucker had to die.

CHAPTER THIRTY-FOUR

Piper

The demon I was riding had begun to fight Abel's will in earnest when I heard Rhys scream Jack's name.

I sucked in a breath in shock, wondering why she was calling his name. She already knew that he was dead. But my hesitation nearly got me thrown off.

Pissed, I thrust the tip of St. Michael into the demon's back, shoving deep enough to reach his heart.

As the demon turned to ash, I jumped to my feet, then turned to run back to the others, freaking out when I heard Ellie start to scream "no." I'd never heard her sound so desperate. Rhys was hysterically calling out Jack's name, which made me even more anxious.

I bolted toward them with Abel on my heels. When I finally reached the edge of the horde, Collin was holding back a sobbing Ellie as Rhys stood next to Abel's car, hysterical.

In the middle of it all stood Jack, holding a bloody sword over David's still body.

"No," I gasped, stumbling over a pile of ash.

"It's not him, Waboose," Abel whispered in my ear, wrapping an arm around my waist and pulling me close. "He's being controlled by a demon."

A squatty demon approached, and we turned to face it together, working in a unison that I was sure usually took years of practice. But I was shaken by the sight of Jack's possessed body, and it made me sloppy. I knew Abel was right—that *wasn't* Jack—but anger roared to life inside me when I saw Collin go at him with his sword and spear.

We finally took care of the demon in front of us, but another quickly took its place. As soon as I got the chance, I broke free and ran to Jack, my heart aching as I ran past David's body. Ellie stood to the side, watching Collin, and I could see he was beginning to tire. He'd been fighting demons for nearly an hour and Jack seemed to have limitless energy.

"Jack," I called out to him, my voice breaking.

He swung his gaze to me, a huge smile spreading across his face.

"Collin," I said calmly, moving toward them. "Let me have a turn."

He started to protest, then abruptly stepped back, leaving me to take his place. I could feel Abel behind me, watching but ready to jump in if need be.

"Jack," I said as we both began circling one another. "Lookin' good for being dead."

"I could say the same about you," he said with a grin.

"Oh, but I wasn't really dead," I said, studying his footing as Abel's instructors had trained me to do. Looking for weaknesses. Looking for patterns.

He laughed. "You can tell yourself that, but you were dead all the same. Your witness to creation power brought you back."

"And what brought you back?" I asked.

His grin spread, but he didn't answer.

"I thought we were friends, Jack," I said, waiting for him to make a move, but I realized I was only giving him a chance to catch his breath.

"How could I be friends with a slut like you?" he spat. "Spreading your legs for the demon behind you. Does he know you would have spread your legs for me only days ago if I'd been willing to screw you?"

I gasped in shock.

"Don't listen to him, Waboose," Abel said. "He'll say anything to hurt you."

This wasn't Jack. I needed to remember that. The demon was counting on me to react emotionally to his assault.

"I only kissed you out of pity," I lied, moving closer. "Poor pathetic Jack, desperate to find his place, when he never had any hope of finding one." The words ripped my heart to shreds, but his confusion, evident on his face, bought me the moment I needed.

I tackled him to the ground and shoved St. Michael so hard into his right shoulder it pinned him to the patch of hard ground where he'd landed.

"Ellie!" I shouted. "Come here."

She approached, wariness in her eyes.

"Kill him," I said, my voice breaking. "Kill him for David." She needed this. She needed the release she'd been denied with the Great One.

She pulled her sword over her head and released a soul-ripping scream of grief and fury as she shoved the blade deep in his chest, killing him.

The fight went out of her then, and she removed her sword and stumbled over to David.

The demons had taken advantage of our distraction, and we were now surrounded.

"Waboose," Abel said in warning.

We were in deep shit.

Okeus began to clap, grinning ear to ear, as his cloud lowered. "That was worth it, all of it." He stepped off the cloud, still smiling. "I've changed my mind about you, slayer of demons. Perhaps I'll make *you* my queen."

"Go back to hell," I snarled, ready to launch myself at him, but Abel held me back.

"Run, Waboose," he whispered in my ear. "Let me hold him off while you take the others and run."

"I'm not leaving you." I risked a glance back at him. *I stand with you, Abel. We belong together.*

Abel shot me a frown.

Okeus started walking toward us, offering Ellie a look of mock sympathy. "Sorry about your paramour, Ellie. I offered you a chance to save him weeks ago, and you selfishly chose not to take it. You only have yourself to blame."

She got to her feet, seething. Her hand loosened then tightened around her sword hilt. "It was blackmail, Okeus."

"Call it what you like, but he could be here now, his arm around you like Abiel is holding Piper."

Abel slowly dropped his arm and stepped in front of me.

"Enough games, Abiel," Okeus said, sounding weary, but then his voice hardened. "On your knees."

Abel took a defensive stance. "First, I wish for your word that you won't harm her."

"That is impossible, my son," Okeus said. "An example must be made of her to show the demons and other supernatural beings that there are consequences for disobedience. However, I won't kill her, and after she is impregnated, I will let you keep her as a pet."

Abel's body stiffened.

"And," Okeus added, a grin teasing the corners of his mouth, "*you* will administer the punishment."

"And if I don't accept your deal?" Abel asked.

"Then Attila the Hun will administer the punishment." He paused. "You haven't met Attila, have you? He prefers the delights of hell to the freedom of this world." His gaze landed on me. "He's very much looking forward to meeting the slayer."

Abel released a low growl.

"One way or the other, she will be coming with me *now*." Okeus reached for me, but Abel lunged with his sword, striking the god in the gut then quickly stepping back.

He looked down at the bloodless wound and he *laughed.*

We were in a world of shit.

Abel shoved me back several steps as Collin grabbed Ellie's arm and pulled her to him.

Okeus released a guttural sound, and the demons surrounding us began to advance in a rush.

Create a world, Waboose.

"No."

Frustrated, I pushed out a wave of power, hoping to boost the effectiveness of my blows, but instead I blasted a shock wave that froze all the demons in place.

Okeus's eyes widened and he took a step toward me, pushing over the demons in his way, crushing one of the gremlins. "Aren't you a surprise. What kind of power is that?"

I strode toward him, ready to finish this off, forever, remembering after the fact that my power hadn't affected him.

I saw movement beside me and noticed Ellie was advancing on him too.

"Piper!" Abel shouted. "Stop!"

Okeus cast a glance to his son then to the frozen demons around him, assessing the situation. "One day, we will be together, daughter of the sea," he said, "but today is not that day."

He cast a wave of energy toward my cousin, sending her stumbling backward, but I absorbed it and held my ground.

He looked thrilled. "What are you?"

I held St. Michael over my head, ready to attack. "Your worst nightmare."

He didn't look scared, but he didn't look as amused as before. "What has Ahone been up to?"

I took another step closer.

"Obviously, I greatly underestimated you," Okeus said. "Perhaps we should renegotiate."

"There's no need to bother," I said, "because I plan on killing you." For the first time, I thought I might actually have a shot.

Abel reached my side, casting a wary glance at me. The others were all staring at me too, and I suddenly realized why. I was literally glowing again.

I didn't wait. I lunged at Okeus's heart with my dagger, wondering too late if this would work as he deftly stepped aside so that my blade missed its mark by mere inches. I recovered quickly, but an oily sheen of dread washed over me. What if I could only kill Okeus after the mark of the crescent moon appeared? Abel would be impossible for me to kill without it, and he was Okeus's son. It terrified me how right that felt, but I didn't let myself dwell on it. Maybe I with my daggers and Ellie with her god-subduing sword...maybe she and I could do it together.

I only knew we had to try.

As though on cue, Ellie was on her feet, making her way past stunned demons that were slowly starting to rouse. Which meant my window of opportunity would quickly close.

Okeus produced two daggers of his own, wearing a huge smile. "I haven't fought a worthy adversary for centuries. I've forgotten how invigorating it can be."

From the corner of my eye, I caught a shadow of movement, but Okeus was faster than the shadow, whirling around to parry a blow from Ellie's sword with his dagger, his reflexes impossibly quick.

Collin joined the fight as well, and Okeus shot him a furious glare as he easily deflected attacks from the three of us, with Abel standing guard behind us at the ready.

"I take no pity on traitors, son of land."

The demons were slowly getting to their feet. I lobbed another wave of power to freeze them again, but this wave was much less powerful and barely affected them.

Okeus laughed. "Wish to renegotiate?"

"Fuck you," I roared, leaping toward him with St. Michael held aloft, only just missing his shoulder.

A new wave of winged demons were headed our way, and a thought from Abel filled me in on the devastation they'd caused in the police station. They were in Okeus's elite personal guard, and Abel suspected Okeus was calling them in to separate me and Abel from the others. He feared they had the power to do it.

Abel stood at my back, fighting furiously. *Create a world, Waboose!*

No," I panted between lunges and jabs. Creating a world would mean admitting defeat, and I wasn't ready to do that.

"Piper."

Another swarm of demons—reinforcements for the original front line of squatty foot soldiers—headed toward the curse keepers and their Tsawasi's army, and I heard Ellie calling out for a retreat.

Okeus had brought out the second wave.

I turned to Abel, knowing full well what would happen. As soon as the others retreated, the swarm of demons that had been fighting them would turn on us. We'd never escape.

"Okeus," Abel called out. "I will willingly go with you if you'll leave the slayer alone."

"You are not in a position to negotiate," Okeus said. "You're surrounded."

I looked up from the bloody battle and realized that at some point, Okeus had stepped back and let his minions take his place in combat. He stood there smiling smugly, his arms spread wide at the scene before him as the battle continued on without him.

"I said I'd go *willingly*," Able shouted.

"No!" I shouted at him. Then lowering my voice, I said, "I'll create a world." Why had I been so stubborn before? Had I really thought I could defeat a god single-handedly?

"No," he said. "You were right. They'll wait forever for us to emerge. It has to be this way." Turning back to his father, he shouted, "What must I pledge for you to leave her alone?"

"Nothing," Okeus said, moving closer to us again, his eyes glittering. "There is nothing you can give me. I want her."

"Kewasa…" A woman's voice carried through the air, making my hair stand on end. I knew who it was, and the look on Abel's face told me he knew too.

Helen is here to kill me, I sent to him. *She killed Jack, and she's sworn to kill me too.*

Abel froze, his thoughts racing.

"She's stronger now," I said, scanning the sky for her. She was close, but I couldn't feel exactly where.

"What is this?" Okeus asked.

A shimmering light appeared about thirty feet across from us. And just like that, the battle came to an abrupt halt. Something had paralyzed the demons around us, and Abel and I went still, exchanging wide-eyed glances.

"I believe it is a ghost," Ahone said, materializing from within the light. He appeared in his old man image, directing a wink my way. "Good to see you again, Piper."

"A ghost?" Okeus said in confusion. His gaze shifted to me.

I shot a quick glance to Abel, firing off a series of rapid thoughts toward him, and he gave a small nod in response. I turned back to Okeus, infusing my words with a confidence that flourished from something greater than even my power. "You said you were bored, Okeus, so I present a new distraction."

"And what is that?"

"Watch me wrestle a ghost into hell."

He grimaced, then shook his head. "Where's the fun in that? I could do it myself with a snap of my fingers."

"But have you seen *me* send a ghost to hell?" I asked, straightening with self-assurance and utmost conviction, but with a little tilt of my head and the sweetest, most virginal smile I could muster, I projected nothing but the purest innocence "It's a spectacle. I'm sure you'll be amused."

He scanned the scene before him—Ellie, Collin, Abel, and I surrounded by two gods and several hundred demons. The Nunnehi warriors and the Little People had fled and were nowhere to be seen.

"Kieran…" Helen called out, floating over the demons' heads and coming toward him. Tonight she wore a sapphire blue ball gown, but it was obvious it wasn't hers. The fabric was stained and it was too big for her, one sleeve drooping over her shoulder and a sash cinching up her waist. Her long brown hair hung loose and a blue ribbon was tied around her neck in place of the usual noose.

"Come to me, Helen," Abel said, reaching out his free hand.

She glided gracefully toward him, taking his hand, her form solid.

"You look beautiful tonight, Helen," Abel said, his voice strong and sure. "What is the occasion?"

"Kieran," Helen said with a pout, lifting her hand to his face and running her fingers down his cheek. "He says you love me, but she stands between us." She pointed her finger at me with an accusatory glare.

"Who says this, my love?" Abel asked, now resting his hand on her hip.

The monster in me rose, and I saw red, needing to kill the object of his affection.

"Him." She pointed above at nothing.

Okeus watched, enthralled but confused.

"Why would he tell you that?" Abel asked in a seductive voice.

Helen's image shivered. "Because she stands between us. She's stolen your heart from me, so I must cut hers out."

She lifted a blade from her side, a kitchen knife about eight inches long, still red with Jack's blood.

"The ghost wishes to cut out the slayer's heart because she's in love with Abiel?" Okeus asked. "Is she insane?" He looked delighted.

327

"Yes," I said, fighting back the monster and telling it that it would get its chance. "She's mad." I cast my hardened gaze to the god. "Give me the opportunity to send her to hell."

His brows shot up in amusement. "For daring to love my son?"

"And for killing my friend."

"What do you have to lose?" Abel asked, his hand now on her cheek, stroking lightly. She tilted her head back, giving him full access to her throat should he choose to take advantage of it. I knew this was for show. His thoughts told me he was distracting her so I could negotiate my terms, yet I had to clench my fists around the blood-slicked handles of my daggers to hold on to my tenuous grasp of control.

Okeus stared at me with new interest.

"You must give me ten uninterrupted minutes to deal with her," I said. "I don't have my usual implements to help me, and I'm used to having the confines of a room to contain them."

"Too long," Okeus said with the wave of his hand. "I'll give you five."

Five minutes to send her to hell with no sage or holy water?

I caught Abel's eye. *You don't need the sage or holy water. Not anymore.*

Okeus watched us, curious and excited, and it struck me that Abel and I'd had multiple telepathic conversations, and Okeus hadn't shown any sign that he'd heard us.

Had my growing power blocked him out?

I will kill my father and spread his pieces around the earth so he will never rise again, Abel thought, and Okeus continued grinning like a fool.

"I'm not sure it can be done, but I get five uninterrupted minutes," I said. "You will not intervene until the time is up."

"Fine," he said with a wave of his hand. "Agreed."

"Agreed," I said, sealing the deal. I felt something lock into place supernaturally, as though the universe recognized our arrangement too.

"What did you do?" Okeus asked, sounding worried.

"You made a deal," Ahone said with a grin. "Now you are bound."

I moved to the center of the twenty-foot-in-diameter ring organically created by the gods, Abel, and the curse keepers. The Little People and the Nunnehi warriors were still nowhere to be seen, but I could feel them now at the rear, fighting the winged demons.

"Helen," I called out in a lilting tone, "get your hands off of him."

Her head jerked up, her bliss instantly gone.

"Kewasa," she snapped, anger flooding her eyes, "your time draws near."

I gave her a mocking grin. "Then let's usher it in."

She floated toward me, and I could feel that she was stronger than before. Had a demon boosted her power? I didn't think so—this felt different. Memories rushed back to me of the ghosts who had died issuing warnings to me popped up. With my new abilities, I could review our interactions. These ghosts had possessed the same power filling Helen now. Only none of them had the stench of Ahone.

Who had done this?

The others had issued warnings before disappearing. Had she just delivered her warning? And if so, would she fade to dust without my intervention?

She growled and lunged for me, but I instinctively sent a wave of power toward her, hurling her backward to the edge of the circle. Releasing a new growl, she charged me again, her knife raised above her head in a tight grip.

"I will kill you, Kewasa," Helen snarled. "I will stab you over and over and over just like I did to the priest who dared to think he could help me."

"You killed Jack because he wanted to help you?" I asked in dismay, my defenses weakening.

Helen took advantage of my shock and slashed my arm, drawing blood. My body acknowledged the pain, but the power in me refused to address it.

This ghost had to pay.

"You're stronger," she said. "He said you would be. He said the demon souls feed your power."

"Who?" I asked as we began to circle each other. My lessons about studying the footing of my opponent wouldn't help me now. "Ahone?"

She laughed. "There are other gods, Kewasa." She spat my title as though it left a bitter taste on her tongue.

Another god was in play?

I cast a glance from Okeus to Ahone, and both looked just as surprised as I felt.

Once again, Helen took advantage of my distraction and jabbed her knife toward my gut. I dodged to the side, missing an incapacitating blow. She grazed my side instead.

"Piper!" Ellie called out in terror.

"You can do this!" Collin shouted.

Abel remained silent.

Do not get involved, I sent toward him.

This is your gift, not mine, Waboose. He didn't sound happy about it.

Nearly a minute had been wasted with the circling and her trash talk. I'd learned some valuable information, but it was time to end this. I'd negotiated for five minutes, and I planned to use the last one or two to grab my friends and get the hell out of here.

"What did Jack want to help you do?" I asked, letting the power in me build.

"He said he could bring Margaret back from hell. He said you would help us cross into the light, but he was a liar."

"Jack was many things," I said, my anger building. "But a liar wasn't one of them. Why wouldn't you let him try?"

"He did," she sneered, rushing toward me.

I considered trying to open the portal now, but the air didn't feel right, and deep in my soul, I knew I needed to enflame her hatred and darkness before I could send her off. And I knew exactly which buttons to push.

"You fight for Abel, but he doesn't love you," I sneered. "He laughs at you behind your back."

Her dark gaze turned to Abel, but he remained expressionless.

"He was never your friend. He was only using you for your power." Lies. All lies, and my heart tore at the obvious pain on her face, but her anger was building. The wall between our plane and hell was thinning.

"Liar!" she screamed, rushing toward Abel, but I cut her off, standing between the two of them.

"He doesn't want you, Helen. He never did. Just like your lover didn't want you. He let his wife kill your daughter."

I heard Ellie gasp, but my insults were working. Helen's humiliation and pain twisted the hate in her heart, making it mushroom with rage and a need for revenge.

The wall thinned all the more.

She pulled her arm back to stab me in the chest, but I shoved Ivy into her stomach.

"Is that what you did to Jack?" I snarled, and the monster in me reared up. I pulled the dagger out and plunged it in again. "Did you get as much pleasure stabbing him as I'm getting from stabbing you?"

She staggered back, and to my surprise, blood seeped through her dress.

The darkness in me delighted in her pain and torment, and the thin sliver in me that cared started to fade.

"No one loves you, Helen. No one. Not even your daughter."

She screamed, releasing her rage, and the trees around us shook. She was strong, so much stronger than I'd realized, and my soul leapt at the thought of possessing all that power. With that power, I could kill Okeus. I could kill Ahone. I could take on the new god who'd orchestrated this and so much more.

I could rule all the creatures both supernatural and human. I could become the most powerful being in the universe—and it started with sending this ghost to hell.

The darkness in me grew, and I felt the final layer between our realms fade to nothing, leaving behind only a thin barrier. And in that moment, I realized it wasn't Helen's hatred I'd been waiting for—it was my own.

Lifting Ivy to shoulder height, I made a slit in the air, cutting the last layer between the worlds. The agony of thousands of souls poured out through the hole, along with an overwhelming feeling of despair and hopelessness. Ice crystals seeped from the tear, spreading outward.

In my peripheral vision, I was vaguely aware that Ellie and Collin were jumping out of the way.

"Helen," I called out in a dark and empty voice. "It is time for you to pay."

"Margaret," Helen sighed, her anger fading as she faced the portal.

Standing in the center was a small girl with blonde ringlets and a lacy white dress. Worms crawled from her empty eye sockets and her grin was lopsided and so very wrong, but then her face changed, as though a mask had appeared—her bright blue eyes, flushed cheeks on ivory skin, and a pink Cupid's bow mouth. She reached out her hand. "Momma."

Helen walked toward her, euphoria on her face, and the monster in me protested. This was punishment! She was supposed to beg me for mercy!

"Piper," Abel whispered in my ear, his hand on my shoulder. "Do not give into this."

"She must pay," I growled, my voice not sounding like my own.

His arm wrapped around my waist, pulling me close. "Let her go, Waboose. She has suffered for a century. Let her have her daughter."

The monster in me roared and I sent out a wave of power to push him away, but he took it all in and held me gently. "Piper."

Helen walked through the portal and it instantly closed behind her.

"My love," he whispered with so much tenderness the monster in me cracked and my knees buckled, but he simply held me close.

"Abel," I whispered in horror. "Help me. I don't know what's happening to me."

"I will, but we still have two minutes in your bargain. We have time to escape."

And in that moment of gentleness, my hand began to burn, a pain different from the burn that I'd been feeling from being so close to demons. I shoved St. Michael into its sheath, the pain too intense to hold the weapon. The burn was in the upper left corner of my palm, and I knew exactly what it meant.

"Abel!" I cried, growing frantic and pushed my power toward the mark in a desperate attempt to stop it from appearing.

He turned to me with wide eyes. What he saw must have told him everything, because he immediately glanced down at my palm. The outline of a crescent moon began to appear, and the monster inside me roared to life, hungry for blood. Hungry for Abel's life. Hungry for his power.

"No!" I cried out, taking several steps away from him to put distance between us. I turned to face him, panic making me stumble.

"What's happening?" Okeus demanded. He sounded out of sorts. Almost apprehensive.

Abel dropped his sword onto the ground with a clatter and held out his hands in surrender. Tears filled his eyes. I could see fear there too, but not for himself—he was worried for me. "Don't fight it, Kewasa. This is our fate."

"No!" I shouted, more to the monster inside me than to him.

I pushed all my energy and power toward my hand, fighting the mark, and the monster in me roared in protest. Still gripping Ivy in my right hand, I fell to my knees.

Abel dropped down with me, cupping my face with his hand, searching my eyes.

"Run," I forced out through gritted teeth. Tears of frustration streamed down my cheeks as it all became so clear, too clear. Whether or not this was fated to be, I gave rise to this mark with my own actions. This was the cost of sending Helen to her fate. I'd blackened my soul and scorned my humanity to do it, releasing the mark under my skin.

The last of the battling demons fell silent and lowered their weapons, and all stood watching the spectacle with curiosity. For a moment, the only movement was in the sky, two ravens circling overhead.

"It has come to pass," said a familiar voice. The mysterious voice in my head that had been guiding me.

Manipulating me.

"Who the fuck are you?" I screamed, leaning onto my bent legs as I tried to rein the monster in.

"Is this your doing?" Okeus snapped.

"There must always be balance, brother," Ahone said. "But this is not me. Surely you can recognize his handiwork."

Okeus gasped. "Odin?"

Who was Odin? The Norse god? Frankly, I was too busy fighting the rising force inside me to care.

"Run," I grunted as Abel gathered me in his arms. "Run, goddammit. I need you to live."

He sat on the pavement, straddling me across his lap. "Don't fight it, Waboose," he repeated with a broken voice. "You're only making it worse."

"Abel, run," I pleaded. I was starting to lose ground. The curve of the moon had already etched into my skin.

"I love you, Piper. Not because of your power or your titles, but because you've made me feel again. You've made me feel human. I will love you until the end of eternity. Now fulfill your destiny."

I started to sob as I lifted my right hand, compelled by a force outside my control. The dagger pointed toward his chest. "Please don't let me do this, Abel. *Please.*"

His voice lowered so only I could hear him. "After you do this, you have to run. Run and hide." His voice turned stern. "Do you understand me?" When I didn't answer, he sank his hand into my hair. Holding my face inches from his, he repeated, "*Do you understand?*"

The dagger was pressed against his chest now, and still I fought the monster in me with everything I had. "*Abel...*"

Relief filled his eyes. "I sought you out for this reason, Piper. This is what I wanted. Remember that."

"Even now?"

"No," he admitted with a soft smile. "I wish I could have forever with you."

The monster in me roared with impatience and forced the blade partially into his chest before I managed to stop it.

"Stop her!" Okeus shouted, finally understanding. Several demons tried to rush me, but some invisible force kept them out.

"She is still within her five minutes," Ahone practically sang with happiness.

"Stop fighting it, Piper," Abel said softly. "Just give in." Then he kissed me, his lips gentle on mine, a sharp contrast to the violence in my soul begging for release.

I squeezed the dagger hilt with all my might, trying to pull back, but the power surged, driving the blade deeper.

His body stiffened. I tried to pull the dagger out of his chest, but my hand refused.

Okeus's anger exploded, but the invisible force field held everything at bay.

"*Abel.*" I'd been so sure I could save him, that there had to be a way to stop the mark. I'd never let myself believe this would actually happen. Never realized I'd held the power to prevent it all along. Even now, as his blood pumped from his body and he started to slump backward, I waited for my miracle.

He stared up at me and smiled, but the monster in me wasn't satisfied. It wanted his soul.

"No!" Crying uncontrollably, I twisted my hand, and his eyes widened as he released a gasp of pain.

"*I'm sorry*," I sobbed.

He lifted his hand and covered mine as the light faded from his eyes.

My hand was magically freed. I stared at him in a stupor. This was one shock too many, but somewhere in the back of my mind, I told myself to catch him before he crossed over. If I couldn't save his life, I could at least save him from hell. But the moment he died, the barrier that had been protecting us dropped and the demons swarmed us.

Okeus was losing his mind, ordering my capture and torture.

I got to my feet and spun around wildly, trying to find Abel's spirit, but all I saw were hundreds of demons and they all wanted me. Ellie and Collin were near caught in the madness.

My grief and agony combined with my power, building to a boiling point. A shock wave exploded from me, and the demons' bodies fell where they stood.

"Abel!" I screamed, stepping over the demons as I searched for his spirit, my hand still drenched in his life's blood. He had to be here. He had to cross over.

Only then, as I stumbled around the parking lot, did I realize what I'd done. As far as I could see, Collin and Ellie, who'd made their way back to David's body, were now the only living souls remaining in the wake of the bloodbath. Somehow I'd murdered hundreds of demons. I knew I should try to comprehend the fact that I'd channeled this much power, but all I could focus on was Abel.

He was gone.

I'd failed him. I'd failed me.

"Abel," I said half-heartedly, knowing that I would have found him by now if his spirit were present.

"The demigod is no longer on this plane," I heard a small voice say, and I knew before looking it belonged to Tsagasi.

My heart caught in my throat as I turned to face him. "Is he in hell?"

"You knew he was destined to go there."

So I'd been wrong about that too.

I glanced around, realizing I'd missed something else. Okeus and Ahone were gone. "I suppose it's too much to hope I killed Okeus when I killed those other demons."

"No, you didn't kill him, but you sent him running. He's frightened and confused by your power. He's regrouping to figure out how to handle you." He paused. "He will be back for you."

"And I'll be waiting." Ahone was equally culpable in Abel's death. He would pay with his life too.

I ran a hand over my head, feeling more broken and alone than I'd ever felt. I glanced to the side and saw the wadded-up paper Collin had tossed away. Leaning over, I picked it up and opened it, realizing it was Tommy's picture. Collin had had it all along, and now I knew why it had made him so driven. In the middle of the drawing, David was lying on the ground in a puddle of red blood while Ellie leaned over him, Collin looking over them both, clutching his sword and spear. Off to the side, Abel and I stood facing Okeus.

Had Collin agreed to fight to try to save David or to rid himself of his rival? The grief I saw on his face now and the agony in his eyes as he watched Ellie sob over David's body convinced me he'd done it to save David for Ellie.

Only I'd failed them all. The swirling black circle in the background of the drawing confirmed it.

I stared at Abel's lifeless body slumped to the side in the center of a bloodied parking lot, surrounded by hundreds of dead demons I'd failed him, but as I examined the drawing more closely, I realized I had another option.

This wasn't over. Not yet. "I can still save him."

Tsagasi stared at me as though I'd lost my mind. "The demigod is dead, and Okeus will torture you for killing him. You need to focus on what you can control, not what you can't."

My stubbornness kicked into overdrive. "I still plan to kill Okeus. But now I plan to kill Ahone too."

He remained silent.

"I told Abel I'd save him from hell, Tsagasi." My voice broke, but my back was rigid with determination.

"Kewasa," he said. "I'm sure you meant well, but you—"

"No," I said, dropping the drawing to the ground. "I may not have been able to stop the mark and prevent myself from murdering him, but I will not fail in that."

"It's too late." The sympathy in his voice surprised me.

"Is it?" I asked, marching toward the curse keepers' car.

Ellie was on the ground, lying over David's bloodied body, his lifeless eyes turned up to her as though he was watching over her, even in death. And then I realized Abel wasn't the only one in hell. We'd never freed David and Jack's souls. They were there too.

"Ellie," I said with a firmness that took us both by surprise.

She looked at me with her tearstained face, her expression an equal mixture of awe and fear.

Collin stood to the side, fighting his own tears, but my harshness provoked him into raising his sword in warning.

I reached for her, squashing the monster in me. I'd find a way to harness it. Never again would I give it free rein.

"Ellie," I said more gently, extending my hand closer. "David's not here. Let's go." She let me help her to her feet and I cupped her cheek, looking deep into her eyes. "We will get him back."

Fresh tears filled her eyes.

"Are you ready?" I asked, my voice cracking. "Will you come with me?"

She nodded without hesitation. "Yes."

"Where are you going?" Collin called after us as we strode to the car, both of us filled with new purpose.

I turned back to face him, the beast in me fighting against its yoke, eager for the next fight. "We're going to get them back. We're going to hell."

Coming September 27, 2019
The end of the Curse Keepers saga
Of Death and Ruin
Piper Lancaster #4

About the Author

Denise Grover Swank was born in Kansas City, Missouri and lived in the area until she was nineteen. Then she became a nomadic gypsy, living in five cities, four states and ten houses over the course of ten years before she moved back to her roots. She speaks English and smattering of Spanish and Chinese which she learned through an intensive Nick Jr. immersion period. Her hobbies include witty Facebook comments (in own her mind) and dancing in her kitchen with her children. (Quite badly if you believe her offspring.) Hidden talents include the gift of justification and the ability to drink massive amounts of caffeine and still fall asleep within two minutes. Her lack of the sense of smell allows her to perform many unspeakable tasks. She has six children and hasn't lost her sanity. Or so she leads you to believe.

For more info go to: dgswank.com or denisegroverswank.com

D.G. Swank

Made in the USA
Coppell, TX
08 December 2019